# Wilmington Manor

James E. Laws, Jr.

To the Creator for Life


To My Parents for Love and Nurturing

# ACKNOWLEDGMENTS

**Thank you to friend and author, *David Robbins* for being a wonderful mentor.  Thank you for your scathing reviews, suggestions for rewrites, and continued encouragement.**

Thank you to the first focus group for taking the time to read the first draft and providing valuable feedback on the concept and direction of the storyline:  Joseph Casazza, J. C. Faulk, Bradley Green, Elaine Robnett Moore, and Dr. Bill Woodson.

Thank you to the first editor, Ingrid Navid for wonderful comments and phrasing suggestions.

Thank you to Beverly J.R. Tyler and Chuck diGiacomantonio for reading and commenting on the second draft of this book.

Thank you to Joni Albrecht for editing the third draft.  Your suggestions on character development and setting were perfect.

Thank you to the Museum of the White House of the Confederacy, Richmond VA; the Virginia Historical Society, Richmond VA; the Valentine Museum, Richmond VA; and Diane Jacobs from the Museum and Archives Department at Virginia Military Institute.

Also, thank you for research materials loaned to me from JoAnn Ellsberry of McGuire Funeral Home, Washington, DC; Gary Hyde; Lage Carlson; and Dr. Morgan Jackson.

English translation of Tschaikowsky's Wieder –wie fruher by Dr. Ernest Roan
French edits by Dr. Sonia Feigenbaum
Cover design by Steven Previter

## Prologue

**MawNancy** paced around her shanty. The floorboards mourned under each step. She rubbed her leathery black hands and mumbled an old African chant. Her mutterings turned to words. "Dey took him, beat him, and hung him. Dey gonna pay. Everyone of dem gonna pay." Tears poured and mingled with snot. She wiped her face with the sleeve of her torn blouse. Her body ached with each movement. She'd tried to help her man fight off the nightriders, but they had beaten her too. The door slowly opened. She sprang for her walking stick, ready to swing. "Oh, Daisy, it's you. I thought they'd come back fer me."

"I brought you some food. Would have come sooner, but I had to finish cooking for the family."

"Thank you. Don't feel much like eating."

"I'll just leave it. Yo hands is bleeding. Dey swollen, too." Daisy put the tray on the table.

"I tried to hep Sam fight 'em off. It was five of 'em with sacks over dey heads and the eye holes cut out. Between my stick and fists, I got in some good licks. We put up a good fight." She covered her face with her hands and cried. "But dey got him anyway." She composed herself. "T'was all because of her they killed my Sam."

"What you mean? All because of who?" Daisy reached out to comfort MawNancy.

"Don't matter none. Dat whole family gonna pay. I'm gonna make 'em pay." MawNancy paused and rubbed her hands. "When you gonna kill that old rooster?"

"I might fry him up tomorrow for Sunday dinner."

"When you kill him, bring me de head. I need it fresh, still dripping."

"All right. Soon as I kill him, I'll bring it to you."

The next day, MawNancy set out for a walk through the high weeds down by the river. She'd seen them there before and suspected what might be going on. She needed proof that young Master Andrew was meeting a man – a married man and friend of the family – to undress and do Lord knows what. She didn't care what they did. But it was different for white folk. If word got out, the family would be destroyed. She'd have to get in cahoots with the overseer to have the proof she needed, but it would be worth it to see the Gordon family shunned by all their friends. She liked the young master and didn't mind his habits, but if ruining him was the key to her revenge, she'd sacrifice him.

As she had hoped, MawNancy came upon two horses tied to a tree. Weary of vigilantes and nightriders, she gripped her stick tight, ready to swing at a moment's notice. She walked off the path toward a commotion in the grass. She craned her neck to see what first looked like two men tussling. Both had their pants pulled down around their ankles. Their sounds were not from fighting but from passion. She backed away before they saw her but not before she knew without a doubt one was young Master Andrew. "Every Sunday at the same time. I got 'em now."

## Chapter 1
### July 1856

**Andrew** looked out over the parade grounds at families gathered to congratulate the newest batch of cadets. It was the first day of the two-day graduation ceremony. He spotted Ross and Joseph in the distance. He would miss them and their arrangement but would say goodbye later. He pushed those concerns from his mind. Right now, he needed to find his family. He meandered through the crowd of mothers showering sons with congratulatory kisses and fathers offering hardy handshakes and backslaps. Marches played by a crisp military band punctuated the air with brass and tympani. Winded from the drill he'd just finished with his corps, he searched for his father, mother, and sister. Andrew squinted into the midday July sun finally spotting his mother's hideous parasol and his sister's ugly hat. He swallowed hard, took a deep breath, and made his way to them through a sea of ridiculous attire.

"Hello Daddy, Mother, Anna — how did y'all enjoy the ceremony?"

"I do declare, I think I saw the Fairchilds," said Mother. "I'm sure that was Camilla Fairchild and her husband, Sidney, walking over yonder. If they're here, I must be introduced," she said, smoothing her lace collar. "I saw them once at a barbecue, but I was never properly introduced. I wonder why they're here. Is there a Fairchild in your class, Andrew? Now that I think of it, their son must be close to your age. I do hope you made friends with him."

"Oh for heaven's sake, Victoria, simmer down," Daddy cut her off.

Andrew admired his father's ability to take control of any situation.

Daddy continued, "you're carrying on like a wet hen. Don't nobody but you give a damn if the Fairchilds are here. I come to see the great Virginia Military Institute. Now, I see exactly where my money went." He bit the tip off a cigar and retrieved a match from his coat pocket. "I hope all this military training done turned you into a real man." He struck the match and puffed the cigar, blowing pungent smoke in Andrew's face.

The comment landed like a well-placed punch to the stomach. He hadn't been with him two minutes, and Daddy had already taken a jab.

"Andrew, I do hope to meet some of the eligible young men from your class," said Anna. "Yes," Mother continued. "It is time Anna married. Let's make the most of tonight's ball."

No handshake, no backslap, and certainly no congratulatory kiss.

"I see," said Andrew biting his bottom lip to fight back anger.

They stood in uncomfortable silence. Finally Daddy said, "That damn politician y'all had for a speaker went on for two hours."

"Senator Hunter did go on for a while," Andrew agreed.

"It's hot out here. Aren't there any refreshments?" Mother asked fanning with a lace handkerchief.

"Yes. Let's go over to the tents for a cool drink," Andrew suggested.

"Good. Perhaps we'll see the Fairchilds," said Mother.

Andrew led the way in silence, too hot to speak. His thick brown hair was wet and clinging to his scalp. He ran his handkerchief around the back of his neck to catch the sweat pouring from his head.

His classmate, Ross McCabe, walked briskly toward him with an outstretched hand and big grin. "Andrew, promise me we'll keep in touch. I want you to come visit us in Connecticut. My folks sure enjoyed meeting you last night."

Finally, a handshake, a backslap.

"Thank you, Ross. Permit me to introduce my daddy, John Gordon. And this is my mother, Victoria, and my sister, Anna."

"I'm pleased to meet all of you. You have a mighty fine son, here. He has been a good friend to me, and he's one of the best sharpshooters in our class. You all must be mighty proud. I'm sorry I can't visit; I've got to find my folks. Nice meeting you all. Andrew, write me, you hear," he said.

"I will, Ross." Andrew didn't want to let go of Ross's firm grip. He finally did and watched him hurry off, hoping that it would not be a

2

final farewell.

"My goodness, Andrew. Friends with a Yankee?"

"Yes, Mother. Friends with a Yankee. I'll get us some punch."

The heavy cut-glass cup almost slipped from his gloved hand when the slave handed it to him, the black hand in stark contrast to his white glove. Andrew passed cups to each of his family members, careful not to spill.

Mother sipped then grimaced, setting the cup on the table. "Well, there's certainly nothing special about this. After all the money we've spent, you'd think they could at least come up with a decent punch."

Andrew couldn't bear the thought of going back to that plantation; day after day nothing but bickering and complaining. He tried to calm himself, to control his childhood stutter trying to make a reappearance. He didn't answer, his words thumping in his throat.

Sweat streamed down Daddy's red face. Andrew turned to ask if he needed more to drink when the cup slipped from Daddy's hand, splashing the sleeve of Andrew's uniform. The cigar fell from Daddy's mouth and cartwheeled down the front of his coat landing in the grass. He dropped to his knees, breathing heavily. Kneeling beside him, Andrew loosened his father's collar, fanned him, and wiped the sweat from his brow. Others gathered around.

"Somebody get me some water, please." Andrew stretched his daddy on the ground and, holding his head, slowly poured a little water into his mouth. After a few seconds, he coughed and sat up.

"What's going on? What are y'all looking at?"

"You fainted, Daddy. It looks like the heat got to you."

"Daddy?" He gave Andrew a strange look.

"I'm just fine. Get me up from here," he barked.

Andrew looked to his mother and sister for some explanation. They offered only blank stares.

Daddy brushed the dirt from his knees. "Get me some more of that punch. Where the hell's my cigar?"

The crowd of on-lookers dissipated, and Daddy straightened his jacket.

"My goodness. I'm glad the Fairchilds weren't here to witness that spectacle," said Mother.

"Indeed," said Anna.

Andrew's concerned eyes remained on Daddy. His color and breathing seemed to have returned to normal. "Come on, ya'll. I'll give you a tour of the place. I thought we'd start over near the quadrangular court, where we had the ceremony. Then we'll make our way to the classrooms, mess hall and over to my barracks. I've grown to love this place. You feel up to walking a bit, Daddy?"

"I feel just fine," he blustered, acting like he had no idea why Andrew would ask.

Major Thomas Jackson strolled the grounds greeting graduates and their families, dapper in his blue uniform. Andrew hoped the Major would come their way. "Daddy, one of my professors is on his way over. I want y'all to meet him."

"Andrew, my boy, how are you?" Major Jackson said. "Congratulations on completing our rigorous curriculum. You've excelled at everything we put in front of you. This is a day you will never forget. We're expecting great things from you."

"Thank you, sir." Andrew introduced his family.

"Indeed," said Major Jackson. "The pleasure is all mine." He nodded to Mother and Anna. "Mr. Gordon." He extended his hand to Daddy. "Andrew has done you proud, but I'm sure you know that."

"What do you teach, Major Jackson?" Anna asked.

"Natural and Experimental Philosophy," he responded. "I also teach Artillery Tactics."

"I declare. It all sounds so complicated," said Mother.

He turned to Andrew and grabbed his shoulder. "Now, I hope you'll consider the offer the Board of Visitors made to you. It's a good opportunity, and we need a talented young man like you. We're expecting great things from all of our graduates of the class of 1856."

"Yes sir. You'll be hearing from me."

"You all have a good day," Major Jackson said. "If you'll excuse me, my old friend, Fairchild, and his family are waiting for me."

"Offer? What offer?" Mother questioned Andrew through a

4

smile that failed to mask irritation.

"They've offered me a teaching position – Assistant Professor of French *and* Mathematics."

Mother looked at Daddy. "John!" She huffed.

"Not now, Victoria. Let's enjoy Andrew's success."

They spent the remainder of the afternoon touring the school's campus before retiring to their rooms to rest and freshen up for the Military Ball.

Andrew returned to his room to find Joseph waiting. He'd already stripped off his uniform. "Anybody see you come in?"

"Of course not." Joseph drew the drapes. "No need to start being careless now."

"Is Ross joining us?"

"I think he's still with his family."

"What's going to become of us?" Andrew unbuttoned his uniform jacket. "I can't give this up. This is the only time I truly feel free."

"I guess we'll have to find wives."

"I can't do that." Andrew kicked off his shoes and unbuttoned his pants.

"Someone's at the door," whispered Joseph.

They scrambled to gather their clothes. Three simple knocks came then a brief pause then two knocks. They exhaled.

"It's Ross," said Joseph.

Andrew rushed to the door, unlocked it, then slid back the extra bolt they had installed against regulations, and Ross rushed in.

**********

The Mess Hall had been transformed for the ball, the capstone of graduation exercises. Crisp linens atop proper buffet tables lined a straight path to a dance floor where cadets and belles hoped to stray. Banners representing the school and the class of 1856 festooned the beams overhead. Andrew stood in the entrance, admiring the hallowed sanctuary and its countless secrets and traditions, the ball one of its most cherished. He was now part of this family history. The feast of ham, stewed oysters, potatoes, asparagus and sweet grapes adorned buffet tables lining the far wall, while side tables along the opposite wall offered pound, sponge, fruit and sugar cakes, fruit puffs, fresh oranges, raisins, ice cream, and lemonade. It was a spread to impress even the likes of Mother. Andrew mingled with fellow cadets, their families and amorous females who seemed to outnumber graduates two to one.

Andrew reminisced and talked about the future with classmates, especially Ross and his family, but kept one eye trained on his own relatives. Daddy, Mother, and Anna occupied one corner of the room and had for most of the evening. He walked over to check on them.

"Well, what do you think? Y'all having a nice time?"

"Oh, yes," a giddy Anna responded. "It's everything I thought it would be. The list of dances is simply breath taking. This band can play anything."

"The dance card includes marches, several quadrilles and waltzes and even a few polkas. They're ending the evening with the *Virginia Reel*," said Mother approvingly.

"I'm hungry," grumped Daddy. "Ain't nothing on that table I want to eat. How much longer is this gonna go on?"

"Not much longer," said Andrew. "We can go back to the hotel and get supper in the dining room." A tap on the shoulder turned him.

"Joseph, where have you been? I've been looking for you all evening." Andrew grasped the cadet's hand in a warm shake. "Allow me to introduce you. This is my father, John Gordon and my mother, Victoria. And permit me to introduce my sister, Anna. Daddy, Mother, Anna, this is my friend, Joseph Carter, from Covington, Virginia."

Joseph nodded to Daddy and Mother. "How are you, Mr. and Mrs. Gordon? I hope you're enjoying the evening." He extended his hand to Anna. "The pleasure is all mine, Miss Gordon. I hope I'm not being too forward, but might I have the honor of the next waltz with you, if your dance card has a space for me?"

Anna looked at her dance card, which Andrew knew was far from filled.

"Why yes, Mr. Carter. The next waltz will be just fine."

"Thank you," said Joseph.

"Covington?" Daddy questioned. "That's in the Blue Ridge Mountains ain't it?"

"Yes sir, it is. Alleghany County."

"Mighty pretty country up there. When I was much younger, I traveled throughout Virginia," Daddy recalled.

"My family has been there for several generations. We like it. We'd be mighty pleased to have you all come for a visit. Andrew and I will keep in touch and make sure our families get to know each other."

"I'd like that very much, Mr. Carter," said Mother.

"It's been my pleasure meeting all of you. Andrew, walk with me for a spell. Let's talk about the opportunities which lie before us. Miss Anna, I shall return in time for our waltz."

Andrew and Joseph headed off for a private talk.

Joseph whispered, "I'd much rather waltz with..."

"How long before you travel back home?" Andrew cut him off.

"I'll be here a few more days and then I return home for a month. After that, I come back here to prepare for my new responsibilities. I plan to accept the teaching offer. I hope you'll be back too." Joseph raised his bushy eyebrows."

"I'm gonna try. My folks don't understand." Andrew released a heavy exhale. The start of a new song broke the silence. "There's the waltz. Thanks for agreeing to dance with Anna."

"I best go get her."

As the evening drew to a close, the bandleader took center floor.

"Everyone," he announced with dramatic flair. "It's time for the final dance of the evening, and we expect full participation. It's time for the *Virginia Reel*!" The crowd clapped and hollered. The bandleader, assisted by a few band members, divided the celebrants into four groups and lined them up, men facing women. Daddy didn't have time to object before the bandleader herded him into line facing Mother.

"Let's begin," the leader announced. And with a flourish of his right hand, the men bowed, and the ladies curtseyed. A single fiddler struck up a jaunty tune, joined by a bagpipe and a flute. The dancers clapped, and the gentlemen and ladies began the ritual dance they had learned in primary school cotillion.

\*\*\*\*\*\*\*\*\*

After the ball, Andrew and his family returned to the hotel for a late supper. Andrew was pleased Mother and Anna had selected modest gowns instead of the flamboyant dresses they were known to wear. A waiter escorted them to a table.

"The fireworks were simply divine," said Mother, peeling off her long white gloves.

"Dazzling," agreed Anna. "I waltzed with several fine gentlemen. I danced with one of your classmates twice, Andrew." She opened her beaded handbag and pulled out an embroidered handkerchief and dabbed her neck. "His name is Arthur Wise of Albemarle County."

"I do believe I know the family name," said Mother. "We'll have to ask about them when we get home."

Mother had behaved for most of the evening. Andrew finally dared to relax after a day on full alert. He enjoyed the meal.

"This has been a mighty good day," said Daddy, as he placed his fork at four o'clock on his empty plate and rubbed his belly. "You've learned a lot here, and you seem to have really taken a liking to the place."

"I love it here. I feel free."

"Free? You ain't no slave."

"I know. What I mean is they respect me and my opinions."

"Perhaps that explains why we didn't hear much from you the entire time you've been here, except for when you needed money. It's been five years, Andrew. You hardly ever came home on your furloughs. I got the circular, which reported your progress. I was glad when you stopped getting so many damn demerits," said Daddy.

"You read those?" Andrew was surprised.

"Of course I did. How else was I supposed to keep up with you and know that you were all right?"

"Sending me here wasn't a waste of your money if that's what you were wondering. I've done well. I was always first, second, or third in my classes. I'm good at recitations and examinations. I did well in chemistry, mathematics, and debate."

"Debate?" Mother almost laughed. "You? Debate?"

"Does that surprise you, Mother?"

"Yes it does, considering how nervous you are, not to mention your ... condition."

"I used to be nervous, but not anymore. As far as my condition is concerned, I got that under control before I came here." He paused long enough to let the anger rising in his chest subside. He would not let her rile him or ruin his celebration. "I'm particularly good in French, which is why they offered me the teaching position. I wouldn't mind living in France for a while." He hadn't planned on mentioning his idea of living abroad, but decided to test the waters.

"Your time here has come to an end, and you have responsibilities to your family at Wilmington Manor," Mother reminded him. "Tell him, John. We have spent a great deal of money sending you here. You can forget about this professorship *and* your absurd idea about living in France. Really, Andrew," she huffed. "It is time for you to come home. I forbid anything else."

"Forbid," he responded. "You forbid? Need I remind you that I am a grown man?"

"And need I remind you that you have no finances of your own, except what your father and I give you."

"I'm aware of that, but surely you mean except for what Daddy gives me."

"It is time you took a wife and settled down." Mother leaned forward to maintain eye contact. "Yes, Andrew. *A wife.*"

They sat in silence for a moment. Seething at the sight of his mother, Andrew rubbed the vein on the side of his neck, his chest heaving.

"I'd like some coffee," said Mother. "Anna, wouldn't you like coffee?"

"Yes. That would be nice. I would like some coffee," parroted Anna.

"Y'all enjoy, but you'll have to excuse me," said Andrew. "I want to get back to my room to get a good night's rest before tomorrow's commencement exercises."

"Certainly, son. I think it's time we all turned in, but before you leave, let me give you this." Daddy handed him a small box wrapped in blue paper. Andrew looked at his mother and sister. The surprised look on their faces revealed they had nothing to do with the gift. He tore through the paper and opened the box. It was a silver pocket watch with his full name engraved on the back and the date of his graduation.

"Thank you," he said looking directly at Daddy, deliberately not acknowledging his mother or sister.

Daddy slurped at the remains of his bourbon. "Maybe one day you can tell me more about sharpshooting? I never thought I'd see the day."

"I'd be happy to," said Andrew. "Y'all have a good night's sleep, and I'll see you early in the morning."

As Andrew was about to stand to leave the table, Sydney Fairchild entered the dining room with his family. Mother clearly spied them, too, and jumped as if she had been stuck with a hatpin.

"The Fairchilds are here. I didn't see them at the ball. I must make their acquaintance. Andrew, don't leave just yet."

"Victoria, don't disturb those folks," said Daddy.

"John Gordon, if it weren't for me, we wouldn't know any of the right people. Besides, they need to know how important we are. Anna, look at that dress and those jewels." Andrew hoped the Fairchilds didn't notice his gawking family.

Mother pinched her cheeks, smoothed her bodice and made her way to their table on the opposite side of the room. Andrew busied himself with the pocket watch, taking it out of its box again.

"Andrew, it ain't proper, your mama going over there alone. Go on over there with her. I don't need to meet those people," said Daddy, puffing on the stub of a cigar and shaking his glass toward the waiter. Andrew cringed but obeyed, hoping to avoid any more of a scene.

"Good evening, Mr. and Mrs. Fairchild. I'm Victoria Gordon. We have not been properly introduced, but I saw you once at a barbeque in Richmond." The Fairchild men stood. "My son is a member of this year's graduating class at Virginia Military Institute, as is yours." She nodded to Sidney IV.

"Hello, Mrs. Gordon," said Mr. Fairchild. "This is my wife, Camilla, and our son, Sidney IV.

"She seems to know who we are, Sidney," hissed Camilla.

"Are you from Richmond, Mrs. Gordon?" asked Mr. Fairchild seemingly attempting to make up for his wife's rudeness.

"We are from Charles City, Virginia," said Andrew moving closer to his mother. "Good evening Mr. and Mrs. Fairchild. I'm Andrew Gordon. Hello, Sidney."

"If I recall, they own a little farm outside of Richmond," said Sidney IV. "Is that right, Mrs. Gordon?"

"A three-hundred-acre tobacco plantation can hardly be considered a little farm," retorted Mother.

"Very impressive, Mrs. Gordon," said Mr. Fairchild, remaining a gentleman in spite of his wife and son. "Is Mr. Gordon here?"

"Yes, he is," said Andrew. "He is not feeling well, and we are about to return to our rooms." He exaggerated his father's condition to cover his mother's unescorted, uninvited, and clearly unwelcome advances.

"No doubt this is a special time for you and your family, Mrs. Gordon," said Camilla.

"Yes it is. We are very proud of Andrew."

"How nice. Then you'll appreciate our desire for privacy during our special family time." Camilla's cold stoic face spread into ghastly smile, exposing corn-yellow crooked teeth.

"Of course," Mother replied.

Mr. Fairchild gestured as if he wanted to apologize but withdrew and said nothing.

"Mother, I see our coffee has arrived. Let's return to our table. Have a good evening," said Andrew.

Mother grabbed his arm and walked away, head held high. But she wore the rejection like a mask. She had been thrashed by the *right people*.

Andrew wanted to knock the smug look off Sidney the Fourth's face for insulting his family but relied on self-control to contain the situation. The last thing he wanted was to embarrass the Gordon name any more than his mother already had.

"I want to leave," Mother said.

"No," Andrew snapped. "You are going to sit with Daddy and Anna and enjoy your coffee. I am going to my room. When you leave, you are not to look in that direction. Do I make myself clear?"

"I'm sorry if I embarrassed you, Andrew."

Mother took her seat, visibly shaken by the reception she received from Camilla Fairchild.

"Good night," Andrew said. "Remember the commencement ceremony is at the Presbyterian Church. We cadets march in at 11:00; you will need to get there early to get a seat. It will be crowded."

Andrew walked back to his room holding the gift tight and hoping that his graduation was something that had finally made Daddy proud.

The second day of the ceremonies was hot as the day before. Andrew and his classmates processed into the cavernous hall. The wood floor and chairs creaked with every movement. The tall windows on each side were opened wide, providing some ventilation and sunlight. Flies, too. After they had taken their seats, Rev. Smith from the Union Theological Seminary stepped forward and gave the opening prayer. Andrew was next. Third in his class, he had been selected to read the Declaration of Independence. He hadn't told his family about the honor, determined to remain calm and not stutter. He would show Mother, before all assembled, that he had beaten his condition. He stepped to the podium, spread his legs for a firm stance and placed both hands on the podium. A bead of sweat trickled from his neck down his back. He swallowed and relaxed his throat. The first word was the hardest. He took his time and formed it perfectly in his mind and let it roll off his tongue. After that, every word came. It was a perfect oration. When he finished, everyone clapped, including Daddy. He stood perfectly still and let the applause wash over him. Mother and Anna sat in stunned paralysis, their mouths slightly agape like two stale corpses.

## Chapter 2
### July 1856

**Andrew** rode horseback alongside Daddy while Mother and Anna rode in the carriage driven by two slaves. They stopped in Fluvanna for a short rest and lunched on hardboiled eggs, bread, and jelly. They got as far as Richmond, spent the night at the Spotswood Hotel and continued on to Charles City the following day. Andrew's back ached over the last miles of the trip. He was no longer used to long rides.

As they topped the hill overlooking Wilmington Manor, Daddy trotted up next to Andrew. "She's a sight to behold ain't she? I done made a lot of changes since you've been gone. I had them crepe myrtle trees put in to flank the road up to the main house. It's been a few years, and they've taken root a might nice. Your mama worried me until I had the portico and the four columns painted last week. I have to admit, that fresh white paint looks nice against the brick."

"This place is truly a reflection of Mother."

"What do you mean?"

"Majestic to the eye." His voice trailed, "But void of depth."

"Andrew, you're home now. You got to try to get along with your mama and your sister. I know they can be difficult. That's why I agreed to send you away."

"That's just it, Daddy. I've been away, and I've grown up some. Military school was home to me. I have changed, and things can't be like they used to be."

"Look down yonder, Son. I done bought twenty more slaves since you've been gone and got about seven or eight more from breeding."

Andrew looked to the south of the main house and down the hill where a cluster of shacks, humble but proud, stood at the center of the social fabric of the slave community, hemming in the distinct culture within its borders. It was there the slaves jumped the broom, set up house, made love, and mourned and buried their dead.

"Now, look up yonder to the north. We got acres and acres of tobacco. Look at those barns and stables filled with horses and farm equipment. On up beyond that, I done cleared some land for raising chickens, a few cows, pigs, fruit trees, and vegetable gardens. I ain't selling any of that. That's just for us."

"You've done a lot since I've been away. It looks good."

"We got a nice place here, and one day it will all be yours. With the James River right here and Richmond only twenty miles upriver, you can go up there anytime you want to visit friends. You can have any woman you want, but that don't seem to interest you none."

Andrew looked away, stung by the comment.

"We got plenty of time to talk about your future here. Come on. I know they're all waiting to see you."

"I can't wait to see Georgie."

"That's something else we got to talk about."

"What do you mean?"

"It's hot. I'm going on in. We'll talk later."

"Daddy!"

The carriage and Daddy went on ahead. Andrew took a deep breath, exhaled in defeat, and followed them down the lane to the main house.

After unpacking and settling in, the excitement of graduation and the trip home quickly faded. Andrew looked for Georgie to come welcome him. After waiting impatiently for a bit, he headed out to find her. He paused at the top of the staircase and looked around the house. He had been away for a while and had visited other fine homes in the North and South. He looked at Wilmington Manor differently now. The place reeked of Mother's desperate need for acceptance.

Andrew slowly descended the stairs, each step reacquainting him with place he called home and reminding him why he left. The interior of the house was as picturesque as the exterior. Fourteen-foot ceilings and large rooms gave Mother plenty of space to show Virginia her fine ways. An impressive staircase descended from the second level into a large foyer. Andrew rubbed the rich, walnut banister. It gleamed, polished daily by slaves. The railings were supported by ornate spindles, freshly painted white, an eye-catching contrast between the glossy brown banister and the equally high-polished steps. At the foot of the staircase, each banister encircled itself. His fingers trailed off the banister as he walked off the bottom step. The first floor was home to two grand parlors, a dining room, and a vast library, which also served as Daddy's office. He strolled into each room. A doorway, piece of furniture, or whatnot unlocked a childhood memory. Each room had its own color scheme with complementing drapes, upholstery, wallpaper, and paint. The parlors were different shades of blue, the dining room hunter green, and the foyer and stairwell old gold. With the exception of the library, the formal rooms and the foyer were adorned with chandeliers that were raised and lowered with gold braided ropes in order to light the candles. In her fervor to become one of Virginia's elite, Mother failed to realize that her decorating efforts had crossed the line of good taste.

Andrew made his way to the brick outbuilding, which housed the kitchen a few feet away from the main house. His steps lightened as he approached the place of comfort. Aunt Daisy's back was to him when he stepped in the door. She stirred a pot and hummed a familiar slave song. He cleared his throat, and she started and turned. A smile stretched across her round face. She flung her arms open, and Andrew rushed to her.

"Lord have mercy. Welcome home."

He buried his face into doughy flesh. They held each other, rocking, her ample bosom pressed against him.

"Oh, Aunt Daisy, I've missed you so much."

He stepped back to look at her. "You haven't changed at all." He cupped her face and kissed her forehead. She was plump but shapely and high yellow, not light enough to pass.

"They feed you good up at dat thar school?"

"Not as good as you."

"When they told me you was coming. I got ready to fix all yo favorites. Yes, I did. I got a special meal this evening just for yo homecoming. I'm so glad you back. Cause Lord knows we needs you 'round here."

Andrew took a seat at the table. "Where's Georgie? She hasn't been to see me."

The gleam left her.

"What's wrong? Is something wrong with Georgie?"

She wiped her hands on her apron and took a seat across from him. "Things ain't the same with Georgie." She seemed to choose her words carefully. "She fixing to have a baby."

"A baby! Who's the daddy? One of the field hands?"

"Simmer down, now. Dat's what I'm trying to tell you. Since dis here done happened, she ain't been herself. It's like she done taken an ailing in her mind."

"What do you mean?"

"I don't know," she said sniffling and wiping her eyes with the hem of the apron. "She won't talk. Won't say nothing 'bout it. She just walk around looking far off. She won't eat. Sometimes I think she trying to kill dat child 'fore it's born. I know something terrible happened to my baby. I just know it. Maybe she'll tell you."

"What's Daddy done about all this?"

"He done tried to talk to her, I done tried too, but she won't say nothing. Yo daddy questioned the menfolk. He even threatened to whip some of 'em, but don't nobody know, and Georgie ain't talking."

"I don't want to believe this. It explains why she hasn't come to greet me." He grabbed her hands, the hands that soothed him when he was a scared little boy. "Don't you worry none. I'll get to the bottom of this. Is she in her cabin?"

"Yes. We can't git no work out of her. Others been doing her chores so Massa John and that old overseer don't take notice. She just sit thar looking far off."

"I'll go down now. Don't you worry. I'm home."

She smiled. "But is you gonna stay? It's been hard here wid you away."

"I don't know, Aunt Daisy," he sighed. "But let's not worry about that now. We got to see about Georgie."

*********

Andrew knocked on the cabin door but got no response. "Georgie. Georgie, you in there?" He opened the door. She sat at a small table staring at a plate of untouched food. She saw him and retreated to the corner of the room, her back pressed against the wall.

"Georgie, it's me, Andrew. I'm home. I've come back home."

The large bump in her belly told him she was near the end. Haggard and frail, cheekbones visible, clothes hanging on her, she was a ghost of the pretty girl he had left behind.

"Georgie, this breaks my heart. You are the one person I expected to greet me with open arms, a hug, and a smile. Why are you cowering from me as if I were a villain? Georgie, it's me, Andrew. I'd never hurt you. What has happened to you?"

She moved toward him, a wild-faced child he almost didn't recognize. He held out his hand, and her bony fingers reached for it. She rested her head on his chest and sobbed. He held her, not wanting to injure her frail body or hurt the baby. Her tears soaked his shirt. He rocked her until she calmed. "Can you tell me what happened?"

"No," she said shaking her head, panic-stricken. "No."

"Yes you can, and you must. Something terrible has happened to you, and I want to know."

"But..."

"What happened, Georgie? Who did this to you? No harm will come to you if you tell me."

She composed herself and pulled away from his embrace. "You left me." She sank back into her despondence and returned to her seat at the table.

"Please forgive me. I didn't know that my leaving would allow this to happen to you. I'm back now and will do everything in my power to protect you. I will not rest until you are well, and we've gotten to the bottom of this. I'll be back with food and milk." Tears streaked his cheeks, and his voice trembled. He pointed his finger at her. "If I have to stay all night, I will not leave you until you have eaten and told me what has happened." He rummaged through her trunk and found a fresh dressing gown and placed it on the bed. "I'll send Aunt Daisy down with fresh water. She can help you clean up. If you won't let her do it, I'll wash you myself." He wiped his cheeks and nose with the back of his hand. "I love you, Georgie." He headed for the kitchen to find

Aunt Daisy.

Andrew returned to Georgie's cabin with a tray loaded with warm broth, milk, and mashed potatoes. She sat in a chair by the fireplace wearing the fresh dressing gown. Her hair was combed and in a long plait, cascading across her shoulder down her breast and resting on her swollen stomach.

"I told you I'd be back with food."

She didn't respond. She just stared at him as he placed the tray on the table and uncovered it.

"You look so much better."

"Mama helped me clean up," she mumbled.

"Come on." He took her hand and led her over to the table. He got her seated and pulled up a chair beside her. "I thought it best not to put too much on you right away. We'll ease our way back into regular food." He poured broth into a teacup. "Sip this," he said putting the cup up to her mouth. "It's warm. Not gonna burn you." She swallowed and licked her dry cracked lips. "That's it. Take a little more. Now, let's try these mashed potatoes." He scooped up a fork full and put it to her mouth. "Come on, Georgie. Open up. Like I told you, I'll stay as long as I have to."

She opened her mouth and ate the potatoes, and soon they found a rhythm.

She finished the meal.

"Let's rest. He put her in the bed and covered her. He took off his shoes and crawled in behind her, wrapping Georgie in his arms like when they were children. "Now it's time to tell me what happened."

She said nothing.

"I know you're not asleep, and I know you hear me. Tell me what happened."

Andrew swatted at a mosquito buzzing around his ear. The flame in the oil lamp flickered, causing early evening shadows to dance on the walls. Everything else was still until Georgie's exhale. "All my life, I've had you, and then you just up and left."

"You know I had to go to school. We talked about it."

"But even when you had a chance to come back to visit, you

18

rarely did. I heard Massa Gordon complaining to my mama about how you spent your time off visiting your new friends rather than coming back home. You forgot about me. Now you come back expecting me to be here waiting like nothing has changed. It's been hard without you. My people don't like me 'cause I'm the Massa's daughter. The white folks don't like me 'cause I look too much like them. Look at what they've done to me."

"I'm back now, and if I leave again, I'll take you with me. I promise you. Now tell me what happened."

She turned to face him, exhaled, and pressed her face close to his chest. "The overseer, Onie Johnson." More sobs came. "He got drunk and came to my cabin. He told me I was uppity and needed to be taught my place. Said I needed to be taken down a notch or two. He beat me. I fought back as best I could. I bit a plug out of him, scratched and kicked, but he was too strong for me." She stopped to compose herself.

"Go on."

"I even threw the lamp at him. It started a fire. I ran for the door while he was stomping it out, but he caught me. He tore my dress off. I tried to fight." She started to cry.

"That son of a bitch. I ought to kill him."

"I begged him to stop, but he wouldn't. After I missed my timing, I had to tell Mama about the baby."

"It's all right. I'm gonna take care of you." He stroked her brow. "I don't know how you have carried a baby this far in this condition. Why didn't you tell Daddy or Aunt Daisy what he did right after it happened?"

"Massa Gordon was away. It don't matter none. I couldn't tell."

"Why?"

"Mr. Onie say, if I tell, he would kill you the first chance he got. After he found out about the baby, he said if I told, he'd make sure the baby got sold away. I'd never see it again."

"I should've come home more often. Oh, Georgie, I'm sorry. This might not have happened if I had been here. I've got to figure out how to handle this. Don't say anything to anyone. I might just blow his brains out myself. Now, you've got to eat to get your strength up. And, don't you worry about me. I've learned how to protect myself, and I can take care of Onie Johnson." He slept beside her for a few hours and then returned to his own bed.

\*\*\*\*\*\*\*\*\*\*

The next morning, Mother and Anna's gossip dominated the breakfast table. Andrew and Daddy sat at opposing ends. Daddy slurped coffee, sucked his teeth, and rubbed his chin amidst the clang of dishes being removed. "I reckon you done seen Georgie and Daisy."

"Yes, sir. I have." Anna stopped chewing and Mother's coffee cup chipped the edge of her saucer, the question and the clank jarring the still morning air.

Daddy continued. "What you think of Georgie?"

The clatter stopped. Two female slaves froze in place waiting to hear the response.

"Looks like the baby will be here any day now."

"You gentlemen will have to excuse us. Anna and I are expecting our gowns for tonight's ball to be delivered momentarily," interrupted Mother. "Come along, Anna. We'll wait in the front parlor. Luther, bring coffee to the front parlor for Miss Anna and me."

"Zula," Daddy called to one of the slave girls. "Y'all come back later and get them dishes. Go on back to the kitchen. I'll send for you."

"Ya sah. Welcome home, Mr. Andrew."

They sat in silence until the room cleared.

"So, you gonna answer my question?" Daddy seemed anxious.

Andrew moved to the chair next to him. "You know she hasn't been able to work?"

"Course I know. I know everything that goes on around my plantation, except for this thing. I done tried to talk to her, but she just done shut down. If she don't get no better, I may have to send her away after the baby is born. I wrote to the folks at the state asylum. They know she's part Negra, but they'll take her if I say so."

"Don't do that. She's down mighty low, but she's not crazy.

You know Georgie has always been delicate. I got through to her last evening. I got her to start eating."

"I knew if anybody could reach her, it would be you. Which one of them field hands took her? Did she tell you? After all my ranting about it, I still ain't got no answers."

"It wasn't a slave."

"What you mean? Ain't no free niggers been on this plantation. You know I don't believe in mixing the slaves with the free."

"Now, Daddy, I need you to be calm until we figure out how to handle this."

"Handle what?" He spit a crumb off the tip of his tongue and leaned forward to hear what Andrew had to say.

"It was Onie Johnson. He got drunk. He beat her, and he took her."

"Goddamn it. Goddamn it!" He pounded the table with his fist, his face red, and his brow furrowed.

"Please calm down. I don't want anyone else to know just yet."

Daddy's nostrils flared, and his breathing labored. He pointed his finger at Andrew. "Everybody 'round here knows she's my daughter, and, slave or not, she ain't to be treated like a common field hand. He could have any wench he wants except her. That's disrespecting me. I'll kill that piece of trash."

"Let's just get rid of him. We'll escort him off the land and be done with him. You and I can run things until we get a new overseer."

Laughter and raised voices came from the front parlor, needling Daddy. "What's all that racket going on in the front room? It must be the dressmaker delivering them damn dresses. They cost me a fortune. Listen to them in there carrying on like school girls." The distraction calmed Daddy a little.

"Remember, let's think this thing through and make a plan for getting rid of Onie."

Daddy didn't respond. He just sat motionless with his fists clenched and jaws tight.

Andrew got up from the table. "I'll be back directly, and we can go check on things in the fields. I know what your temper is like when you get riled. Let's take time to think this through."

He passed through the parlor. "Look, Andrew. Aren't they lovely?" Mother held one of the dresses up to her body and waltzed around the room.

"Andrew, you're back just in time for the Annual Richmond Dogwood Cotillion. It's tonight. We've been planning for it for months," said Anna. "We made at least three trips to Richmond trying to find the right fabrics and patterns. We couldn't find a thing. These have come direct from Paris, France. We'll be the only women in original Charles Worth designs."

"We'll be the envy of every female in the room," said Mother as she hummed and continued to waltz around the room.

He didn't respond. Mother's pretense was just one of the many things he disliked about her.

Later Andrew returned to the parlor carrying a trunk.

"You going somewhere?" Mother stared at the large trunk.

"Not yet. This is taking up too much space in my room. I thought I'd store it in the cellar. Where's Daddy?"

"Where else would he be except out in the fields with his precious darkies," said Anna gazing up from her book.

Mother looked up from her needle point, "He stormed out of here cussing and fussing about something and went on out to the fields."

Worried, Andrew hurried back to his room and picked up his pistol. He strode out of the manor and rode his horse to the fields. He stopped close enough to see the two men arguing. Onie stumbled and fell dodging one of Daddy's shots.

"Why'd you do it? You ungrateful son-of-a-poor-white-trash-bitch." Daddy took aim at Onie.

"Please Mr. Gordon, don't shoot. I can explain," he begged.

Andrew was too far away to stop the shooting. His father stood over Onie, sunlight reflecting off his pistol; Onie struggled to get up. Andrew fired his pistol in the air twice and galloped toward them. He dismounted. "That's enough, Daddy. That's enough." Andrew walked up to Onie. "Get your things, and get off our land. We'll pay you what you got coming."

"And don't you bring your no 'count ass to the house to get it. We'll bring it to you," said Daddy. "Georgie might be in the kitchen or the house, and I don't want her running into you."

Onie shuffled to his feet, shaking. He started to protest, backing away, his wild eyes fixed on both pistols. He turned and started to run, stumbling before taking off in a dead sprint.

Daddy and Andrew returned to the house in silence, counted out fair pay for Onie and walked to his quarters to see him off the land. Onie had tied up a few belongings in a satchel and flung it across the back of his horse. Andrew wondered if the man had stolen anything.

"I done good work fer you, Mr. Gordon. I made them niggers work hard. This just ain't right. All because I fucked a nigger."

Daddy's fist sprang to Onie's mouth. Onie stumbled back, red drops spotting his shirt. He straightened his stance and wiped his bloody mouth with his sleeve.

Andrew was stunned at how quickly Daddy threw the punch and the power with which he did it. He could never be that kind of man, and Daddy would always be disappointed in his lack of brute strength.

"It's your wife and daughter you ought to be hitting. It was them that put me up to it. Now, I'm the one who's got to suffer."

"What the hell are you talking about?" Daddy's mouth hung open, as if the answer might need a landing place.

Onie continued, "That's right. They paid me a hundred dollars to do it and gave me a bottle of your best whiskey to prime my pump."

Daddy drew back to land another blow. Andrew stepped between them. "Hold on, Daddy."

Andrew shoved the money into Onie's chest.

"Get the hell off my land," said Daddy.

Onie mounted his horse and spit a wad of blood at their feet. "You ain't seen the last of me. I swear to God, you gonna regret this." He kicked the horse and rode off.

Daddy walked up the back yard with fists clinched and huffs of angry breath marking each step.

"Calm yourself. Remember you fainted at my graduation. Don't wear yourself out."

"I ain't old and useless yet, Boy."

"That's not what I meant."

As they neared the house, pinewood smoke stung Andrew's eyes. Zula was boiling laundry in a large pot over an open fire in the back yard.

Daddy yelled to a couple of the male slaves, "Move that pot and git more kindling. I need a strong fire. Now!"

"Massa say move de pot," one of the boys repeated.

Andrew followed Daddy up the steps and into the house where Daddy found Mother and Anna still with their needlepoint and reading. He stormed into the parlor, his face red, his breathing harder and faster than outside. "Why'd you do it? Why'd you put him up to it?"

"What are you going on about?" Mother looked over her spectacles as she worked silk threads into a ribbon of flowers on linen fabric.

"You know what I'm talking about. That Onie Johnson told it all. It seems the two of you put him up to taking Georgie."

"I have no idea what you're talking about."

"You're a liar." Spit flew from Daddy's mouth, inches from her face. "You paid him with money, whiskey, and Lord only knows what else."

Mother didn't flinch. She stood. "How dare you accuse me?" Trying to appear in control, she pointed her finger at Daddy. "Yes. Yes, goddamn it, yes!" Each word moved her closer to hysteria, her background she tried so hard to hide, clawing its way to the surface. "She walks around here like she's as white as me. Just because she's your bastard don't change the fact that she's still a nigger slave."

He drew back to slap her.

"Daddy!" Andrew's voice stifled Daddy's anger. He lowered his hand.

"Where are they? Where are they?" Daddy ran up the stairs and Andrew followed. He went from bedroom to bedroom slamming doors. He skipped back down the stairs two at a time, the dresses draped across his arm.

24

"John, what are you doing? This is absurd, and I will not stand for any more of it," Mother said. He pushed her aside and headed out the back door.

"Daddy, please don't," begged Anna.

The pot which Zula was using to boil clothes had been removed, and two slave boys had put more wood on the fire. Daddy tossed in the ball gowns. The wind caught them, and, for a moment, they appeared suspended in mid-air. Lace, taffeta, and silk ribbons floated before landing on the hot cinders and flaming wood. The material almost snuffed out the fire. They lay for a minute smoldering. White smoke crept up from the mound, and a few flames flickered.

"Get me some kerosene from the barn," said Daddy.

A slave boy came staggering with a can so heavy he could hardly carry it. It wasn't needed. By then, the dresses were in a full blaze.

*********

Georgie stood behind the cabin and watched them run off Onie. She had heard everything and was shook to her core. She turned to head up the path toward the kitchen but pain like a knife stabbed at her stomach. She doubled over, stumbled back, and retched. She steadied herself against the side of the slave house and wiped her face with her apron. After a few minutes, she tried walking again.

Holding her swollen belly, she reached the kitchen and sat down, the taste of vomit still in her mouth. She strained to stand up out of the chair, walked to the door, and spit into the yard.

Mama beamed when Georgie turned back into the kitchen. "Well. Thank ya, Jesus. I sho am glad to see you up and about. Ya hungry?"

"Maybe a little."

"Sit right here, and I'll cut ya some of dat corn bread I made last night for Mr. Andrew's home coming. You be all right once dat baby pop out ya," she said sawing the bread. "I'm so happy you done come back to yo right mind."

"They paid him to do it." Georgie sat staring at the plank that made up the tabletop.

"Paid who to do what, Honey?" Mama handed Georgie a saucer holding a slice of bread.

"Miss Victoria and Anna paid Onie Johnson to rape me. I told Andrew everything last night. Massa Gordon and Andrew just run him off."

"So dat's who done it. Is dat why ya kept quiet 'bout it fer so long? How you know dey paid him?"

"I heard everything. That's what all the fuss is outside."

Mama walked to the door and looked out. "I need you to be strong, Georgie. We gots to protect dis chile you carrying."

"How am I gonna protect this child, when I can't even protect myself. I'm gonna have this baby, but I can't stay here much longer."

Mama spun around and rushed to the table. "Hush yo mouth, chile. Don't go talking no foolishness."

"It ain't foolishness. But first, they gonna pay for what they've done to me."

"Now, dat's even more foolish. You have always had your daddy's spirit, and dat's dangerous for a colored chile."

*********

Andrew found his father in the library making notations in the ledger. "Hopefully, we've seen the last of Onie," he said walking up to Daddy.

"If he shows his face around here again, I'll blow his brains out. If you hadn't stopped me, we'd be burying his ass right now."

"What are you recording?" Andrew looked over Daddy's shoulder.

Daddy smiled. "Thought I'd start a fresh page for the little one. I want to record the birth right away. Never thought my first grandchild would be half Negra."

"Listed with all your other property." Andrew flipped through several pages.

"If it's a girl, I hope Georgie will name her after my mother, Sally."

"What if it's a boy?"

Daddy turned and looked at Andrew. "You know damn well, if it's a boy, she will name him after you."

Andrew smiled. "I'm going on back to the parlor. I'll reload in case that fool comes back looking for trouble."

He sat in a corner chair – one designed for impressing – and studied his mother and sister while he readied his pistol.

"Come away from the window, Anna. Come on back in here," said Mother. The dresses were nothing more than ashes now.

A solitary tear rolled down Anna's face. Mother grabbed her by both shoulders and turned the distraught girl to face her. "Don't cry! Don't ever cry! Never give him that satisfaction."

"But Mama, they were Charles Worth," she said as more tears fell.

"We'll get more dresses, and we'll get even with him." Mother stared at Georgie, who had just stepped into the kitchen doorway.

Andrew snapped the pistol's chamber closed and leaned back in the chair. His body tensed at his mother and sister. He'd seen kinder copperheads.

### Chapter 3
### July 1856, Oaks' Plantation, Bowie, Maryland

**Edward** set up a makeshift table in the pantry where the sterling he was to polish stood within reach, along with the family's fine china and crystal. He buffed candlesticks in time to organ music in the background, the same tune playing over and over. Mrs. Oaks practiced her Sunday morning hymns each day at this time. Today's practice came to a sudden stop, right when Edward accidentally clanked the silver ladle against the punch bowl. The organ's wheezing bellows ceased as did the dreadful tune. Edward feared it would ring in his head the rest of the day. The music was replaced by the murmur of Mrs. Oaks' soft slippers on the carpets.

"Edward, you in there?" Mrs. Oaks peered around the cracked door. Her frail hand opened it wider. The old woman stood before him, pale as ever. "I'm practicing for Reverend Oak's Sunday sermon," she said, wearing her Christianity like a badge of honor. "I hope you didn't harm the silver."

Edward had always been curious about the self-proclaimed God-fearers like Reverend and Mrs. Oaks who remained silent about the beatings, rapes, and lynchings that were regular occurrences in the world around them.

"No, Ma'am. Everything's just so. I'm sorry for the noise."

Mrs. Oaks' crucifix rested on her bosom against her burgundy plaid dress. "Well, good. I wanted to make sure. Put a good shine on that bowl. I'm having Susie make her special punch for my luncheon tomorrow."

"I'll see to it."

"All right. I won't disturb you." She shuffled off singing *"we shall come rejoicing, bringing in the sheaves"* with a voice as shrill and frail as she looked.

Wonderful. Now, he had words to go along with the tune. His left hand hurt and was slightly swollen from the scuffle the night before. The fight revisited his mind. Mahala, the field hand, had mouthed off in front of the slaves when Edward walked through the shanties looking to deliver a message to the overseer.

'Lookie, y'all. Its de pretty house-nigger in his fancy clothes,' Mahala had said jumping in front of Edward and blocking his way.

'Let me pass. I got no business with you.'

'You working in de big house, eating good, got fancy clothes, and dey say you 'posed to be fucking, too. But, we done heard dat you don't like womenfolk. What kind of man is you?' He slapped Edward.

Edward punched Mahala hard, and the man fell into the cook fire. His ragged pants caught the blaze. He danced around like a fool trying to put them out. Everybody laughed. Edward had kept walking.

Edward tried to forget the accusations, but they were true. Reverend Oaks couldn't afford to buy more slaves. He sought to breed his own, and Edward had been purchased for that purpose. He recalled the three women who had been told to lay with him. They had been obedient to Reverend Oaks' orders. It was Edward who had not performed. No matter how hard he tried, he wasn't aroused by the women. The first one was plump with large breasts. No matter how much she rubbed, kissed, and licked on him, he was not interested; there was no pretending. Finally, she put her mouth on his cock, something she said the overseer taught her to do. That worked. He quickly put it in her before it lost its firmness. But he wanted it to end. He lurched, moaned, and faked an ending.

A few weeks later, the next one to knock on his door was a girl he recognized as help in Miss Susie's kitchen. She smelled of cooking grease, and her kisses tasted like fresh dough. She refused to use her mouth like the first one. After massaging and tugging to no avail, he told her he was tired and sent her back to her cabin.

The third and most recent visitor was a field worker. 'They tell me dem little girls dey sent here don't know how to please a man. Well, you 'bout to have a real woman now.' She stepped out of her dress.  After a half hour of more pulling and tugging, she slipped from the bed and stepped back into her dress.  'Ain't no man ever refused what I got to offer.'  She left in a huff.

Evidently, the three women must have talked.  The encounter with Mahala was probably only the beginning.

Edward finished the old lady's silver, went about his chores around the house, then headed to the kitchen to check on the evening meal.  "How's everything coming along, Miss Susie?" he asked the aging cook as she scurried around the small kitchen. He was the only one who called her *Miss*.  She seemed to appreciate the small ray of respect.

"Everything be ready on time.  You come on and get it when dey ready to eat."

"I'll be back in about an hour."

"All right.  Now, you watch yo self.  You hear me?  Dey tells me you knocked Mahala flat on his ass."  She laughed, her bosom shaking in rhythm.  "You be careful.  Dey dem vengeful niggers. It's three of 'em.  Dey try to hurt you.  If dey come after you, you got to hurt them first."

"Thank you, Miss Susie.  I'll remember."

"One thang dey say 'bout you is sho nuff true."

"And what's that?"  He braced.

"You do talk all proper like white folks," she grinned.  "De way you talk, it's a wonder you can't read, too."

\*\*\*\*\*\*\*\*\*

Edward retreated to his cabin, built close to the big house. He wanted to sit for a moment before his supper duties.  He would be back in that chair after dinner was cleared to sleep for the night, next to the bolted door, in case any trouble came up. The problems with the other slaves could mean big problems for Edward.  Reverend Oaks needed field workers more than he needed a fancy-talking butler to keep a shine on the silver.  If the others kept after him, Oaks would get rid of him before he would any of the field hands.

That night, his troubled mind took him back to childhood where he grew up fighting. A skinny little orphan, the other children beat him down whenever they could. No one looked out for him until one day an old slave woman pulled him aside and said 'Boy, I catch you crying one more time 'cause of what dem little no-good pickaninnies done to you, I'll beat you myself.' She took him behind a cabin and taught him how to make a fist and swing it. 'Ain't no such a-thang as fighting fair,' she told him. 'You kick, bite, and use whatever weapon you can find. Don't matter none if you win. When dey find out you'll fight back, de little bastards will leave you alone. 'Course winning is good.' The old woman's words were one of the few things he'd ever been given. Sure enough, after he'd inflicted some wounds, the bigger boys left him alone.

The force against the door was so powerful it knocked the top hinge loose, and the bolt flew across the room. Mahala and his minions had found a tree limb strong enough to ram the door. Edward jumped up. The open door hid him long enough to gather his wits. Miss Susie's warning to 'hurt dem first' flashed in his mind.

"Where de hell is he?" One assailant entered the room.

"Drag him out here. I'm gonna put my foot up his ass," said Mahala.

Edward reached for the kerosene lamp resting on the mantle. The lowered wick cast a dim light over the room. The flame flickered at his movement.

"Behind the door," the man alerted the other two. Edward slammed the door just as the outside two tried to enter; they ran face-first into it. The one in the room was Clem. Edward smashed the lamp against his head, the flame catching his collar, soon engulfing his entire shirt. The other two came in throwing punches. Clem staggered into the yard and rolled in the dirt. Edward recognized the other man as Aaron. Edward picked up the chair and splintered it across Aaron's head and back, rendering him helpless.

"It's just me and you now, fancy nigger," said Mahala. "You won't be so fancy when I finish whipping you." He charged Edward, and they tumbled through the door and into the yard. The ruckus roused the other slaves. Mahala broke free from the tussle. He swung at Edward and missed. Edward landed two punches square in Mahala's face. Dazed, the man didn't defend. Edward kept punching until Mahala fell to the ground and stopped moving.

**\*\*\*\*\*\*\*\*\***

Edward sat in the front seat of the buckboard beside Reverend Oaks. Mrs. Oaks stood by clutching her crucifix.

"I'm sorry about this, Edward, but it's got to be done," said Reverend Oaks. "My plantation is small. I need every able-bodied slave I can get. It's going to be weeks before Clem's burns heal. Aaron can't lift much of nothing since you cracked that chair across him, and you beat Mahala so bad, his mind might not ever be right."

"He was defending himself," protested Mrs. Oaks.

"I know," Reverend Oaks snapped. "It's bad blood between them. You think they gonna let him be after this, aside from all the unnatural things they saying about him? First chance they get, they'll come for him, and somebody is gonna end up dead."

"Unnatural things? What are you talking about, Reverend?" Mrs. Oaks took a step closer to the wagon. "Edward has been a jewel and a tremendous help to me."

"Some things you best not know about." Reverend Oaks directed his gaze to Edward. "Mr. Fairholm over in Annapolis done offered me a fair price, and I'm selling him. It's for the best." He slapped the horses' backsides, and the wagon lurched forward.

"Good bye and Godspeed, Edward," said Mrs. Oaks, wiping a tear.

"Good bye, Mrs. Oaks, and thank you for your many kindnesses."

Miss Susie peeped from behind her shack and waved goodbye.

## Chapter 4
### July 1856

**Andrew** rested his head on the carriage window, lulled into a bumpy doze on the quiet ride to the cotillion. Mother and Anna were still smarting over the dress burning. Daddy had initially refused to attend the dance. He and Mother had fought most of the day about Georgie. Andrew convinced him to attend, saying it would be good for business. Tobacco buyers loved those things. As the carriage rounded the corner to the grand hall, lanterns illuminated Broad Street, and musicians performed near the front of the building. The family descended from the carriage into a swirl of party goers.

"I will never live this down, John Gordon, never," said Mother.

"Never live what down, Victoria?"

"Anna and I are wearing the same dresses we wore two years ago. Everyone will talk. They will assume we have no money."

Daddy stopped. He faced Mother, held her by the shoulders, and leaned in. He studied her, wet his lips, and said, "Do you really think I give a good goddamn about what you have on or about what people think? They can assume whatever the hell they want. I know what I have, and that's all that matters. Now, we can put up your pretense of being a happy family, but I'm here tonight for business reasons and business reasons only."

Mother stepped back and composed herself. She took Daddy's arm, and Anna took Andrew's. They swooshed through the large glass double French doors and cascaded down the grand stairwell into the ballroom. The crowd hushed, but the orchestra continued to play. Andrew took a seat where he could watch the crowd. Mother and Anna quickly engaged in what he supposed was idle gossip with their circle of friends. Daddy was cornered by a group of men fussing about abolitionists and bragging about the good crop they each were expecting to harvest. Within moments, Mother and Anna approached with the rustling of petticoats and a debutante in tow.

"Andrew, I want to introduce Miss Abigail Winston," said Mother. "She's visiting these parts from Atlanta."

"We've been having a delightful conversation. Mother and I

34

have invited her to visit us at Wilmington Manor before her return home," announced Anna.

Andrew stood. "Pleased to make your acquaintance, Miss Winston. I do hope you are enjoying your stay in Richmond."

"Why yes, Mr. Gordon. It's lovely here. There is so much to see. I don't know if I can get it all in before I return to Atlanta."

"Yes, it is an exciting city."

"Andrew just graduated from the Virginia Military Institute a few days ago," interjected Mother. "It was a lovely ceremony with a reception on the lawn and a military ball. He's the best sharpshooter in his class, and he read the Declaration of Independence at commencement."

"Well, I do declare, Mr. Gordon," said Abigail.

The orchestra began a Strauss waltz. "Oh, how I love this music. Andrew, isn't this one of your favorite waltzes?"

Abigail lowered her eyes obviously embarrassed by Anna's transparent suggestion. He couldn't add to the embarrassment by *not* asking her to dance.

"Yes, Anna. It is. May I have this dance, Miss Winston?"

"Oh dear. Why yes, Mr. Gordon."

"Mother, will you and Anna excuse us?"

"Of course."

He held her tiny waist, and they moved to the music. The bass drum kept a steady three-quarter beat. Abigail's stale breath reeked of onions and garlic. He angled his head so the scent would not be in his face.

"How long will you be in Richmond, Miss Winston?"

"Until early August," she said, singeing his nostrils. "I'll be back in November for the Annual Ball of the Young Bachelors' Association."

"How nice." He asked no more questions and instead, concentrated on the dance steps.

They returned to Mother and Anna. "Thank you so much, Miss Winston. I hope you enjoy the remainder of your stay. Now, if you will excuse me, please, I want to speak with an old friend before he departs."

"Of course, Mr. Gordon. I understand. Perhaps I'll see you when I call on your mother and sister."

"Perhaps."

Andrew drifted through the next few hours engaging in light conversation with old acquaintances. The stiff collar constricted his breathing. He stepped into a parlor room used by the musicians to store instrument cases and took a seat in a large wing chair in the far corner. Out of sight, he loosened his tie and collar. He put his feet up on a stool in the dim room and exhaled, finally able to relax. The door opened, and Miss Winston and two other young ladies walked in. He recognized them: Emily Johnson and Lovey Masterson. Both were from Anna's circle of simple-minded friends. They did not see him in the dark corner.

"What a charming room. And it's not being used tonight. Let's talk here in private," said Lovey. "I saw you dancing with Andrew Gordon, earlier, Abigail. You know he is one of the most eligible bachelors in these parts."

"Yes. I was told about him the moment I arrived in Richmond," said Abigail. "Everything I heard is true. He's handsome and tall with strong shoulders. And he has the most interesting brown eyes. I must admit, I have an affinity for tall men. He doesn't look at all like his homely sister."

"Well, the rumor is that she is only his half-sister. It seems their mother is not as virtuous as she puts on," said Emily. "By the way, can you believe they came here tonight in those old ball gowns?"

"Abigail, you are not the only woman with an eye on Andrew Gordon," said Lovey using a more combative tone.

"I can be very persuasive," retorted Abigail.

"Really?" Lovey snapped her fan open causing a loud pop and fanned herself with much fervor.

"Oh dear, I've completely lost track of the time. I'm sure my hosts are ready to depart," said Abigail. "I must bid you ladies good night."

"Good night, dear."

Abigail hurried off.

"I'm glad she's gone, with that horrid red hair. Jezebel," said Lovey. "I've had my eye on Andrew Gordon for years."

"Don't worry, Lovey dear. She'll never catch a man with that breath," said Emily. "Thank heavens we had our fans."

Laughing, amid the whisper of crinoline and lace, they strolled back to the ballroom.

Andrew waited a few minutes, then left the room. Daddy walked up. "Your mother is ready to go."

"Good. So am I. I've seen and heard quite enough."

"Did you have a nice time, Son?"

"I find these things to be such a bore. I have very few close friends, except Jessup, and he wouldn't be caught dead here."

"The less you see of Jessup the better. He's gotten quite a reputation as a dandy since you've been away." Daddy puffed his cigar.

"Let's go. Mother and Anna are waiting."

Andrew leaned his head on the side of the carriage wall and settled in for the ride back to Wilmington Manor.

"It was awfully rude and abrupt of you to walk away from Miss Winston like that, Andrew. You would do well with a wife like her," Mother informed him before she had even settled into her seat.

"Thank you, Mother. When I decide to marry, it will be someone I've selected. Not someone you have selected for me."

"Well, I see you have found your voice. It appears you have learned more than sharpshooting at that military school."

"Yes. I have."

They rode in silence. Daddy slept.

Luther was waiting when they arrived home. He extended a shaky wrinkled hand to Mama and helped her step over the threshold and then directed his attention to Daddy. "I beg your pardon, Massa Gordon, but I thought you ought to know about Georgie.

"What's wrong? Is it the baby? Andrew asked.

"Ya sah. She done had a little girl. They both mighty weak, but we praying they gonna pull through. They done named her Little Sally."

"Y'all hear that?" Daddy said to Mother and Anna, who were midway up the staircase. "Your handiwork done come full circle. Now, both of you better hear me, and hear me good.  Either one of you do anything to harm Georgie or that baby, and I'll do more than burn a damn dress."  He pointed his finger.  "You hear me?" He roared.  "Answer me!"

Anna lowered her head.  "Yes, Daddy."  She turned and continued up the stairs.

Mother stood with one gloved hand on the bannister.  She stared at Daddy — daring him.  He didn't flinch, and his finger didn't waiver.  Mother snapped her body around, the train of her dress cascading down the steps, and she followed Anna up the stairs.

## Chapter 5
## May 1859
## Three years later

**MawNancy** prepared to venture out after the Sunday afternoon storm subsided and the sun peeked through. She tied a red scarf around her baldhead, topped it off with a wide-brim, straw hat and grabbed her satchel and the walking stick she had whittled into a two-pronged fork. Inhaling deeply the scent of wet earth, she struck a steady stride west. She'd heard of a nest by the riverbank. The slave children had been told to stay clear. She walked the well-worn path, stopping every now and then to pluck horehound leaves or ragwort. At the river's edge, she rummaged with the stick through soggy brush, looking for a grown one, not a baby. She focused on the reeds closest to the river, where mama water moccasins made secure homes for their babies. When she parted the stalks, nice-sized coils gleamed in the mid-day sun, motionless. MawNancy raked the sleeping creature toward her to snare its head between the prongs. The moccasin squirmed awake and bared its fangs. Keeping one eye on the trapped snake, MawNancy dug in her satchel for the glass jar. She grabbed the snake by the neck and shoved the jar in its mouth catching its fangs on the rim to milk it. The serpent fought back, but MawNancy's grip was firm. "Dat ought to be 'nuff. I thanks ya, ma'am." She walked to the bank and flung the angry thing into the river. It slithered upstream, rippling the calm waters.

She sealed the jar tight and walked in the direction of the big tree. The amanitas grew there and, by her estimation, should be ripe. With their white caps alongside the other mushrooms they looked similar, but she knew the deadly difference. She picked six large ones and put them in the jar to soak up the fresh venom.

The recipe originated with the African shamans and had been handed down through generations. According to the old man who taught her, the first African to bring it to these shores said the American serpents didn't have the potency of the pit vipers and other African snakes. Still, if done right, the potion could bring about a short or prolonged painful death, depending on the frequency of the dosage.

Having used it once before, she knew the concoction worked. A lifetime ago she had fed it to a young master who had beaten and raped her. During his fevers and stomach pains, she pretended to nurse him while slowly poisoning him more and watching his lingering, suffering, and death. Her first taste of revenge was sweet.

In her business of vengeance, she'd learned that patience was the most important tool. Five years had passed since the lynching, and her hatred had grown stronger. Now without warning, fate had provided her with an accomplice.

She hurried to her cabin to prepare the deadly brew, the necklace of human bones beating against her breast with each deliberate stride. She muddled dry ingredients in a make-shift mortar, then, spread the brown powder on her table. With a withered finger, she traced a circle in the dust. Over and over, she drew the same line, entranced. With each pass, her low humming increased. Groans became words, a chant: "Curse my enemies, whose noose bruised my Sam's neck. Crush my oppressors, who choked his breath and striped his back. Bring forth yo' winds of death and destruction on those who left him hangin'. Surround 'em, terrify 'em, kill 'em." Tears fell silver in the mixture.

A ruckus outside broke her concentration. She stepped to the window to look out. Miss Anna was after Georgie, again. She was after her with a whip, last time it was the broom. Being half white and the master's daughter, Georgie stood up to the folks in the big house, the only slave to do so.

Georgie dodged the lash, which wasn't much of a problem, since Miss Anna was as skilled with the whip as the half-dead hound dog that had taken to hanging around the slave shanties.

"Come back here, you lazy wench." Miss Anna cracked the whip toward Georgie.

Georgie dodged the lash and ran between the shanties with Miss Anna in pursuit. They came around the other side. MawNancy stepped outside, and her mouth flung open.

"I'm going whip you if it's the last thing I do." Miss Anna made another feeble attempt at cracking the whip.

Georgie grabbed a bucket off one of the shanty stoops and flung the water at Miss Anna, dousing her square in the face.

"You bitch. Stand still. You hear me, stand still!"

Georgie pelted Miss Anna with a hand full of gravel. She took off running, but her foot tangled in the hem of her dress, and she fell. Miss Anna stood over her ready to lash out.

Master Andrew galloped up. "Anna!" Beet-red and sweating, he dismounted, yelling with his teeth bared. "Daddy and I warned you about coming after Georgie. Didn't we?"

"But, Andrew, she..."

He snatched the whip from her. "Get on back up to the house."

Miss Anna ran off crying and dripping wet.

Mr. Andrew turned to Georgie. "You all right? She didn't hit you with this thing, did she?"

"I'm fine." Georgie brushed the dirt from the front of her dress.

The excitement ended, the other slaves disbursed, and MawNancy returned to her business. "Have mercy," she chuckled. "When dat dumb chile gonna learn. Whenever she come after Georgie, she de one ends up bruised and battered."

MawNancy pricked her finger with a knife and dropped blood into the mixture. "Don't you worry, Sam. De time done come for her to pay fer what dey done to you." She rubbed her leathery hands together. "I gotcha now you jackal bitch."

## Chapter 6

### August 1859

**Georgie** stepped into the library with a dinner tray. The ledger lay open in front of Andrew, and he was scratching out something. The sight of the worn leather-bound book angered Georgie from deep within. "What are you doing with that?"

"I never got around to recording old Jerimiah's death. He's been buried over a week."

"I've always wondered where I'm listed. Am I with the hogs or the cows? And my baby, is she with kittens or the puppies?"

"Georgie, you know we don't think of you like that."

"Is my name in that book, my mama, my baby? Just how much are we worth? Does it say?"

"Please don't do this, Georgie. Not today."

With heavy breathing, she managed to ask Andrew if he was hungry, softening as she spoke.

Andrew pushed the ledger aside and rubbed his temples. "I don't know. I don't feel much like eating these days." He closed the book and shoved it on the shelf above the desk.

"What's wrong?"

"Just feeling sorry for myself I guess." He rubbed his face. His stubble sizzled. "I can't believe it's been three years since I came back from school, and I'm still here. I had grand plans to get away and see the world. Most of my classmates secured good military positions. I wish I could have accepted the teaching position the school offered me, but with Mother sick and Daddy's mind gone, I'm stuck here. I'm nothing more than a glorified overseer. All that hard work and education for nothing."

"We need you here. Before you came back, I wanted to die," she reminded him. "You came back just in time."

"Look at you now." He took her hand, interlocking his fingers with hers. "Motherhood suits you well. Since giving birth to Little Sally, you've grown even more beautiful. You look a lot like Daddy, more so than Anna. Your hair is the envy of every white woman who visits here. It's almost down to your waist now. I think Daddy's mother had hair like

42

that."

"That's why I keep it tied up most of the time. I done had enough of white women hating me."

Andrew lowered his head. "Daddy done taken a real liking to Little Sally."

"She seems to like him, too. She follows me to his room when I take his tray. She hops on his lap and just sits there. Every now and then, I see him stroke her brow or kiss her forehead."

"They have a real fondness for each other. I think having her around is good for him. I'm sure he knows she's your child. Little Sally's his only grandchild."

He looked at Georgie. Concern and sadness shadowed his face.

"What else is on your mind?" She asked.

"I reckon it's been hard for you to take care of Mother, after all she's done to you."

"Mama says it's my Christian duty. Why you think Miss Victoria always been so mean to me?"

"You're Daddy's child, born exactly one month after Anna. I guess she's angry that Daddy preferred Aunt Daisy to her. You remind her of that. Daddy clearly preferred you to Anna when you were children. Even I could see that, and I was just a child. He had a cabin built for you when you turned seventeen. How many slaves have that?"

"None of them, and they let me know it. I can't help how Massa Gordon feels."

"What about Miss Anna? What I ever done to her?"

"Anna is a tortured soul. When y'all were still little, she once came to the kitchen and saw Daddy playing with you, holding you up, and saying you were his favorite little girl. Anna ran back to the house crying and told Mother what she saw. They continue to hold that against you."

"I was only a child, no more than four or five years old."

"I know." He pulled the lid from the dinner tray. "That smells good. Maybe I am a little hungry after all." He stuck a fork full of mash potatoes in his mouth. "You best get some sleep. We might be up with her again all night. Looks like she's not long for this world."

"I know. Mama's gonna sit with her for a while. Then I'll take over."

********

Georgie awoke to her mother's gentle tug on her shoulder.

"Time for you to go on up and sit with her, Georgie. I hate to wake you, but I need to rest a spell 'fore I starts cooking breakfast."

"How's she doing tonight?" Georgie sat up and tied her hair in a white cloth.

"She down low. Ain't gonna be much longer. Lots of pain," said Mama.

"Good."

"Now, that ain't Christian, Georgie."

She didn't respond but headed up the path to the big house.

Georgie entered the bedroom. An overwhelming stench filled the air, and she gagged, her eyes watering. The grand mistress had lost control of her bowels, again. Georgie covered her nose and mouth and made her way across the room to raise the window.

"Who's there?" Miss Victoria demanded, gasping for breath and sweating profusely.

"It's Georgie. I'm here to sit with you."

"Here to gloat. Shut that window. And I need a fresh wrapping. I know you can smell it."

Georgie pulled back the covers. Shit had seeped out of the swaddling and stained the sheets. She teetered back, unsteady on her feet.

"I said I need changing. Now get to it."

Georgie threw the covers back over Miss Victoria and took a seat by the open window.

"I told you to shut that damn ... Oh," she screamed. "Oh. Have mercy," she moaned. "Why me? What have I done to deserve this pain?"

Miss Victoria continued to gasp for air. Some of her moans were barely audible, and others were violent screams heard around the plantation. Georgie sat by the window fanning herself.

\*\*\*\*\*\*\*\*\*

Aunt Daisy sat on the side of the bed rubbing her hands. She tried not to stir too much, afraid she'd wake up Buck. She may not have loved the man when they'd jumped the broom but after all his help raising Georgie, she took care of him now. Maybe even loved him. Massa John had arranged the union after Buck's third escape. Massa said settling down would keep Buck from running away. May have, but the union didn't keep Massa John out of Daisy's bed.

"What's wrong wid ya?" Asked Buck propping himself up. "Ya joints hurt?"

"Nothing, Buck. I can't seem to get no rest tonight. You go on back to sleep. I think I'll walk out and get some air."

"You needs yo rest," he warned.

"I know. I be all right. You go on back to sleep."

She walked into the darkness and waited for light. When it dawned, she bathed in the sunrise, its warmth and beauty soothing her unsettled spirit. She walked down to where MawNancy sat outside her cabin door. "Look at her. Got me mixed up in all dis mess." Aunt Daisy mumbled as she walked toward the old woman who chanted an old African curse while fingering a necklace made of human bones she'd sawed into small pieces and strung together.

"You gonna sit? Or you gonna stand thar a-looking at me?" MawNancy crowed.

"I need to get on back to the house. She down low."

"I know. I been a-sitting here listening to her scream fer mercy. Asking why her. Why her," MawNancy cackled. "Death is a-working. He's a-riding her some'm terrible."

Miss Victoria's screams grew more frantic. MawNancy stood and looked up the hill. She pointed her bony finger toward the house, her fingernails caked with dirt and tobacco resin. "Ride her," she said. Her eyes glistened with anticipation. More screams of pain came. "Ride her," her voice even more animated. "Ride her!" She raised her arms and danced around stomping up dust. She threw back her head, looked to the heavens and commanded, "Ride dat bitch all de way to de dungeons of hell. May Satan himself meet her at the gate and shove his red-hot pitchfork up her ass. Burn her in hell's fire for *all* eternity. Suffah. Suffah! Suffaaah!!"

"MawNancy!" Aunt Daisy raised her voice, overwhelmed by such an evil vision. "Ain't no cause fer taking pleasure in dis."

MawNancy shook her fists at the heavens and laughed a loud devilish laugh as she continued to chant and dance around the yard. "Oooh Faah Kaay Moe Teeh Nah, Oooh Faah Kaay Moe Teeh Nah." She laughed so hard she doubled over and held her belly.

"I best git back up there. Georgie be needing me 'bout now. You best mind yo self, MawNancy."

"I ain't worried none 'bout dem white folks. Oooh Faah Kaay Moe Teeh Nah, Oooh Faah Kaay Moe Teeh Nah. What can dey do to me?"

"Dey can kill anyone of us any time dey wants to."

MawNancy ceased her incantation and stood still. "Dey kilt me a long time ago." Her eyes widened, and she beat her breasts. "I'm dead inside, Daisy. Now, I'm a-working on a-killing dem."

The exchange was interrupted by Miss Anna's scream followed by her uncontrollable sobbing echoing around the plantation. MawNancy sat down. The cloud of dust she'd danced up floated off and dissipated. She fingered the bone necklace, which she claimed protected her from white people. The bones were all that remained of her dead husband. She rubbed her ugly hands and looked up the hill transfixed on the big house. She rocked and whispered the chant, "Oooh Faah Kaay Moe Teeh Nah, Oooh Faah Kaay Moe Teeh Nah. Forces of darkness come to me. A vessel of evil I shall be. Curse my enemies. Crush my oppressors. Bring forth thy winds of death and destruction. Death and destruction." Her voice trailed off to nothing more than a purr. She fingered the necklace and rocked. Her eyes rolled back in her head.

Aunt Daisy turned and walked toward the big house. "Thank ya, Jesus. It's over."

\*\*\*\*\*\*\*\*\*

Georgie was busy helping prepare food for the family. A constant parade of slaves moved in and out of the kitchen, buzzing about Miss Victoria's death.

"Was you in de room when she died?" Zula questioned Georgie.

"I was."

"Oh Lord, I'm scared of dead folks," Zula exclaimed. "What was it like?"

"If you so scared, what you want to know all about it fer," Mama needled Zula.

"I could tell the end was near," Georgie answered against Mama's caution. "I sent for Andrew and Anna. Miss Victoria jerked and tossed with each scream. Her arms flailed, and she lashed out like she was fighting off something."

"She was fighting off the devil and his helpers. They had come fer her," said Mama.

"She sat up, her hair wild and crazy, eyes wide as saucers," Georgie continued. "With one final yelp her eyes rolled back. She took her last breath and fell to the pillow. It looked like she just gave up."

"I hope Miss Anna don't put me out in the fields," worried Zula.

"Don't you fret none 'bout dat. I guess she be in charge of us for a while 'til Mr. Andrew take a wife. He gonna look after us like he always do," Mama reassured her.

"I sho hope he get hitched soon," said Zula.

"Or maybe somebody will marry Anna and take her away from here," said Georgie.

They all laughed.

"Lord have mercy. What man you think gonna marry dat ugly thang? She don't' look nothing like her mama or daddy," Mama said laughing so hard, tears came. "Ugly as a cake of homemade soap she is."

"Maybe a blind man will marry her," said Zula between laughs.

"What happened to dat cousin from South Carolina? Dey was trying to arrange a marriage 'tween him and Miss Anna?" Mama recalled.

"Don't you remember," said Georgie. "He come a-courting. Said he was gonna be here for a few weeks. He got a good look at her and was gone in three days. Ain't been back since."

"All right now, y'all. We ought not to talk like dis. The Lord don't like ugly," warned Mama, grinning.

"Then why he make Miss Anna?" Zula snickered.

Georgie let loose a belly laugh. "She might make some man a nice bride as long as he don't raise the veil."

The rare light moment came to an abrupt end with Mama's orders to deliver food to the mourners.

"Zula, you take dis tray of sweet cakes and buttermilk on up to 'em. Dat should hold 'em till I can get something else ready," said Mama still chuckling.

## Chapter 7
## August 1859

**Andrew** sat in his bedroom sipping whiskey, lost in his thoughts. The knock startled him.

"What is it, Zula?" Always three soft raps from Zula. He put the glass on the table and turned his gaze toward the door. She pushed the heavy door open while somehow maintaining control of the tray.

"Aunt Daisy sent me up with some'm cool to drink," she said halfway in the room, still struggling with the door.

He walked across the room in his stocking-feet, suspenders hanging at his sides, the whiskey dancing on his tongue and down his throat; he opened the door.

Standing in a white dress and apron, with her hair tied in a kerchief, she held a tray with a pitcher of cold buttermilk and Aunt Daisy's sweet cakes. Condensation ran down the side of the pitcher like sweat and gathered in a pool at the bottom of the tray. The weight of the tray was a bit much for the petite girl to handle.

"How old are you now, Zula?"

"I'm 13, Sah."

"You growing up fast."

He took the tray, set it on his dresser and poured himself a glass. The milk went down sweet and cold, just the way he liked. He bit into one of the cakes.

"You tell Aunt Daisy I said thank you. I don't know how she keeps ice in this August heat. Make sure you tell her what I said, you hear?"

"Ya Sah," she said as he handed her the tray. "Ya want me to take dat glass back and wash it?"

"No, that's all right." His face warmed with color. Even if it was just by a slave girl, he didn't like being caught drinking so early in the day. Sometimes he wondered just what they thought of him.

"I's gonna take some of dis down to Massa John and Miss Anna."

He held the door open, and Zula headed down the hallway to Anna's room. After a few steps, she stopped. "Mr. Andrew, I sho is

49

sorry 'bout Miss Victoria. I reckon she ain't having no moe paining now. Oh, and Mr. Nim, he downstairs waiting to see you."

"Thank you, Zula. Tell Nimrod I'll be down directly." He shut the door.

Andrew reached the top of the stairs. He smelled Nimrod. "Damn," he mumbled. "That man ain't had a bath since I hired him. He smells worse than a polecat."

"Afternoon, Mr. Andrew," Nimrod said, fidgeting with his hat and showing his snuff-stained teeth. "Everything is ready. Just like you asked. I had two of 'em dig the grave where you told me."

"That's fine. Come on back to the library. Reverend Grandison will be here at 9:00 tomorrow morning, and we'll begin the service at 10:00. I don't want us out in that heat too long, especially Daddy." Andrew walked over to the desk to fiddle with some papers to put some distance between himself and Nimrod in the hopes of getting a couple of deep breaths of fresh air. "After the service, have a few of the slaves fill the grave. I guess that's all." He wanted Nimrod and his stench out of the house.

"I thought you ought to know that old one was dancing around and mumbling mumbo-jumbo voodoo stuff earlier this morning."

"Who you talking about?"

"That old woman, black as soot, bald head, got them bones around her neck."

"Oh, you mean MawNancy. She thinks she can cast spells and charms, but we don't pay no attention. It's just nigger superstition, that's all. She's harmless. Let her be."

Nimrod headed to the foyer. Andrew called, "Nim."

"Ya Sah?"

"Make sure the slaves are at the service. They can watch from a distance."

"All of 'em? Mr. Andrew I don't see no reason for niggers to be at a white woman's funeral. Besides, it gonna take time away from their work."

"It ain't your decision. All that want to come, can come."

Nimrod left mumbling to himself.

**\*\*\*\*\*\*\*\*\***

Aunt Millicent, along with her husband, Henry, arrived from Richmond. Andrew waited outside the bedroom door while Aunt Millicent, Anna, and two female slaves finished washing and dressing Mother's body. The door opened.

"We're done," said Aunt Millicent. "I drew the drapes to keep the room as cool as possible."

"Yes. Death and this insufferable August heat are not a good combination. Thank you for coming so quickly and helping out."

"You're welcome, Andrew." She touched his arm. "In spite of our differences, she was my sister. What was the cause? I saw her at the Spring Cotillion in April, and she seemed fine."

"We don't know. In May, she took sick all of a sudden and went downhill fast. Doc Prichard says these things happen, but even he's baffled by it. He tried all kinds of treatment, but nothing helped. She was in such pain."

"Yes. I can tell she suffered. How are you doing? With your daddy's mind failing and Victoria's sickness, you've had a lot of responsibility on you."

"I reckon I'm holding up as best I can." Andrew followed his aunt into the room. Mother was laid out on the bed wearing one of her best dresses, her hair combed down to frame her face – a distraction from all the weight she had lost. "She looks nice. I hope she finds some peace. Nimrod and I set up this makeshift table." Andrew indicated a large plank over three wooden horses. "We'll put her there. It can serve as her cooling board until the undertaker arrives with the coffin."

Later in the day, Andrew and Georgie inspected the gravesite. Andrew peered into the deep hole. "It looks like everything is in order. Long time ago, Daddy picked this spot for the family cemetery. Mother's gonna be the first occupant." The undertaker's wagon turned the corner and headed up the road to the house. The crepe myrtle trees provided some much needed shade for the driver. "It must be a special kind of person to be in the business of caring for the dead."

"I reckon so." Georgie shielded her eyes from the sun and

watched the dead-wagon make its way to the house.

"Theopolus Martin. He's been the undertaker round these parts for nearly twenty years." Andrew rambled to Georgie, his thoughts needing a place to land other than in his scattered mind. "He and his brother Hurley started off as cabinetmakers, making coffins on the side with the excess wood."

"Always a need for coffins, that's fer sure."

"According to Daddy, the coffin business became so successful they put Hurley in charge of wood-working and Theopolus in charge of undertaking. I best get on up to the house to meet with him."

"Me too. I need to help Mama in the kitchen." Georgie grabbed his hand. "How you doing?"

"I reckon I'm all right. I have all kinds of mixed feelings about this."

"If you need me, I'll be in the kitchen."

"Thanks. Mother would appreciate your kindness."

"I ain't doing it for her. I'm doing it for you."

Andrew walked back to the main house. The wagon stopped in front. The large black wagon pulled by two fierce looking black horses decorated in black plumes unsettled him. Nimrod and two slaves unloading the coffin nearly overwhelmed him. Andrew followed them up to the bedroom, each step a struggle. A stench greeted them when they opened the door. Despite careful preparation, Mother's body was expelling gases and fluids. Andrew covered his mouth with a handkerchief.

Mr. Martin walked up to him and whispered, "Don't worry, son. This is natural. I brought extra flowers, enough to cover the smell."

"Thank you." Andrew exhaled.

Mr. Martin went to work preparing the viewing and operating with a quiet dignity, referring to Mother as Mrs. Gordon, as if she were still alive.

After setting up the coffin, Nimrod, Mr. Martin and Andrew lifted Mother into her final resting place. The two male slaves moved forward to help, but Nimrod yelled for them to get back. "What you think you boys doing trying to put yo hands on a white woman?" The slaves nodded an apology and waited to be told what to do.

After she was securely inside the coffin, Nimrod motioned for the slaves to carry it downstairs. They set her up in the front parlor, where Mr. Martin draped black bunting around her coffin to cover the wooden horses that served as the bier.

"I've learned the new technique of arterial embalming. It preserves the body so you don't have to rush the burial," Mr. Martin's explanation barely audible. "I'll have to carry Mrs. Gordon back to my shop to do the work. But, it's no trouble. I can have her back by tomorrow evening. I studied the technique under the tutelage of Thomas Holmes, a pioneer of the process." Mr. Martin placed a small piece of wood under Mother's chin to keep her mouth closed. "She will look natural, like she's sleeping."

"No thank you, Mr. Martin. I want to move things along and have the burial tomorrow."

Neighbors and friends came to offer condolences throughout the evening and into the night. Most waited until after sunset to venture out. Each visitor bestowed accolades on Mother. The wonderful woman they described was not the person Andrew knew. He smiled and shook each hand, thanking them for their kind words. After hours of playing host, he said good night to the last callers, grateful to call it a day. "We could all do with a good night's sleep."

They agreed. To his relief, Anna and Aunt Millicent did not expect the family to perform the traditional ritual of sitting up with the corpse all night.

**********

Aunt Daisy rose early the next morning to start cooking before the sun got too strong. She stirred around the kitchen, moving pots and pans and fretting over what to start first. "Whar is dat serving bowl," she mumbled. "I needs it for dem turnip greens. Zula done put it in the big house. Dat gal can't never put thangs back whar I tells her."

She crossed the yard and entered the back of the main house. It was dark, and a few kerosene lamps lit the downstairs rooms. More lamps lit the front parlor where Miss Victoria rested. A motion in the front parlor startled Aunt Daisy. She entered the foyer and looked into the parlor, the viewing room. A figure stood beside the coffin. Aunt Daisy stepped inside, onto a creaky floor board. MawNancy started.

"What you doing in here, MawNancy? Git out 'fore somebody catch you. It's done. We finished. We done wid it!" she whispered. "Is you done taken leave of yo senses? After all the careful planning we done, you gonna be so careless as to come in here to see fer yo self."

"I be going." MawNancy didn't seem at all worried about Aunt's Daisy's concerns. "I needs a few more things, and den I be done."

MawNancy snatched two clumps of hair from the corpse, fists full and pulled hard. "I hope de bitch felt dat." Each forceful grasp caused the upper part of the corpse to shift. The wood wedged under the corpse's chin slipped out, causing the mouth to open. Clear liquid flowed out, staining the lace collar. MawNancy shoved the wood back in place, then took a small knife and scraped shavings off of Miss Victoria's fingernails into a pouch, collecting from two fingers. "I needs to make sho I got 'nuff."

Aunt Daisy grew impatient. "I want dis day to come and go. Go on from here, now. What you gonna do if Massa John or Mr. Andrew come down and catch you here? You fixin' to get us both kilt."

"I's done." MawNancy tied the pouch to secure the hair and nail shavings and shuffled to the back door.

She reached for the doorknob, but Aunt Daisy grabbed it. "What you up to now? I put it in her food like I told you I would. Don't nobody know 'bout dis but de two of us. Now she dead. We got to let it go 'fore we gets caught."

MawNancy turned to face her. "I don't 'tend to let her have no peace, even in death."

"What you mean? Got me mixed up in all yo voodoo. I got to ask God to forgive me fer dis killing."

"Dis ain't no killing. Dis is justice. My spells ain't no different from yo Jesus. Wasn't he casting out demons into hogs and raising dead folks?"

"Ain't the same."

"Yes 'tis. If my work so bad, why ya hep me?" MawNancy

54

folded her arms across her flat breasts and struck a defiant pose. Her tongue moved around like a cow chewing cud.

Aunt Daisy relented. "After what she done to my Georgie, I wanted her to suffer. I wanted her dead. When you came to me and asked me to hep you, 'course I said yes. It took us a long time. It was hard to get it in her food without hurting the rest of the family. Once she got down low and started taking her meals in her room, it was easy to feed it to her."

MawNancy smiled. "Spent pert near three years trying to get at that bitch, but we got her."

A few seconds of silence lapsed before Aunt Daisy ventured, "I been wanting to ask you fer a long time. Why come *you* hate her so much?"

MawNancy smacked her gums and chewed more imaginary food. "'Twas her lies that got my man, Sam, killed." Her bottom lip trembled. Her voice cracked. "You know how they came and took him."

"I remember. 'Twas a terrible thang what dat lynch mob did to Sam."

"'Fore they come fer him. He told me what he seen."

"What did he see?" Aunt Daisy's curiosity surfaced. She thought she knew the whole story.

"Sam came up on Victoria and dat other plantation owner, Jim Williams, just a-fucking in de cornfield. Ya know he that gal's real daddy. She ugly just like him. Anyhow, 'fore Sam could tell what he seen, Victoria said my Sam was trying to take *her*. Dat Jim Williams spread de word with dat trash in town, and de mob came and took Sam. I tried to hep Sam, but dey beat me, too. After dey hung him, dey cut him 'tween his legs. By de time Massa John got thar, it was too late. When I walked up on my Sam swinging from de big tree, dey had beat him so bad, I didn't know 'twas him." Tears flowed down her face. "I knew his pants, 'cause I'd patched 'em. Those pants was pulled down, his cock was on de ground, blood runnin' 'tween his legs. Right den and thar, I vowed to kill her. I was gonna get at her through the boy."

"Mr. Andrew? You leave him be."

"All right now. I know you likes him. I like him too. When it come out dat she paid Onie Johnson to rape Georgie, I knowed ya'd hep me. Dat's when I come to ya wid my new plan."

"Dear Jesus, forgive us and hep us." Aunt Daisy clasped her hands.

"Don't need no Jesus. Gots all I needs right here." She raised the pouch. "I be going now."

"MawNancy, just what was you planning that involved Mr. Andrew?" Aunt Daisy put both hands on her hips.

"Don't worry yo-self wid it. De boy all right by me. I got what I wanted." MawNancy pointed to the corpse in the other room and closed the door behind her.

Aunt Daisy went back to the dining room to get the serving bowl. She heard someone walking and thought MawNancy had returned. She went back to the front parlor. "What you doing down here so early, Massa John?"

"Morning, Daisy. Thought I might come and sit with her before the others get to stirring around, before they put her in the ground."

"Well, praise be. Looks like you done come to yo self. Mr. Andrew be mighty happy to know it."

*********

Andrew awakened at 5:00 that morning. Unable to sleep, he rested in bed until 6:00 when one of the slave boys came in to put fresh water in his pitcher and wash-basin and empty his slop jar. He washed, shaved, and surveyed the black suit he had laid out the night before. "All of us in all this heavy black material standing in the heat don't make no sense," he mumbled as he stuck his leg in the britches. He finished dressing and headed down to Daddy's room to help him get ready. He found the room empty. Andrew walked down the stairs and into the parlor, where he found him seated next to the coffin. "You all right, Daddy?"

"I'm fine. Just want to sit a spell with your mother."

Andrew walked to the foyer. "Luther, did you help Daddy get dressed?"

"Naw Sah. He was sitting there when I came up. Said he didn't need nothing."

"He picked the right day to be in his right mind."

"Yas Sah. Seems so."

Later, Andrew and Daddy stood by the open coffin and greeted family and friends. When it looked like everyone had said their goodbyes, Mr. Martin closed the coffin and he, Nimrod and a few of the slaves carried it out of the house and down the path to the family cemetery. The family followed two-by-two. Andrew held Daddy's arm. Anna and Millicent followed. Behind them walked Millicent's husband and two sons followed by an assortment of cousins and close friends. It was only a short distance to the graveside, but the mourners arrived there drenched in sweat.

Reverend Grandison stood ready, the Holy Bible tight in his hand. A large group of slaves gathered on one side and members of the community on the other. Reverend Grandison opened with the Twenty Third Psalm. He spoke eloquent words about the Gordon Family and the respect they garnered throughout the great Commonwealth of Virginia. He went on to talk about the good woman Mother had been and how kind she was to everyone, even the slaves. Andrew noticed that Aunt Daisy and Georgie did not attend. After the brief lauding of Mother and descriptions of the suffering she had endured, the Reverend ended with the Lord's Prayer. The designated funeral hands lowered the coffin just as the Reverend ended his sentence about committing the body to the earth, ashes-to-ashes and dust-to-dust. Anna cried.

The group dispersed; Anna stood alone, weeping. Draped in black, her long veil moved in the hot breeze. She muffled her sobs with a white handkerchief clenched in her fist. No one went to comfort her. The other mourners made their way back to the house, and the slaves shoveled dirt into the grave.

"Uncle Henry, will you help Daddy back up to the house? I need to see about Anna," said Andrew.

Andrew walked up to his sister and put his arm around her shoulder; the two of them stood there until the grave was filled. Arm and arm they walked to the house. He rubbed her hand, and she rested her head on his shoulder.

**\*\*\*\*\*\*\*\*\***

Georgie strolled from her cabin. Another still night settled in. The breezes that did manage to rustle were too hot to bring relief. She watched Zula leave Nimrod's cabin, silent like a prowling animal.

"What you doing out here?"

"Georgie!" Zula turned abruptly. "You scared me."

"I'm sorry. I didn't mean to. Just didn't expect to see nobody else out here."

"I come out here late at night sometime to be alone with my thoughts. It's the only time I feel at peace. After Mr. Nim finish wid me, I need time to come back to myself. Walking out here helps. I hope the rain or the air will wash him off me," said Zula.

"I know." Georgie placed her hand on Zula's shoulder.

"He tells me he's helping break me in fer breeding."

They walked out close to the gravesite and stared into the darkness. MawNancy appeared out of the blackness like the apparition some accused her of being. Zula gasped.

"Hush now," said Georgie. "She doesn't see us. Let's watch."

MawNancy walked around Victoria's grave seven times, the earth over it fresh and unsettled. She stood over the grave mumbling strange words and fingering the bone necklace. She opened a small pouch and shook dust over the grave. She spread her legs, pulled up her skirt, squatted and pissed over the grave, chanting with her head back, eyes to the moon. She stepped back, looked at the grave and said, "I ain't done wid ya yet, Bitch." She spat on the grave and disappeared into the night, like her mysterious curses into the air.

58

## Chapter 8
### August 1859

**Andrew** sat mounted on the palomino. The field was full of black bodies glistening with sweat. The mid-morning sun beat down causing their clothing to cling to them like dew on leaves, outlining the women's breasts. Some of the men were shirtless – black muscles and torsos moved in rhythm picking pole beans, tomatoes, and digging potatoes. Andrew's straw hat did little to shade him from the unrelenting sun. He dismounted and picked up a potato. "I reckon they look pretty good," he said to Ryland. "Good enough for us, since we are not selling most of this."

"Ya sah." Ryland shoved the spade into the ground.

For a minute, Andrew let go of the horse's reins, and the mare walked away. He whistled at her. "Get back over here, horse." He struck out in a trot to catch her, lost his footing, and tumbled forward landing on his shoulder. "Goddamn it," he yelled. "Somebody stop that horse." He sat in the dirt massaging his shoulder. A shadow came over him, and he looked up at MawNancy.

"Let me see it." She knelt in the dirt and pawed her hard hands into his shoulder blade. "Ain't nuttin broke. Take off ya shirt."

She spit in her hands, rubbed them together, and placed them on his shoulder. A powerful heat took over the injured spot. The pain left.

"Dat better?" She stood and brushed the dirt from her skirt.

"Yes it is. Thank you, MawNancy." He moved his shoulder around. One of the workers retrieved the horse, and he mounted up.

That evening around sunset, Andrew knocked on MawNancy's door.

She peered out. "Ya sah, Mr. Andrew."

"I just want to thank you for what you did for me this morning. My shoulder's been feeling fine. I thought you might like this cold butter milk." He offered her the tin can covered with a white cloth.

"Thank ya, sah. That's mighty nice of you."

He shifted his stance, not fully comfortable around the old slave. "You have quite a gift for healing."

She grinned, toothless. "Most folks don't understand my gifts." She paused. "Kinda like you. You got gifts too that you might not understand."

"I don't know what mine are."

"Ya sah. I think you do. You just don't see it as a gift."

Andrew stood dumbstruck. He feared her meaning.

She continued. "Most Sundays, I strolls down by the river through the high weeds – off the main path."

Andrew felt the color drain from his face. He was speechless. She's seen them. As careful as he had been with is dalliances in his secret place, she had found him out.

"MawNancy understands thangs better than most folks." She took the buttermilk.

"But you misunderstood..."

"Hush, chile. MawNancy likes you. You got a good soul. Ain't no need to fret. Yo secret is safe with MawNancy. You just be careful."

"But..."

She raised her weathered hand to silence him.

"Thank you." He lowered his head and turned to walk away.

"Mr. Andrew, sah."

"Yes." He stepped back toward her.

"Raise yo head. Ain't no shame."

Andrew smiled.

"One moe thang. If'n you don't mind, when dis winter come, it be mighty nice to have a good blanket and some shoes." She stuck out a foot exposing a tattered shoe.

"Of course, MawNancy. Enjoy that buttermilk."

## Chapter 9

### September 1859

**Anna** bumped along the dry road in the open carriage, fanning off flies, gnats, and dust. She adjusted the parasol to shield the sun. No fanning could cool the fury still raging inside her. Andrew sat opposite, his long legs stretched out. She seethed at the sight of him. "It *would* be nice to get some support from you every now and then, Andrew."

"Not this again," he sighed. "You …" he sat up and jabbed his finger at her "… you made Zula spill coffee on the table cloth. It was your abrupt movement that caused the whole thing. You didn't get burned. It did not even get on you. There was no cause for you to slap her."

"You always take the side of the slaves. It was wrong of you to criticize me in front of her. They will never respect me as the mistress of the house. They will certainly never fear me as long as they know they can run to you."

"Is that it?" He chuckled. "You want to be feared?"

"Do not mock me. I will not be made a fool by you in front of the slaves, and I will discipline them as I see fit."

"Oh for heaven's sake. Can't we at least try to enjoy this happy occasion? Think about the wedding and the honor of serving as bridesmaid for Lovey. Let's put the bickering aside for a few hours at least."

"I'll not look fit to do anything after sweltering in this heat. Why did you have that old man hitch up the open carriage? The closed one is better suited."

Andrew remained quiet. He stretched his legs out, rested his head on the back of the seat and closed his eyes.

After riding in silence for what seemed like an eternity, Anna said, "We're almost there. I see the house up ahead. Several carriages have already arrived."

"Uh huh."

"Lovey always thought that one day she would marry you." Anna's tone was less combative.

Andrew did not move, didn't even open his eyes. "I know she

did, but she's marrying Artemis Woolfork. He's from a good old family with lots of good old money. I'm sure she'll be very happy."

Their carriage pulled up to the house. Mr. and Mrs. Masterson stood out front greeting guests.

"Andrew. Anna. How wonderful to see you," said Mr. Masterson, extending his hand to help Anna down.

"Thank you so much for coming," said Mrs. Masterson. "And thank you, Anna, for helping us out at the last minute. You are such a dear."

"What do you mean?" Anna did not want to appear unappreciative of their thanks, but she was not aware of anything special she had done.

"Stepping in as a bridesmaid at the last minute," said Mrs. Masterson. "After a year of planning, Lovey's cousin wrote us two months ago that she could not travel up from Tennessee. Can you believe it? Then we asked Emily Johnson, and she had to back out because of health reasons. But we all know better than that. I do wonder how they intend to conceal the child after it's born. They'll probably say it's a cousin they're raising. Her poor mother must be mortified. Anyway, then Lovey approached you. It is so sweet of you to step in like this."

Anna tried to contain her shock. A year's planning? She had only been informed last month and had rushed to have the special dress made.

"All the girls are gathered in Lovey's bedroom. You make eight. One of the house slaves will direct you. Go on in," said Mrs. Masterson. "Pick up your bouquet. They're on the credenza in the hallway."

"Andrew, we're serving juleps on the veranda. Go on up, and help yourself." Mr. Masterson gripped Andrew's shoulder. I hope y'all are getting on all right after your mother's passing. How is your father?"

"He's doing fine, Mr. Masterson. Thank you for asking." Andrew took Anna's arm. "I'll escort you up to the house."

Anna struggled to fight back her tears. After they were a few steps from the Masterson's, she murmured, "They only wanted me after the others bowed out."

"I'm sorry, Anna. Try to enjoy yourself." Andrew pulled her arm closer to him.

She pulled away. "I don't' need your pity."

Lovey's bedroom was buzzing with excitement when Anna entered. She looked around at the other girls from their circle of friends.

"Anna, come in. We'll be ready to start in a few minutes," said Lovey.

Miss Bingham, Lovey's spinster aunt was making the final adjustments to Lovey's veil. The lace draped across the top of her head, down the back of the ivory colored dress and merged with the long train. The bridesmaids' dresses were in alternating colors—four light blue and four pink. The bouquets were pink and blue flowers accented with baby's breath. Lovey's bouquet was all white and cascaded down the front of her dress.

"All right young ladies lineup," Miss Bingham announced. "Pink, blue, pink, blue," she counted off and lined up the eight girls according to the color of their dresses. "You, Dear. Miss Gordon, you're in pink. Right here. You'll be last."

"How appropriate." Anna looked at Lovey.

They processed down the front staircase, outside, and onto the south lawn. It was a beautiful September afternoon. The leaves were beginning to turn various shades of yellow, red, and orange. There were so many trees, the entire lawn was shaded. A string quartet played underneath a large maple, the sun accenting its red leaves. The groom and his groomsmen were all in place. Each man seemed more handsome than the one before him. Lovey beamed as she walked down the aisle on her father's arm. Anna wondered if she would ever have her own wedding, her own man. A soft breeze swept under their petticoats, stirring their dresses.

After the ceremony, Miss Bingham took charge, delivering more instructions. "Ladies and gentlemen, I need you to line up in front of the house. Mr. Portman is here with his brand new daguerreotype. This is so exciting." She clasped her hands. "We're going to have a photograph made *right here*. This way everyone," she motioned.

After the photograph was taken, Anna searched out a glass of punch and sat on the veranda, a voyeur to the happiness and excitement around her. The flirtations between the single men and women eluded her. Andrew towered over her, "I'm going to give my good wishes to the happy couple. Would you like to join me?"

"No." She sipped the punch. "I want to go home, now."

"But..."

"Now, Andrew."

"All right. I'll wish them well and have the carriage brought around."

They rode home in silence. The sun was setting when the estate came into view. Anna lowered her parasol. "I want to go away for a while. Aunt Fannie wasn't able to visit Mother before she died. I'd like to visit her for a few months. I'll write her in the morning."

"I think that's a good idea," said Andrew. "She's mother's sister too, and we rarely see her. Mississippi might be a good change for you."

## Chapter 10

## Late September 1859, Fairholm Plantation, Annapolis, Maryland

**Edward** had been a slave at the Fairholm Plantation for three years, but this would be his first time inside the mansion. Reverend Oaks had told Mr. Fairholm about Edward's skills as a butler when he sold him, told him right in front of Edward. He held out hope they would use him in the big house someday. After all, he'd been summoned today to meet the old man. The grass and shrubs glistened from the late afternoon rainstorm. Birds fluttered overhead, venturing out after the storm. Edward followed Porter Hickman up to the porch of the white frame house, large drops of water from overhanging magnolia leaves landing on their heads.

"Come on in, Hickman. Pour yourself a libation," Fairholm yelled from the front room. The foyer was much grander than at Oaks, gleaming with polished wood and silver and brass.

"Thank you, Mr. Fairholm. Don't mind if I do. I brought the fighter up for you to look over like you asked. You may not remember him, but we've used him in some local bouts around town. If we decide to take him, this will be his first time to travel out of state."

"I see." Fairholm walked around Edward, looking him up and down in the bright light of the foyer, while Hickman poured himself a drink. Fairholm came close, lining his yellow eyes up to Edward's. Edward held a steady gaze back. "I'm always glad to see you, Hickman. You done made us both rich men. How long you been training my fightin' niggers, three or four years?"

"Oh, I reckon it's more like five since I come up from Louisiana." Hickman reentered the foyer, a glass of whiskey in hand. "I didn't expect to stay long, but there's a real interest in pugilism in these parts. More so than I expected."

"We got us some of the best fighting bucks in this neck of the woods thanks to your training." Fairholm's small hands ran over Edward's shoulders and back. He stifled a shiver.

"Thank you, Sir. That's what I want to speak to you about. We got that match set up next week in Virginia. I figure it would take us a couple of days to travel from here in Annapolis down to Spotsylvania."

"Two days? Hell, Hickman, Maryland ain't that far from Virginia." He stopped examining Edward and took a seat on the bench by the door.

"I know. I want to build in a day to get the bucks rested and do some training."

"That makes sense. You make all the arrangements. You gonna let this one fight?"

"I think I'll take him. Go on out on the front porch and wait for me, boy." Hickman motioned for Edward to leave.

Edward stood on the porch, watching slave women in the side yard boil and hang laundry, their hands like black stars on one white sheet after another. He waited near an open window and was surprised to hear the men's conversation drift out.

"We got to watch him is all," Hickman continued.

"Ain't he ready?"

"Oh, he's ready. He can fight. He's a strong son of a bitch. He ain't as big as the others, but he's solid and can throw a punch. He can beat any of the other four we got with no problem. He just got an attitude. He's one of them uppity niggers, used to work in the big house at the Oaks Plantation. I think he was the butler. He don't act like them regular field hands. He's kinda smart."

"I know how to handle that."

"I can handle him, Mr. Fairholm. I just want to keep him shackled when I ain't got my eyes on him."

"You think he'll run off?"

"Don't know. Can't take the chance. I can't prove it yet, but I think he can read some."

"What? How do you know?"

"Like I said, I ain't for sure."

"Well, I'll leave this up to you. I just want that prize money. If he worked in the big house, how'd he learn to fight?"

"As I hear it, Reverend Oaks bought him to breed his wenches, but it seems he don't have no interest in that. The other field hands were jealous that he was working in the big house and had a nicer cabin to live in. When word got out that he didn't want what the females had to offer, let's just say he had to defend himself. He learned to fight the hard way. Three field hands jumped him one night. He beat the hell out of all of 'em. Damn near killed one, using only his fists. That's when Reverend Oaks sold him to you."

Edward peered through the window.

"I kinda remember something like that," said Fairholm. "That fool preacher knew of my interest in fighting bucks. Sold him to me for half of what he's worth. Just wanted to get rid of him."

"I'll take him with the other four, and we'll see what he can do with some real competition." Hickman stood and swallowed what was left of his drink. "That's good stuff, Mr. Fairholm.

"When it comes to my women and whiskey, I only like the best."

"Yes sir," Hickman chuckled. "I'll be on my way. Thank you for the rye."

"Good to see you, Hickman."

Edward walked away from the window and stood by the door as Hickman came out. The man's arrogance, swagger, and overall sense of superiority made Edward want to pound him. He hated Hickman and Fairholm too. Fairholm used slaves like animals to tend his fields, he fucked the women whenever he felt like it, and he used Edward and men like him to fight like animals to increase his wealth. He wanted them all to die. Even Reverend and Mrs. Oaks for not standing by him.

"Come on," Hickman ordered. "I got more training for you."

**\* \* \* \* \* \* \* \* \* \***

Edward and four other fighters were chosen to make the trip to Spotsylvania, Virginia. Driven there in a livestock wagon, they were delivered, tired and sore, to an old warehouse that had been converted into a makeshift arena. The night of the fights, planters and farmers from the surrounding area filled the building and grounds. Edward, in ankle shackles, kept his eyes to the ground or off in the distance, on the groups of men who stood in the loft for a bird's eye view. He did look up a few times to see four women, strolling the place, offering sex for sale. The place reeked of cigar smoke, sweat, blood and remnants of horse shit. It made Edward gag; he was near retching.

"You all right, boy?" Hickman asked.

"I'm just fine, Mr. Hickman."

"You better be. We got a lot riding on you. Let's' move on up to the front." Hickman unlocked the shackles.

Fairholm walked up. "This is our last fight. Two of our boys won, and two got licked. I done made a little money, but not as much as I expected. We need this last fight."

"Get on in there," Hickman said to Edward.

The crowd yelled when Edward stepped over the ropes. He looked at all the white faces with cigars and pipes clenched between teeth and money wadded in fists.

"Wallop his ass, boy," yelled a bystander.

Another said, "I'm betting on you. Don't you disappoint me. Ya hear?"

His opponent stepped in on the other side. The crowd roared. He was a big black man with arms the size of tree limbs. Both fighters were naked from the waist up.

"I've seen him fight before. Lucifer's his name. He's big and mean, but he's slow. Tire him out, and then go in for the kill," advised Hickman.

His opponent sized him and looked back at his owner, "Not to worry, Massa. I'm gonna send this nigger to heaven or hell in the next few minutes. Won't take long. Won't take long t'all." He put up his big fists, bent his knees and walked around Edward. Edward waited, staring his foe in the eye. The man charged, took his first swing and missed. Edward tripped him, and Lucifer tumbled into the dirt. He struggled to get up. When he did stand, Edward landed his first blow, knocking the big man back down. Blood squirted from his lip. The crowd cheered. Lucifer wiped his mouth with the back of his hand. "You're gonna pay for that lucky punch."

He charged Edward, again, grabbing him around the waist with one arm. Edward had oiled his body, and Lucifer couldn't hold the grip. Edward slipped away and landed another blow.

Lucifer grabbed Edward with both arms around his waist and

attempted to raise him off the ground. "I'm gonna snap your back in two."

Edward managed to get one arm free and plunged his elbow into the strong man's nose. The man yelled in pain, and Edward landed another elbow to the side of his nose. It snapped. He released his grip, and Edward slipped away. Lucifer held his face with both hands. Blood oozed through his fingers.

"Finish him," yelled Hickman.

Edward landed a few blows to Lucifer's sides. The bloodied man regained his composure but seemed surprised and outmaneuvered by Edward's skill. Lucifer's owner threw a knife into the ring with the instructions: "Kill 'em."

Lucifer grabbed the knife and lunged at Edward. Edward went for the nose again. The big man held his face. Edward sank his teeth into the man's wrist, causing him to drop the knife. Hickman climbed over the rope and into the ring, grabbed the knife, and ran out.

"You mine now," said Edward, landing blow after blow to the big man's face until he fell to the ground.

Edward stood over Lucifer, and Hickman tossed him the knife.

"Now, use it. Cut his fucking throat." Hickman stared at Lucifer's owner.

Edward picked up the blade and knelt by Lucifer.

The big man opened his eyes. "Pl ... pl ... please. D ... d ... don't," he muttered.

"You still want to send me to hell?" Edward pressed the blade of the knife against the big man's jugular.

The crowd roared. Fairholm smiled and flicked ash from his cigar.

The big man raised his head and looked at Edward. "Pl ... pl ... please," he said before falling back exhausted.

Edward threw the knife at feet of the big man's owner and walked out of the ring.

**\*\*\*\*\*\*\*\*\***

Edward and the other fighters washed up and did the best they could do to mend their cuts and bruises. Fairholm walked into their backroom with a half bottle of whiskey. He whistled and danced a little jig. "Good job, boys. Most of you anyway." He glared at the two losers.

"Mr. Fairholm, I think we ought to head on back tonight," Hickman said.

"What? What the hell for? I got plans. One of the best brothels around is up in these woods. Didn't you see them whores tonight? You can come, too."

"I'm worried about that buck Edward beat. His owner didn't take too kindly to loosing. He lost a lot of money on that fight. I fear there may be trouble if we stay the night."

"Has something been said? It was a fair fight."

"When Edward was about to cut that buck's throat, his owner reached for a derringer in his coat pocket. I saw it in his pocket when they came in. I was behind him with my pistol in his back. I whispered in his ear that if he touched the gun, I'd blow his ass to west hell. Then I reminded him that he was the one who put a knife in the fight."

Fairholm sighed and relented. "You may be right. There could be trouble. Gather up the boys, and let's head on back. Damn it all. I was planning on a good time."

Edward and the other fighters climbed into the back of the wagon. He thought about the black man he had just beaten and how the man had pleaded for his life. All of this to make Fairholm and Hickman rich men. The five fighters outnumbered and Hickman and Fairholm. We could kill them and escape. Would the others follow if he attacked, or would they turn on him and protect the white men? Surely he wasn't the only one who felt this way. Fairholm was half drunk, and Hickman was focused on the road. He could easily overpower Hickman and get his gun. If he killed Hickman and Fairholm, the others would have to follow his plan. One of the fighters was light enough to pass for White. Would he play along? Could he play the part of a white man? He talked like a dumb field hand. Edward rubbed his swollen hands contemplating his escape until he fell asleep in the back of the wagon.

It was early the next morning when they arrived back at the plantation.

"Y'all boys get on out, but don't go nowhere. I got something for Edward," said Hickman, as he jumped out of the wagon and went into the barn.

Fairholm headed on up to the big house. The five fighters stood around nursing their wounds: cracked ribs, swollen knuckles, bruised eyes, split lips, and missing teeth.

Edward's head was down when the whip cracked across his back. He turned to see Hickman ready to lash a second time.

"When I tell you to finish off an opponent, you do what I say." The lash came down around Edward's legs. "Don't you ever defy me. You hear me, boy?" He drew back to fire off another lash. "That goes for every one of you. When I tell you to do something, you do it. Goddamn it."

Edward raised his arm to protect himself. The lash wrapped around it. Edward grabbed it and pulled. Hickman stumbled forward.

"You done lost your mind, boy?" Hickman said.

Edward knocked Hickman to the ground with one fell blow to the face. Hickman's jaw hung slack. Edward stood tall, squaring his shoulders.

"Nobody whips me." He grabbed the weapon and thrashed Hickman with it. The lash tore through Hickman's shirt and split his skin. Blood stained the fine white cotton. After three strikes, the other fighters subdued Edward. Hickman squirmed on the ground like a wounded snake. Edward wrestled away from them and ran for the fields. The dew had slicked the grass, and he stumbled a few times. He headed deep into the woods toward the creek, finally stopping to gain a sense of direction. His hands hurt from the fight, and his feet bled from the sharp stones underfoot. He ran on, resting only moments at time, hiding in thick brush or riverbeds.

At night fall, he didn't have the strength to keep running. He rested in some thickets in an overgrown cemetery. The hounds barked, and the light from the vigilantes' torches illuminated the hillside. He climbed a pine tree and hid high above them in the darkness. The mob, led by Hickman and Fairholm, passed below him. The dogs scratched at the tree but moved on. Edward found two limbs that held him under the arms and knees, his seat drooping in between. It supported enough of his weight that he closed his eyes and relaxed a little. "I should have killed them when I had the chance," he mumbled.

"Looks like he's been this way," Fairholm yelled to the group. "Keep searching. We'll find him." Shouts from the ground made their way up, but Edward remained hidden in the high limbs.

With all quiet at dawn, Edward climbed down to search for a better hiding place and to hopefully find some food. Out of nowhere, a hound sprang on him and tore at his flesh. In a moment's time, he snapped the dog's neck. The bitch yelped before taking a last breath. Two searchers galloped toward him. Edward ran, jumping over headstones, before the men circled him. One flung a net over him. "Fire off a couple of shots to let the others know we got him," he said.

Edward struggled to get free, but was securely trapped. The searcher dismounted and whacked him up beside the head with the butt of the rifle. "Keep yo ass still."

*********

Back at the plantation, Edward was tied to a whipping post, his arms spread above his head.

Hickman paced. His jaw tied with a white rag. "Nobody whips you, huh?" He spoke through clinched teeth trying not to irritate his jaw. "Well, we'll just see about that."

Hickman landed the first lash to Edward's back. The pain seared to his bones, white heat flashing. He gritted his teeth to take it. He refused to scream. His mind left as the lashes kept coming. Blood ran down his legs, warm, replacing the morning's cool dew. And then nothing.

He regained consciousness to one of the slave women applying ointment to his wounds. "You done taken leave of yo senses, boy," she chastised him. "What you thinking 'bout hitting dat white man. Dey kill us for less."

"Water, please."

"Massa say you can't have nuttin'. Lord have mercy. Dey done took de flesh clean off ya." She applied more ointment. "You rest. I'll see what I can sneak back."

The fever broke on the morning of the third day. "Get him on out here," Fairholm yelled to the slave woman who had been charged with his care.

"Massa, he still mighty weak. With the fever and no food and all, he just ain't got no strenf."

"Hickman, go on in there after him."

Edward staggered out into blinding sun. The slave trader's wagon rolled up, and the trader jumped down.

"Well, take a good look at him," Fairholm said to the trader. "I done told you what my price is."

"Open yer mouth, boy," said the trader.

He inspected Edward's teeth and grabbed his balls.

"I reckon everything down there works," said Fairholm. "He don't seem too interested in using it, though, other than to piss."

The trader looked at Edward's back and then at Fairholm.

"I told you why I'm selling him. I think we done whipped that drapetomania out of him. He won't be no trouble to you. You just let him know who's boss."

"Maybe, but a potential buyer might not want him when they see his back. Signs of whipping is a sure sign of a problem nigger."

"I told you my price. Do you want him or not?"

"Yes siree. I believe I'll take him. Not sure what I'm gonna do with him, but a buck like this for the price you asking is a mighty good deal."

"I'll tell you what you gonna do with him," said Fairholm tapping his ridding crop to his boot. "You gonna sell his black ass on deep down south."

## Chapter 11
## October 1859

**Andrew** sat at the head of the dining room table while Zula cleared the dinner dishes. He thought she had dropped something on the mahogany surface, a spoon maybe, then realized the sound was a faint, abrupt knock on the front door.

"Luther, you in there?" Andrew raised his voice to make sure the old slave could hear him.

"Ya sah. I'll see who 'tis." Luther came back to the dining room. "Massa Jessup Tillman is here to see ya, sah."

"This is a nice surprise," Andrew said hurrying to the foyer, where Jessup stood, reeking of wealth and excitement.

Jessup took off his gloves and hat and untied his cape, handing them to Luther. "Here, boy." He shook Andrew's hand and grabbed his shoulder, smiling broadly. "It sho is good to see ya. Damn good to see an old friend. I hope y'all don't mind my coming by unexpected like this, but I was on my way up to Richmond for a late supper and wanted to stop in. I was down in Savannah checking on some of the bank's holdings when your mama died. I do hope you got my lettah."

"I did. Thank you for sending it. You are always welcome here. I was just thinking about some plans for next year. I've got several acres of land down on the southern end I might use for growing fruits and vegetables. I'll need extra slaves to clear the land, and I might need a loan from that bank of yours first." Andrew laughed and slapped Jessup's back.

"Anytime you need anything, just let me know."

"I'm just fooling with you. I'm fixed pretty good right now. I just finished dinner, but I can have Aunt Daisy fix you a plate if you'd like."

"Naw. I don't want nothing to eat. I just wanted to see how you was doing."

"At least have a whiskey with me. Come on in the front parlor."

"I think I'll pass on the whiskey, but I would love some of your daddy's dandelion wine."

"Daddy's been ailing more and more these days. He wasn't up

to making wine this spring. He showed one of our slaves how to make it. She made a batch, and it's pretty good. Some say it's better than Daddy's." Andrew's voice trailed, and his shoulders slumped with a heavy sigh.

"What's wrong?"

Andrew rubbed his face. "You're the first person I've told about Daddy's condition. Hearing the words makes me sad."

"I haven't seen him up in Richmond in quite a spell."

"Luther, bring us up from the cellar some of that wine Georgie made," Andrew instructed.

"It's mighty quiet around here. Where's Anna, out at one of those blasted cotillions with the high-and-mighty bluebloods?" Jessup smirked.

"She's in Mississippi visiting family. Finally I have some peace in the house. I'm able to enjoy these warm days and cool autumn evenings."

"Oh?"

"Come on now, Jessup. We've been friends since childhood. You know how difficult she can be. After Mother died, Anna got worse. We fought everyday about one thing or another, from the running of the house to the disciplining of the slaves. She'll stay down there for a few months and be back in time for Christmas."

Luther returned with a decanter of wine and two stemmed glasses on a silver tray. "Luther, that'll be all. You go on to bed now. I've got everything we need here."

"Good night, Mr. Andrew. Mr. Tillman."

"I want us to speak privately," said Andrew after Luther's departure.

"You ought to come on up to Richmond with me tonight. I guarantee you'll have a good time at Miss Maggie's. You can find anything ya want at Maggie's, Andrew. And I do mean *anything*."

Andrew smiled. "I know what you mean, Jessup. But no thanks."

"Why?"

"Makes life easier. Do you know what they would have done to us if we had gotten caught together like that?"

"But we didn't get caught," Jessup seemed pleased to point out. "Now, we're grown men and can do whatever we damn well please."

"I've heard about Maggie Dumont and her establishment, but I've never been."

"Her place is about a mile east of Richmond, off the main road. It's a grand, old structure that served as the main house for a plantation before the owners went bankrupt. You should know it. Remember the Smith's. The old man was nothing but a drunkard. The family lost everything. Pappy's bank held the deed to the place. I convinced him to sell it to Maggie. She paid half the price in cash and took a loan from the bank for the rest. She's a good business woman."

"Who goes there?" Andrew's curiosity surfaced.

"The clients are mostly businessmen, plantation owners, or visitors to the area. Every now and then, a couple of farm hands save up enough money, get a hot bath and shave in town, put on some clean clothes, and stop in for an evening. The atmosphere's respectful. Maggie has a couple of good old boys to keep patrons in order. She pays them with a little money and an hour or two with one of the girls. The *peace keepers*, as I like to call them, get their pay at the end of the evening."

"Not tonight, Jessup, but I promise I'll make it up to you. We'll go out soon for a night in Richmond."

"I'm gonna hold ya to that promise."

"Aren't you worried about your reputation?" Andrew asked, both out of concern for Jessup and also for himself should he keep his word and go there sometime.

"Hell naw. Those bluebloods won't turn on me. When Pappy died, I inherited one of the biggest banks in these parts. They all respect and need money, and I control a lot of it. I associate with whomever I please, and if some of those upstanding hypocrites don't like it, they can kiss my ass."

Andrew chuckled. "I do envy you, and I have missed our friendship."

They talked about old times, mutual friends, and finances

before Jessup announced, "I got to be getting on. Tell that gal she made some mighty fine wine." He set the glass on the table. "We just won't tell yo daddy I said so."

They laughed as they walked to the foyer. Andrew retrieved Jessup's cape, hat, and gloves. They gave each other strong handshakes and backslaps as they said goodnight. Jessup held on to Andrew's hand, his demeanor suddenly somber. He leaned in toward Andrew and gently rubbed his forehead on the side of Andrew's face. He whispered, "Life is too short, my friend." He stepped back and flashed a sly grin, "If ya change yo mind, I'll be at Maggie's."

Jessup's carriage disappeared into the darkness; the cadence of the horses' hooves muffled by the night's heavy silence. Andrew went back to the parlor, poured another glass of wine, and sat by the fire, alone.

## Chapter 12
## October 1859

**Jessup** rushed up the steps of the bordello. Wind caught the folds of his cape, flaring it up. The figures inside looked blurred through the heavy lead glass panels in the door. A servant boy saw him coming and opened the door. The crowd turned.

"Jessup! Good to see you," a few regulars greeted him. He sauntered through looking for a good spot to watch and be watched. Making his way to the middle parlor, he leaned against the large mahogany bar, his favorite place in the ornate room. It didn't' take long for all eyes to find him. He looked back, surveying the patrons, most of whom he knew socially or through business.

He softened when he saw her walking toward him. Regal in a royal blue gown with gold trim and a hooped skirt, she was lovely, her thick blond hair pulled back into its customary chignon, her lips painted crimson. It was her familiar and accepting nature that had captured Jessup the most.

"Why Jessup Tillman, you handsome devil, I thought you were going to ignore us this evening. You're later than usual." She kissed him on each cheek with a grace that eased his last nerve.

Her mere presence snuffed out his facade. "Hello my dear Maggie. I stopped by to see an old friend on my way out this evening."

"You should have brought him with you," she said as she motioned for Silas, the black bartender, to bring Jessup a drink.

"I sho tried, but he ain't much for having a good time."

"What a pity. After all, isn't that why God put us here?"

He laughed. "And I intend to have as good a time as I can."

A loud, passionate and prolonged scream traveled from an upstairs room. They paused, smirked, until the noise stopped.

Jessup raised his eyebrows. "Sounds like somebody else is having a good time."

She smiled. "We aim to please."

"Indeed. And from the looks of you, business must be quite good." He fondled the pleats in her dress. "Looks like you redecorated the place, too. Quite elegant, my dear." He motioned toward the expensive settees, chairs, and large palms decorating the saloon.

"I want to keep those high level planters and exporters coming back."

"Everything looks mighty good."

"Thank you, honey. I'll be back to talk to you a little later. I've got to check on some things."

"Maggie," he said, trying not to sound desperate. "You got anything for me this evening?"

"That's what I'm going to check on, darling." She winked and headed toward another room.

He took his favorite seat in the middle parlor where he could see all the goings and comings. Maggie's girls meandered around the room in negligees or revealing undergarments, waiting to be selected by eager clients. Others were already engaged in the upper rooms. The house smelled of cigar smoke, whiskey, and perfume. A string trio consisting of a guitar, banjo, and violin played in an adjoining room.

Jessup started when Maggie's hand touched his shoulder. Her other arm was interlocked with a man whom he had seen there before but had not yet met.

"Jessup, permit me to introduce you to Mr. Thelton Taylor. He visits these parts quite often from up north."

"Pleased to meet ya," said Jessup with his cigar clenched between his teeth.

Maggie released Thelton's arm and slipped back into the crowd.

*********

Jessup descended the staircase and walked to the bar to get another drink. The place was mostly empty. A few final customers said their good nights to the girls. Jessup took a seat in one of the new settees and sipped his whiskey. Ten minutes later, Thelton came down and headed out the front door .

"You still here?" Maggie asked walking up behind him.

"Yes. It's late. I think I'll spend the night in my room. 'Less, of course, you have another need for it."

"Of course not. We have an agreement for nights just like this.

79

You disappeared on me, darling."

"Yes," he said, a big grin spreading across his face. "I spent some time in my room getting to know Mr. Taylor. Then, we fell asleep." He raised his eyebrows.

"Good. We found out that he has a liking for both."

"Indeed he does." He took another sip. "Maggie, you and me, we get on just fine. I respect you, and you don't judge me. How you come to be so acceptin'?"

She smoothed the skirt of her dress and sat beside him. "Honey, I'm in the business of making people feel good, not in the business of judging. I've seen and damn near done it all. I don't care nothing about these hypocrites who fuck my girls at night and flaunt their pure upstanding wives by day. All I want is the money they pay to spend time here."

He raised his glass. "Amen and hallelujah. You give the men what they will never experience with their wives. Old prudes."

"The stories I could tell, darling." She took the combs from her hair and let it fall. The golden locks hung to her shoulders and framed her face, making her appear more youthful than she was.

"I appreciate our arrangement," he said. "I have a real fine time." He held her hand, and they sat in silence. "How did you come to be such a rich businesswoman? I inherited my money. I didn't have to work. Pappy did all that for me. But you made yours, and that's more respected, regardless of how you made it. I remember you telling me you had it hard growing up in the North Carolina mountains. How did you do all this?"

"Mine ain't an easy story," she said. "Silas, bring me a whiskey, so I can have a proper visit with my friend here." She kicked off her shoes and repositioned herself to get more comfortable.

"Here ya are, Miss Maggie," said Silas handing her the drink.

"Thank you, honey. Why don't you call it a night and go on to bed? We can finish up here later." She waved her hand toward the stairs.

"I think I will, Miss Maggie. Y'all have a good night."

She stared at the glass as if it would conjure up her past. "I think my life began the night I made up my mind to get away from Floyd. I was fourteen years old. I was lying in bed staring at the ceiling. I'd spent the better part of the early evening settling two of Floyd's gambling debts. The second man was so drunk, he couldn't perform. I knew enough about prostituting to know how to trick an old drunk into thinking we'd had sex. That's what I did to him and kissed him before sending him on his way. He slipped into his trousers, tucked in his shirt, and staggered out the bedroom door. When I thought the house was clear, I peeked through the door to make sure Floyd didn't have anybody else waiting for me. He wasn't in the house. I relaxed a little when I realized my work was done for the night."

Captivated by details of her life he had not heard before, Jessup asked, "Who's Floyd?"

"Floyd was my daddy. I just can't bring myself to call a man like that daddy. I told you, mine ain't no easy story." She took a sip of the drink and continued. "The house was empty. The light from his lantern flickered deep in the back yard, illuminating the lower branches of the big oak tree. I saw him out there, digging. I guess he hadn't heard the last customer ride off. I watched through the back window until he was through. When he started back to the house, I ran to the bed and covered myself with a quilt, pretending to sleep, hoping I wouldn't have to service him too. He placed the shovel against the side of the house with a loud clang. His heavy boots thudded on the steps leading to the back door; the hinges let out their familiar sigh. He had not tied his boots, and they clopped loosely, each step leaving its own sloppy echo. For a moment, there was silence. I think he stood at the bedroom door listening for the bed springs heaving. He cracked the door, looked in, and I'm sure was surprised to find the man gone. I lay still, trying to become invisible. He kicked off his boots. They slipped off easily and fell to the floor. He unhooked his overhauls. I felt his weight on the bed and heard the springs cry as they adjusted to his presence. I was resting on my side, and he pulled the quilt from me. He turned me over and spread my legs."

"My God," said Jessup. "What a worthless son of a bitch."

She went on with her story, sometimes looking down at her

drink, other times directly into his eyes. "The awful truth has been bottled up in me for a long time. You're the first person I've ever trusted to tell." She took a sip and continued. "Floyd left early the next morning to go into town to do whatever he did all day, which I assume amounted to drinking, gambling, and rounding up men for me. I waited until he had been gone for about an hour, then grabbed the shovel, and headed for the oak tree. The earth was still fresh from where he had been digging the night before. I focused on the sound of the shovel penetrating the earth. After a few minutes of digging, the shovel hit something hard. I dropped to my knees and brushed dirt from the top of a homemade box, removing it from its grave. A mason jar filled with coins and cash was stored inside. I thought about leaving some so that he wouldn't know right away that the stash had been stolen. But then I thought better of it; I had earned most, if not all, of the loot by submitting to the men he brought home. I emptied the jar and reburied it in the box, careful to pat the earth tight so that he wouldn't notice it had been disturbed. I placed the shovel beside the house just as he had. I packed a few meager belongings and left. I didn't know where I was going, but I knew I was leaving the God-forsaken place I had called home. I walked in the opposite direction of town. I knew Floyd would go there to look for me first, and too many people there knew me, especially the men. I walked all day and night, staying off the roads as much as possible. The sun had been up for several hours when I arrived in Asheville the next day. I was scared, hungry, and looked like the ignorant ragamuffin I was. Shopkeepers were opening for the day. The looks and stares of disapproval made me dare not ask for assistance. I didn't want folks to know that I had money for fear that they might try to steal it." She paused for a few minutes, maybe to collect her thoughts.

Jessup wanted to ask a question but thought it best not to prod. While he regretted the terrible details of Maggie's story, the account and the way in which she told it mesmerized him. He had not intended to bring back a painful past, but she seemed to need to purge and continued.

"At the end of the main street was the local church. The tall white steeple gleamed, and sunlight reflected off its fresh paint. I kept my head down and walked toward it in hopes of finding sanctuary. I pushed the large doors open, and will never forget how the morning sun danced off the maple pews and stained-glass windows. It was like sacred sunshine, there to make me clean. I walked down the aisle to where a man was sweeping. 'Excuse me, sir. Could you tell me where I could get some food and a bath,' I asked. He turned and looked at me. He was a big man with a big, thick handlebar mustache. His eyes flashed fire at me. 'How dare you,' he roared. His white face turned burnt orange. 'How dare you enter the house of God! Get out! Get out! This is no place for the likes of you.' He walked toward me. Now, usually, I ain't scared of no man, but his massive build and thunderous voice frightened me. I turned and ran toward the doors. He threw the broom at me. It missed me, the handle whizzing past. I picked it up and flung it back at him, knocking over a cross and candles sitting on a nearby table. I burst through the doors into the bright sunlight and ran. I later found out his name was Harry Jackson, and he was one of those ignorant, religious zealots who run around proclaiming the word of God, but know nothing about its true meaning. He preached fire and brimstone but had so little education he couldn't actually read a scripture if his life depended on it.

"Once safely away from Reverend Jackson, I slowed my pace and walked toward the edge of town. As I got farther away from the main street, the buildings sat far and few between, with little activity on the road. I came upon a house of sorts isolated from the rest of town; the sign out front read *Dumont's Saloon*. Three women in robes and undergarments talked to two men on the front porch. The men were tucking in their shirts and fastening their trousers. They seemed in a hurry to get somewhere. 'Excuse me. Could y'all halp me? I need some food and a bath.'

"Finally, the Negro woman in the bunch said, 'Where you from, honey?' I answered her, 'I been walking for pert near two days. I'm awful tired and hungry.' One of the men told the Negro woman to take care of me. He said he would be back later that night.

"The Negro woman said, 'Come on in, honey. We'll get you

some food and a place to sleep.' I was struck by the kindness of these women, compared to the scorn shown to me by the reverend and the good townspeople.

"'What's yer name, honey,' she asked me.

"'Lula. Lula Higgins,' I responded. 'What's yo name?'

"'Maggie,' she said.

"'You got a last name,' I asked.

"'I don't know. Don't reckon I got a last name. Folks just call me Maggie. Come on, Lula. Let's get you some food.'

"She led me through the main part of the saloon and into the kitchen in the back. I will never forget the smell of the eggs, bacon, coffee and fresh bread. Another Negro woman cooked and cleaned the place. A bunch of white girls sat around the large wooden table, drinking coffee, smoking tobacco and waiting for a plate of food. After breakfast, Maggie took me to her room and prepared a bath for me. I leaned back in the tub and enjoyed the warm water. For a moment, I foolishly believed I could wash away my past. Soaking in the tub, I looked around the room. A large four-poster bed was the center of attention. The room was accented with two nice armchairs and a dressing table. I had never seen such perfumes, bath oils and fine toiletries before. This Negro woman named Maggie was my savior.

"'You can sleep in my bed today, but I'm gonna need it tonight,' she told me as she tossed a simple cotton nightgown on the bed. 'You can rest in that. I don't have much use for it, except in the winter if I'm sleeping alone, and that don't happen much.'

"'Thank you,' I said. 'Who was that man who told ya to look after me?'

"'That was Thomas Dumont. He owns this place but has a farm outside of town. I run things during the day. He'll be back tonight.'

"'You his woman?' I asked.

"'Well, I ain't just his; I got to make a living. But, we do have a special friendship. I'm his whenever he wants me to be, and that's most of the time.'

"She was real pretty, the color of coffee with lots of cream mixed in. Her thick curly black hair framed her face and rested on her shoulders. Slender and shapely, she was the kind of woman I wanted to be. I slept most of that day, with the satchel full of money under my nightgown, safe next to my body. Although the people seemed nice, I had learned to trust no one. Many hours later, I was awakened by her gently shaking me.

"'You got to get up now,' she told me. 'The men be coming in, and I'm gonna need the bed. Get dressed and go on down to the kitchen for something to eat and to help Stella. You got to earn your keep. We found a dress for you. It was left here by one of the other girls. It ought to fit. None of us wanted it.'

"You should have seen the thing. I was glad to have the matronly, light blue, long sleeve dress with white cuffs and collar. It looked respectable, just right to begin a new life. I pulled it on and went to the kitchen. After I'd eaten, I helped Stella with the dishes. And that's when Thomas Dumont walked in.

"'Well, you look a hell of a lot better than you did this morning,' he told me.

"I took my hands from the water and dried them on my apron." 'Thank you, sir. Thank you for ya halp.'

"I had been so weak from hunger that morning when I first met him that I really had not paid much attention to him. Standing before me now, I saw that Thomas Dumont was tall with dark brown hair and clear blue eyes. His beard was thick, and he took the time to groom it. The line on his neck where his beard ended and white skin began was razored to precision. His deep, rich voice commanded attention.

"'What you running from,' he asked.

"'My daddy. He beats me and ...  Well, he just don't treat me right,' I said.

"'Where you headed?'

"'I don't rightly know. All I know is, I got to get far away from him. I want to get to a big city.'

"'Well,' he said. 'There's Charleston, Atlanta, New Orleans. Which one you interested in?'

"'Which is the farthest away?'

"'That would be New Orleans.'

"'That's where I want to go. Can ya tell me how to get there?' I asked.

"'We can put you on a stage to Greensboro, and you can get a train from there to New Orleans.

"'Can I leave tomorrow?'

"He chuckled." 'You could stay here and work for me. Maggie could teach you all you need to know.'

"'Thank you, but I need to move on. I got a little money. I can pay my way.'

"'All right, Lula. We'll see you off tomorrow.'

"Now, I had never told him my name was Lula. I reckon Maggie must have told him.

"The next day, Dumont checked on the stage departure schedules and around 2:00 that afternoon, I was headed to Greensboro, where I was to catch a train. I settled into the back of the coach, and for the first time, felt safely away from Floyd.

"Between the stage and the train changes, it was a long trip. When I finally arrived in New Orleans, the streets were swarming with people. Music filled the air along with thick French accents. Like a foreign land, streets with exotic names like Rue Dauphine, Rue LaSalle and Rue Dorsiere held one mystery after another. I found lodging in one of the city's boarding houses and started looking for work. The city was loaded with slaves, and most merchants used slave labor rather than paid employees. I had a difficult time finding work.

"New Orleans was filled with wealthy white residents *and* had a population of successful free Negroes who were financially well off. One day I stumbled into a nice area of well-kept homes. To my surprise, it was the Negro section of town. I later found that many of the free colored people were educated merchants, shopkeepers, undertakers and other professionals. I also learned that some of the homes were occupied by the Negro mistresses of wealthy white planters. These free mulatto women bore the children of the planters, and the planters kept their half-white, half-Negro families in almost as fine a style as their legitimate white families.

"I was taken with New Orleans; although the city was not so

impressed with me. My thick hillbilly accent and lack of sophistication hindered me from getting work in the millinery shops, boutiques and other places I looked. I tried to keep fed and as clean as possible, but my money was running low.

"Once, I entered a local restaurant seeking work. A man seated at a small table looked official with several papers scattered before him on the table and on the floor. The place was empty, but the workers were preparing early for the morning rush. The wonderful aroma of sausage and bacon cooking in the back reminded me I was hungry. I walked up to the man and said, 'Exc'use me. I'm looking fer work. Y'all need any halp. I can do just 'bout anythang.' The man took his eyes off the papers and looked me up and down, me in my dirty blue dress with the white collar and cuffs.

"'Bonjour, mademoiselle,' he said. 'Que veux-tu?'

"I stared at him. I didn't understand his words.

"'What do you want,' he asked in a heavy French accent flavored with contempt.

"'I'm looking fer work,' I again explained. 'I'm new here, and I need work.'

"He stared at me a moment longer then said, 'We have no need for you here. Au revoir, mademoiselle.'

"'But I ...'

"'Au revoir sortez d'ici! Go!'

"My spirit sank. I turned and left the establishment. I realized that with no money, no friends, and no place to go, prostitution was quickly becoming my only option. The owners of the boarding house in which I was living would not extend credit to me until I found work. After a few more days of rejection, I found my way to Gallatin Street. When I sought work in one of the whorehouses, the madam slowly looked me up and down just like that Frenchman in the restaurant.

"'You got a name' she gruffed, still sizing me up through jaundiced eyes. She took a puff from a small cigar she held between withered fingers with cracked nails. She blew smoke in my face and grinned, bearing brown teeth caked with the remains of the day.

"I thought about the two people who had helped me most —

Maggie and Thomas Dumont. I straightened my spine and looked the old bitch in her yellow eyes, and with the most sophistication I could muster, I said, 'My name is Maggie. Maggie Dumont.'

"In the summer, I worked as a dance hall gal on the riverboats. In the winter, I worked as a whore in one of the famous houses in New Orleans, all the while saving money. When the *New Orleans Daily Picayune* began its campaign urging the police to clean up the brothels on Gallatin Street, several of my friends were arrested. I was fortunate to escape the raids. After a couple of close calls, I thought it time to leave New Orleans. By the time I got to Richmond, I had the money and the know-how to own and operate a gentleman's club." She paused and rested her hand on his arm.

"After I got here, I had the good fortune of meeting you."

Jessup leaned over and kissed her on each cheek. "Maggie Dumont. So that's how you come by the name. Well, let me tell you something, Maggie Dumont. I respect you, and I'm damn proud to call you my friend. I'll always be here for you."

"And, I'm always here for you. We're family." She smiled and took another sip. "I remember the first time I saw you," she chuckled. "I had only been in town a few days but long enough to be shunned by everyone. I was crossing the street headed to the bank to see your daddy about getting a loan to buy this place. That drunkard, Jim Williams, almost ran me down with his wagon. You seemed to come from nowhere and pulled me out of the way. After composing ourselves, you tipped your hat and asked 'are you all right, Miss Dumont?' We had never been introduced. Somehow you already knew who I was, but it didn't seem to matter to you. You extended your arm and escorted me across the street, treating me like a lady in front of all the town's blue bloods. I knew right then and there that I liked you."

"I remember. I had just left Pappy's office and had been ridiculed by him. He had called me a worthless dandy with questionable habits that would destroy the family name. How about that? I was feeling mighty low."

Maggie nodded.

"It was actually later that same day when you found me beaten up pretty badly in the alley beside the Spotswood, where you were staying. I had mistaken the friendliness of a farmer for more than he was willing to give. A few days later, I found out it was you who paid the bellman to get me to a room and send for the doctor."

She lowered her head. "I will never forget the horrible name that bumpkin called you as he walked away. I immediately knew what had happened."

He rubbed the side of his face. "After my bruises healed and my pride was restored, I called on you to thank you for your kindness and discretion. You told me about Pappy's reservations about making you the loan so I intervened."

They sat quietly.

"It's so good to be here with you. I'm glad we talked." Jessup yawned and stretched his long arms. "I'm gonna go on up to my room and get some sleep."

"Good night, darling. Rest well," she said.

"You too, Maggie." He looked back as he climbed the stairs, grateful for Maggie. She and Andrew were like family to him.

## Chapter 13
## October 1859

**Georgie**, Mama, and two other slave women struggled carrying a tub filled with hog intestines. They dropped it at the river's bank. Shit splashed, staining Georgie's white apron. "I hate hog-killing time. Means more work for us." She wiped the mess from her apron and rinsed her hand in the river.

"I don't mind it. I likes dis kinda cooking," said Mama.

"Course you do. Curing meat gives you a chance to be bossier than usual. Ain't no one but you know how," said Georgie.

"Mind yo manners, Georgie. The field hands gets to eat a little better."

"If you call scraps better, crackling, meat skins, and chittlins ain't exactly a ham or a chop," Georgie reminded Mama.

The kill was fresh. Steam rose from the intestines into the cool air. Each woman picked up a piece, walked to the edge of the water and squeezed the shit out into the river. Each washed an intestine in the current and then placed it in a tub of fresh water.

"Dat ought to do it fer now," said Mama after they had cleaned the entire tub full. Let 'em soak tonight, and tomorrow we'll wash 'em again before I start getting de fat off."

"Cleaning chittlins in this cold water ain't good for your joints, Mama. It's mighty cold these days for the middle of October. Must gonna be a long winter."

"My joints be just fine. I'll warm 'em by de fire tonight."

*********

"I done washed my hands four times, and they still smell like chittlin shit," said Georgie relaxing by a fire in Mama's cabin.

"You'll get used to it."

"I don't want to get used to it, Mama."

"You getting might uppity, Georgie." Mama glared across the table.

"That's what Onie Johnson told me."

"Oh Baby, you know I didn't mean ..."

"I know."

Georgie sighed, exhausted. She untied the fabric that held her hair in bondage.

Mama looked at the mane. "It's getting mighty long. Time to cut it back."

"I ain't cutting it. I'm going on over to my cabin. It's getting late, and we've got more of them nasty things to clean tomorrow."

Uncle Buck rocked in front of the fire and sucked on his corncob pipe. Little Sally slept curled up on a pallet beside him.

"Might as well leave her here she sleeping so good," suggested Mama.

"All right. Thanks for the cornbread. Good night, Uncle Buck."

"Night, Georgie."

"You all right, Uncle Buck? You' been mighty quite all evening."

"Oh Baby, I'm just fine. Just sitting here thinking."

"Thinking about what?" Mama placed both hands on her hips. "What you got to be thinking 'bout?"

"Eating dem good chittlins," he said, his voice roiling into a chuckle.

Georgie rolled her eyes and shut the door behind her.

"She mighty particular about dat hair, ain't she," said Uncle Buck.

"Yes she is," huffed Mama.

"I can hear y'all out here," Georgie yelled through the door. "You could have waited until I got away from the door to talk about me."

Georgie walked back to her cabin, the smell of Uncle Buck's corncob pipe in her nose, and the taste of cornbread in her mouth. A figure stood by the willow tree stopped her on the path. "Who's there?" she commanded. "Is that you, MawNancy?" Georgie stared at the apparition, keeping a safe distance. "I ain't never seen no haunt before. Is you one?"

The figure started to sing softly, a nightingale's pitch.
*Steal away, steal away, steal away to Jesus.*
*Steal away, steal away home.*

*I ain't got long to stay here.*

The woman hummed then asked in a husky voice, "You ready to go wid me, gal?"

"Go where?" Georgie asked.

"Freedom."

"They'll kill me if I try that. I done seen what they do to runaways." Georgie sprinted to her cabin. She turned to look back; like a phantom, the woman was gone. Only the tree, and the pitch black remained.

## Chapter 14
## November 1859

**Andrew** stood outside Nimrod's door and called to him. "I'm going up to Richmond. I'll be back around night fall."

"You think everything's clear, Mr. Andrew? That terrible rain might have washed out the road. It's been mighty cold, too."

"I think the road is passable. If not, I'll come back. By the way, I heard from Anna. She won't be home until after Christmas." They stood in silence, Andrew in reverence of the news. He wondered if Nimrod might also be grateful. "I sent for another horse," Andrew continued. "Blue had thrown a shoe. The horses aren't well groomed. It's time we get another slave to work the stable. Uncle Buck is getting too old to do it alone."

"I'll see what I can do," grunted Nimrod.

"Don't need to decide right away, but think on it. And Nimrod, let him be. He's an old man."

The buckboard pulled up, and Andrew climbed in. "I shouldn't be long. I want to pick up a few things and meet with some business acquaintances. I'm seeing Millard Horsley about space in his warehouse for next year's tobacco crop when auction time comes."

The muddy road was not impassable but made for a slow trip. He was in no rush, and the chill and dampness did not snuff out his energy stoked by the excitement of the city.

*********

"How do, Mr. Horsley?" Andrew yelled over the din of slaves and free blacks unloading spools of twine used to tie bales of dried leaf. Andrew inhaled the heady scent of high-dollar tobacco that lingered in the warehouse.

"Andrew. What can I do for you?" Mr. Horsley extended his stocky hand.

"I'm just stopping through. Thought I'd say hello and let you know we want to store our tobacco here, same as usual."

"I'm always glad to do business with the Gordon household. You just let me know when you're ready to bring it, and I'll have space for you.  How was your ride up?  With all the bad weather we've had, I'd thought the roads would have been full of muck."

"It wasn't too bad, other than a bit chilly. The rains haven't hurt trade up and down the river.  It looks pretty busy."

"Business is good these days."  Mr. Horsley brushed dirt from the front of his pants and walked closer to Andrew.  "Shockoe Warehouse District and Tredegar Ironworks got lots of immigrants working for 'em now."

The cavernous warehouse seemed empty despite the hauling and loading equipment stored along walls. Come harvest time it would be stuffed from rafters to floorboards with Virginia gold.  Andrew inched his way toward the door.

Mr. Horsley followed.  They reached the door, and Mr. Horsley extended his hand.  "Just let me know when you're ready to bring your crop in, and I'll be waiting for you."

"Thank you.  Nice seeing you, Mr. Horsley."

He held a firm grip on Andrew's hand, "It's good to see you, son. How is Mr. Gordon? Make sho you tell him I asked about him."

"I will," answered Andrew, avoiding discussion of his father's well-being.

"You going to the auction?"

"Didn't hear about it."

"Slave trader's in town.  Got a bunch of niggers to sell.  Starts in about an hour.  Just down the block yonder, in a warehouse across from Lumpkin's Jail."

"I got a little shopping to do, but I'll be back."  Andrew waved goodbye.

He returned at the auction's start and made his way up front for a good view.  Seven Negroes stood on display as the auctioneer began the sale. A tall, skinny, dark brown boy walked up to the block.  His long arms dangled at his sides.  He seemed excited about all the attention.

The auctioneer yelled to a crowd of twenty-five or so planters, "First up we got a Negro boy about 10 years old.  He's young now but is a sound investment.  You will get years of good work from this one, and in a few years, he'll be ready to stud.  He's healthy, with strong bones, and he's got a fine temperament. Yes sir, he won't give you no trouble."

His cadence roared to start the bidding. "Who's gonna start? Do I hear two thousand dollars? Two thousand? Anybody for two thousand dollars? What about fifteen hundred? Who'll do fifteen hundred? Fifteen hundred dollars? Come on gentlemen. This boy is gonna give you years of hard work. One thousand dollars then. Anybody for a thousand? What about five hundred dollars? Who's gonna bid five hundred?

The bidding started at one hundred dollars. There was little interest in the boy. He sold for $275 to the owner of a small farm in Covington. Andrew knew it as a little lumber town nestled in Virginia's Blue Ridge Mountains. He wondered if his military school friend, Joseph, still lived there. They had not kept in touch like he had hoped they would.

"Next up is this handsome, young female about 20 years old," the auctioneer bellowed. "She's strong, and you won't have no trouble breeding her. And gentlemen, she'll make a good bed warmer on cold winter nights."

Most of the men were interested. The bidding started at three hundred dollars, moved around the room on fifty-dollar raises until it stopped at Jim Williams and his winning bid of twelve hundred dollars.

"One thousand, two hundred," crowed the auctioneer. "Going once. One thousand, two hundred going twice."

"Thirteen hundred dollars," a woman's voice from the back rose above the auctioneer's.

The room fell silent, and everyone turned to the new bidder, a lady dressed in fine silk, demure under a proper hat. The auctioneer looked at Mr. Williams for a counter bid.

"Fifteen hundred dollars," Williams bellowed.

"Two thousand dollars," the new bidder countered.

Williams was about to open his mouth when the woman usurped him, "Twenty-five hundred dollars."

Visibly angry, Williams did not bid more. "I guess I'll have to get what I want from her at your place, Maggie," he said.

The men laughed.

"Well, well," mumbled Andrew. "That's the famous Maggie Dumont."

The slave trader prodded a walnut brown male up to the block. Unlike the others, shackles bound his hands and feet. Dried blood caked his swollen ankles; the shackles dug into his flesh. Pus oozed from sores, and he grimaced with each step. The slave trader opened his shirt and exposed his chest. "He's good and fit fer field work."

The auctioneer brought out the usual selling points. "This is a fine specimen. You can get good work out of him now plus immediate stud use."

"Fine specimen my ass," Andrew said to the man standing next to him. "He's been mistreated. Just look at his feet. Without proper care, the infection could kill him."

The bidding started at five hundred dollars and went to two thousand, five hundred, Mr. Williams' bid.

"I've got twenty-five hundred dollars," yelled the excited auctioneer. "Do I hear three thousand? Anyone for three thousand?"

Andrew stared at the slave's bloodied ankles and rag-wrapped feet. His hand raised, guided perhaps by some supernatural force. He heard a voice — his own — utter "three thousand dollars." The sound of the auctioneer's gavel smacking the wooden podium jarred him from his trance.

"Sold to Mr. Gordon for three thousand dollars!"

Andrew had had no intention of bidding. Now, he was the owner of a male slave, a three-thousand-dollar-male slave. He approached the trader, a scrawny man trying to pass himself off as a gentleman by wearing a suit. The sleeves and pants were too short, and the jacket so tight it appeared the seams might burst. "I'll have to go to my bank and get the money. I'll be back directly," Andrew told him.

When he returned to the warehouse with the money, the auction was over, and the buyers were settling accounts.

"Mr. Gordon," said the trader. "I wasn't planning to sell that one here. I was gonna take him on down south. Virginia is too close to the northern line fer a nigger like him. He was owned by the Fairholm

Plantation in Maryland, trained by Mr. Fairholm as a fighting buck."

Andrew stood speechless.

"I'm sure you know what that is," said the trader. When Andrew didn't respond, the trader continued, "Some well-to-do men, like yerself, train their male niggers to fight. Sometimes kill fer sport."

"I've heard of it. Don't approve."

"You ought to know, this one needs watching. He broke a white man's jaw up in Maryland. They damn near kilt him fer it. I think he's learned his lesson, but I'd keep them shackles on him, if I was you. You can keep 'em, but I'll have to charge you extree."

Andrew remained silent.

"You want the shackles?"

"Take them off his feet, but leave the ones on his hands."

"That'll be ten more dollars," said the trader through a snaggle-toothed grin.

Despite being overcharged, Andrew wanted to get himself and the slave away from the weasel-looking trader.

The trader unlocked the foot shackles. He and Andrew walked to the wagon; the slave followed behind, unsteady on his newly freed legs.

"Where are his shoes?"

"Ain't got none. Here's the key to them hand shackles fer when you's ready to take 'em off." He handed Andrew a rusted key.

"Raise the back of his shirt," Andrew told the trader.

"What fer?"

"Just do it," ordered Andrew. "You told me they whipped him."

The trader lifted the back of the shirt. Scabs covered the slave's back, still healing from the most recent beating.

"Why didn't you show his back when you were parading him around?"

"A deal is a deal." The trader fiddled with his hands. "I told you he might be a problem. You can't say I didn't warn ya."

"You told me after you took my money. I'm not trying to back out of the deal, but you should have shown all of him during the auction."

"I think he's got that drapetomania. You know, the hankering to be free. They say the only cure is to whip it out of 'em. If that's true, they done cured him," the trader sneered at the slave. "Nice doing business with you, Mr. Gordon." He extended his hand to Andrew and again flashed a mostly toothless grin.

Andrew remained silent, his arms at his sides. He could not let this slave know that he was afraid. He remembered his daddy's tactics and turned to the slave and said, "Listen to me, boy, and you listen good. You give me any trouble, and I'll blow your goddamn head off. You understand me? Now get in the front seat." He knew how to be a white man when the time called for it.

The slave tried to climb into the wagon but couldn't manage unassisted. Andrew put a hand on his back to hoist him up. The wounded feet, in plain view now, needed immediate attention. Andrew reached into his satchel, pulled out a pair of wool socks he had brought for himself and handed them to the slave. "These will have to do until we get you some shoes."

Andrew grabbed hold of the reins and, just before pulling off, studied the battered black man sitting next to him. The man was struggling with shackled hands to put the socks over his bleeding feet, his sad eyes begging the stockings for some relief.

"You got a name?"

The slave stopped fiddling with the socks, sat up straight and looked Andrew in the face. "Edward."

Andrew slapped the horses' backsides. The buckboard jolted, and Edward lost his balance. He flashed a menacing look. Andrew ignored it as the wagon pulled forward. He glanced toward the warehouse across the street and locked eyes with none other than Onie Johnson. Onie stared back with both fists on his hips and his legs spread wide. Andrew drove on, ignoring the bile that had risen in his throat.

The two rode in silence. After a while, Edward asked, "You mind if I sleep in the back of the wagon, sir?"

"You stay in the front where I can see you. And, my name is Andrew. Andrew Gordon."

A cold blast of wind hit them. Edward shivered and crossed his arms over his upper body.

"I was so focused on your feet I didn't notice you don't have proper clothing." Andrew reached in the back of the wagon. "Here, put this blanket around you. These palominos will make good time. We'll be home soon."

"Thank you, Mr. Andrew."

"You're' welcome, Edward."

While Edward dozed, Andrew looked at his new property, another name to add to the ledger. His body was strong, but the mistreatment evident. As they got closer to home, Edward awakened with a pained expression.

"Something ailing you?" Andrew asked.

"My feet hurting a little more than usual."

"The feeling must be coming back now that you're wearing warm socks. Aunt Daisy will know what to do."

Andrew pulled up in front of the stable just before nightfall. Uncle Buck came out to take care of the horses and wagon. Edward rolled onto his stomach on the wagon's bench seat and slid off the wagon, wincing when his battered feet touched the ground.

"This here is Edward. I bought him to work in the stable and barn with you," Andrew announced, the thought of pairing Edward with Uncle Buck just occurring to him. Up to that point, he hadn't known what he was going to do with Edward. Andrew took the key out of his pocket and unlocked the shackles.

"Let him sleep in the barn tonight. Tell Aunt Daisy to feed him and look after his feet. And have a plate sent up to my room." Andrew stopped by Nimrod's cabin. "Nimrod, I purchased a new slave today at an auction while I was up in Richmond. I want him working with Uncle Buck for now. He's got some problems with his feet. They need time to heal."

"Ya sah. I'll look in on him."

A slave girl sat in the shadow on the bed. In the dim light, Andrew tried but couldn't make out who it was. Nimrod only cracked the door and seemed eager to end the conversation. Hungry and tired, Andrew closed the door and made the short walk home.

Back in his room, Andrew ate and put away the few items he had purchased — socks, a new straight razor, long johns and a rag doll, an upcoming Christmas present for Little Sally. He rummaged through one of his trunks until he found an old pair of boots. He went to his office and retrieved the Wilmington Ledger. He added Edward to the count while the information was still fresh in his mind. On the next available line he wrote: Edward, Male, approximately 30 years old, purchased October 15, 1859 for three thousand dollars. After the ink dried, he returned the book to its place on the shelf, pulled on his coat, grabbed the spare boots, and walked out into the frigid night.

Andrew found Edward in the barn with fresh bandages on his feet; the distinct aroma of Aunt Daisy's eucalyptus balm mixed with that of dried fescue. Edward sat on a pallet of straw and a few blankets. Aunt Daisy had mothered him, as Andrew hoped. He threw the boots to Edward, who lifted his eyes.

"They ought to fit."

Edward's eyes met Andrew's.

"You know, most white men don't take kindly to being looked in the eye by a nigger," Andrew spat out.

"Thank you for saving me from that trader and for your kindness. It's been a long time since I've had a blanket, socks, and boots."

Edward spoke with a quiet elegance despite his station and condition.

"There's another blanket up in the loft," said Andrew, softer.

Edward rose and hobbled to the ladder. He put one foot on the first rung, but the pressure on his ankle was too much. He stumbled, catching himself. Andrew helped steady him, holding his arm and leading him back to the pallet.

"It's gonna be a while before your feet are back to normal. I'll get the blanket. That trader ought to be horse-whipped for letting your feet get in that condition."

Andrew climbed the ladder, grabbed a blanket and handed it to Edward.

"You rest easy. The overseer is Nimrod. I told him you get your orders from me, for now. I don't want him ruining you by working you too hard before your feet have healed." He stood at the door with his hands in his coat pockets, suddenly at a loss for words. He stared at the ground, trying to push away nerves. "Huh. Well, uh. I think. Wha … wha … wha … what I mean to say is, I ho … ho … hope." His tongue and mouth worked against him, obeying a mind of their own. "Wel … wel … wel … well, you'll be all right here," he managed.

Edward lay back and pulled the blankets up to his chin. Andrew turned and walked to the small barn door. He opened it, and the autumn wind rushed in cooling his hot cheeks. He closed the door and made his way back to the house.

## Chapter 15
### Early December 1859

**Andrew** made the first few weeks easy for Edward, allowing him time to heal and get used to his new surroundings. Uncle Buck seemed to appreciate the help, and Aunt Daisy had clearly taken a liking to him. Andrew checked in on him daily. The swelling in Edward's ankles was gone, and the wounds on his back healed, leaving pink stripes. Andrew gave him an old pair of long johns in the hopes they would help the slave's body focus on complete healing and rather than on keeping warm in the damp quarters.

A light frost silvered the ground causing the few faded brown and yellow leaves still clinging on limbs to glisten in the warm morning sun. At the sound of gravel crunching, Andrew strode out to the front porch to find Old Man Benson from down the road driving a wagon up to the house. The creaking wheels came to an abrupt halt. "Good morning, Mr. Gordon."

"How do, Mr. Benson? What can I do for you?" Andrew walked to the side of the wagon.

"I got a message fer you. I been up in Richmond the last few days and saw Millard Horsley. He knows we're neighbors and asked me to stop and tell you that the chain on your pocket watch come loose, and the watch dropped on the floor when you was in his place a spell back. He knows it yours being that your name is on the back and all."

"Thank you, Mr. Benson. I hadn't missed it. It was a graduation gift from my daddy. Mr. Horsley could have just given it to you to drop off."

"I told him I'd bring it, but he said he wanted me to deliver the message only."

"Well, thank you for coming out of your way."

"You welcome. It weren't no trouble. Y'all have a good day now." He slapped the horse with the reins, and the rickety wagon pulled off.

\*\*\*\*\*\*\*\*\*

Andrew finished breakfast and pushed his plate aside signaling

Luther to clear the table. "It's been over a week since I got that message from Mr. Horsley about my watch. I reckon I'll go on up to Richmond today to get it and a few other things."

"Yes sah," said Luther, refilling Andrew's coffee cup.

"Tell Aunt Daisy those biscuits were mighty good. That was right filling."

"I'll tell her. She'll be glad to hear it."

"Have Uncle Buck and Edward hitch up the buckboard. I want to leave right away, so I can get back before nightfall."

Andrew nursed the coffee until it went cold. He pulled on his coat and headed out into the bright, chilly day. He looked forward to the crisp wind against his skin. "The horses look good with their tails and manes brushed. They seem well rested and fed, eager for the trip. Don't you think?" He looked to Edward who was standing in front of the animals checking on their harnesses. "Are you responsible for this grooming?"

"You have some mighty fine horses. I enjoy taking care of them."

"You seem to be getting along quite well. Your ankles look healed, and you're walking pretty good. Those boots fit all right?"

"Yes sir. They fit fine. I'm feeling much better. Thank you."

"Good. I've got a better winter coat for you. I'll find it and get it to you." Andrew climbed into the buckboard and took the reins. He looked at Edward before snapping the horses forward. "Get in. You'll ride with me." Andrew pointed to the seat next to him, and Edward climbed in.

Andrew tipped his hat to Nimrod, who watched them leave. He and Nimrod disagreed about the work assigned to Edward. "I don't see no reason why an able-bodied slave is wasted on stable work that a crippled old man was capable of doing by himself," Nimrod had grumbled to Andrew a few days after Edward's arrival and a few other times since.

The trip started out quietly, the silence broken by only the heavy clops of the horses' hooves and the creaking wagon boards. Andrew wasn't in the habit of making small talk with slaves, but for some strange reason, he was comfortable with Edward. Light conversation followed, mostly about Edward's recovery and their mutual admiration of fine horses. When they arrived in Richmond, Andrew made a quick stop by the bank to see Jessup. Edward tended to the horses and wagon while Andrew visited. Afterward, they made their way to the Shockoe Warehouse District to retrieve the watch.

Mr. Horsely addressed Andrew the instant he walked through the door. "I'm sorry you had to make a trip all the way up here to get it, but I could tell it was expensive with your name on the back and all. I wasn't gonna put it in anybody's hands but yours," he said as he rummaged through a drawer.

"Thank you, Mr. Horsely. I appreciate you looking after it for me. My daddy always said you were a fine man.

"You're mighty welcome. Have some coffee or a nip?"

"I can't stay. Nightfall is going to catch me for sure."

The trip home started the same as the trip out. The quiet comforted Andrew. He pulled out his tobacco kit and lit his pipe. "You smoke?"

"No sir. Mr. Fairholm never let me around tobacco. He wanted me in good shape for fighting. Before Mr. Fairholm, I was owned by a preacher who didn't believe in tobacco or strong drink."

Andrew handed him the pipe, "Try it. Careful, don't take too much. It'll strangle you."

Edward sucked on the end and coughed.

"You took in too much." Andrew laughed, and Edward, between coughing fits, did, too. "Try again. This time take it slow."

Edward tried again, more careful, and blew the smoke out of his mouth without coughing. Andrew smiled at Edward's success and was about to ask him if he liked the taste, when horses coming from behind startled him to attention. Andrew didn't realize they were right up on them until they rode up in front of the wagon, forcing Andrew to stop and reach for his pistol. One of the horsemen had already drawn his. The other dismounted and walked toward the wagon.

"Git out," he told Andrew.

Andrew didn't move but studied the mean face showing from

under the hat. Andrew recognized it as Onie's. "What the hell do you want?"

"I said git outta that wagon, you son of a bitch."

"I'd get moving if I were you, mister," said the man with the revolver. He cocked it.

Andrew put one foot on the ground, and Onie landed a blow to the side of Andrew's face, knocking him out of the wagon. Andrew struggled to get up, but Onie hit him again and said, "You and your daddy run me off your plantation like I was nothing but trash. I've waited all these years to pay you back. And then today, I see you pull off back yonder with your fine horses and a nigger beside you."

He kicked Andrew in the stomach. Andrew looked to Edward for help; the slave moved to intervene, but the mounted horseman pointed the silver revolver at Edward's head. "Move again, nigger, and you're dead,"

Onie jumped on top of Andrew, trying to pin him down, but Andrew grabbed a hand-full of dirt and rocks and threw it in Onie's eyes. Andrew shoved him off and tried to collect himself, but Onie came at him again. This time, Andrew landed a couple of blows. Onie lay on the ground dazed, holding his head. Andrew walked toward the wagon, thinking the fight was over. The mounted gunman pointed his revolver at Andrew. Edward jumped from the wagon, and the gunman swung his gun toward Edward and fired. Andrew looked to make sure Edward was not hurt. The gunman dismounted and went after Edward. Edward tackled him, sending the gun flying. Edward grabbed the man by the collar and stood him up only to knock him down again. Edward landed two more punches before the gunman was out cold. Onie stood again and came after Andrew, tackling him. Onie climbed on top of him and began choking him. Edward grabbed Onie by the back of his coat, pulled him off, and knocked Onie against the front wagon wheel. Onie reached for Andrew's gun on the front seat of the buckboard. He turned to aim but was met by Edward's solid, black fist. The gun hit the ground, and so did Onie.

A pain cut Andrew from the inside, making him stumble. He suspected that a few ribs were broken from Onie's boot. He hoped his thick coat had cushioned the blow enough, so that there wouldn't be much damage. Onie and the gunman lay on the ground, and Edward stood over them, his fists balled tight. He looked ready for the next onslaught, but the men didn't move.

Edward walked to Andrew and put his arm around his waist. The support helped, and Andrew put his arm around Edward's neck. They made their way back to the wagon, and Edward helped him in. Every time he shifted on the hard bench or moved his legs, a jab shot through his side. Edward went back to Onie and the other man. He took the gunman's pistol and then removed the one from Onie's horse.

Panic swept through Andrew, as Edward walked toward him, a gun in each hand. Andrew looked for his pistol; it was on the ground beside Onie, out of Andrew's reach. He was alone and defenseless with a heavily armed slave trained in fist fighting. "Wh … Wh … Wh … Why'd you take those?" Andrew asked, trying to mask fear.

"By the time they come to, we should be almost home. But if they do happen to catch up to us, it'll be a fair fight this way," said Edward. He picked up Andrew's gun, climbed into the wagon and handed the three revolvers to Andrew. Andrew's shame rose to his face. Edward had risked being shot and had beaten two men to save him. He set the two revolvers on the floor, and put his in his coat pocket.

Andrew held his side and tried to move the horses and wagon forward. He winced at the smallest movement. Edward took the reins and said, "I'd better do that." He slapped the horses, and the wagon pulled off with a jolt. The lurch caused Andrew to cry out in pain. "Brace yourself here," Edward said motioning to his right side. "You won't feel it as much."

## Chapter 16
## Early December 1859

**Edward** drove the wagon home with Andrew leaning on him asleep. The events of the evening stirred up all sorts of memories. When Onie and the gunman first descended on them, Edward thought they might be nightriders like the vigilantes who had chased and captured him for breaking that trainer's jaw. The brawl conjured up his days as a fighter. Visions of his opponents on hands and knees struggling to get up and the sound of white men cheering, money clenched in their fists, still haunted him. Some rooted for him, and others yelled for his opponent to get up and fight. Once again he was face-to-face with the image of Fairholm, his smug expression and lust for his buck to win, lining his pockets with the winner's purse. Edward wanted to pound every one of them. He had just beaten two white men. They could kill him for that. He wanted to run but wasn't sure where he was and didn't know which way to go. Andrew had been kinder to him than anyone had been in a long time. He desperately wanted to run, but slapped the horses' backsides and made way for home.

By the time they reached the plantation, Andrew was waking. Edward pulled the wagon up and ran to the kitchen where he found Aunt Daisy and Uncle Buck. "Go get Nimrod. Mr. Andrew has been hurt."

Edward was lifting Andrew off the wagon when Nimrod showed up. Georgie and Zula ran toward them. Georgie gasped at the sight of Andrew's bruised face.

"What the hell's going on?" Nimrod demanded.

"Two men ambushed us on the way home."

"Oh Lord, he's hurt bad. We need to get him in the house," said Aunt Daisy.

"Let's get him to his room," said Nimrod. "He can hardly walk." Nimrod moved to help, but Edward didn't need assistance, lifting Andrew like a baby. "I got him."

Aunt Daisy and Georgie led the way. Edward carried Andrew into the house, up the stairs and to the master bedroom. Nimrod and

Zula trailed behind.

Old man Gordon came out of his room into the hallway. "What's all the damn ruckus out here?"

"Mr. Andrew is feeling poorly," Aunt Daisy told him. "We looking after him. You go on back to bed now. He be just fine."

The old man grumbled and retreated to his room.

Aunt Daisy barked out orders. "Zula, go to the kitchen, and put some wood in the stove. I need to get some hot broth in him."

"Georgie, try to get him to drink some water then find some clean sheets to shred, so I can wrap his ribs. And, I need some clean gauze to dress his wounds."

"Edward, get his clothes off."

Nimrod peppered Edward with questions. "What the hell happened? Who did this? Did you get a good look 'em?"

Edward struggled to get the boots off Andrew without causing him more pain. "I don't know. It all happened so fast. Two white men on horses came out of nowhere and attacked us. One held a gun on me while the other one went after Mr. Andrew. He said something about getting even for being run off from here a few years ago by Mr. Andrew and Master Gordon. Mr. Andrew called him Onie."

"Oh, my Lord," said Aunt Daisy. "Georgie, did ya hear dat."

"I heard him," said Georgie.

They got Andrew in bed, and Aunt Daisy gave him a couple of spoons of brandy.

"Ain't no more for us to do. You come on outta here with me, boy," said Nimrod.

Edward wanted to protest, but thought it best not to anger Nimrod. He took one last look at Andrew then left to unhitch the wagon and care for the horses. Afterward, he went to the kitchen, hoping to find Aunt Daisy or Georgie. They could fill him in on Andrew's progress. Edward's exhausted bones and muscles relaxed in the warmth of the kitchen stove. He stretched out in a corner next to the fire and slept, but awakened soon after to the sound of the door opening. Georgie started.

"What you doing in here?" she demanded.

"How is he?"

"Still resting," she said, pulling her shawl around her shoulders and softening her tone. "It feels good in here, don't it? She paused and looked at Edward. "You want to see him, don't you?"

He shook his head yes.

"I know who did this," she said. "It was the old overseer. He's the one who raped me. That old trash still working his evil against us."

"I'm sorry, Georgie. This must bring back all your bad memories. Lord knows it done brought back mine."

"It's not your fault. I'm just glad you were there to help him."

"They could come for me for beating two white men. They could hang me for that."

"He'll protect you," Georgie reassured him. "Just like he looks after Mama and me. Come on. You sit with him the rest of the night. Mama is too old to be sleeping in a chair anyway."

"First I want to show you something." He stood behind her. "What?"

"Ball your fist, and let me see you swing."

She did.

"Ain't enough power to it. When you swing put your shoulder into it, and aim for a weak spot. I like the nose. It's easy to break."

She tried again.

"That's better. We'll work on it in our spare time, if you like. If anybody comes after you again, you can at least fight them off enough to get away."

She smiled. "All right. I'd like that. Thank you."

They went back into the house, where they found Aunt Daisy asleep. Georgie roused her with a whisper, "Come on to bed, Mama. Let Edward sit with him."

Edward watched Andrew sleep and eventually drifted off himself.

**\* \* \* \* \* \* \* \* \***

Andrew stirred and opened his eyes to see Edward sleeping in the chair next to the bed. The morning sun shone through the window on both of them. He smiled, pleased he was nearby. Andrew noticed Edward's physical features in detail for the first time, his skin the rich brown of walnut shells and his black hair thick and heavy like wool. Eyebrows so perfect they looked drawn, framed his closed eyes, lashes curling up to his eyelids. His clean shaved face was smooth. He was tall—only an inch or so shorter than Andrew.

The pain in his body took over, and last night's fight flashed in his hurting brain. He relived the blows he had taken from Onie. His ribs ached.

Slumped in the chair, Edward shifted and then woke. He straightened, rubbed his face and looked at Andrew. "How you feeling?"

"Like hell." Andrew tried to get up, but the pain proved too much.

"What are you trying to do? Let me help."

"I am not the kind of man to sit around helpless. I've got to piss."

Andrew struggled out of bed and tried to walk over to the slop jar. He made it with the help of Edward's steadying arm but was too weak to stand on his own. Edward stood behind him with his arm around Andrew's waist to hold him up. With his other hand, he reached from behind and held up the slop jar to Andrew until he finished. The stream of piss hitting the porcelain was harsh at first but changed in timbre as the pot filled.

"While we're at it, is there anything else you need to do?" Edward asked.

"I'll let you know after breakfast," Andrew responded with a half smile as he buttoned his drawers.

They made their way back to the bed, and Andrew sat on the edge.

Finally, Andrew said, "Thank you for all you did last night. You saved my life. Onie intended to kill me."

"I'm glad I was there to stop those two," said Edward. He paused then ventured, "Ain't it against the law for a slave to raise his hand against a white man? They whipped me when I hit that trainer."

"I hadn't thought about that," said Andrew. "If anyone asks, we say I did all the fighting. You never touched either of them because there was a gun drawn on you. I took the gunman by surprise while he had his eye on you. That's what we tell them."

A knock at the door announced Zula with Andrew's breakfast tray.

"What you got for me, Zula?" Andrew asked.

"Aunt Daisy done cooked everything in de kitchen. She say you needs to git yo strenf up. You got bacon, eggs, bread, jelly, and coffee." She placed the tray on the bureau and closed the door behind her.

"Thank you, Zula," Andrew called out.

"Edward, you go on down and get some breakfast. Tell Aunt Daisy to give you the same things she gave me."

Edward hesitated.

"You go on now. I'll be fine."

"All right," said Edward. "But you should get that dried blood out your nose."

"Hand me that handkerchief from the dresser." Andrew wiped under his nose. "Did I get it all?"

"No. It's caked up in there." Edward took the cloth and dipped it in water from the wash basin. "Hold your head back." He held the side of Andrew's head and cleaned the dried blood. "Hurt?"

"No. It's all right." Edward rinsed the handkerchief in the basin, moved the tray to Andrew's bedside table then opened the door to leave.

"Edward," Andrew said from the bed. "Will you come back when you've finished and help me shave and dress before Doc Prichard gets here?"

"I'll be back directly."

*********

Georgie witnessed all of the goings and comings that morning. Doc Prichard arrived around mid-morning. She followed the doctor up to the bedroom to hear the diagnosis. Andrew, with Edward's help, sat waiting, cleaned, and dressed.

"Don't look like no major damage has been done," said Doc

Prichard. His drawl so slow, it seemed those listening could leave the room, complete a task, and return before he finished a sentence. "You got a couple of bruised ribs but don't look like nothing is broken. I'm gonna leave some liniment and laudanum. Other than that, only proper rest and time will do the healing."

Georgie headed back to the kitchen to report to Mama. She stood beside the house, resting a minute, when Doc Prichard left, and the Sheriff rode up. Nimrod was out front when the Sheriff dismounted. Georgie froze to listen to the conversation.

"Can I help you, Sheriff?" Nimrod asked.

"I'm looking for Mr. Gordon, the owner of this place."

"He's feeling a might poorly. I'm the overseer, in charge when he ain't around. What you need?"

"Onie Johnson and Clayton Barlow done issued a complaint against a male Negro slave from the Gordon Plantation for attacking them last night. I come to pick him up."

Nimrod sucked his dirty teeth and smiled. "I'll get him."

At that, Georgie ran in the house and straight up to Andrew's room to tell him the law had come for Edward.

"Georgie, help me to the window. I'm still unsteady." Andrew mustered his strength to stand, and the two shuffled across the room. The Sheriff had put handcuffs on Edward and was about to lead him away.

"I can't get down stairs in time to stop him. Hoist the window." Georgie pried the resistant sash up, straining to get it high. Andrew yelled down, "Sheriff Watson, what you mean by taking my property without my permission?"

The sheriff hollered back, "I don't need your permission to take in a criminal. This boy's done broke the law. He beat two men — two white men — almost to death last night. I'm taking him in."

"That's a lie," Andrew shouted. "He was with me last night, and he didn't raise a hand against either one of those bastards. They fought with me and only me."

"Help me get down stairs," he told Georgie as he reached for his shirt. "You wait there," he yelled down.

With her help and a cane he made his way down the staircase. She opened the front door, and Andrew stepped onto the porch in his bare feet wearing nothing but a shirt and trousers. In the rush, Georgie had forgotten her shawl. The cold wind whipped her hair in all directions and under her skirt causing it to flair.

"Now, what the hell is going on here?" Andrew asked.

"Like I done told you. This boy beat two white men last night, and he's gonna pay for it."

An anger flashed through Andrew's eyes the likes of which Georgie had never seen before. "My family is one of the most upstanding in this community. Do you mean to stand here on my property in earshot of my daddy and tell me that you take the word of two no-good, drunken thieves over mine? I beat both of them, and I got the bruises to prove it. Doc Prichard just left here from 'tending to me."

He opened his shirt to show his wrapped ribs. "Now, whose word do you intend to take on this matter, Sheriff Watson, mine or that trash that tried to rob and kill me last night?"

"Well," the sheriff shifted his arrogant disposition. "If you say he wasn't involved ..."

"That's exactly what I say."

"I guess I'll have to release him."

Andrew kept quiet until the cuffs were off Edward, motioning him to go on back to the stable. "Sheriff, what made you think you could come here, take one of my slaves, and not say a damn thing to me?"

"Well your man here ...," he nodded toward Nimrod, "... he told me you were sick, and he was in charge."

Andrew snapped his head in Nimrod's direction. Nimrod dropped his glance and shifted his weight from one foot to the other. Andrew raised his cane and pointed to the acreage that made up Wilmington Manor. "Ain't but two men ever going to be in charge of this plantation. One is my daddy, and the other is me." He looked at Nimrod and asked, "You understand me?"

Georgie was not accustomed to Andrew demonstrating strength and confidence. She was glad he was coming into his own.

Andrew continued, "Since you're so bound and determined to make arrests, jail those two bastards for attempted robbery and attempted murder." He walked into the house and slammed the door behind him.

"You'll catch your death of cold standing outside like that wearing next to nothing," Georgie said helping him back up the stairs.

"I'll be all right," he reassured her. "I couldn't let them take Edward. I'll kill them before I let them take him."

"Would you now?" Georgie paused and gave him a curious look.

"What I mean is it wouldn't be right to punish him for protecting me. Come on. I need to rest. That wore me out."

When he was settled back in to bed, he said to Georgie, "Tell Nimrod I want to see him, now."

Georgie found Nimrod in the kitchen eating a piece of dry bread and drinking coffee.

"Mr. Andrew says for you to come to his room right now," she took pleasure in informing him.

"I reckon this is about that goddamned new nigger he likes so much." He took a final sip and mumbled, "I might as well get this over with."

Neither Georgie nor Aunt Daisy answered him. Aunt Daisy continued her rhythm of kneading dough. The fire sizzled as Georgie threw a couple pieces of kindling on it.

*********

Andrew rested, his thoughts racing back to his childhood with Georgie. He recalled the many times they had looked out for each other. As children, he saved her from Anna's fury on several occasions, and she had provided him sanctuary from Mother and Daddy. When he wanted solitude with his books, she showed him some of her hiding places. When Daddy wanted him to hunt or watch him whip a slave, it was Georgie who lied and said that he was playing on the other side of the plantation.

He received no affection from Mother, didn't like Anna, and had very little in common with Daddy. Just as he was a misfit in his household, Georgie was a misfit among the slaves. She was much lighter in complexion than most, was pampered as far as a slave's life was concerned and was the plantation owner's daughter. Therefore, she had very few friends and confidants. Andrew found in Georgie and Aunt Daisy the love and kindness that were missing in the big house. The kind of caring, he came to realize early in his life, that his mother and sister were incapable of giving. Now, he was beginning to believe that he had found that kind of caring in Edward.

The knock on the door brought him back to reality.

"Enter." His bed faced the door; he sat up with his eyes fixed to meet Nimrod's as soon as he entered the room.

Nimrod began a desperate, stuttering rant. "Mr. Andrew, I didn't mean no harm by telling the sheriff about ..." He lost his words. Andrew let him squirm in his search for something to say.

Nimrod began again, "I mean ... I thought ..."

Andrew cut him off. "I own this plantation, every tobacco leaf and every slave that picks them. You don't have the authority to turn any slave or any other piece of my property over to anybody. I pay you to keep the slaves working. You make damn sure you understand that you never have and never will have the authority to speak for me."

Again, Nimrod tried to explain. "Mr. Andrew, I ..."

"That's all, Nimrod. You can go. Now!"

Nimrod lowered his head and skulked out of the room.

*********

For the remainder of the day, Edward hung around the kitchen every chance he got to keep up with the news of Andrew's recovery. Later that evening, he stopped by as Aunt Daisy was preparing the supper trays for Andrew and Mr. Gordon. "Zula take dis tray up to Massa Gordon. Edward, I got Mr. Andrew's tray ready. Do you want to take it up to him?"

"Sure." He tried not to appear too eager. He had not seen Andrew since that morning when the Sheriff came.

Edward knocked on the door but got no answer. He slowly opened it wide enough to see Andrew sleeping. He put the tray on the dresser and thought he ought not disturb him. But, then again, if he didn't rouse him, the food would be cold by the time Andrew awakened. Edward sat and watched Andrew sleep, wondering about the past weeks, how Andrew was at that auction and ended up purchasing him, why he had fought so hard to save Andrew last night when he could have beaten all three of them and escaped, and why Andrew lied to the sheriff to save him. He was lost in questions. When he came back to reality, Andrew's open eyes, fixed on him, startled him.

"How long you been here?"

"Just got here. Brought your food but didn't want to wake you. You was sleeping so good."

"What are you thinking about so hard?"

"You."

Andrew looked surprised at his candor. "What else," probed Andrew.

"Me and how I come to be here with you."

Andrew sighed, "I told you it'll be all right. Now, what did you bring me? I believe I am a little hungry."

"Aunt Daisy fixed a little of everything," Edward said as he got up and reached for the tray.

Andrew moved around in the bed, propping up to eat. Edward placed the tray across Andrew's lap.

"Hold still. Let me put the pillow behind you."

Andrew removed the lid and said, "Good Lord, Aunt Daisy. I can't eat all that. You eat yet?"

"Naw. I'll get something when I go back."

"Help me to eat this. "Aunt Daisy will be mad and think I don't like her cooking. Come on. Pull that chair up beside the bed."

The two sat with little conversation and shared chicken, lima beans, corn pudding and rolls. After they devoured the meal and Edward was preparing to leave he said, "I'll stoke that fire to keep it warm in here for you tonight."

"Don't leave just yet. Fix me my pipe," said Andrew. "Everything's on the dresser."

Edward got the pipe, filled it with tobacco and handed it to

Andrew. He walked over to the fireplace, struck a match on the hearth, and walked to Andrew with it.

Andrew handed Edward the pipe. "You light it," he said. "See if you remember how to draw on it and not choke."

They shared the pipe and talked about the many uses of tobacco until Andrew drifted off to sleep. Edward lowered the flame on the lamp and quietly closed the door behind him.

*********

Aunt Daisy decided to take in some night air before going to bed and walked toward MawNancy's cabin. The old woman sat on a stump outside the front door, whittling a hickory stick.

"My joints hurt a little more each day. Thought I'd walk around a while 'fore going to bed," said Aunt Daisy.

"How de boy doing?" MawNancy asked.

"He be all right. Just gonna take a few days of rest."

"Good. He de only decent one in the whole bunch. Come on in. I was a takin' a break but ready to finish now." MawNancy welcomed her.

"Finish what?" Aunt Daisy stepped in the door and met a strong odor. The place was a junk pile. Bones and strange items hung from the ceiling. Glass jars containing rooster heads, a couple of dead snakes, tin cans filled with ointments and other types of liquids filled the shelves and tabletops. MawNancy had meticulously constructed a doll made of sackcloth. The crude effigy was stuffed with shredded cloth, and she was busy stitching it closed. "I put bits of that bitch's fingernails inside. And these are her own hairs. Got 'em when she was laying in the parlor." The strands of hair from the dead body were sewn onto the doll's head.

Aunt Daisy looked for a place to sit. "Old woman, what you up to now?"

"Hush now. You break my thinking." She finished stitching the doll's back to keep the stuffing intact then sat it on a small table beside two candles, a tin can filled with a ruddy brown liquid, two large bones and a lady's hatpin. The candles cast a dim light in the otherwise dark room. MawNancy picked up the two bones and clanged them together in a steady beat and chanted, "Oooh Faah Kaay Moe Teeh Nah, Oooh Faah Kaay Moe Teeh Nah. She closed her eyes. After a few minutes of the monotonous beating and repetition of words, she stopped and opened her eyes wide as if the underworld had provided her with the revelation she sought. She spat on the doll and poured the brown liquid over it. The effigy soaked it up. She chanted again, then picked up the long pin and held it above her head then lowered it to examine the sterling and ivory keepsake. She mumbled some strange words and plunged the pin in to the center of the doll. A cold wind rushed into the cabin and blew out the candles. In the pitch black, MawNancy giggled devilishly. "It's a-working. I told you I wasn't done wid her."

"I best be on my way. Them dark forces you messing with ain't nothing to play wid," Aunt Daisy warned. "You best let Miss Victoria rest."

"No peace," whispered MawNancy. "As long as I'm alive, she ain't gonna have no peace."

## Chapter 17
### December 1859

**Anna** returned to Wilmington Manor from her trip to Mississippi determined to make a place for herself amongst Virginia's most sought after families. She dug her hands deep into her fur muff as her carriage entered the estate grounds. She missed her mother, but now *she* owned the title of mistress of Wilmington Manor. While away, she had been entertained by some of the finest families in the South, and now she would give her own lavish parties for all the right people. She would have gowns made in Paris and would challenge her feeble-minded father to burn them. She would dare her spineless brother, with his affection for slaves, to impede her plans. She would succeed where her mother had not.

The slave children in the yard and on the porch whooped, hollered, and broke into song as the carriage approached the main house. Some danced and jumped. "I do declare, you'd think they'd never seen a carriage before. Pickaninnies. Oh, by the way, dear, I'd better go in first. You wait a minute and come on in after me," she said to her friend, Mae, as she descended from the carriage. Her dark green velvet cloak swept a path behind her through the fallen leaves.

"Welcome home, Miss Anna," Luther greeted her and ushered her in.

As she came through the door, Andrew entered the foyer and stood speechless.

"Well, that's a fine greeting. Aren't you happy to see me, Brother?" She strolled into the house removing her muff, gloves, hat and, cloak. She scanned the room. "Merry Christmas. Not that you could tell it from the looks of this place." The house was void of holly, wreaths, or any symbols associated with the season. "I know we are earlier than I said we would be in my letter, but hopefully we've arrived in time to make this place look like Christmas."

"We?" Andrew questioned.

"So you can speak after all. I was afraid that you had regressed back to your childish ways."

Mae stepped through the doorway and behind her Luther with

their bags.

"Andrew, this is my friend, Mae Bradford. I've invited Mae to spend Christmas with us. Mae, this is my brother, Andrew Gordon, Lord and Master of Wilmington Manor." Anna gave him a deep curtsey with bowed head just in case her sarcastic tone had not taunted him enough.

He hobbled over to Mae, took her hand and bowed; he grimaced at the movement. "Welcome to Wilmington Manor, Miss Bradford."

Mae responded with a curtsey. "Why thank you, Mr. Gordon. I am glad to be here."

"What in heaven's name has happened to you?" Anna asked.

"It's nothing," he replied then turned and limped down the hall.

Anna took complete control of the holiday festivities, planning menus and parties to finish the year, paying particular attention to Christmas Eve and Christmas Day. Wilmington Manor, and Mae for that matter, must have properly trimmed holidays. She invited a few family members and friends to join them for dinner on Christmas Eve.

Anna had the slaves cut down a large pine tree and set it up in the front parlor next to the Chickering, and she dispatched Zula to the attic to find decorations. Pine roping decorated the banisters and mantles, and wreaths made of cedar branches and magnolia leaves graced the doors. The greenery filled the rooms with a sweet fragrance, bringing a much-needed freshness inside. Anna was quite sure her holiday décor surpassed all other years.

Worried that all went perfectly for the Christmas Eve dinner, Anna decided to visit Andrew in his office one afternoon after the mid-day meal. Deep in thought, he was pouring over the ledger. His pipe lay on the desk. It looked as though it had gone cold, no smoke rising from its bowl. "Counting up?"

"Yes, as a matter of fact, I am."

"I'm in need of some of it."

"Do you need more beef or chicken for the holiday meals?"

"No. I'm speaking of human property. We'll need to assign a couple of slaves to the kitchen to help that old woman prepare the meals."

"Aunt Daisy has handled meals for this house since before we were born. She's an excellent cook. Besides, she's got Georgie." He struck a match and lit his pipe, sucking on it until the end flamed red.

"Georgie," she huffed. "I doubt that wench can even fry an egg. I'll not have my special plans ruined. Send those two that cook for the field hands in to help."

"Aunt Daisy won't take too kindly to other cooks being in her kitchen."

"Her kitchen? Perhaps she needs reminding that I am the mistress of this plantation, and she is a slave, nothing more than a check mark in that ledger. It is not *her* kitchen. Maybe some field work would do her and that Georgie some good."

"All right. If you want Mary and Sadie to help Aunt Daisy, you tell them, all three of them. By the way, who's going to cook for the field hands? Figure that out, and let me know, Mistress." He went back to the ledger.

**\*\*\*\*\*\*\*\*\***

Aunt Daisy stood with her arms folded across her breasts in the sweltering kitchen. "I don't needs no hep with *my* cooking."

"I know you don't most days, Aunt Daisy, but we got extra special guests coming, and I want to make sure you have all the help you need." Anna looked to Georgie for support. Georgie stood stone-faced.

"Done told ya. I don't needs no hep." Aunt Daisy emphasized each word.

"Well, it's been decided. Mary and Sadie will help you, and that's all there is to it." Anna stood firm.

Aunt Daisy relented. "All right den. Dey can clean and chop, but ain't no mixing of spices and tasting. Dat's up to me." She pointed her finger at the two women. "I ain't gonna have dem two ruining my meals, and den I be blamed fer it."

"Y'all will get along fine. I knew I could count on you. It's just for a little while, until Christmas is over, and our guests have gone." Anna smiled at Georgie who remained cold. "I'll be back with more instructions."

Christmas Eve morning Anna awoke to the sounds of a crackling fire. She yawned, stretched, and collapsed deep into the pillow, content thinking about the day she had orchestrated and how it was all about to come to fruition. Snowflakes danced outside the window. She rushed to look out. A light snow covered the ground. She threw on her robe and rushed to Mae's room. "Mae, can I come in?" She knocked softly trying to contain her excitement. "Mae, it's Anna. Can I come in? It's snowing."

"Yes, Dear. Come on in." Mae was propped up in bed having her morning coffee.

Anna jumped on the bed, almost toppling the tray. The scalding coffee sloshed and nearly spilled.

"Have you looked out? It's snowing. It's not very deep, but everything is covered. It's simply beautiful."

"Yes, I looked out earlier." Mae took another sip.

"We'll take a morning stroll around the plantation before breakfast. It will give you some time with Andrew. I told you he'd make a fine husband. Don't you think?"

"Oh yes. He's very handsome."

"He's also the kind of man we can control."

"We?" Mae tilted her head.

"Of course I mean you, dear."

"Have you said anything to Andrew about the special guests expected for tonight's dinner?"

"No," Anna pouted. "He can be surprised along with everyone else."

"Anna." Mae took a sip of coffee. "Senator Jefferson Davis and his wife will be joining us tonight. Don't you think Andrew has a right to know that such impressive guests will be dining at his table?"

"Our table."

"As you put it, he is the lord and master of this plantation and I think..."

"There's no need to discuss it further. I'll think on it. Now hurry and get dressed. I'll be back shortly." Anna rushed from the room.

"Zula. Zula, where are you? I need you to lace my corset."

After coffee and dressing for snow, Anna, Mae, and Andrew, walked the plantation grounds. The red brick of Wilmington Manor looked piped in frosting.

"What a beautiful estate you have, Andrew. The fresh coat of snow came just in time for Christmas. Look yonder, I believe that's a deer running through those trees." Mae pointed toward a wooded area.

"Thank you, Miss Mae. We're fortunate to be located in a part of the county that captures the beauty of each season."

"May I take your arm?" Mae asked. "I'm not accustomed to walking in snow. I'm afraid I might slip."

"Of course," he said. "Perhaps we should head back to the house. I'm sure breakfast must be ready."

"It's so pretty out here. Let's walk a little more, then head back," Mae requested.

"Yes. Just a little longer," interjected Anna. "Mae, tonight's dinner guests will be my mother's sister, Aunt Millicent, and her husband, Uncle Henry. We have not seen them since mother's funeral a few months ago. They are bringing Cousin Betsey. She's Daddy's first cousin. I've also invited Jim and Caroline Shelton. They own a small plantation not far from here."

"Inform Mae about Cousin Betsey's hearing," said Andrew.

"Oh, yes," said Anna. "She's mostly deaf and carries a horn shaped device that she holds up to her ear. You will have to speak into it. I don't know if the thing works. She never seems to fully understand anything. Hopefully, speaking with her will not be too frustrating for you, dear. Come to think of it, I really don't know why I invited her."

"Anyone else?" asked Andrew.

Mae was about to respond, but Anna interrupted. "There may be a surprise guest or two."

Andrew exhaled. "I don't like surprises, Anna."

They walked down close to the river and then turned back. The stable doors were open. "Who's that Negro in there with Uncle Buck?" Anna asked. "I've never seen him before."

"His name is Edward. I bought him while you were away. I've

got him helping with the horses."

"Another addition to the ledger," she mumbled. "Why does he keep looking over at you?

"I saved him from a trader who was mistreating him. He's grateful, that's all."

They returned to the house, walking under the snow covered trees that lined the main entrance.

"What a refreshing walk," said Anna as they entered and removed their cloaks. "That's a very fashionable cape, Andrew. I don't recall seeing it before. Is it new?"

"Yes. I let Jessup talk me into buying it. Since we haven't been to any of the fancy dress balls in Richmond this season, I haven't had a chance to wear it. Being Christmas and all, I thought I'd put it on. I'm glad you like it."

"We been holding breakfast for you," Georgie greeted them. "Didn't know how long you was gonna be. I hope it's still hot."

"I'm going to serve Mr. Andrew. You two are not needed," Mae said, dismissing Zula and Georgie.

Andrew seemed as if he was about to object, but Anna interrupted. "Why thank you, Mae. You seem right at home here. Doesn't she, Andrew?"

Mae served up the plates for everyone. Anna observed that she took special care to give Andrew large helpings. After they took one bite, it was clear the food was cold. Fire flashed through Anna.

"Where are they?" she demanded.

Mae tried to calm her. "Well, one of them said it might have gotten cold while we were out walking. We did walk longer than planned. I'm sure they can heat …"

Anna picked up her plate and stormed toward the kitchen. She pushed the door hard until it flew open, a cold wind rushing in with her. The five slave women hushed their chatter, their eyes fixed on Anna as she walked in and flung the plate on the table. The bone china cracked in two, and grits seeped onto the wooden table. Anna smoothed her skirt and brushed the hair from her eyes, both blown about by the wind on her march from the house to the kitchen. "You expect me to eat this slop? You expect me to eat cold food? You wanted to embarrass me in front of my guest, didn't you?"

Anna wanted to make sure Georgie understood. She positioned her face inches from Georgie's. "I'll have every one of you whipped. I'll beat you right now." Fueled by blind rage, she grabbed the broom and knocked over glassware, pots and pans, swinging at the women. They backed away, but Georgie grabbed the broom and wrestled it from Anna.

"How dare you," Anna screamed. She wanted to slap the smug look off Georgie's face.

Aunt Daisy stepped between the two. "Now, Miss Anna, you know we didn't 'tend to serve you, Mr. Andrew, and y'all's guest no bad food. I takes pride in what I cooks. Now, y'all went out, and it sat there and got cold. Georgie and Zula can get it, and I'll put some mo heat to it."

"I told Miss Mae that it might be cold," interjected Georgie. "But she told us to leave and let her do the serving. You were there. You heard it all."

"That's right," said Zula.

Mary and Sadie moved in closer. Anna squared her shoulders and looked the slave women in the eyes, determined not to shrink back. But the slave women seemed to be encircling her. Overwhelmed by their closeness and feeling outnumbered, Anna panicked. "Get away from me."

Aunt Daisy moved closer and reached out to her. "Calm yo self, Chile."

Anna shoved her toward a rickety set of shelves, screaming, "Leave me alone."

Aunt Daisy fell hard, and the shelves collapsed. Anna stood, frozen. The slave women cried out as a large cast iron pot careened from the top, its round lip landing in the center of Aunt Daisy's head. She fell to the floor, her head hitting with a thud. Blood splattered the wall. The stew pot bounced twice before coming to rest next to Aunt Daisy, who lay motionless in a mess of pots, pans, broken bowls, knives, forks and a pool of blood.

Anna couldn't speak, move, or make sense of what had just happened. The slave women cried out and crouched next to Aunt Daisy. Georgie screamed for Andrew and ran out. In a matter of seconds, Andrew rushed in and grabbed Anna by the shoulders. He shoved her against the door, yelling, "What have you done? Oh my God, Anna, what have you done?" She couldn't answer. She wasn't sure what she had done. Cold food, embarrassment and rage were all she could remember.

She wrestled away from Andrew and ran back to the house, to the safety of her room. There, she combed her hair and recomposed herself for her guest. She sat staring in the mirror, trying to get Aunt Daisy's bloodied head out of her mind. There was a timid knock on the door.

"Come in."

Zula entered the room but remained close to the door. "I'm just checking to see if you need anything, Miss Anna. They done carried Aunt Daisy to her cabin, and Miss Mae still sitting in the dining room all alone."

"I'll be down in a minute." Anna attempted to engage Zula in conversation. "Don't you think Miss Mae would make a nice wife for Mr. Andrew?"

"I don't know about those things."

"Well, I think she would, and I intend to make it happen."

"Yes ma'am." Zula turned toward the door. "I'll tell Miss Mae you'll be down directly."

After some time, Anna returned to the dining room, where Mae had eaten her cold meal.

"You took a while. Is everything all right?" Mae asked.

"Yes. Everything is just fine. Mary and Sadie will have to finish the cooking for tonight's meal. We should go pick our dresses for the party."

Later, Anna sat at her dressing table applying perfume and powders preparing for dinner, when Andrew knocked and entered without waiting for her response. "Aunt Daisy has not regained consciousness. I've sent for Doc Prichard, but I'm sure this doesn't matter to you. For the sake of appearance and the family name, I will come to your party this evening. But I warn you, Anna, do not cross me."

His manner unnerved her, but she was determined to stand up to him. "I cannot be bothered with your news of that old woman. I have final details to which I must attend. Guests will be arriving soon."

"Some have already arrived."

"What? It's too early."

"Aunt Millicent, Uncle Henry, and Cousin Betsey are downstairs. I am going to my room to get dressed. You heed my warning. I am in no mood for your games."

Before she could speak, he turned and shut the door.

Anna called for Zula and quickly finished dressing. Flustered, she now had to rush. She selected one of several new gowns she'd purchased in Mississippi, a gold dress with wide pleats. The full hooped skirt made her tiny waist seem even smaller. She wore her mother's diamond earrings and necklace.

Descending the staircase, she was greeted by the low hum of the guests' chatter rising from the front parlor. Cousin Betsey was the first to see her when she entered the room. "Anna, my dear," she said, lumbering toward Anna, her hearing device in tow. Her dumpy frame and pigeon-toed walk made her appear more as a caricature than a human being.

"Oh God," thought Anna. "She would be the first to greet me." Anna extended both hands. "How are you, Cousin Betsey?" Anna spoke into the horn with a raised voice.

"What say, dear?" Cousin Betsey frowned.

"How are you?" Anna enunciated each word even louder.

"Oh thank you, dear. This is one of my favorite dresses. You look lovely too." Cousin Betsey smiled.

Anna rolled her eyes and moved to the next guests. "Aunt Millicent. Uncle Henry. Merry Christmas. So good of you to come."

"Thank you for inviting us," said Millicent. "Henry misjudged the time and got us here early."

"Yes, it's all my fault," Henry kissed Anna on the cheek. "Merry

Christmas, and please forgive me."

"Of course. It's just fine. It gives us some private family time before the others arrive."

They gathered in the front parlor by the Christmas tree. The conversation centered on the few social events that had already taken place, the upcoming growing season and the well-being of extended family members.

Finally, it was Uncle Henry who asked, "How's John? Is he joining us tonight?"

"The excitement might be too much for him," said Anna. "We thought it best not to involve him this evening."

Bill and Caroline Shelton arrived. With Caroline as a guest, all of Virginia society would soon know about the elegant evening she had hosted. Anna particularly wanted the word out that she had entertained Senator and Mrs. Davis.

Mae finally finished dressing and joined the party. Anna made the introductions, starting with Cousin Betsy. "Betsy, this is my dear friend, Mae, visiting from Mississippi," to which Cousin Betsy responded, "Why yes, Miss, I would like some punch to sip."

Andrew entered and welcomed each guest with a Christmas greeting. He spoke with ease and grace, much to Anna's relief. She grew fidgety during his toast, however, impatient for the special guests to arrive. Only Mae knew, and she was sworn to secrecy.

"Are you concerned about the arrival of your final guests?" Andrew asked.

"Yes. Everyone else is here. I wonder why they are so late."

"It's not that they are late, Anna. It's that the others arrived early. Who are you expecting?"

"That is a surprise."

Just then, the last carriage arrived, the driver's voice carrying inside. Anna clasped her hands together. She was giddy but had the presence of mind to check her hair and smooth her dress. Luther opened the door, and Anna greeted the latest arrivals, taking the gentlemen's spare arm, as his wife held the other. They entered the parlor, and she announced, "Ladies and gentlemen, may I present to you Senator Jefferson Davis and his lovely wife, Varina. These are my other special guests visiting from Mississippi. Senator Davis is traveling through these parts on his way to Washington on business. So, quite naturally, I insisted they spend Christmas Eve with us."

It crossed Anna's mind to thank Mae for introducing her to the Senator and his wife in Mississippi. A look of disappointment showed on Mae's face. "I'll make it up to her later," thought Anna. "I'll tell her I was so excited that I forgot to mention it." She then proceeded to escort the Senator and his wife to each guest to make individual introductions, first to Andrew, master of the house, who officially welcomed the distinguished couple to Wilmington Manor. She intentionally introduced Bill and Caroline last, in the hopes that tomorrow's gossip would be accurate. Life did not afford her many, but this indeed was one of Anna's shining moments.

Luther served his special eggnog, and Mae played Christmas Carols on the Chickering as she and the ladies discussed the latest social news. The men took the opportunity to get inside political news from Senator Davis.

After much beverage and light conversation, Luther announced dinner, and they all moved to the dining room. As the guests were seated, Anna marveled at the elegant ambiance, the stylish party she had created. Everything was perfect from the women's dresses, to the men in long tailcoats with white bow ties, to the house decorated so beautifully, and the delicious aroma of holiday recipes mixing with the fragrance of cut greenery and the Christmas tree. The table was set with the family's finest crystal, china, and lace, all imported from Europe. Andrew sat at the head of the table, and Anna at the other end. This was the kind of event her mother longed for at Wilmington Manor. At that moment, she missed her father at the table, sad that he was tucked away in his bedroom unaware that it was Christmas and that his family and friends were under Wilmington's roof. In spite of their differences, he belonged at the Christmas Eve table.

Luther filled everyone's glass with homemade wine, and Andrew raised his to make a toast. "To this glorious holiday," he said. "May it always be filled with joy and shared with family and good friends."

"What'd he say?" Cousin Betsey whispered to Uncle Henry.

Luther served the first course.

Although the men had already engaged in many politically charged conversations, they continued to pepper Senator Davis with questions. Anna felt sure the conversation would remain safe and polite, what with the mixed company and all, until Uncle Henry ventured, "Tell us Senator, what is your opinion on the strain the issue of slavery is causing between the north and the south."

The Senator put down his knife and fork, placed both hands on the table, straightened his spine. "We have a way of life here, in these southern states that is like no other. Slavery is a part of that way of life, and it is vital to our economy. I will not stand by and allow Yankee northerners to dictate the way we live. I would rather us secede from the Union before I witness my beloved South controlled by northerners and abolitionists."

Cousin Betsey had put her horn up to her good ear to hear the senator's monologue. To which she replied, "Secede from the Union! My dear, that would be too much to bear."

"Madame, I tell you, I love this great country, but I will fight to the death before I see our very lives changed by outsiders."

The evening's lively tone was being quashed by his somber, combative tone, and a panic rushed through Anna. Her elegant evening was about to be ruined by talk of politics and slavery. She shot Andrew a look of desperation.

Andrew obediently changed the topic to tobacco, always a favorite amongst growers. "I'm pleased to tell you gentleman that I have some mighty fine cigars I have been saving for an occasion such as this. And, Senator, they are made from tobacco grown on this fine southern plantation. We will enjoy them after dinner."

The main course arrived on time, but Anna could see lumps in the thick gravy as soon as it was ladled onto plates. The mouth-watering aroma she expected from the venison and turkey was nonexistent.

After the dessert and coffee, Anna announced, "Ladies, will you join me in the front parlor for more eggnog."

"And, Gentlemen...," said Andrew, "...follow me to the library, and we'll enjoy those cigars I promised."

He and Anna lingered in the foyer directing the guests to the proper places.

"The meal was terrible." she said, fighting off tears.

"Mary and Sadie are not accustomed to cooking for this kind of evening. They cook for the field hands," Andrew reminded her. "Aunt Daisy is the only one who knows how to season wild game. But in case you've forgotten, she's been unconscious since this morning," he bit.

"The pound cake was good. Most had second helpings." Anna ceased talking to Andrew long enough to point Mrs. Davis in the direction of the parlor.

"Of course they had seconds. They were hungry from not being able to eat the main courses. Aunt Daisy made the pound cake yesterday." He turned his back to her and headed toward the library. "Gentlemen, I'll be right with you. I have a special brandy I know you will enjoy."

The evening drew to a close, and the guests said their farewells, Senator and Mrs. Davis the first to depart. The final guests to leave were Bill and Caroline. Anna suspected that Caroline lingered on to savor every moment.

"Thank y'all for a truly fine evening," said Bill as he offered Andrew a handshake. "Caroline and I wish you both a very Merry Christmas."

"Oh yes, it has been quite an evening. By the way, dear, I noticed that you have a new cook," Caroline added.

Anna, stunned, offered no reply.

Bill grabbed Caroline by the arm and said, "Y'all have a good night," and ushered her out the door.

Anna and Mae started their ascent up the staircase but were interrupted by Luther. "I beg your pardon, but I thought I ought to tell you that Aunt Daisy is dead."

## Chapter 18
### December 1859

**Andrew** remembered Anna's same guilty look from childhood when he would catch her in one of her many lies. He looked in her eyes for remorse but found only contempt. Andrew's anger was only out-measured by his sadness.

"Dear God. I've got to check on Georgie," Andrew mumbled. He headed to the cabins, walking fast, his ribs aching.

Sobs from the women permeated the darkness along the hardened path to her cabin. Word of Aunt Daisy's death must have circulated among the slaves. The cold wind whipped his face, chilling his hot tears.

A kerosene lamp cast dim light in the one-room cabin. Uncle Buck sat at a table in the corner. Georgie sat by her mother's body, which was laid out on the bed, her head wrapped in gauze. Andrew walked to Uncle Buck. "I'm so sorry, Uncle Buck. Lord knows, I'm so sorry."

He walked up behind Georgie and rested his hand on her shoulder. "She was like a mother to me," he whispered.

Aunt Daisy's skin had taken on the ash-gray color of death. Andrew cursed Anna for her part in it all.

"I'll have Nimrod build a box for her and the grave dug in the slave cemetery. I think we ought to bury her in the morning."

At Andrew's words, Uncle Buck sobbed, his whole body shaking. Georgie walked to him and put her arms around his shoulders. With her cheek pressed close to his, she sang softly.

*Swing low sweet chariot, coming for to carry me home.*
*Swing low sweet chariot, coming for to carry me home.*
*I looked over Jordan and what did I see, coming for to carry me home.*
*A band of angles coming after me, coming for to carry me home.*
*Swing low sweet chariot, coming for to carry me home.*
*Swing low sweet chariot, coming for to carry me home.*

Tears rolled down her face. She moved to the bed and knelt by her mother's lifeless body, holding her hand, moaning deep, guttural sounds. It broke Andrew's heart. He didn't know what to do; he couldn't find words to comfort her. He needed air. He kissed Georgie on her forehead. "I'm going to see Nimrod. I'll be back shortly," he whispered, choking back more tears.

He walked to the stable, where he found Edward brushing a mare.

"Edward."

He kept working.

"Edward!"

Andrew walked up beside him and took Edward's hand in his and held it still. "You gonna brush the hide right off her."

Edward rubbed the horse. "Easy girl." He turned to face Andrew.

"I guess you know what happened," Andrew said.

"I know. When I got to the kitchen, Mary and Sadie had wrapped her head with their aprons to stop the bleeding. I helped carry her to her bed. I was there when she died. Doc Prichard told us there was nothing he could do. There was nothing any of us could do but wait and hope. Uncle Buck sat by her the whole time holding her hand. The bleeding stopped, but swelling came. MawNancy did the best she could do with ointments and chants. Georgie bathed her head with a wet towel, trying to keep the swelling down. Then she just stopped breathing."

Andrew let the story sink in.

"It ain't right. It just ain't right," said Edward.

"I'm as angry and hurt as you are. She was like a mother to me."

"What you gonna do about it?"

"What can I do? Whip Anna? Put her in jail? As much as I hate what she did, I can't do anything about it."

"It ain't no different here than at any other plantation. We just slaves to be whipped and killed."

Edward's words stung. Andrew had done his best to take care of his slaves. He had given special care to Georgie, Aunt Daisy, and now Edward.

Edward went back to brushing the mare. Andrew moved closer

to him and again put his hand over Edward's, holding it still. Andrew slipped his arm around Edward's waist and drew him closer. Edward didn't pull away but turned and faced Andrew in the embrace.

Andrew lost all thoughts looking into Edward's eyes, only that he wanted to stay right there.

Edward swallowed and said, "Can't. Just Can't. I'm sorry Mr. Andrew. Too dangerous. This time they'll kill me." He stepped back. The brush fell to the floor, and Edward walked away.

Andrew dropped his head. "I'm going back to the cabin to see about Georgie."

Andrew had trouble falling asleep. When he finally drifted off, he was awakened by sawing and nailing. Edward and a few slaves were up early making a box for Aunt Daisy, working outside of her cabin. Andrew groomed himself to the rhythmic sound of hammering then went to Daddy's room to help get him dressed.

When he received word from Nimrod that they had put her in the box, Andrew took Daddy over to the cabin to say goodbye. Georgie and Uncle Buck were seated on one side of the simple pinewood coffin. A steady stream of slaves continued in and out of the cabin to pay their respects. Andrew kissed Aunt Daisy on her forehead and rubbed her hand, tears falling on her white cotton dress. Daddy stood beside the box. He didn't seem to be fully aware of what was happening. Edward placed the lid on top and drove in the nails. Edward and Ryland, the field hand and slaves' self-ordained minister, and a few other male slaves carried Aunt Daisy outside where their entire community was waiting to proceed to the burial site. Andrew and Daddy walked behind Georgie and Uncle Buck. Little Sally trailed along. Snowflakes gently swirled, and one of the men began to sing in slow cadence:
*Ride on King Jesus. No man can-a hinder me.*
*Ride on King Jesus, ride on. No man can-a hinder me.*
One by one, they all joined in, creating a rich, a cappella, call-and-response chorus as they carried Aunt Daisy to her final resting place.

Ryland stepped forward to say a few words about Aunt Daisy. He quoted a little scripture, probably what he remembered from the few times white ministers had held services for the slaves. He reminded

them that Aunt Daisy was now living in freedom with Jesus and God. "*Freedom*," he repeated, looking at Georgie. They lowered Aunt Daisy into the ground, and the snowfall got heavier. They sang.
*Steal away, steal away, steal away to Jesus.*
*Steal away, steal away home. I ain't got long to stay here.*
*My lord he calls me. He calls me by the thunder.*
*The trumpet sounds within-a my soul. I ain't got long to stay here.*

The men lowered the box into the grave, as the singing rose and then trickled off. Three slaves set to work filling the grave. By the time the burying was finished, only Uncle Buck, Georgie, Little Sally, Edward, Andrew, and Daddy remained.

"I'll be around later to see you," Andrew said to Georgie. He took Daddy by the arm and led him to the big house. They came upon MawNancy who had watched the burial from a distance. She had stood alone far away from the others in the cold with her arms folded beneath her sagging breast. She held a stoic, steely gaze on the grave and seemed unbothered by the winter wind that whipped around her. A single tear rolled from her eye. It followed a path down her leathery black cheek to the bottom of her chin before it dropped on her shawl.

"You all right, MawNancy?" Andrew asked.

"I be just fine, Mr. Andrew. Hi you, Massa Gordon?"

Andrew kept walking. Daddy had been out in the cold long enough.

That night, Andrew distributed the gifts he had bought for Anna and Mae, the exchange between Anna and him was minimal and cold. The festive atmosphere that existed only a few days before was long gone; a solemn veil hung over the plantation. He debated whether to take his gifts to Uncle Buck, Georgie, and Little Sally. It seemed inappropriate so soon after burying Aunt Daisy. Nevertheless, he wanted to get out of the house, and he wanted to see Edward. He grabbed the items and headed to the cabin. He found Uncle Buck and Georgie sitting quietly with Little Sally playing in front of the hearth.

"I know it's a sad time, but I got y'all a little something for Christmas."

They received the packages and thanked him. Wool socks for

Uncle Buck and a rag doll for Little Sally.

Georgie took her package, broke the string, unfolded the paper and examined the royal blue material.

"I know how you like to keep your hair tied up. I thought you might like this fabric for it."

"It's beautiful. Thank you," she murmured.

Andrew left them to their private grief and went to find Edward, who was in the stable working. Steam rose off the horse's back and nose. "How are you?" Andrew asked, his reserve apparent.

"Fine," Edward's terse response was laced with anger.

"I got something here for you." Andrew pressed a package in Edward's chest. "I brought you something for Christmas."

Edward caught the bundle before it slipped to the ground. He opened the gift, a new pipe and a small pouch of tobacco. He stared at it. "I've never received a Christmas present before."

"I ho ... ho ... ho ... hope you like it," said Andrew. "I th ... th ... th ... thought. What I mean to say is I ho ... ho ... hope. Maybe sometime we can share so ... so ... so ... some to-ba-cco." He turned to walk away, feeling like a fool. Damn stuttering.

"Andrew," Edward called. "I mean *Mr.* Andrew. Thank you. I'd be proud to share tobacco with you anytime you say. Um ..." Edward seemed to lose his words.

"What is it Edward?"

"About last night. I...um."

"Don't' worry about it."

Edward stood still staring at Andrew.

"Is there something else, Edward?"

"Well ... um. That woman I saw you walking with yesterday. You 'bout to get married?"

"No. I'm not getting married."

"Oh, I see. Well, Merry Christmas."

"Merry Christmas to you, Edward."

## Chapter 19
## December 31, 1859

**Andrew** laid out a suit of clothes, and Zula and Ryland set up the tin bathtub in his room, filling it with hot water. He had promised Jessup he would meet him at Maggie's to ring in the New Year. Andrew preferred a different place, but Jessup wouldn't hear of it. Depression clung to the house, and Andrew wanted to get out, if only for the night, to forget and celebrate with Jessup and a bunch of strangers.

Anna and Mae had left for a small party hosted by Cousin Betsey, their absence lifting his spirit some. Andrew had been invited but sent his regrets, not in the mood to spend time with the Virginia bluebloods he knew would be invited. Andrew lowered himself into the warm waters. His thoughts were stuck on Cousin Betsey, who like his mother and sister, prided herself in rubbing shoulders with only the *right* people. She had always made it clear that her cousin, Andrew's father, had married beneath the Gordon family standards when he married Mother. Cousin Betsey had conveniently forgotten they were all born poor and that her long-dead husband had made his fortune as a dishonest gambler, which is why he was long dead. Cousin Betsey had lost her hearing while still a young woman running from her husband during one of his drunken, violent tirades. Her foot had caught in the hem of her petticoat causing her to hurl head first down a flight of stairs. With the passage of time, she had managed to erase these sordid details from her memory of the family history.

Andrew soaked, forcing his thoughts away from his dreadful family and the past, only to land on a worry about tonight. He wondered whether it was a good idea to meet Jessup after all. A knock on the door brought him to. It was Edward delivering supper. Andrew was glad to see that Edward had taken on more work around the kitchen. It might stifle Nimrod's complaints about not putting him in the field. Since Aunt Daisy's death, the work assignments were unclear and in transition. Georgie wasn't capable of much work as she grieved for her mother. Uncle Buck sat in the stable staring most days, lost far off in his mind. By default, Edward orchestrated many of the duties that fell on the kitchen staff.

Edward sat the food on a nearby table. "I thought you might be hungry, so I brought you some food. Zula took supper down to your daddy earlier."

"Thank you." Andrew splashed water on his upper body, rinsing suds off his chest. "I'm done here." He stood and grabbed the towel to dry himself.

Edward stared at the tub.

"When was the last time you had a bath?"

"I got in the wash tub sometime back before it got too cold.

"The water is still hot. Why don't you get in?"

"I'm not going to turn down the chance for a hot bath. Thank you." Edward kicked off his boots and unbuttoned his shirt.

Andrew finished drying, put on a robe and walked over to inspect the tray of food. "I'll eat these peach preserves and the bread, but I think I'll pass on the beef. Mary and Sadie have a few things to learn about cooking meat."

Edward stepped into the tub. "They sure can't cook like Aunt Daisy. This water feels good."

Edward's back was to Andrew; he stared at the lash marks. They were mostly healed but still looked painful. Andrew took a drink of brandy to wash down the bread and peaches and carried a glass over to Edward. "Drink it. It'll warm you up inside."

Andrew knelt beside the tub and felt the water. "It's still warm, good." He picked up the cloth, lathered it with soap, and washed Edward's back, gently so as not to aggravate the wounds. With his free hand, he massaged Edward's neck. Edward reached out his hand to Andrew's face and held it there. Andrew leaned in closer, meeting Edward's eyes with his. The kiss was awkward, but sweet. He tasted the brandy Edward drank. He suspected that Edward tasted the residue of peaches he had just eaten. Andrew pulled back, and they looked at each other. Edward grabbed the collar of Andrew's robe and pulled him closer — this time the kiss was longer, deeper. Edward stood and stepped from the tub. His brown skin glistened with water. Andrew stood, too, marveling at Edward's exquisite body. He took a towel and dried Edward's body, the contour of Edward's muscles hard under the cloth. He ran the cloth across Edward's chest, arms and torso, then knelt on one knee and dried Edward's legs. As he rose, Edward's semi-erect cock brushed against Andrew's cheek. Andrew blushed, and Edward smiled.

They stood facing each other. Edward untied Andrew's robe and pushed it off his shoulders. Silk crumpled to the floor. Edward explored Andrew's body with his strong hands. They pressed close together, the stiffness between their legs touching, arousing them more. They stood, suspended in time it seemed, kissing and feeling each other's bodies. Andrew led Edward to the bed. He lay on his back, looked up at Edward and opened his arms. Edward climbed on top of Andrew and held him tight. They kissed and moved together, Andrew's arms traveling from Edward's shoulders, down the curve of his back to his muscular ass and back up again. The two quivered together as warm liquid erupted from them both, running down their legs and seeping into the sheets. They continued to embrace and share peach and brandy kisses. Andrew had never known such sweetness. His dilemma was solved. He would not meet Jessup at Miss Maggie's place after all.

## Chapter 20
## December 31, 1859

**Jessup** arrived at Maggie's place early hoping to make a full night of New Year's Eve partying. The music was lively, the wine and liquor plentiful, and the lipstick and rouge heavier than usual. The optimism of starting again permeated the merriment; maybe the stroke of a clock could somehow cleanse the previous twelve months. Roaring laughter, clinking glasses, and lust filled the atmosphere, setting the stage for 1860 to enter on frivolity. Because it was Saturday, the crowd was even larger this year. Thelton Taylor, the gentleman Maggie introduced to Jessup a few months earlier, was back in town. They spotted one another and nodded. Jessup walked to the bar and ordered a whiskey from Silas. By the time he leaned against the bar and took the first sip, Thelton was standing next to him.

"I was hoping I would see you here tonight," Thelton said, extending his hand.

Jessup offered him a firm grip. "How long have ya been in town?"

"Just got here a few hours ago."

"Didn't ya get my lettahs? I sent two."

"I did, but I ain't much on writing. I thought it would be more fun to tell you what I have to say face-to-face and show you what I mean." He smiled and squeezed Jessup's upper arm.

Jessup's demeanor softened. "Still, it would have been nice to hear from you. Where you staying?"

"My usual place, the Powhatan House Hotel on Eleventh and Broad. Do you still have your room here?"

"'Course I do."

"We'll meet there later and talk."

"Just talk?" Jessup raised one eyebrow.

Thelton didn't respond to the flirtation. He just smiled and walked away.

Jessup spotted Maggie headed his way. He couldn't wait to greet his friend and wish her a very Happy New Year. Her red gown and diamonds sparkled in the candlelight; she was regal. He kissed her cheek and hand. "Happy New Year, dear Maggie."

"Why thank you and same to you. I hope we can help you ring in the New Year properly."

"There is no place I'd rather be." He looked across the room at Thelton, who was laughing with two of the girls. "You got a full house tonight. The holiday sure is good for business."

"Business always picks up this time of year." Silas walked up behind Maggie and whispered in her ear. "Jessup, I've got to look after something, but I'll be back to visit with you some more before the evening's over."

"All right," he said and watched her make her way through the crowd and disappear into a room that he had never seen used before. She looked around to see if anyone saw her unlock the small door. Silas stood behind her, as if standing guard to keep patrons from seeing or entering. "It must be where she keeps the money," Jessup mumbled out loud, the whiskey already sending a tingle to his lips. He went back to sipping and watching the crowd.

As the evening inched toward midnight, Jessup wondered if Andrew would show. He was looking forward to toasting in the New Year with his best friend and also wanted to introduce him to Thelton, who was still busy laughing with all the ladies. Annoyance crept up Jessup's spine. He downed a few more whiskeys then walked to the other parlor rooms to survey the guests. Maggie darted into the odd room again. Silas wasn't standing guard this time, so Jessup followed her in. He stumbled down a small set of steps. At the bottom, he couldn't see much but heard hushed voices. Maggie met him before he could fully enter the room. Over her shoulder, he made out two figures and another door. The room's size surprised him, much larger than he expected. A small lamp lit the area, barely. He thought one of the figures was Silas. The others were the Martin brothers, he felt sure, the two undertaker-cabinet-makers. Maggie stood in front, a blood-soaked cloth in her hand. Other people were gathered in the room, but the undertakers and Silas stood in front of them.

"Darling, you shouldn't be down here. You should be up enjoying the party," she said. "In my haste, I must have forgotten to lock the door behind me."

"What's going on? Are you all right?" Jessup asked, looking at the dripping cloth. "Careful. Don't stain your dress."

"Yes. Oh, my yes, I'm fine. Mr. Martin was delivering a cabinet that I ordered and injured his hand. We didn't want to alarm the other guests. So, we're fixing him up down here."

Jessup looked at the Martin brothers. One of them quickly put his hand behind his back.

"You go on back upstairs, and I'll be up shortly," she told him.

He staggered up the stairs and returned to his favorite seat in the front parlor. Why would a cabinet be delivered this late on New Year's Eve? Neither one of those Martin brothers looked injured. And who were all those people behind the Martins and Silas? He recalled an incident involving that weasel, Jim Williams. A few years back, Williams beat up one of her girls pretty badly for refusing one of his unusual fetishes. He's been barred from Maggie's ever since. He kept pondering and drinking whiskeys, wondering about the strange circumstances he'd witnessed. He was lost in thought when Thelton walked up and whispered, "You go on up, and I'll be there shortly." Jessup finished his drink, forgetting about the goings on in the cellar. He climbed the stairs, a slur in his step. He walked down the long hall, trying to straighten but swaying between the two walls until he came to his room at the end. He unlocked the door and collapsed onto the four-poster brass bed, his legs dangling over the side. He reached for and missed the whiskey bottle on the bedside table. Maggie always made sure he had his whiskey and a clean room.

Thelton showed up forty-five minutes later reeking of perfume. The smell irritated Jessup from his relaxed state. "You've been with one of the girls," said Jessup sniffing the front of Thelton's shirt and touching the smeared rouge on his cheek and neck. Angered, Jessup backed away. "I shouldn't have to play second to a local prostitute."

"I told you before, I like both. If you got a problem with it, I can leave." He stumbled toward the door.

Desperate and lonely, Jessup would have to accept the whore's leftovers. "No. Please don't go." He looked at Thelton and then to the bed.

Thelton jumped on the four-poster. "Well then, pour us a drink."

About midway through their tryst, the noise downstairs reached a magnificent crescendo. Thelton leaned forward and kissed Jessup on the back of his neck. "Happy New Year." He smacked Jessup's bare ass and thrust in deeper. Jessup buried his face in the pillow as pain became pleasure.

## Chapter 21
### January 1860

**Andrew** was putting the finishing touches on a note to Jessup, apologizing for not joining him on New Year's Eve and vowing to make it up to him, when raised voices came in from the foyer. He went to the front hall to investigate and found Luther overseeing Mae's trunks for her departure. "Is everything ready, Luther?"

"Ya sah. I reckon Miss Mae be down directly. She best come on 'fore she miss dat train."

"Jim and Caroline Shelton are going to Richmond today. I arranged for them to take Mae to catch the train." Andrew peered out the window. "That looks like their carriage now."

Anna and Mae came down the stairs, Mae clad in a heavy cloak, gloves, hat, and muff.

"Well, dear, this is goodbye," said Anna. "We've enjoyed having you here. I do hope you enjoyed your visit." Anna leaned in to kiss her goodbye, but Mae turned away and walked to Andrew. Extending her hand she said, "Thank you so much for your hospitality, Andrew. If you are ever in Mississippi, do call on my family and me. When I next see Senator and Mrs. Davis, I will give them *your* warm wishes." She strode toward the door without looking back. "Goodbye, Anna."

Andrew put on his coat and gloves and followed. "Jim. Caroline. Good to see you. Thank you so much for taking Mae to the train." He shook Jim's hand through the carriage door and helped Mae get in. "You have a fine trip home."

He waved as they pulled off, relieved to have Mae and her overtures on their way. Andrew checked the porch to see if Luther was back inside then cut across the lawn to the stable. He checked around him as he approached, making sure no one was watching. The pounding of metal on metal came from within. He opened the door and ducked inside, bolting it behind him. Edward, visible through the rafters, was up in the loft hammering on a beam. Andrew climbed the ladder, startling Edward when he reached the top. They both smiled. Andrew exhaled, his breath hanging between them.

"Are we alone?"

Edward nodded yes.

"Where's Uncle Buck?"

"In the kitchen." Edward put the hammer aside and took a step toward Andrew.

They embraced. With gloved hands, Andrew held Edward's face. Edward slipped his arms around Andrew's waist, pulling him close. Andrew closed his eyes, savoring Edward's lips as they crumpled together on a soft bed of hay. It was cold, but they each got their pants down. Andrew drew Edward on top of him, wanting his pressure, his weight. They moved together, in one motion, Andrew's belt buckle clanking in rhythm against the floor where the hay had spread thin. He didn't try to stop the noise and risk interrupting what seemed like perfection, what he'd been waiting for since their first time together. A week had passed, and they had not had a private moment.

They finished and lay still. Quiet. Finally Edward rolled over and Andrew sat up, his back against the wall. Edward moved to rest between Andrew's legs. Andrew wrapped his arms around Edward, his chin on Edward's shoulder. "Mae is gone back to Mississippi. Her visit wasn't so good. She seems like a nice lady, but she and Anna did not really know each other that well."

"She came all this way to visit someone she didn't know?"

"She came all this way because Anna must have told her she could find a husband, and as you can tell, I'm not available."

Edward arched his neck back and kissed Andrew. "What's gonna become of us? What will happen if we get caught?"

"We can't get caught. We'll figure out how to be together. Just got to be careful. When you bring my dinner tray tonight, bring enough for us both."

A knocking on the door down below made them both jump. "Edward! You in there?"

"It's Uncle Buck," Edward whispered. "Hold on I'm coming," Edward yelled.

"Damn," said Andrew adjusting his clothes.

"Why you got the door bolted?" Uncle Buck yelled.

Edward opened the door. "Trying to keep the cold air out. It kept blowing open."

Andrew smiled at Edward's quick response.

"Hi you, Mr. Andrew," Uncle Buck greeted.

"Just fine. Thank you."

"Mr. Andrew, you sho you all right. You didn't hurt your head or nuttin did you?

"I'm just fine. What do you mean?"

"I thought maybe you bumped up against one of the bales. All dat hay in the back of yo head. We got 'em stacked everywhere."

"I'm all right. Edward was just showing me how you got things rearranged in here. Everything looks mighty nice. I'm gonna head on back. Thank you, Edward." Andrew opened the door, brushing the hay from his hair.

"Anytime, Mr. Andrew," said Edward shaking off hay from his shoulders.

Andrew spent the remainder of the day anticipating their evening meal together. He had taken so many meals alone, avoiding Anna's company. Supper hour finally arrived, and Edward brought up a tray, enough for two. They ate, smoked pipes and made love. At five o'clock the next morning, they awakened to a steady knocking on the door.

"Mr. Andrew, wake up," a muffled voice beckoned through the door.

"Just a minute. I'm coming. He fumbled for his robe. "Stay in the bed and cover yourself," he whispered to Edward. He cracked the door to find Madie, the slave woman assigned to Daddy.

"Mr. Andrew, I'm powerful sorry to have to wake you. It's Master John. He done run off. I can't find him no where. I came in to check on him like I always do, and he ain't there." Poor Madie was frantic.

"You search the house?"

"Ya sah. I did. He ain't here."

"Go on out and find Uncle Buck and Luther. Tell them to light some lanterns and torches. I'll get Nimrod and some of the others. We'll find him."

"Ya sah." She scurried away.

"We got to go out and find Daddy." He looked for his shirt and britches. "His mind is so far gone. I knew this might happen."

"I'll help you search," said Edward, rummaging through clothes, their clothing a mixed pile on the floor.

"Let me go down first. You wait until the house is quiet and come down the back stairs. Meet us out front." Andrew bolted out the door.

The small search party consisting of Andrew, Edward, Nimrod, and Ryland searched most of the morning with no sight of Daddy. By noon, they enlisted the whole slave community to comb the plantation. Smaller groups spread out in different directions. Uncle Buck saddled horses for Andrew and Nimrod.

"We'll search the southern end," said Andrew.

"Mr. Andrew, ain't nothing down there," said Nimrod trying to control his mount. The mare bucked and resisted his control of the rein.

"I know that, but we've got to search everywhere. He won't last the night in this cold. You go up north, and oversee the others. Edward and I will search the south. He looked at Edward. "Saddle yourself a mount."

The two galloped away from the group. They came upon Big Tree, as it was known, a 90-year-old pecan tree that grew at the far southern end of the plantation. Known because of its size — it made the full-grown oaks around it look like saplings. At harvest time, it yielded plenty. It had a long history of providing nuts for cakes and pies.

"Is this part of the plantation?" Edward asked.

"This is all ours. We just haven't gotten around to developing out here."

"It's a good thing we came this way. I see him. Look yonder." Edward pointed to the tree. "He's hiding behind it."

They spurred the horses and trotted up. Daddy, completely naked, ran toward the woods.

"Daddy!" Yelled Andrew. "Stop, Daddy! It's me, Andrew."

Daddy stopped and turned. Andrew dismounted and ran toward him.

"Andrew, they're after me. I can't get home." He ran toward Andrew, crying like a small child. "They're after me. I tell you they're after me." Andrew embraced his father. The man was shaking, tears streamed down his face.

"Who's after you?"

"The slaves. They've revolted. They're hunting me down."

"No, Daddy. We're all looking for you. We're worried about you." Andrew took off his coat and put it around Daddy's shivering body. Edward brought a blanket to cover his lower body.

"Let's get him on my horse." Andrew helped hoist Daddy up and got in the saddle behind him. Both were shivering.

Edward walked his mount up beside them. "Here, put this on." He handed Andrew his coat.

"You keep that on. I'll be all right," said Andrew.

"You gonna have to take it slow. I can ride back faster. Go ahead, take it," Edward insisted.

Andrew slipped on the coat.

"See you when you get back. I'll let the others know we found him."

"Edward, I'll need you to bring up some more fire wood to my room before I turn in tonight. Restock Daddy's room first." Andrew made eye contact with Edward, sure there was no risk. Barely awake, Daddy slumped in front of him, clearly exhausted from running from phantom slaves.

Edward held his gaze. "Yes, sir." He spurred the horse and galloped toward the big house.

Edward helped Madie calm Daddy and get him settled. Georgie made hot soup and fed it to him.

The house finally quiet, Andrew returned to his room and waited for Edward to bring firewood. Andrew stood warming his backside by the fire when the knock came. Edward entered without being summoned.

"Finally," said Andrew. "I thought you'd never get here."

"Settling your daddy took longer than I thought it would. How you feeling?"

"I'm chilled to the bone." He shivered. "Thanks for helping get Daddy settled in. He's gotten to be too much for Madie to handle. His mind is gone, but his strength has not. You must be chilled, too. You rode back without a heavy coat."

"I've been in the kitchen. It's nice and warm in there. I feel better now. Eat some soup. It'll help warm you." Edward moved toward the fire to warm his hands.

Andrew reached for Edward's hands. "It's not soup I need to warm me." He pulled Edward close.

The next morning Andrew met with Nimrod in his office. "I've decided to move Edward from stable work," he said.

A big grin spread across Nimrod's face. "Well that's fine, Mr. Andrew. I got just the place for him in the fields where he belongs. I'll tell him soon as I leave here."

"I'm not putting him in the fields. I'm assigning him to look after Daddy. He can care for Daddy's personal needs better than a woman. Daddy is still strong enough to overpower Madie. After yesterday, it's clear he's a danger to himself. We'll put a cot in Daddy's room for Edward."

"I see," said Nimrod. His expression hardened. He leaned back in the chair, sucked his dirty teeth and rubbed his chin stubble. "You still think the old man needs help in the barn and stables?"

"I do. Assign Ryland to help Uncle Buck. Anything else we need to talk about?" Andrew asked.

"No. Not unless you want me to tuck them in at night, too," Nimrod grunted. "Maybe I'll sing 'em one of their coon songs."

Andrew ignored the comment. Nimrod swaggered out leaving his stench behind.

That night Andrew left the door to his room unlocked. Edward slipped in after Daddy was asleep. "Is Daddy resting all right?"

"He's fine. I gave him a swig of brandy to help calm him," said Edward, unbuttoning his shirt. Andrew had already memorized Edward's chest, its muscular curves and thin coat of black curly hair.

After making love, they lay together on their sides, Andrew tracing the whip marks on Edward's back with his thumb. "Do these still hurt?"

"It was a lot of pain when I got them, but I don't feel them much now. They've mostly healed."

"So unnecessary. Don't make no sense." Andrew rolled to his back, exhaled, and changed the subject. "You ever do it with a woman?"

Edward turned to face him. "I tried it a few times. It don't do nothing for me. I like what we do. What about you?"

"I let some friends talk me into going to a whorehouse a couple of times back when I was in military school. It didn't go well. I mean, I appreciate a beautiful woman, but I don't need one in my bed. I like this." He groped between Edward' legs and massaged him. "What about other men? Am I your first?"

"You're the first that I have cared about," said Edward. "The first time I thought about it, I was 12 or 13. I came upon two slaves, both men, doing it in the woods. Then at Oaks Plantation, there was this man, a cousin to Mrs. Oaks, who visited often and requested a certain male slave wait on him every time. I was the butler there before I started fighting for Mr. Fairholm. Once I was taking fresh linen to the man's room and walked in on the two. The man wanted to buy the slave from Mr. Oaks. I heard him ask about it more than once, but Mr. Oaks wouldn't do it. I think he knew."

"You ever aim to be free?" Andrew jumped from subject to subject, wanting to learn as much as he could about Edward.

"Yes," said Edward. "I ran after I broke that trainer's jaw and whipped him. They caught me. I vowed I would run again. My mother died just after I was born, and my father was sold away while I was still young. An old slave woman looked after me, but she soon died. You, Georgie, Aunt Daisy, and Uncle Buck are the first people who have been kind to me in a long time. And Mrs. Oaks, she was nice to me when I was there."

Edward rolled to his side, and Andrew returned to rubbing his back, careful to run his hand lightly over the scars. Edward cared for him. Of this, he was sure. Edward could have left him to die that night Onie and the other man attacked them, or he could have killed them all and escaped.  But he didn't.  Instead, he brought him home and nurtured him back to good health.  Maybe putting Edward in Daddy's room with better sleeping accommodations and giving him the duty of being caregiver would decrease his desire to leave.  He nuzzled his head in the well of Edward's shoulder and held him tight.

"I better get on back to your daddy's room," said Edward. "Tomorrow, I'll oil the hinges on his door and yours, so they don't squeak so much when I come and go."

"You think of everything, don't you?"

Edward winked.  "I try."

## Chapter 22
## Spring 1860

**Georgie** beat rugs with a large stick. Early spring had been warm, and Anna hadn't stopped with cleaning orders: wash the bedding, air out the mattresses, clean all the floors. A cloud of dust rose with each whack. Georgie sneezed just as Ryland walked up with a fishing pole in one hand and a string of fish in another.

"Afternoon, Georgie," he said.

"What you doing with all them fish?" She swung the stick, and more dirt flew from the carpet.

"I went fishing this morning and caught a few. Can't nobody fry fish like you. I thought maybe after I clean 'em, you could fry 'em up for us."

*Us.* She wasn't sure what she thought about that. "You clean them, and I'll fry them for you. You can pick them up this evening."

"You ain't gonna join me? Come on, Georgie."

He was a good man, and she hated to reject him. "I ain't ready yet." She hit the carpet a couple times. How'd you find the time to go fishing anyway?" She tried to lighten the conversation.

"It's Sunday."

"Oh, that's right. Us house workers don't get Sunday off. We got to work every day. But y'all say we got it better than you out in the field." She swung the stick hard.

He turned to leave.

"Ryland," she called. "Thank you. I just need a little time."

"It's been over three years, Georgie. Look at her." He pointed to Little Sally playing with the other children. "We all love her. I'm a good man." He spread his arms open, fish dangling in one, and the fishing pole in the other. "I'll do right by both of you."

"I know. Bring them fish back, and I'll fry them. I'll fix some corn bread, and *we* can eat tonight."

He smiled and turned on the dirt path, a spring in his step as he walked to his cabin.

She went back to beating the rug. She knew the others called her uppity and high-yellow. They said she thought she was better than them because she was the Master's bastard. Massa Gordon had built a cabin for her, and Andrew protected her from Nimrod and Anna. She wasn't light enough to escape and pass, but the dark slaves resented her because of her color. She had closed herself off from most folks. Maybe she would open her heart to Ryland. Lost in her thoughts, she barely noticed the children running by, chasing each other. Little Sally caught her eye. She was clutching the doll Andrew had given her for Christmas. A little boy snatched the doll and ran away. Little Sally chased after him, crying.

Georgie yelled to the boy, "Give that doll back to her, boy. You hear me?"

He stuck out his tongue at Georgie and threw the doll in a tall pile of wood, then turned and ran off.

"Come back here, boy! I'll box your ears!" Georgie yelled.

Georgie put down the stick and ran to help Sally, who had climbed up on the woodpile. She reached into a crevice to retrieve the doll then screamed, her eyes wide, face red. Georgie ran to her and saw a snake trying to slither back down through the chinks between the logs. It writhed but didn't go anywhere, drained from the bite. Blood ran down Sally's hand, two puncture wounds directly in her prominent vein. The two holes swelled red against the child's white skin.

"Oh, God, no!" Georgie pulled the child away from the woodpile and bashed the snake's head with a log. "Somebody help me. Oh, please help me," she yelled, trying to comfort her child who was still screaming and crying.

Ryland was first on the scene. The large snake was wounded but still alive. He finished it off with a large rock. He took Little Sally from Georgie, who was trying to suck the venom from the wounds. He cut the wounds, despite Sally's kicking and screaming. He sucked out the poison and spat it on the ground. Sally lay in his arms, limp and quiet now.

Andrew came running out the back door with his pistol. "It's a copperhead," he said.

"I killed it," said Ryland before sucking on the cut again. "I need to dress the wound."

Georgie ran to the wash line and tore down a clean sheet. She brought it to Ryland, who tore a strip and wrapped it around Sally's wrist.

"Let's be sure it's dead," said Andrew, and then he shot it in the head. "Take her to the cabin, and I'll go fetch Doc Prichard."

Edward rushed over. "What's wrong?"

"Copperhead done bit Little Sally," said Andrew. "The damn thing must have come up from the riverbank and got under that pile of wood. I'm going for Doc Prichard."

Ryland carried Little Sally. Georgie followed, walking in a dream state. She could hear the conversation but seemed to float above it all.

It wasn't long before MawNancy came running with her bag of ointments and potions. By the time she arrived, Little Sally was unconscious. Georgie didn't know if she should let the old crone near her child, but she was desperate for anything that might save her. MawNancy pried open Little Sally's mouth and poured a clear liquid into her. Her breathing grew shallow, and her fever raged higher.

Georgie cradled and rocked Little Sally, singing and moaning *Fix Me, Jesus*, but life was leaving her baby; she could tell. Georgie stopped singing and rocking and drew Little Sally's mouth near her ear. Little Sally's last breath was but a whisper of warmth. Georgie hugged the lifeless child close, tears landing in Little Sally's hair. Just as she had watched life leave her mother, now she watched it slip away from her child. All of Georgie's secret plans for her baby evaporated with that last breath. Little Sally could easily have passed for white. Her porcelain skin, hazel eyes, and whispery-thin black hair favored the Gordon side. Georgie had planned to teach her the refined skills of white ladies, and ask Andrew to see to the child's education, possibly up north. And maybe when Little Sally was old enough, they could have escaped together. She could have pretended to be the child's maid. She was determined that her daughter would not be subjected to a life of slavery. But this had not been a part of her plan.

An hour later, Doc Prichard and Andrew rushed in.

"It's too late," said Georgie, still cradling Little Sally. "She's gone."

When they tried to take the child from her, Georgie fought them off — the two slave women who came to prepare the body, Andrew, Edward, and Ryland. She screamed, yelled, kicked, scratched and bit them. Andrew and Edward held her down, and the others removed Little Sally from Georgie's clutch. Too exhausted to fight anymore, Georgie lay screaming, "She's all I have. Where are you taking her? She's all I have."

Ryland and Uncle Buck sat with Georgie all night, the loneliest, coldest night of her life. The next morning Ryland and Uncle Buck walked with her to the barn where they had built the small coffin and placed the child in it. Ryland removed the lid. Little Sally had turned ghastly white; even her lips had lost their color. She did not look peaceful. Her mouth was twisted. Georgie reached to comfort her baby. She was stiff, hard, and ice-cold. Georgie pulled her hand back. Ryland put his arm around her. Georgie pulled away.

Later that day, they buried Little Sally beside Mama. Before they lowered the coffin into the ground, Georgie pleaded with Ryland and Edward to open it one last time. They obliged. A small clump of dirt fell from the lid onto Little Sally's white dress. Georgie thought about removing the dirt but did not. She kept her gaze on her baby's distorted face. She looked nothing like the happy child Georgie remembered. "She's still in pain," she whispered.

Georgie retreated to the comfort and solitude of her cabin. She sat for days humming, rocking, and singing *Steal Away to Jesus*. She longed for Mama. She ached for Little Sally. She stopped eating except for when hunger pains became unbearable. Andrew came two or three times a day; the others checked in on her, too. She could not bring herself to respond to any of them. The knocking only reminded her of swatting the rugs the day Little Sally died. Or the sound of nails being driven into the coffin lid.

Again, she heard the knocking but could not bring herself to move from her chair. The hinges seemed to cry with her as the door opened. It was Ryland with a tray of food. "Georgie, please eat something. I know you're hurting. Let me help you," he pleaded. He reached for her hand. She pushed him away.

"Georgie, you can't keep on like this. Nimrod knows you ain't working," Ryland warned. "Don't make Mr. Andrew have to send you away to one of them places."

"Let them beat me 'til I'm dead." She commenced humming and rocking.

After a few days, she decided to eat. Georgie walked to the kitchen after the sun set. The crickets' lullaby annoyed her, as did the fireflies, which Little Sally loved to chase. Mary and Sadie ceased their chatter when she walked in the door.

They seemed afraid of her. "I'm hungry," she said.

"Thank you, Jesus," Mary clasped her hands and looked out toward the heavens.

"Come on, baby. Sit right here, and we'll get you something," said Sadie.

They brought her a plate of fried chicken; she hadn't known how hungry she was until she was on her second piece. She was finishing off a wing and some buttermilk, when Anna stepped in the door.

"I'm looking for Zula," she sneered. "Any of y'all know where she is?"

"No, Miss Anna. We ain't seen her," Mary quickly responded.

"Well, I need my bed linens changed. Georgie, come change my bed!"

"I'll do it, Miss Anna," Sadie volunteered.

"And I'll help so we can be quick about it," said Mary.

"Georgie can do it," said Anna. "She ain't been doing much else lately."

Mary persisted. "Miss Anna, you know Georgie been feeling poorly. It ain't no trouble t'all. I can…"

"I said I want Georgie to do it," Anna said looking at Mary and Sadie. Georgie recognized the same fire in Anna's eyes the morning she caused Mama's accident. "Come on girl, now!"

Georgie got up slowly and followed Anna into the big house and up to the bedroom. Georgie waited for instructions, her head down.

"Well, what're you waiting for? I said I want that bed changed.

Now, be quick about it. You know where the fresh linens are kept. I'm going to visit my friend, Caroline Shelton, and I want a fresh bed to sleep in when I return." She sat at her dressing table applying powders and perfume, but no amount could fix that kind of ugly.

Georgie struggled with the bed coverings; she moved slowly, listless from lack of food. Anna slammed a bottle on the dresser and stormed over, snatching the pillow from her hand. "I told you to be quick about it, you lazy wench!" She slapped Georgie hard across the side of her face.

For a second, the room went dark. In that moment, Georgie's mind relived the rape that Anna and Miss Victoria orchestrated, then the pot careening down on Mama's head and the pool of blood on the kitchen floor. She saw the serpent pump its venom into her daughter's veins, then a vision of her dead daughter's twisted face in a pine box. Her sight returned, and there was Anna standing in front of her cloaked in arrogance and superiority. Georgie fought to quash the rage inside her, but it burst through. Heat churned in the pit of her stomach and spread through her limbs. The hot rage reached her head, and all of her suppressed pain erupted. She slapped Anna as hard as she could across the face.

Anna stumbled back in shock. "You bitch! I'll have you whipped."

Georgie swung again, with her hand closed in a tight fist like Edward had showed her. Anna fell across the dresser. Anna ran for the door, her eyes wild. She had just opened the door when Georgie grabbed her by the back of her dress and flung her into the room again. Anna opened her mouth, maybe to scream, but before a cry for help came out, Georgie pummeled her again, and again, and again. She grabbed her by the neck and shoved her against the fireplace. Anna's head hit the wooden mantle, the blow knocking her out. Georgie came back to her senses. She surveyed the room, taking it all in. Anna lay in the corner of the room by the fireplace. Blood stained the front of Anna's torn dress and Georgie's hands. She removed the key from the nightstand and quietly stepped into the hallway. She was careful to make sure no one saw her leave. She locked the door, slipped the key in her dress pocket, and escaped down the back stairs out into the night.

With a steady pace, but not so fast as to draw attention to herself, she headed to her cabin to gather a few belongings. She would take her chances and run north. If she stayed, they would kill or beat her so badly she would wish for death. She tried to contain the panic that was building inside her, when a figure stepped out of the darkness in front of her. Before she could scream, a hand covered her mouth and shoved her against a tree.

"I'm gonna ask you again, gal, is you ready to go wid me? You been humming and singing my signal song for a long time now. I come back for you."

It was the woman Georgie saw by the tree months ago. Her voice husky, she was strong as any man. She removed her hand from Georgie's mouth. The woman's eyes reminded her of Mama's. How could someone who appeared so hard and tough have such kind eyes. "Yes, I'm ready to go," she told the woman. As the words fell from her mouth, tears streamed from her eyes. All that she ever knew, good and bad, was about to be left behind, and she had no idea what the future held for her. "I beat her. I beat my missus bad, and I got to go before they find her."

The woman looked at the blood on Georgie's hands and studied her for a moment. "You don't look strong enough, but they'll kill you for sure if I leave you here. The slave catchers will really be after you. Now, I'm gonna tell you, when you go wid me, I gets you to freedom. Ain't no turning back. I'll kill you dead 'fore I let you turn back. Now, is you going wid me or not?"

"Yes," said Georgie. "I want to get my things."

"Ain't no time for that. Just more things they can use to catch your scent."

Georgie took one last look at the main house then turned to follow the woman into the blackness. They made their way through the night, avoiding the roads. The woman seemed to know every path, tree, and rock along the way. The terrain was thick with vines, trees, and brush, and the smell of honeysuckle strong.

They walked for what seemed like hours, sloshing through creeks and hiding in and around abandoned buildings. They noticed every sound. Slave catchers were always out looking for runaways. The slightest noise sent them running behind a tree, crouching in tall thickets, or lying prone on the ground until the threat of danger subsided. Just before daybreak, they arrived on the outskirts of a small town.

"Wait here behind this tree until I come back for you. Keep your head down and don't make a sound. You hear me, gal."

She vanished. For a moment, Georgie stood frozen with fear. For the first time, she was away from Wilmington Manor, and completely alone. She sat down and rested her back against the tree. She trusted that the woman would return. Without meaning to, Georgie drifted off to sleep.

A hand nudged her shoulder, rousing her from deep slumber.

"Wake up," the male voice said.

"Quick, get her up," said the other male voice.

Two white men stood over her. They wore thick black boots and holsters with gleaming pistols. Slave catchers. Her spirit sank. She wanted to run, but there was nowhere to go. And if she did run, their bullets would get her before she got too far. The woman, her savior, had abandoned her.

One of the men said, "Don't be afraid. You're safe. She sent us back for you. It was too near daybreak and not safe for her to be out."

Confused, Georgie tried to make sense of what was happening, of the white men speaking kindly. They motioned her toward a wagon. Too exhausted to resist, she got into the back. They covered her with a blanket and told her to be still and quiet. One reached back to cover her face with the blanket. In the moonlight, she caught a glimpse of him. She'd seen him before.

The short ride in the back of the wagon was rough. Her body ached, and she felt every bump in the road. The fight with Anna, and the night's journey took their toll on her already frail body. When the wagon finally came to a stop, the two men got down and walked around to the back.

One of them whispered, "Don't move. We're going to carry you in."

"In," she thought. "Where is in? Where am I?" She fought to suppress the panic welling up inside her.

They lifted her like a sack of flour. One carried her legs and the other her torso. The timbre of their boots on the wooden floor let her know they had entered a building. They adjusted her between them, and she felt herself on a diagonal, headed down. The men struggled to maintain control of her down the steep steps. She squirmed. "Hold still," one of them said. "We've got you. We're trying to be gentle." At the bottom, they stood her up and removed the blanket. She took a few moments to adjust to her surroundings and the fear she was fighting to overcome. Her eyesight came into focus, and she realized the woman was standing across from her. Next to her were the two white men, and behind them was a stack of coffins. They were well made like the one they buried Miss Victoria in, not a box made of spare plank like the ones Edward and Ryland had to put together for Mama and Little Sally.

"This is a safe place," the woman said softly. "It's one of many we use to hide escaping slaves. It's a funeral parlor. This is Hurley, and this here is Theopolus."

Georgie recognized Theopolus as the undertaker who brought the coffin to the house for Miss Victoria's burial. The men brought her food and a change of clothing — a man's britches and shirt. She'd never dressed in britches before. Mama always said it was bad luck for a woman to wear britches. She pulled off her dress. Anna's room key clanged to the floor. Georgie looked at the key for a moment then kicked it to the other side of the room.

Georgie's head throbbed. She untied the fabric concealing her hair.

"They're gonna be looking for you extra hard on account of what you done. You got to look different in case slave catchers stop you. We gonna have to cut that long hair, too." The woman touched Georgie's hair.

"Oh," she gasped.

"It'll grow back," one of them said.

She loved her long hair. She gathered it in her hands and swept it over one shoulder. Losing it temporarily was a small price to pay for freedom.

"Can I keep this?" she asked meekly, holding up the blue fabric Andrew gave her for Christmas.

"Wrap it around your waist, on the inside next to your body," they told her.

Hurley began cutting Georgie's hair. Georgie watched as large clumps fell to the floor around her.

"She'll have to stay here until tomorrow. We'll head out in the morning. We'll have to move quick 'cause they gonna be looking for her."

"Yep," said Theopolus. "The farther up north we get her, the better. With the haircut and the new clothes, the dogs will have a hard time picking up her scent, and the catchers won't recognize her."

"I'll meet you there," said the woman. "I'll sleep here today and head out tonight. We'll meet at the next stop tomorrow. I want to gather a few more from Berkley."

"How should we take her, cabinet or coffin?" asked Hurley.

"Coffin," said Theopolus. "Since she's alone."

"Coffin?" thought Georgie as she rubbed her hand across her almost baldhead. She was horrified at how prickly it felt.

Hurley whipped up a warm lather in the shaving bowl and slathered it over her head. He guided the razor with seeming precision over the contours of her head, navigating it around her ears. Her head was as smooth as the palm of her hand. She could no longer hold back the tears.

## Chapter 23
## Spring 1860

**Edward** leaned over Massa Gordon, shaving him when a knock on the door interrupted his focus causing him to nick the old man below his jaw. "Come on in."

Zula opened the door. "I been to Miss Anna's room three times this morning, and she won't let me in. She won't even say nothing when I call through the door."

"Go on in. Maybe she's out," said Edward whipping up a good lather.

"The door is locked. She got to be in there. She done missed breakfast and lunch."

"Let me finish up here, and I'll come help you."

Zula and Edward knocked on the door to rouse Anna. Their knocking progressed to pounding and yelling. Luther came up to help then retrieved the extra keys Andrew kept in his office. After much fumbling, one finally unlocked the door. They were stunned at the mess they found. The room was filled with broken lamps and vases, and overturned furniture. Blood spattered the floor, walls and draperies.

"Miss Anna!" Zula shrieked, running toward Anna, slumped in the corner near the fireplace.

Edward had overlooked Anna when he first entered the room. He crouched next to her now and checked for a pulse. "She's alive." He and Luther lifted her onto the bed, and Zula retrieved towels. She wet them with water from the pitcher on the dressing table and placed the cloth on Anna's forehead.

"You better go get Mr. Andrew," Luther said to Edward.

Edward walked out to the field, where he spied Andrew and Nimrod on horseback, off in the distance. Edward motioned to them, and they galloped toward him, Andrew in the lead.

"What's wrong, boy?" Nimrod said.

Edward ignored Nimrod and directed his gaze to Andrew.

"What's wrong? Is it Daddy?" Andrew asked.

"You need to come on back to the house. Something is wrong with Miss Anna. She's been locked in her room all morning. Luther used the spare key to get in, and we found her on the floor. The whole room is torn apart."

"You stay here, and I'll head back," Andrew told Nimrod.

Edward walked back to the house with Andrew on horseback trotting beside him. Andrew seemed to slow the horse so they were able to go side-by-side.

As they walked, Edward imagined what it would be like to climb up on the saddle behind Andrew. In his mind, he felt Andrew seated in front of him. He smelled the soap he'd washed with that morning and his body pressed close. Andrew stopped his horse in its tracks and suddenly dismounted. The two walked back together. It was as if Andrew had read his mind.

Edward retold how they found Anna and the condition of the room.

"I don't understand. Maybe she's had some type of mental fit," said Andrew.

"I don't know either."

"In spite of Anna's constant bad behavior, she is my sister and I have worried about her. Now I have to worry about her and Georgie. If Georgie doesn't come back to her right mind soon, I may have to put her away. Daddy had made those arrangements years ago, but she got her mind back. I fear the asylum for her. They would experiment on her and do things they would not do to a white patient. If she don't get right soon, I won't have a choice."

"I hope it doesn't come to that," Edward didn't want any more heartache for Andrew.

"I'm glad you're here." Andrew gave Edward a quick look.

They entered the bedroom, where Luther was still putting things back in order. Anna drifted in and out of consciousness. Zula had cleaned her up as much as possible, but her face was distorted with swelling.

"These wounds were not self-inflicted. She's been in a fight," Andrew said as he examined her. "I want to know who did this. Get some smelling spirits. Maybe that will bring her around. I'll send Nimrod to fetch Doc Prichard."

Edward wanted to comfort Andrew but knew not to draw attention to their closeness. Andrew paced the room, pondering what had happened. "Who would do this to her? Plenty of people on and off the plantation have reason to dislike Anna but not to the point of this. Did any of you see or hear anything?"

"Not until we came in here," said Edward.

Luther agreed.

"Where's that smelling salts?" he snapped at Zula.

Zula retrieved the bottle from down stairs and waived it under Anna's nose. She coughed and flailed her arms but did not fully come into consciousness. Andrew talked to her, but she didn't answer his queries as to who had attacked her.

"We need someone to help you 'tend to her. Do you think Georgie is strong enough to help?" Andrew asked Zula.

"Ya sah," she said. "But we can't find her — been looking for her all morning. Ain't nobody seen hide naw hair of her."

"Check in the kitchen," said Andrew, who then turned to Edward and asked, "Have you checked in on Daddy lately?"

"I haven't had a chance since we've been tending to Miss Anna, but I can go in there now."

Edward was still in Old Man Gordon's room when Doc Prichard arrived. From down the hall, Edward heard the doctor's boots clomping up the stairs.

"Edward," Andrew called. Come on in here, and tell Doc Prichard how y'all found her.

Edward repeated the story.

"She's taken a good whipping, but she'll be all right. She doesn't appear to have any broken bones," said Doc Prichard.

"Doc," said Andrew. "Has she been, uh, you know, violated?"

"No. You can rest easy about that. Nothing like that has happened."

He left laudanum and more smelling salts. As he was about to leave, Anna groaned. The doctor waived some salts under her nose, and she coughed. Her eyes opened, and she appeared half aware. Andrew and the doctor talked to her and encouraged her to stay awake.

They prodded her with questions about what happened and who had attacked her.

In spite of her swollen mouth and eyes, an eerie, determined look came over her and she muttered, "Georgie. I want that bitch whipped, and I want to be the one to do it." She stared at Andrew. "Find her."

"Georgie!" Andrew gasped. "Georgie did this? How did she find the strength? Her mind's not right. I knew I should have sent her to that asylum. We've got to search for her before she gets hurt." Andrew rushed from the room.

Edward did not participate in the search. He spent the remainder of the day taking care of the old man who had taken to relieving himself in his clothes. They gave up the search at nightfall. Edward spotted Andrew and Nimrod out of the window, returning the horses to the stable.

Edward went to Andrew's office to tell him about his father's condition. Andrew hadn't come in from the stable, but Edward knew it wouldn't be long. He looked about the room, and his gaze landed on the ledger laying closed on the desk. Georgie had told him about it. He stepped out into the hall to make sure no one was near, then went back to the desk. He stared at the book, gold-leaf lettering spelling out "Wilmington Manor" on its cover. He opened its well-worn pages and thumbed through, wondering where he was listed. He closed it when he glimpsed a notice on the desk. He picked up the paper and studied it. When he was a boy, he and several other slaves used to sneak off to the cabin of an old school headmaster who taught them letters and words from his books. One of the field hands caught them and reported them to the overseer. Edward and the other slaves were beaten, and the schoolmaster's books confiscated and burned. But he'd had enough training to make out words and meaning. Edward took his time and studied each word, sounding them out.

Runaway Slave

Female Mulatto

26 years old

Answers to the Name of Georgie

$500 Reward if Returned Alive
Wilmington Manor Plantation
Andrew Gordon, Owner

 A creak in the floorboard startled him, and he turned to see Andrew staring back, his face red and brow furrowed. "Well, I'll be damned," said Andrew. "What other surprises you got for me?"

 He snatched the paper from Edward's hand, causing it to rip. Edward stepped back, surprised at Andrew's manner. Andrew shoved him against the desk. "Do you realize you could be killed if anyone finds out you can read?" He pushed Edward's chest between every three for four words.

 Edward grabbed Andrew by the front of his shirt to stop the shoving.

 Andrew broke free from his grip and looked around quickly. "You mind your place. What if Luther had seen us?" Andrew hissed.

 "Mind my place?" Andrew's words stung.

 "Get out. Get the hell out of my sight."

 Edward moved passed Andrew to leave. "So, what are you gonna do when they bring her back half dead, beat her some more?"

 They stared one another down for a few seconds.

 Andrew glared, his nostrils flaring and chest heaving. "Out," he said.

 Edward walked out to the stables to calm himself. He missed the horses. He brushed the palomino. She whinnied at the touch. "Easy girl," he said.

 Ryland walked in. "I was hoping it was you in here," he said. "I need your help."

 Edward hadn't spent much time around Ryland. Most of the male slaves were jealous of Edward's closeness to Andrew. "What you need me for?" Edward continued brushing the mare.

 "I'm trying to help Georgie."

 Edward turned abruptly to face him. "You know where she is? Is she all right?"

 "I don't know where she is. But I do know that catchers gonna be looking for her, and they gonna need something to catch her scent.

The wash women will boil her clothes in lye soap this evening, if I can get Georgie's stuff to them. I heard Nimrod say them catchers won't be here until around noon tomorrow. The clothes will be dry by then. I need you to help me get the clothes and bed linens to the washers. Will you help me?"

"I'll help you."

They gathered Georgie's few items of clothing and bed coverings and carried them to the wash-house, where two slave women were fanning the fires. The women accepted the bundles without saying a word and tossed them into the large pot. The older woman threw in a cake of lye soap and stirred.

"Thank you," said Ryland as he and Edward left the washroom. "That stuff can dry in the night air, and I'll take it back early in the morning before the day starts."

"What if they don't dry?" Edward asked.

"They will. We've done this before when it was colder than it is now."

Edward realized that he was not a part of the slave inner circle. Much happened that he did not know about. "I best get back to check on the old man."

"Thanks for your help," said Ryland.

"Anything for Georgie." Edward headed back to the house.

*********

Andrew reprinted the announcement. He made two copies and would have Nimrod deliver them to the *Richmond Examiner* the next day. They would make handbills. He walked to Nimrod's cabin to give him the notice and instructions to make the trip up to Richmond early in the morning.

"All right, Mr. Andrew. I'll head out at first light," said Nimrod. "You know, I used to be a slave catcher. I'll get my boys together. Don't you worry. If she's alive, we'll find her."

"Make sure they understand they are not to hurt her," Andrew warned. "She's not in her right mind."

"Well, I'll tell 'em." Nimrod hocked and spit in the yard. "But you know them boys don't follow no rules."

"If they harm her, the reward gets cut," said Andrew.

That night Andrew left his door unlocked as usual, but Edward did not come. Andrew rested in bed reliving their earlier exchange and wondered why Edward's ability to read had angered him so much. Was it because he thought he knew everything about Edward? What other secrets did he keep? Maybe Edward was planning to escape, too. He wouldn't. He couldn't. But Georgie had. Georgie, his half-sister whom he loved more dearly than his own sister, had attacked Anna and fled to freedom. Edward could easily forge a pass and slip away, and he would lose them both. The thought tightened his chest. He hugged his pillow and wished for sleep.

## Chapter 24
### Spring 1860

**Georgie** rested in a coffin in the back of the Martin brothers' wagon, on her way to freedom. The box had air holes, and she had been covered with a pall in case they were required to open it. At some point between leaving Wilmington Manor and being carted off in a box made for the dead, she reached peace with her ordeal. She relied on her trust in God and believed that the spiritual realm would protect and guide her. She played over and over in her mind the words she used to hear Mama sing.

*Guide my feet while I run dis race.*
*Guide my feet, Lord, while I run dis race.*
*Guide my feet, Lord, while I run dis race.*
*For, I don't want to run dis race in vain.*

When fear and uncertainty threatened to consume her, she repeated the tune, and it centered her spirit. The wagon creaked and groaned, and the horse's hooves maintained a steady stride. The wagon slowed to a stop. A single horse trotted up. She was getting adept at picturing a scene painted from the sounds she could make out from within her box. Her freedom box.

"How do?" said the horseman.

"Fair-to-middlin," replied Theopolus.

"I'm looking for a runaway, a wench," said the horseman. "She been missing pert near a whole day now. There's a reward. I think they want her back. Don't matter none to me if you bring her back dead or alive. She gave her missus a good walloping before she run off. I'm out scouting around to see if I can find her before I get the catchers looking. If I don't find her today, the catchers will start tomorrow."

"Do tell," said Hurley.

Georgie recognized Nimrod's voice. Her body tensed, and sweat gathered around her head and neck. The hot box became more oppressive. She needed to sneeze. She fought to suppress it. She bit her upper lip to take her mind off the twitching. She moved her mouth and nose from side to side. She had to suppress it. The pall tickled her nose, which made the urge stronger. She fought hard to hold it back.

She couldn't lose her freedom because of something as simple as a sneeze. It was difficult to move, but she adjusted her hand and pinched her nose.

"Well, I won't tarry none. It looks like y'all got plenty to do. I see you got one to plant," said Nimrod. "If you run across her, she belongs to the Gordon Plantation. She answers to the name of Georgie."

"We'll keep a look out," said Theopolus.

"Sure will," grunted Hurley.

Nimrod trotted off, and for the first time since the exchange began, she breathed again. The wagon rolled on. The urge to sneeze subsided.

*Guide my feet while I run dis race.*
*Guide my feet, Lord, while I run dis race.*
*Guide my feet, Lord, while I run dis race.*
*For, I don't want to run dis race in vain.*

Hurley and Theopolus removed the coffin from the back of the wagon. "Hold on." Hurley said. We got to make sure ain't nobody around before we let you out." They lifted the lid, and Georgie stepped out, into dusk. They were in a cemetery beside a shallow grave. The fake burial was easy to pull off in the early darkness. The box was designed so that it could be easily disassembled to look like nothing more than plank boards. They secured the wagon, and the three walked through the woods.

"Its about a mile walk," Theopolus told Georgie. "How you holding up?"

"I'm all right."

"Let's go," said Hurley.

The katydids, cicadas, and crickets sang an evening song. Early blooms fluttered in the warm spring breeze. Georgie's boots were too tight, and her muscles were sore from being in the cramped coffin. Excitement pulsed through her veins. She focused on the insects' sounds to take her mind off her aching feet. She smelled the flowers, which were common at Wilmington Manor, as if noticing their fragrance for the first time. They were approaching a large house, when Hurley said, "That's it, just up ahead."

The three reached the back of the house, where they descended a staircase, which had been camouflaged with vines. Hurley knocked on the small door. Four knocks, one, then one again. There was movement on the other side. The door opened, and a big black man quickly ushered them in.

"She here yet?" Asked Hurley.

"Not yet," said the black man. "We got some more in the back waiting for her."

"How many altogether?"

"With this one here, it makes five."

"That's enough for one trip. This one here," Hurley said nodding toward Georgie, "They gonna be looking extra hard. We got to move, and be quick about it."

"Is there a problem?" A woman's voice came from the shadows.

"Nothing we can't handle," said Hurley. "There's a special reward out on this one. Seems she knocked her missus around a little before she left."

The voice stepped in to the light. She was the prettiest white woman Georgie had ever seen — far more beautiful than Victoria, Anna, or any of the women who came to Wilmington Manor. Her dress sparkled, and her lips were painted red. She stepped closer to Georgie, and looked her up and down. "Well, you could have fooled me. I thought she was a young boy the way y'all got her dressed."

"Had to disguise her as best we could," explained Theopolus.

"Well, y'all done a good job. How you doing, honey." She touched Georgie's cheek. "My name is Maggie, and this is Silas." She gestured to the black man. "We run this safe house. Take her in the back with the others, and get her some food. It's a long trip tonight between here and the next stop."

They walked toward the back, when there was another knock on the door. Startled, no one moved. Four knocks, then one, then one again. Silas stepped to the door and removed the two large pieces of wood that secured it; the woman who had been her savior slipped in.

She always appeared to be calm, despite her illegal business. She scanned the room and acknowledged everyone, then asked, "How many you got for me?" Her husky voice still unnerved Georgie.

"Five, including this one. The handbills come out on her soon. We ran into the plantation overseer on the way up here," said Hurley.

All the talk about Georgie and the special reward for her capture made her feel guilty, as if she would be the cause if anything went wrong. She nervously rubbed her smooth scalp, a new habit. She had not gotten used to the idea of having all of her hair gone.

"We're about to feed them, and then it should be dark enough for you to head out," said Silas as he beckoned Georgie to follow him to the back room.

Georgie paused. She would probably never again see the two men who had helped her get to this point on her journey to freedom. She turned toward Hurley and Theopolus. "I want to thank y'all for all your help," she said.

"Good luck to you," said Theopolus.

Hurley tipped his hat. "You'll be just fine as long as you do what she tells you."

"We got to be going," said Theopolus.

Georgie followed Silas to a poorly lit room where two black men, one woman, and a boy who could not have been more than 10 years old sat on the floor.

"This here is Georgie," Silas introduced her to the group. "She's a woman. She's made up to look like a young boy, and that's how y'all is to treat her if you run into any trouble."

The escapees looked at her staring blankly. One man nodded his head.

"Y'all wait here, and I'll fetch you some food," said Silas.

Georgie, took a seat on the dirt floor and rested her aching back against a wall. The boy scampered over. "Hi. My name is Ebb," he announced. "You come from far down south?"

"No. I'm from Virginia."

"Where in Virginia?"

Hunger and exhaustion overwhelmed her manners. She was in

no mood for answering this boy's questions.

Ebb, full of childish energy didn't wait for an answer. "I used to live here. Miss Maggie bought me and let me work here cleaning and chopping wood to pay off the cost. Now, I'm leaving to be free."

The woman in the group walked over, both hands on her hips. "Ebb, you let her be. Can't you see she's tired?" She plopped down beside Georgie and grunted when her wide ass hit the hard dirt. "My name is Chloe. The three of us is from the Richardson Plantation, just outside of Richmond. That there is my man, Deutney." She pointed to the brown skinned man standing with arms folded and leaning against a wall. The other one is my brother, Lim. We saw us a chance to come north, so we took it."

It was clear that Chloe and Lim were brother and sister. They had the same round face and dark skin, almost skillet-black. Lim wore a beard, but his skin was so dark, and the light so dim, it was hard to tell where the beard began or ended.

"Deutney. Lim. Y'all come on over here and meet Georgie," Chloe called out.

Deutney swaggered toward the women. He bent down and stuck his finger in Chloe's face. "I done 'bout had enough of you giving me orders, woman. I been taking orders all my life. Now, I ain't about to start taking 'em from you. Listening to you what got us is in this mess. Freedom – that's all you can talk about – freedom. Now we running like scared dogs. Got some woman we don't know nuttin 'bout leading us. Now we got this one dressed like a man." He snorted in Georgie's direction. "You mind your tongue, Chloe." He stood and walked away.

Lim walked over. "Don't mind him none. He just scared about getting caught, like the rest of us ain't scared, too. I'm Lim."

"Pleased to meet you, Lim. I'm Georgie."

Chloe stood and brushed the dirt from her behind. She walked to Deutney, who had retreated to a corner. The two exchanged low words. Chloe hit him on the arm with the palm of her hand and walked back over to Georgie, Lim, and Ebb. "Don't pay him no mind."

Silas returned with food and distributed it. They were given two apples, two rolls, and two pieces of meat each with instructions to save half for the next day. The next safe house was two day's journey, and they needed to ration their food.

After they finished their meager meal, the woman came into the room to gather them and begin the journey. Silas and Maggie stood behind her. Her directions were simple and similar to what she told Georgie.

"When you start out with me, I gets you to freedom. You do what I say when I say. Ain't no turning back." Exposing two pistols and looking each one in the eyes, she said, "I'll kill you dead 'fore I let you turn back."

Deutney looked at the woman and snorted. He stood defiant, legs spread and arms folded.

## Chapter 25
## Spring 1860

**Andrew** stepped onto the front porch and inhaled the spring air. The bright crisp morning did not remove the cloud hanging over him. His Georgie was gone. Thanks to Nimrod, word circulated among the slave catchers that the Gordon Plantation was offering a reward for an escaped slave. They gathered that morning on the front lawn like a pack of starved dogs with fresh meat waved in front of them. They waited for Nimrod's word to begin the search, chugging from flasks and loading guns. Andrew surveyed his plantation over run with strangers and their hounds' deafening yapping.

Nimrod paced, barking out orders. The chaos, coupled with the ignorance of the participants, made Andrew wonder if it was all a waste of time. He stepped into the yard and looked up; Edward watched from the upstairs window. Their eyes made vacant contact. Nimrod passed Georgie's clothes and bed coverings to each catcher, so their hounds could pick up her scent. The catchers mounted up, released the dogs, and in a cloud of dust began their pursuit.

Nimrod swaggered up to Andrew. "We got a problem with them crops at the far north end. They looking a might poorly. I'm afraid we might lose some of 'em"

"What? Why am I just being told about this?"

"Just discovered it a couple of days ago. With the escape and all, I reckon I just plain forgot to tell you."

"All right. So, tell me now," said Andrew, still irritated and distracted about the argument he and Edward had and eager to reconcile.

"Be easier to show you. Why don't you ride out and take a look. I'll come out as soon as I finish up here."

"I'll meet you there." Andrew mounted up.

"I'll be there directly." Nimrod grinned.

He'd lost another tooth. Another fight or maybe the damn thing rotted out.

Andrew got to the north end and examined the crops. They looked fine. He waited for Nimrod, deep in thought about Edward and how to apologize to him.  A half hour passed, and Nimrod had not showed.  Impatient and frustrated, Andrew rode back to the house expecting to meet Nimrod on the way back.  Nimrod would have to explain why he had sent him on a wild goose chase.  Andrew galloped back, an anger driving him to ride harder.  Nimrod's behavior was becoming more disturbing as of late; perhaps it was time to find a new overseer.  He arrived at the house and found Ryland working in the yard.  "Have you seen Nimrod?"

"Ya sah.  He took Edward in the back of the wagon, and they headed down yonder a while ago."  Ryland pointed toward the south end of the plantation.

"You sure about that?"

"Ya sah.  I seen 'em as plain as day.  Said he had something for Edward to do.  Edward tried to explain to him that he needed to look after Massa Gordon, but Mr. Nim made him get in the wagon anyway."

"Then why the hell would he send me ..."  Andrew slapped the backside of his horse and took off toward the south end.  He rode hard, kicking and using the whip, following the fresh wagon tracks.  His mind raced.  Why would Nimrod bring Edward out here?

Andrew came to the clearing and stopped. A rope hung taut from the branch of the big tree, and Edward's body swung from it, slowly from side to side.  Everything else stood still except for Edward. His legs twitched.  "Oh God," said Andrew.  He raced to the tree, kicking his horse harder with each stride.  He fumbled for a knife in his saddlebag while trying to hold up Edward's body.  Still mounted and with an arm around Edward's legs, Andrew managed to reach the rope with his other hand.  He sawed at it but feared he wouldn't be able to cut Edward free.  He continued to saw, and finally the rope started to split. The sudden weight of Edward's body was too much for him to hold.  Edward hit the ground hard and with a crack.  He didn't move. Andrew dismounted and felt Edward's neck.  It wasn't broken.  He blew into his nostrils and massaged his neck and chest.  Edward didn't response.  Andrew sat him up and struck him on the back with the palm of his hand then laid him back down.  Edward's hands were bound, and the severed noose was still around his neck.  Helplessness laced with anger came over Andrew. He released a guttural scream that frightened even him as he scooped up Edward's body and held him tight to his chest, hugging and rocking him. "Oh God, no. Oh God, no. Please, no."

Edward spit up and coughed, the liquid soaking Andrew's shirt. Edward tried to move his arms. Andrew sat on the ground and laid Edward's upper body in his lap and wiped his brow. He took the noose from around his neck and untied his hands. Edward lay unconscious but grimaced with pain when Andrew moved him. He took shallow breaths, his chest seeming to search for more air.

Andrew didn't take his eyes off Edward, making sure he continued to breath. How did this happen? Why would Nimrod do such a thing? Maybe it wasn't Nimrod. Maybe they had been ambushed, and Nimrod was hurt, too. He blamed himself for not staying closer to home. Were the culprits still around? Maybe he and Edward were still in danger? He had to get back to the house. But how? He could not leave Edward. He fought to keep his wits. He gently laid Edward flat on the ground, and got up to look for wood to build a stretcher. He found nothing large or sturdy enough.

He kept searching and came across a wagon wheel stuck out from some tall brush. "Oh, thank you, God," Andrew said through tears. He struggled to free the wagon, then hitched it up to his horse. He pulled it close to Edward. Edward's eyes were open, but he didn't speak. He smiled and reached up to touch Andrew. As Andrew lifted him, Edward yelled out in pain and held his right hip.

"You're safe now. We're gonna get you home."

He lifted Edward into the back of the wagon. Andrew wanted to get him back to the house as quickly as possible but took it easy on the rough road. The slightest movement caused Edward to shout out, he tried to hold his right leg steady. Once Andrew got closer to the big house, the road smoothed, and he was able to pick up speed. A young male slave raked in the herb garden gone to seed. Andrew yelled for him to run ahead and get Ryland. The boy took off toward the stable. Andrew pulled the wagon in front of Georgie's cabin. Ryland and a few others came running to help. They began to lift Edward from the wagon, but he yelled out in pain.  Andrew cleared them out of the way and lifted Edward by himself to the cabin.  He pushed the door open with his shoulder and instructed Ryland, "Go get Mary and Sadie to help tend to him.  I'm heading to town to get Doc Prichard.  Tell MawNancy to get over here.  Maybe she can help until Doc Prichard gets here."

"What happened to him, Mr. Andrew?"  Ryland asked.

"Best I can tell, that bastard Nimrod tried to lynch him.  Watch Edward close.  I don't know how long he hung there before I found him."  Andrew walked out the door.  "If I ever see that stinking piece of shit again, I'll blow his brains out," he mumbled.

He'd forgotten that his horse was hitched to the wagon.  "Somebody get me a fresh horse saddled and ready to go.  Now!" he yelled.  His raised voice surprised him.

By the time Andrew was mounted and riding toward the road, Mary and Sadie had come with salves and ointments.  MawNancy came running from another direction, her satchel banging against her hip and that damn bone necklace beating against her breast.  Andrew wished for Aunt Daisy.  She would have known what to do.

## Chapter 26
## Spring 1860

**Georgie** had gotten used to the company of her fellow travelers. The woman led them north toward Washington. As Silas predicted, it would be about two days travel on foot before they reached the next safe house. They walked all night, stopping only once to rest. The soft earth covered by leaves gave way to the weight of each step. It was one noticeable comfort in an otherwise difficult journey. Before daybreak the group settled in a wooded area.

"The time done come for us to get some rest," the woman told them. "We gonna have to take turns being the lookout. Don't eat nothing 'til we ready to head out tonight. You need dat food to keep your strength up for the journey. We're only at the southern tip of Caroline County, and we still got a ways to go."

Georgie's hunger gnawed at her, stomach to jaw. Despite the times in her life when she had refused to eat, she had never truly experienced real hunger. Whenever she felt a little peckish, she could go to the kitchen and get something to eat. Now, she didn't know where her next meal would come from.

The woman instructed them to cover themselves with leaves and branches as camouflage. She sat with her back propped against a large rock with one of the pistols in her lap. She would take the first watch.

Georgie thought about the roll in her pocket. She wanted to nibble on it but remembered the woman's warning that it would be needed to keep up her strength later. She curled up under the leaves and scratched her baldhead.

She was awakened by Lim shaking her. "It's yo turn to take watch," he said. He handed her the pistol. "Don't be afraid to use this but only if you have to."

She tried to gather her thoughts, coming out of a deep sleep. The woman was still leaning against the rock but was now sound asleep. Georgie prayed that nothing would happen while she sat watch. The thought that they could all be caught or lose their lives if she failed to act quickly or overreacted too quickly scared her. She sat tense, alert to every rustle and snap. As time wore on and the woods remained quiet, she relaxed.

She closed her eyes for what seemed like only a second. She opened them to see large black boots beside her. She fumbled for the gun, but he quickly overpowered her and took it. She had been so intent on watching what was coming up in front of her that she forgot to watch for what might come up from behind. The man's hand covered her mouth. Facing her, he looked her straight in the eye and said, "I'm a friend. Are there others?"

She struggled with him, but he was too strong. She didn't want to yell and expose the others. If she were caught due to her own carelessness, she didn't want them to be caught, too.
Again, he spoke. "Are there others? I am a *friend*."

A pistol cocked. The woman stood with her gun pointed at him. He let go of Georgie. "I'm a friend," he said.

By then, the others stirred under their leaves.

"I've come to take you to the next location. My name is Tom Johnson."

He was young and wore a large black hat and carried an even larger shotgun. Two rabbits were tied together and flung across his shoulder. The woman looked him up and down.

"I'm here in place of my daddy, Amos Johnson," the man said. "He's ailing and can't make the long walk." He handed the pistol back to Georgie as if the gesture offered proof that he could be trusted. The woman lowered hers.

"I ain't really out here hunting rabbits. I'm looking for runaways to take to the next safe house."

"I know Amos," said the woman. "I believe you."

"We can make the next safe house by morning if we leave at sunset. I'll be back for you." He looked around at the escapees. "I'll bring food." He nodded to the woman and walked away, the dead rabbits dangling against his back.

Georgie felt wary eyes on her. She had failed the group and

allowed a man to walk up behind her and take her gun, and she had not screamed to notify them of the potential danger. She had broken their trust.

"Y'all go on back to sleep," the woman instructed. And turning to Georgie, said, "You finish your watch, and wake me when the sun dips just below those trees. I'll take over then.

"I told ya," Deutney mumbled to Lim as they both returned to their sleeping spaces.

Georgie lowered her head.

The woman stepped closer. "Just so you know, *friend* means Quaker, and they help us out along the escape route."

"I ... I didn't know."

"That's all right. Now you do. Weren't no harm done."

For the rest of her watch, Georgie looked in front of her as well as behind.

Tom returned later that evening with fried rabbit. Georgie bit into the warm meat, savoring its taste and smell. Chloe sat down beside her and tore into her piece. "How you holding up?" Chloe asked, sucking her teeth.

"My feet hurt. These boots they gave me are too tight. They rubbing my toe raw."

Chloe stopped chewing. She seemed to size up Georgie. "You ain't never done no field work, have you?" Chloe raked her tongue around her mouth and spit out a piece of bone or gristle.

"Well ..."

"I thought not. There been times I'd been so glad to have a pair of shoes, I wouldn't care if they were tight or so loose they fell off. At least my feet would be covered."

Georgie didn't respond. She bit into the rabbit. Maybe she was spoiled like the other slaves said.

"Weren't your fault any more than it was mine. The white folks put us where they wanted us. Hand me your boot." Chloe scraped inside the toe of the boot with a small knife. "Now try it on."

Georgie slipped it on. "Feels some better. Thank you."

"Good." Chloe picked up her rabbit and gnawed around the

bone. "So, how you come by this woman?"

"I was about to start out running on my own, and she was waiting for me. I ran right to her. The Lord sent her at the right time. That's all I can say. How 'bout you?"

"We was all field hands. Lim and Deuntey was out chopping wood one night, and I was gathering it to carry back to the big house. She was out in the woods a-singing and a-humming low. She called us over and said we could go with her. I had heard about a woman who took slaves up north. We dropped everything and left. Deutney didn't want to go. I told him I would go without him. Since we left, he been carrying on about doing right by Massa. Hell, Massa ain't never worried about doing right by us."

"I feel bad that I left the people who love me, but I had to go. I hope they understand and can forgive me." Georgie didn't mention that one of those people was her white half-brother.

"I heard you knocked your missus around before you left." Chloe laughed and slapped her knee. "I wish I could have beat mine good. Maybe I'll meet her up in heaven. I'll knock her around up there." Chloe laughed and examined the clean rabbit bone. "I reckon that's all I can do with that." She tossed it.

After the quick meal, they headed out, traveling off the main road and stopping only a few times to rest. They came upon a tree full of hard green apples and stopped to fill their pockets. The sun peeked through, and they still had not reached their intended destination. They kept walking and hoped that no one would be on the road to spot them.

"That house up yonder," Tom whispered to Georgie. "That's the Quaker meeting house. That there quilt on the railing, with the Jacob's ladder pattern, that's the signal it's safe to approach," he said.

"Y'all wait here. I'll go on up to make sure everything is all right."

He knocked on the door. Four knocks, one knock, then another. The organization of the escape process impressed Georgie. The code words, signs, and secret symbols were known up and down the route. She thought about her own escape, how she had unknowingly started it by simply singing and humming, during her sorrow, the secret song that she didn't even know was a secret. It was that melody that led the woman to her. Most escaped slaves were caught, but those didn't know or have access to this escape process. She cautioned herself from getting too confident. After all, they were still in Virginia and far from freedom. Tom motioned to them from the front porch. They moved toward the house and were ushered in. An old man greeted the woman. Georgie later learned he was Amos.

"Sorry I couldn't meet you, but my rheumatism and neuralgia got me in a bad way," he said struggling up from the chair. "I had to send my son to fetch you."

"He done just fine. Thank you," she said.

Something cooking smelled mighty good. Georgie glimpsed the chicken and rice boiling in a stew pot on the stove. Two women, who appeared to be the man's wife and daughter, prepared the food. The group sat at a large table, and the Quaker women dished up the food. It had been several days since she'd had a hot meal. She savored every morsel and saved the large flakey biscuit to sop the juices from the plate.

Georgie wasn't accustomed to eating with field hands. It had never occurred to her that their table manners would be different until she saw the Deutney and Lim each shove an entire piece of chicken into their mouths and chew the meat and bones simultaneously. They crammed so much in, juice and saliva ran from the corners of their mouths, flowing into Lim's beard and Deutney's unshaven chin and dripping onto their plates. They used their hands, leaving the fork and spoon that had been laid out for each of them untouched. Chloe wasn't much better. At least she didn't try to eat the whole piece in one bite.

After the meal, they were directed to their sleeping quarters in the attic. The opening was a small hole in the ceiling of one of the second-floor rooms on the back of the house. They ascended a ladder one at a time into the dark space, dark except for light from the outside that crept through crevices in the boards on the side of the house. Georgie hoped Chloe's wide ass would make it through the opening. Pallets and pillows were neatly arranged on the floor, as if special guests were expected. The woman explained that they would sleep there during the day and walk again at nightfall. A thick piece of fabric was suspended over a rope and extended across one side of the room. Behind the curtain sat two slop jars. The escape process allowed no room for modesty.

"Where are we?" Asked Georgie.

"This here is called Stafford County," answered the woman. "We still got a good ways to go from here to Fairfax. A boat be waiting there to take us on up and across the Potomac."

In spite of the heavy snoring from the men, Georgie managed to get some rest. Several days had passed since she last slept on a mattress or cushion of any kind, and her body appreciated the pallets the Quaker women had prepared for them. Fortunately, it was an overcast spring day with a breeze, so the attic was not as hot as it could have been.

Just as the sun was setting, the plank covering the opening to the attic moved. Tom stuck his head up through the hole. "Everything is clear. Y'all come on down for supper, and we'll get started."

The old man was still in his chair. "It ain't much, but we got some squirrel, gravy, and biscuits fer ya. I reckon it ought to hold you through the night."

"Thank you for all you done. Your boy did a fine job fetching us, and this is some mighty good food your womenfolk done fixed. We mighty grateful," the woman said to them all.

"If I remember it right, y'all got a good walk ahead of you," said Amos. "Looks like a storm is brewing. It might be a bad one, too, but you gonna have to make it on to the next stop 'fore the sun meets you."

"Does look like bad weather is coming," said the woman. "It might slow us down some, but we'll work through it."

After supper, the escapees bid them farewell. Amos struggled to his feet and walked to the door with them. Georgie looked back and glimpsed him waving from the doorway as the group slipped into the darkness.

They had walked for some time, long enough for Georgie to feel her blister again. She remembered Chloe's word. At least she *had* shoes. The rain came and, with tempest winds, thrashed them unmercifully. The thick trees and other foliage buffered some of the gusts, but the combination of wind and rain was blinding. Georgie struggled to walk, as did the others. They formed a human chain; holding on to one another helped ensure that no one got lost. They were soaked as if they had been swimming in a river. The storm continued throughout the night letting up from time to time only to return with full fury. With each step, water squished through the soles of Georgie's boots. Her clothes hung on her like heavy wet blankets, weighing her down. By the final leg of their journey, the storm had diminished into a light drizzle. They had lost some time, but the woman believed they could still make it to the next stop before the sun got too high. The mud was deep, so they decided to walk on the road, which wasn't much better. The storm and the early hour made it unlikely anyone would see them. It was a chance they would have to take, if they expected to make it to the next stop.

Georgie kept her head down and focused on each step. Keeping pace with the group required all her energy. By the time they arrived at the next stop, the sun was up. She exhaled and surveyed her surroundings. The house was flanked by large trees, hardly noticeable sitting about a hundred yards back from the road.

"Ya see dat there statue," said the woman as she pointed to the Faithful Groomsman, a statue of a little black boy in tattered clothing designed so that a real lantern could hang from his hand.

"Yes, I see it," replied Georgie.

"Dat lantern it's holding, if the flame is lit, we can approach. If dat flame was out, it means it ain't safe, and we keep moving."

Georgie was happy to see the flame lit. The woman approached the house, used the secret knock, and the others waited for her signal to come forward. She motioned and took them behind the house to a small path that led to a barn surrounded by trees and vines.

They entered the barn and disrobed their wet clothes as far as modesty would allow. Georgie stripped down to her undergarments, the blue fabric still wrapped around her waist, a reminder of Andrew. Did he hate her for leaving? Was he grieving, thinking she might be dead? Guilt washed over her. The clapboard barn leaked and held a musty smell, but it was spacious with a loft. The early morning sunlight shown through as the weary travelers did their best to find comfort in their new surroundings.

"We best be mighty thankful for this farmer and his wife helping us out," the woman said to the escapees. They ain't Quakers like the others, but they are willing to do their part. Y'all got to be mindful that not all white folks is bad."

The man's wife appeared in the door with a bucket of hot potato soup. He brought bread.

"Thank you for all your help," said Georgie tearing off a piece of bread.

"Yes, thank you," the others murmured. All except Deutney, who remained silent.

The farmer and his wife did not have much conversation for the escapees. They delivered the food, told them where to find blankets, and said they would return later with more food. As they left, Georgie could see that it was still raining, but the sun was shining bright. She remembered Mama saying when there was both rain and bright sunshine, 'the devil is beating his wife.' She smiled and wondered how Uncle Buck was getting along without her.

The woman followed the farmer and his wife back to the main house. Georgie was grateful for the hot soup that warmed her inner core. After finishing the meal, they searched out and claimed sleeping spaces amongst their wet clothes, which were strewn about over stalls, plow handles, and a pitchfork to dry. Georgie's undergarments were still soaked. She climbed to the top of the loft and took them off, wrapped herself in a blanket and drifted off to sleep.

Although she had been asleep for several hours, it seemed like only a few minutes when Georgie woke to loud voices. The woman and Deutney were arguing. Georgie peered down from the loft. Deutney was pointing a finger at the woman and then in the direction down the road. With effort, Georgie made out their words.

"I ain't going on. I'm going back," he said. "And ain't nothing you can do to stop me. I'm cold, and I'm hungry. As long as I've been with Massa, I ain't never been hungry. I'm going back. I told you we never should have tried this," he glared at Chloe.

"I'll kill you dead 'fore I let you go back," the woman said.

His wet clothes dripping, he headed toward the door.

Chloe ran and grabbed him. "Deutney, please. We got to try. We done come this far. Freedom is waiting for us."

"Freedom?" He shoved Chloe, and she fell hard against the plow. "This is all yo doing."

The woman fired a warning shot at his feet. He turned, squared off and repeated, "I'm going back."

She fired again. The bullet entered the center of his forehead. A look of shock froze on his face as he dropped to his knees. Chloe screamed his name and crawled to his lifeless body, sobbing with her head buried in his dead chest.

The woman motioned for Lim and Ebb to carry him out back. "I told y'all when we started out, ain't no turning back. Them slave catchers will beat you till you tell them everything about the escape route. Now, I mean what I say when I tell you I'll kill every one of you 'fore I let you turn back."

The farmer rushed through the door with his rifle drawn. "What the hell happened?"

"He was trying to turn back." The woman put her pistol back in the holster.

The farmer lowered his gun. "We can't have none of that. We'll all hang if they find out about us."

Chloe stood and looked down at Deutney's body. She wiped her eyes and brushed the straw from her clothing. "I told you. I aims to be free, with or without you."

Doubt and guilt crept into Georgie, but this time she beat them back. Chloe's determination had rubbed off on her. She too was going to be free.

Even with the help of the young farmer, the burial delayed the departure. The extra time gave Georgie's clothes a little more time to dry, but they were still damp and cold when she dressed. Water still squished in her boots with each step.

Before heading out for the next stop, the woman gave them more instructions. "Tonight we got to make it on into Washington. We can breathe a little easier there because there are a lot of free Negroes, but the city is full of slave catchers. It ain't safe to stay there."

Several miles into their trip, Georgie felt sickly, and her strength seemed to fail. Each step became more difficult than the one before. She focused only on walking. To allow anything else to take her attention required energy she didn't want to waste. She developed a rhythm and continued moving in a trance-like state until her boot caught on a small root and caused her to tumble face forward. The group halted. She tried to get up but fell again.

The others came to her aid, and Chloe said, "She got a fever. Looks like it done set in bad. All that rain and then putting on wet clothes, it's a wonder we all ain't sick."

"We all need to rest a spell," said the woman. Prop her against that tree, and give her water. We got a little ways to go. Do you think you can make it?" She rested the back of her hand on Georgie's brow.

"I'll do my best, said Georgie.

"That's all I ask."

The woman assigned each one of them to take turns walking with Georgie to help support her, and they slowed their pace. Georgie's spirit sank. She had not guarded them properly when they were asleep. Now, she was slowing down the group and putting them in danger of not making it to the next stop in time. She lowered her head and labored to keep walking.

After a few more hours, she heard water brushing against a riverbank. They came to a clearing, where the woman told them to rest behind the trees.

"A boat's hidden under dem branches and leaves. We'll use it to take us up and across the Potomac."

"The Potomac? Is we free, now? Ebb asked.

"Not yet, but once we get to the other side of the river, we'll be a lot closer to freedom," said the woman. "You, come and help me get the boat."

Ebb seemed happy to be of some service. He and the woman dragged the boat to the edge of the water. The women got in, and Ebb helped Lim lift Georgie into it. They shoved it in the river and jumped in. The water was peaceful.

"Y'all keep quiet," the woman whispered. "We gonna let the water do the work for us. Just a little paddling. Them slave catchers could be anywhere."

Georgie was weak, but the excitement of being so close to freedom kept her alert. They rode in silence listening to the waves kiss the side of the boat as they approached Washington.

"I know you feeling mighty poorly chile, but we got to keep moving. It won't be much longer, now." They reached the shore, and the woman helped Georgie out of the boat. "Hide the boat in the thickets over there," she told Ebb and Lim.

"We gonna have to change our plans and get Georgie to a bed right away. A group of free Negroes and abolitionist whites got themselves a building in Washington. They send out newspapers about the evil of slavery. We gonna stop there, and they can hide us until tomorrow night."

Georgie's temperature rose. She was sweating and growing weaker by the minute. Two people were now needed to walk with her, one on each side to hold her up.

They entered the city and traveled through its pitch-black alleys. The twists and turns and stench caused Georgie to retch.

"Hold on chile. We just about there. That's the place. It's dark, but somebody ought to be there. After the break-in, dey always have somebody there at night. Looks like the street is clear. Y'all follow me."

The street lamps illuminated the buildings. She led them across the street and around to the back door. She used the handle of the pistol to knock. Four knocks, then one, then another. There was no response. Again, she knocked in the same sequence. Neither she nor the others heard the two men come up behind them, but they all heard the shotguns cock.

"Who are you? What do you want?" one of the men asked.

"It's me," the woman said. "We have a problem, friend."

The men lowered their guns. "Hold on," one of the gunmen said. He went back through the front and came through the building to open the back door.

They rushed into the dark room. One of the men lit a lamp and closed the drapes. More lamps were lit, illuminating the office they had entered.

"Dis one took sick on the way. We can't make it to the next stop 'fore daylight catches us. I didn't have nowhere else to go," the woman told the two men. She gestured toward Georgie, who was slumped in a chair.

"It's all right," he said. "Y'all go on downstairs to the cellar. We going to have to take him upstairs and put him in bed."

"That's a woman," Ebb was quick to inform them.

The two men gave a bewildered look to the woman.

"We had to disguise her," she explained. "Dey looking for her."

"One of you women better come with us to get these wet clothes off her and get her in bed," said the man.

They got Georgie in some dry bedclothes and into a warm bed. She fell asleep grateful for the reprieve. When she awoke, a woman sat beside the bed sewing. She put down her sewing and called for the two men who met them when they first arrived. The men stood in the doorway. "We can all rest easy now. The worst is over," she told them. "Lord have mercy, you gave us a scare. Your fever was so high."

Georgie looked at the three strange faces. The black men were dressed in fancy clothes like she used to see on Andrew and Mr. Gordon. She had never seen Negroes dressed that way. "Where am I?"

"You're safe with friends," said the woman caretaker. "They asked me to come and nurse you. Your sweats were so heavy we had to change the sheets twice a day. Your breathing was so weak, we sent for the white doctor who helps us out when he can."

"Where are the others?"

"They've gone on. You were too sick to travel," said one of the men.

Georgie's spirit sank. Her despair must have shown.

"It's all right," the caretaker said. "You made it to Washington. We can get you on up north. It'll be a lot easier moving one escapee than moving a group. Don't worry. You're in good hands."

"Who are you?"

"My name is Elizabeth Keckley."

"My name is William Wright," said the first man.

"My name is Georganna, but they call me Georgie."

The second man said, "And my name is Ferdinand Helton, and this is my wife, Emma."

The man's wife stepped into the room when her name was called. "Pleased to meet you, Miss Georgie," said Emma.

Georgie smiled. No one had ever called her Miss before.

"Now don't you worry none about getting on up north. That's gonna happen. Right now you need to put your mind to getting better," said Mr. Helton.

"That's right," said Elizabeth. "These colored men-folk 'round here know how to get you where you need to be. Right now, you is right where you need to be—right here with us."

Georgie rubbed her prickly head and looked down, embarrassed.

"Don't worry. It will grow back. In the meantime, I'm sewing this nice scarf for you to wear. I hope you like this material. I picked it myself, especially for you. They told me you had that blue material over there with you. So, I found something close to it in my piece-goods to make this scarf. We can tie it just right so nobody will be able to see your hair until it grows back."

Georgie realized then she had made the right decision in leaving Wilmington Manor.

The next few days of recuperation were also filled with survival lessons from her new friends. Georgie looked forward to her conversations with them.

"There is a sizable population of free Negroes here in Washington, but this city is full of slave traders and catchers," Elizabeth explained. "Enslaved Negroes live alongside free ones."

"She's right," said Mr. Wright as he passed by and overheard their conversation. "It is not unusual to see slaves chained together walking down Pennsylvania Avenue. The city has many popular gathering places for slave traders. In Georgetown, there is McCandless located on Wisconsin and M Streets. On Pennsylvania Avenue and

Seventh Streets, there is Lloyds, and another popular location is LaFayette's on F Street between Thirteenth and Fourteenth. We'll point them out to you. You make sure to steer clear of those places and never go out without your papers."

"It's a damn shame," he continued, his voice more passionate. "Everybody profits off the backs of Negroes. The buyers and the sellers profit. The hotels benefit from the many traders who need lodging. Businessmen own holding cells, charging buyers and sellers a fee to store human chattel in pens. But I tell you one thing," he stepped in the door and took a seat. "Slavery in Washington is increasing the tension between the congressmen from the north and the south. I hear northern visitors as well as those from other countries were appalled at the brutality of slavery and seeing it in the Nation's capitol, one that claims the virtues of equality, liberty, and freedom. Northern congressmen are outraged that their southern counterparts give fiery speeches about freedom while the clanging of chains from slave caravans passes by a window."

The man's anger stunned Georgie.

"I'm sorry Miss Georgie," he said. "I didn't mean to frighten you. I just get so mad when I think about how our people are treated and the hypocrisy of our government. I tell you this thing is going to end in war."

"I do have something I'd like to ask you, if you don't mind," said Georgie.

"Of course, Miss Georgie. What is it?" His tone was softer.

"That woman who brought me here never said what her name was. Who was she?"

He smiled. "You know much about the Bible?"

"I know a little."

"Well, we just call her Moses," he said.

Georgie let the name sink in. "That's strange, ain't it?" She said. "A woman called Moses."

"I'll leave you ladies to your conversation." And with that, he left.

"Actually, I do have something I'd like to discuss with you," said

Elizabeth. "I have a nice home, and you can't continue to rest here in this office. So, I'd like to know if you would like to come and live with me. It would be safer for you there, and I'd like the company."

"Y'all have been so kind to me. I don't know what to say," said Georgie.

"Just say yes. I've taken a special liking to you, and we seem to get on quite well."

Georgie agreed that they did get along quite well. Elizabeth was a light-skinned, soft-spoken elegant woman. She had shared some of her life's experiences, and she reminded Georgie of Mama. Her gentle presentation was not to be mistaken for weakness. She possessed an uncompromising internal strength and fortitude. She had survived the horrors of slavery and managed to purchase her freedom and that of her son. She once told Georgie that she witnessed the large influx of runaway slaves making their way to Washington as they traveled to points beyond. She recognized how unprepared they were for life off the plantations and wanted to help.

"Thank you, Miss Elizabeth. I'd be proud to stay with you."

"Good. Now, you get some rest, and we see about moving you tomorrow."

Georgie snuggled under the covers and marveled at her new friend. Anna, Victoria, and the female slaves at Wilmington Manor had been mostly adversarial toward her. Her only female companion had been Mama. She welcomed her budding friendship with Elizabeth.

## Chapter 27
### Summer 1860

**Edward** sat in Georgie's cabin with his injured leg propped on a footstool Andrew brought from the big house. Rays from the setting sun flooded the small cabin. Andrew stared into the empty fireplace.

"It's the middle of summer, but we could start a fire if you want." Edward said.

"Oh, yea. It's fine," responded Andrew clearly preoccupied.

"What's on your mind, Andrew? Seems like you got something to say."

Andrew rubbed his face, and his stubble sizzled. "Doc Prichard says your hip was not broken but damaged nonetheless. Says you'll always walk with a limp." He lowered his head and rubbed his palms together. "After you're done healing, he says one leg will be a little shorter than the other."

"I'm gonna be a cripple?"

"I've been trying to find the words to tell you. This is all my fault. After we argued when I caught you reading, I never should have left you where Nimrod could get to you. When I cut the rope, I couldn't hold on. I was sitting on the horse, cutting the rope and holding on to you at the same time. It all happened so fast. When the rope gave, I couldn't hold on to you, and then you fell."

"You saved my life. If you had waited a second more, I might be dead. Stop fretting. I'll be just fine."

"Doc Prichard says there are some special shoes that can help balance your walk. I've checked into ordering them."

They stayed in silence a few moments, Andrew still standing. "I'll bring you a couple more lamps from the house."

"This is a nice cabin."

"Yes it is. Daddy had it made special for Geor...gie," his voice trailed. "Oh dear God, I hope she's all right. Why did she leave me, Edward? Why?"

"I can't say. You know she wasn't in her right mind, losing her Mama and then Little Sally. She was suffering. I know you miss her. I do, too. All we can do is hope she's all right."

"You're right. It's not the same around here without her."

"I've noticed that you don't like to talk about her."

"It's too painful." Andrew turned back to the empty fireplace. "Pretty soon we gonna start strengthening your leg with short walks. All right?"

"All right." Edward was happy to change the subject from Georgie because it made Andrew unhappy to think about his loss.

"We never talked about what exactly happened the day Nimrod came after you. He sent me out to the far north end to get rid of me, but what happened next?"

"After you left he came in the house after me. 'Git down here, boy. I need you in the field with me today,' he told me. I tried to explain that I had to look after Massa Gordon because he had an awful bad case of the piles. I looked around for you. He must have known I was looking for you because he said 'He ain't here. You do what I say, and I say git on outside. I got real work for you to do.' You and me had just had the big argument the night before when you caught me reading, and I figured you had told him to come get me. You know, to teach me a lesson about staying in my place.

"I would never turn you over to him no matter how angry I was."

"I didn't know. So I followed him out and got in the back of the wagon. Ryland was there as we pulled off. As we got farther away, I wondered what type of assignment I had been given so far from everything and everyone. We went down a road that is hardly ever used, and the wagon struggled over the path's large rocks and ditches. We came to a clearing, and Nimrod slowed the wagon. I remember that big tree from when we looked for your daddy. At first, I thought I was to gather the nuts, but realized it was too early in the season. Then I saw the noose hanging from one of the branches. Nimrod reached back and hit me on the head with the butt of his pistol. I was groggy from the blow, but I remember another man came from tall brush, and the two dragged me from the back of the wagon."

Andrew balled his fists.

"The next thing I remember was the sun beating down hard and blinding me. I realized I was propped up on the back of a horse. I almost lost my balance and slid off the saddle. Nimrod grabbed me and pushed me back up. 'Naw boy, you ain't going nowhere. I been wanting to get rid of you since you got here,' he said. As my mind cleared, I was able to make sense of my situation. My hands were tied, and I had a noose around my neck. I had to think fast. My head hurt, but I was so scared, I forgot about the pain. I remembered Onie as the man we fought that night on the road, but I couldn't make the connection between him and Nimrod. Onie led the horse and wagon into some tall brush and then unhitched the horse. The noose was tight. I shifted in the saddle looking around for help while making sure I didn't slip and hang myself. 'He can't help you now,' Nimrod said. I was prepared to die, but I was determined to hurt him even if I couldn't kill him. So I spat in his face. The hock of phlegm landed on his nose and streamed down his upper lip. I spat a second time, this time right into his eye. He wiped it off with the sleeve of his shirt. 'You black mothafucker,' he called me. He walked closer to the side of the horse, which is what I hoped he'd do. I braced my right leg tight against the horse to steady myself and hold as tight as possible to the saddle. When Nimrod got close, I kicked him in the face. The heel of my boot landed square on his nose, and blood gushed from both nostrils. The next thing I remember was you holding me and taking the noose from around my neck, and the pain in my hip.

"If I ever see either one of them again, I'll kill them both," said Andrew.

"Right now, I'm just glad to be alive." Edward massaged his upper leg.

"I'm glad, too. I best be getting on back up to the house. I'll be back later." Andrew lit two candles and a kerosene lamp. "The sun is going down. You'll need some light." He kissed Edward and stroked the side of his face before heading out the door.

Edward rested, and his mind raced, pondering his predicament and worrying about Georgie. The knock on the door jarred him. "Come on in."

MawNancy stood in the threshold with her satchel in tow. Her unexpected presence shook Edward, but he tried to hide it.

"You mind if I come in?"

"MawNancy, please do."

Like a haunt, she shuffled across the floor and stood in front of him, setting her satchel on the floor with a clunk. "You mind if I sit?"

"No, ma'am. Pull that chair over and rest yourself."

She pulled the small ladder-back closer. The legs screeched against the floorboards and tried Edward's patience. She sat and gazed at his injured leg. "Still hurting?"

"Some. Mostly at night." Edward adjusted himself in the chair.

MawNancy dug into her satchel and pulled out a batch of jimson weed. "Put dat in yo bed and sleep on it. Heps the healing."

"Thank you."

"Let me see yo hip."

"It's right here." Edward shifted and pointed to the spot.

"I know whar 'tis. I need to see it. Pull down them britches." She cackled. "No need to worry 'bout dat. MawNancy dried up long time back."

Edward obliged her. She spat in the palm of each hand, rubbed them together, and placed both hands on his hip. After a minute, heat radiated from her and warmed his entire leg, calming the ache. She closed her eyes and mumbled strange words. The warmth pulsed over the whole side of his body. He didn't want her to stop.

She came out of the trance. "How dat feel?"

"It felt good. Thank you, ma'am."

She stepped back. "MawNancy ain't gonna hurt you." She dug into the satchel and handed him a jar of ointment. "Put a little of dat on yo leg each day."

"What is it?"

"Some thangs you best not know. Just do it. It'll cut the pain." She gathered her things to leave.

"MawNancy."

She turned to face him.

"Thank you."

She pointed her crooked black finger at him. "De white boy

likes you. You good fer him. I done watched him since he was born, and I ain't never seen him happy 'til you come."

Edward looked the old woman in her face, illuminated by candle-light. She appeared even more ghostly than usual.

"Dat's right. I knows all dat goes on 'round here. Don't you worry none. Yo secret is safe wid me. MawNancy only hurts those who hurt her. De boy all right by me. It's his mama and sister I goes after." MawNancy took a step toward him. "You wants me to fix them dat did this to you?"

"What do you mean?" Edward could hardly find the words to respond.

"You knows what I mean. Don't wait too long to let me know. I'll need some of Nimrod's belongings. I can get at 'em from whar ever they is. I got some of Onie's hair a long time ago. Been saving it for the right time."

"I'll think on it." Edward had never thought of using dark art to get at anybody. He always used his fists. Being a cripple, he might need to familiarize himself with other tools.

"If'n you needs me, send word, and I'll come." She studied his face. "You all right by me, boy." She cackled and walked out.

**********

Edward's healing was slow. Weeks turned into months, and the crisp of fall arrived.

"Cold weather is coming on. I can feel winter's bite in the air," said Andrew.

"It feels good," Edward responded, hobbling beside Andrew on the path.

"Each night you're walking better and better. Getting stronger, don't you think?"

"It's been a few months since the accident. I'm getting along, slowly but surely. These shoes make a difference. I'm getting along pretty well with just the aid of a cane."

"I enjoy these walks with you, Edward. I know it's to strengthen your leg, but I like listening to you. I appreciate you telling me about your days as a fighter. Those must have been hard times for you and the memories still painful."

"And now I know why you loved Aunt Daisy and Georgie so much. They protected you from your mother *and* father."

"You think you can climb the steps?" Andrew asked as they reached the house.

"Don't know. I'll try."

"Let's go up the back steps so we don't run into Anna."

Andrew seemed giddy as they walked down the hallway. Edward had not seen him this way in a long time and wondered what the fuss was about. Andrew opened his bedroom door.

Edward walked in to see two parlor chairs facing the fireplace roaring with a well-built fire. Between the two chairs was a table, and on it were two pipes prepared with fresh tobacco, and two glasses of brandy. Edward smiled as Andrew bolted the door. He turned to face Andrew who was leaning with his back against the door. They stood looking at each other. The fire crackled, and the aroma of fine tobacco sweetened the room. It had been such a long time since they touched each other. Andrew moved toward Edward. The embrace was gentle.

"I have missed you," Andrew said with his lips on Edward's ear.

Edward's cane fell to the floor. The carpet muffled the sound.

Early the next morning, Edward woke and dressed without disturbing Andrew. He roused him as he was ready to leave. Using the cane for support, he sat down on the side of the bed and began to stroke the side of Andrew's face, rough with the beard that had grown overnight.

"You leaving? What time is it?" Andrew asked.

"Hush now. Don't get up. I thought I better get out of here before the others get up and start stirring. They'll be starting breakfast soon."

Andrew propped himself up with his elbow on the pillow and his fist on the side of his face. Edward leaned in for a kiss.

"I think I'll head up to Richmond today. I want to pick up a few things and visit my friend, Jessup."

"Be careful on the road."

"I'll be fine. Don't worry. Onie and Nimrod are long gone."

"I'll see you later tonight for our evening walk," he said, using the cane to push himself up with his good leg. Edward turned and smiled then shut the door.

## Chapter 28
### October 1860 – April 1861

**Andrew** left early for his trip to Richmond. He had no particular agenda but longed to mill around in the city. Hopefully Jessup would be free for lunch. He saddled his favorite horse, a showy deep brown Arabian with a black mane and tail. Andrew had named the horse Sweet because his colors reminded him of the sweet chocolates he liked so much. He welcomed the ride, the solitude and the wind whipping against his face. Daddy taught him young to stay on good terms with good business acquaintances, so he made his usual stop to see Mr. Horsley, who was standing on the porch of the warehouse as he rode up. "Good morning, Mr. Horsley." Andrew dismounted and offered a big grin and an outstretched hand.

"Howdy, Andrew. How are you? You're riding a mighty fine animal."

"Thank you. I thought I'd let him stretch his legs today. I'm fine. And you?"

"I tell you, I don't feel good about nothing no more. Them goddamned Yankees meddling in our affairs again."

"What's got you all fired up?" The usually mild-mannered man's face filled with anger and fear.

"Oh, I don't know. That Abraham Lincoln and them abolitionists are about to destroy this country and our way of life. I declare, the way they go on and on about the slaves. This thing is gonna end up in a war, I tell you. You mark my words."

Andrew didn't want to ask too many questions and seem uninformed; Wilmington Manor kept him somewhat isolated from the rest of the world. He hadn't heard much about the issue since Jim Shelton had mentioned something about it several months ago. He certainly didn't realize that the tension between the southern states and their northern counterparts might be escalating to war. He would ask Jessup to fill him in on the latest news.

Andrew offered only, "I sure hope there's not a war," and continued, "I just stopped in to say hello. I'm on my way up to the bank to see my friend Jessup."

"All right, Andrew. You take care. Tell yo daddy I asked about him."

"I will."

Andrew mounted Sweet and headed to the bank. A strange tension had overtaken Richmond. The inviting air had been replaced with an angry mean spirit. Passersby didn't offer their usual welcoming greeting. Instead, Andrew received glares of suspicion and anger. He wished he'd ridden a more modest horse. He left Sweet hitched to the post in front of the iron-front bank and went in to see if Jessup was working.

"I'm here to see Mr. Tillman," he told the clerk.

"Go right on back Mr. Gordon. He's in his office."

"Andrew." A big grin spread across Jessup's face as he stood to greet him. "This is a nice surprise. What brings you up to Richmond?"

"I needed to get away from the place for a spell. I hope you have time to join me for lunch."

"I'll make time, old friend."

"Good. Let's go someplace nice. How about the Spotswood Hotel? It's not too far."

The grand ambiance of the Spotswood, its carved wood and elegant trappings, were just the backdrop Andrew craved today. It had been a long time since he had partaken of fine hotel dining and relaxed conversation with a peer. He had forgotten how much he enjoyed and missed it.

"What's all this crazy talk about a war between the states," Andrew whispered as they took their seats.

"I don't know, Andrew. Things seem to be getting outta hand." The North's objection to slavery is strengthening, and the South is digging in its heels."

"Is war a real possibility?"

"I hope not, but I just don't know. Tensions are high, and I don't see no compromise in sight. But before we get hung up in all that, I've got something I been wanting to tell you," said Jessup.

"Oh. What is it?"

"I done met someone special."

"Really. Well, tell me, which one of these blueblood debutants has finally hooked you?" Andrew asked with a bit of sarcasm.

"Don't be absurd, Andrew. You know that's not meant for me. I've met a man named Thelton Taylor. He's from Philadelphia, but he comes to town quite regular on business. We spend time together when he's here. I met him at Maggie's. I keep telling you that ya need to come on out with me sometime."

"I see," Andrew said.

"I was hoping you might be a little more excited for me. After all, who else could I tell?"

"I'm sorry. You know I'm not comfortable talking about those things, especially in public. Someone might hear us," he whispered.

"Andrew," Jessup sighed, settled back into his chair, and stretched out his long legs. "You work too hard. You've got to accept this thing as a part of who you are and start to enjoy ya life. Come on out to Miss Maggie's with me Friday night."

Andrew wanted to tell him about Edward but wasn't sure Jessup would understand. "I'm truly glad for you, Jessup. I doubt I can make it out this Friday. Being without an overseer is keeping me tied to the plantation."

"All right. Well, you're here now. So, let's order something good and expensive," Jessup smiled and pulled a cigar from his coat pocket.

Andrew scanned the menu. "I think I'll have the catfish."

"I feel like having the roasted chicken." Jessup lit his cigar.

They laughed, talked, ate, and drank. Andrew finished the main course and then ordered dessert. "I miss these times with you."

"Let's promise that at least once a month, maybe more, we'll get together like this."

"It's a promise." Andrew extended his hand, and they shook on it.

They stood in the doorway saying their goodbyes, but kept finding more to discuss.

"I'll send around a man I know. He might make a good overseer. He's been in town for about a month. We hired him to clean up around the bank, but he's made for outdoor work."

"Send him around. I'm sure I can use the help."

Andrew put his arm around Jessup's shoulder "I'm truly happy for you and Mr. Taylor. One day we'll talk more on this."

"I'm glad to hear you say it. Like I said, I don't have anyone else with whom I can share these things."

**\*\*\*\*\*\*\*\*\***

Christmas Eve arrived without trimming or fuss. Andrew joined Anna for dinner that evening, one of the few times he had shared a meal with her in the past several months.

"I can't believe its Christmas Eve," Andrew said, breaking the silence in the near empty room. "It seems like I was just up in Richmond having lunch with Jessup. But that's now been two months. We agreed to get together regularly, even shook on it, but I haven't been able to get up to Richmond much."

"Yes, it is Christmas Eve," she responded, uninterested. "Any news about the search?"

"No. There's been no word of Georgie's capture."

"They'll get her. I know they will."

"Anna, you've got to move on. Sitting here day after day plotting your revenge on Georgie is not good for you. It has been months."

"You would say that. She was your favorite. You're probably glad she got away. You might have helped her, for all I know. Well, I've got a whipping planned for her when they bring her back. She'll pray for death by the time I'm finished. And you will not get in my way. I don't care what it takes, I want her back. Increase the reward. Have more handbills made." Anna pounded the table.

"Of course, Anna," Andrew replied. "I'll also have a notice published again in the *Richmond Examiner*. But we need to be careful about the attention we give this thing. News is circulating among our friends. Any news about rebelling slaves sheds a negative light on us, our family name. Folks might think I have no control over my own plantation. People are still talking about that Nat Turner, and don't forget Gabriel Prosser.  So, we got to be careful about how much attention we put on Georgie's escape."

"You're just trying to protect her."  I want her back, and I want her punished.  I don't care who knows about it.  I'm not worried about your precious reputation."

Andrew pitied Anna, isolated in her own world with anger and revenge as her only friends.  He changed the subject.  "The new overseer I hired seems to be getting along quite well.  He's a good and honest man.  I'm glad Jessup recommended him."  He tried to find a subject that might interest her.

"I've seen him."

"We should call on some of our friends tomorrow.  I know we would be unexpected, but I'm sure we would be welcome at Jim and Caroline Shelton's."

"I have no friends, and I have no interest in visiting anyone at Christmas or any other day of the year."

"All right."

They finished the meal in silence.

"Well, I'm done here," Andrew said, standing to leave.  "Have a good evening, and Merry Christmas to you."

He grabbed his coat, hat, and a package from his office and headed to Edward's cabin.

"Merry Christmas," he said as he cracked open the door to see Edward standing by the fire warming his backsides.

"Same to you," said Edward with a big grin.

"Did you eat?"  Andrew asked.

"I did.  Mary and Sadie sent me something from the kitchen."

"I was thinking over dinner just now," he said pulling off his coat, "that their cooking skills have improved a little."

"A little.  They will never compare to Aunt Daisy."

"Open this," Andrew said handing Edward the package.
He snapped the twine and folded back the brown paper.  "Socks and long johns.  Just what I need for these long winter days.  Thank you.  I got something here for you, too.  I couldn't find anything to wrap it in."

Edward handed Andrew a small chest with a hinged top.

"This is very nice. What is it?"

"It's for storing things."

"You made this? When did you find the time?"

"Do you like it?"

"I do. Very much. You stained it the same color as my bed." Andrew ran his hand over the chest. "What are these carvings?"

"They're things special to you. See here on top, this is your pipe. And on the front, Sweet, your favorite horse. I thought you could keep our pipes and tobacco in it."

"The detail is amazing. How long did you work on this?"

"I started on it a few months ago while I was sitting around waiting for my leg to heal."

"Such a thoughtful gift; thank you."

**********

Winter moved at a crawl. Edward got well enough to resume his duties taking care of Daddy. On the long cold nights, he and Andrew kept each other warm.

Spring finally arrived, and Andrew welcomed the work it brought. The soft earth was ready for seed, and the house ready for a thorough cleaning. Anna oversaw the household chores, and Andrew surveyed the grounds, supervising the spring planting.

"Mr. Gordon, we just about done plowing that last section on the northern acreage," said Jasper, the new overseer.

"That's good. You've caught on to everything around here real well. I sure need the help, especially this time of year."

"Thank you, Mr. Gordon. I'm glad to be here," he said taking off his hat to wipe sweat.

He was a thin man with only a few wisps of blond hair on the top of his head. Not much older than Andrew, he looked like he'd had a life of hard work. The lines in his face were etched far too deep for a man his age.

"I think I saw your sister the other day. She was sitting looking out the window. I waved to her, but I guess she didn't see me. I done seen her sitting there a few times."

"Yea, she does that a lot. She's waiting on someone."

"I see."

"Don't pay her no mind. She doesn't have a lot to fill her days. She may ask you to post a letter for her from time to time. She's taken to writing to a few of her old friends, most of whom are married now. But if she asks you, try to oblige her."

"I know you've met Edward. He cares for Daddy. He had an accident some time back and has gotten as good as he is gonna get. He walks with a limp, but he gets along just fine. Like we discussed when you first got here, you leave him to me."

"All right, Mr. Gordon. Everything at Wilmington seems just fine to me."

"I'm going in. I've got some papers to complete. If you need me, I'll be in the dining room. Come on in."

Andrew headed back to the house. He'd just settled into his accounting when Jessup entered the house in a frenzy without even knocking or being announced. "Andrew! Andrew where are you?" Jessup shouted.

"I just came in from the field." Andrew met him in the foyer. "What's all the ruckus?"

"I need you to come to a meeting in Richmond tonight. It's mighty important. All the men of influence must be heard." Jessup shook and searched for words. It was not like him at all.

"Come into the dining room. Calm down. "Here, drink this." Andrew poured a shot of whiskey. "Now, tell me what's going on."

Between gulps and trying to catch his breath, Jessup filled in Andrew. "They done fired on Fort Sumpter." He put the glass on the table and stared at Andrew, bouncing his legs. "We are now at war with our northern brothers, and there is talk of secession. Jefferson Davis; or one of his representatives; or somebody; hell, I don't know is speaking tonight. We must be there."

The mention of Davis' name took Andrew back to the Christmas of over a year ago. He stared at the chair Mr. Davis had sat in for dinner and recalled his fiery comments about seceding from the Union. "Let me saddle my horse, and we can ride up together."

They entered Richmond, where excitement bordered on hysteria. Young men hollered in the streets, firing pistols and yelling about walloping Yankees.

"Oh my God," said Jessup.

"Look at these fools. They have no idea what war really means," said Andrew.

"The meeting is over yonder. Let's tie the horses and go on over," said Jessup.

"Do you think it would help if we spoke against this idea of secession?"

"Let's see how things go. They're so fired up, they may turn on us if we speak against it."

They pressed through a crowd of planters, businessmen, and politicians gathered to discuss the future of the Commonwealth. They listened to speeches and arguments, and watched scuffles break out for more than two hours. It looked like it could go on all night long. "I've heard and seen enough. I'm ready to head out," said Andrew.

They struggled to make their way through the standing-room-only crowd to the exit. For a while they walked in silence. While there was disagreement among those gathered at the meeting, it was clear that the majority wanted to break away from the Union and align with other seceding southern states. Andrew pondered what he'd heard and wondered what Jessup thought.

"I'm not sure if secession is the right thing to do," Jessup said, breaking their silent walk.

"I'm pretty sure it is the wrong thing to do, but it seems that most of them have their minds made up. They're thinking with their pride and not with their heads," Andrew answered.

"I'm scared of what all of this means and what it could do to us and this country."

"I'm scared, too."

## Chapter 29
## September 1861

**Edward** settled Old Man Gordon into bed. On most nights, his snoring wasn't too much of a disturbance, and Edward managed to get some sleep, that is, when he wasn't in Andrew's bed.

The door opened, and Andrew peered in. "Is he sleeping yet?"

"Like always, he starts to snore before his head hits the pillow."

"You coming over?" Andrew whispered. He smiled and raised his eyebrows.

"In about an hour. I want to make sure he's in a good sleep. We can't have him waking up and trying to get out."

"It seems like you've got him into a pretty good routine."

"Always breakfast first. In case he spills it or tries to spit it on me, I don't have to clean him up twice. After breakfast, I wash, shave, and dress him. He seems to enjoy our walks around the grounds each day. Sometimes I think he knows what's happening around him but just can't find the words."

Andrew entered the room and closed the door. "Make sure Anna doesn't see you cross the hall. I'm glad you thought to oil the door hinges."

"The carpets silence our footsteps, but I take my shoes off anyway."

Andrew stepped closer, slipped his arm around Edward's waist, and nuzzled his head on Edward's neck. "Make it a half hour." He smiled and headed out of the room.

Edward kicked off his shoes and stretched out on the cot. He awakened from an unintended sleep and bolted upright, longing to be with Andrew and worried he had kept him waiting. He sat up and was met with a hard slap across the face. Old Man Gordon was on him and about to land another blow. Edward fought him off, but the old man was strong. His eyes were wild, and the two tussled, the old man making animal grunts and snorts. Hunks of white spit gathered in the corners of his shriveled mouth. With a powerful thrust, Edward rolled them both off the cot and onto the floor. He straddled the old man and held him down.

Andrew opened the door. "What the hell…"

"He just went off and came after me. Help me keep him down until the spell passes."

They held the old man down until his grunts and fits subsided. He grew limp, meek as a lamb. They got him up and put him back in bed. Exhausted, Edward fell back on his cot.

Andrew eased down beside him. "Anything like that ever happen before?"

"No. This was a first."

"Good Lord." Andrew rubbed the back of his neck. "I hope we don't have to start tying him down."

Edward didn't say anything. He massaged the side of his face. "You all right?"

"Yea. He got me good."

Andrew stroked the mark with the back of his hand.

Edward jerked away. "Careful. The door's open."

"Anna's down the hall asleep," Andrew sighed. "I reckon you ought to stay with him tonight. We'll get together tomorrow. Anna is spending a few days with Cousin Betsey. We'll have the house to ourselves, assuming Daddy acts right." Andrew headed back to his room.

The next day the old man behaved, humble and quiet as usual. He didn't spit out the tasteless corn mush Sadie and Mary prepared for his breakfast. Edward sampled it once, after Doc Prichard prescribed it, and understood why the old man didn't like it. The day followed the routine Edward had worked hard to establish, and promptly at eight o'clock, he settled Mr. Gordon into bed and then slipped across the hall.

Edward and Andrew made up for the lovemaking they had missed the night before. Edward enjoyed exploring every inch of Andrew's muscular body. They lay in each other's arms listening to the quiet, Edward circling his finger around Andrew's thick chest hairs, while keeping an ear honed for movement in the old man's room. Dark thoughts intruded Edward's mind, as they often did. How could he feel this way about this man – a slave holder –his *owner?* He should have been long gone into his freedom, but now his bad leg prevented any thought of escape. The questions beat at him the most after they made love. It was becoming harder to quash them. "I better get back." He kissed Andrew and headed across the hall.

The old man was sitting in the chair waiting for him when he opened the door.

"Not again," Edward mumbled. He backed out of the room and opened Andrew's door. "I need you. He's up again."

They entered the room where the old man sat staring at them. Edward readied for a fight, but the old man didn't move. He looked straight at Andrew. "Your mama thought I was too stupid to know what she was doing. Fucking that Jim Williams and giving me his bastard to bring up as my own."

The old man's eyes had the same wild look Edward witnessed the night before. "I walloped his ass good up in Richmond. Tore that damn saloon apart. He'll go to his grave wearing marks I put on him."

"You don't know what you're saying, Daddy."

The old man kept talking. "Making a fool out of me. You and everybody 'round here knows she ain't my child. Just look at her. That's why I did it every time I got the chance. Slaves, whores, black, white – it didn't matter to me. I fucked them all. Y'all thought I'd come down early to sit with that bitch before ya'll put her in the grave. I didn't give a damn about sitting with her. I came down to tell her to rot in hell."

"Daddy, don't do this."

The old man rubbed his hands. "Don't bury me next to her." He pointed at Andrew. "I want some peace in my grave."

He stood and walked to the foot of the bed and wrapped his hands around the thick walnut bedpost and began thrusting back and forth. "Yea. This is how I fucked 'em. They liked every inch of me. That whore up in Richmond, now, she knew how to please a man. Not like your mama, all dry and tight. Then there was that other one who knew how to use her mouth. And the slaves, don't leave them out. Oh, goddamn." He slapped the bedpost and kept at it. "I always enjoyed my trips to their cabins. Then there was Dai.." The old man stopped moving.

Andrew reached for his daddy.

Edward blocked him. "I know it's hard to watch, but let him purge. He needs the truth to come out."

The old man hugged the bedpost, and tears started streaming from his eyes. "Daisy. Oh, my Daisy." He collapsed to his knees, blubbering like a baby. "Daisy. I want to be buried next to Daisy. You took me to see her lying in that box, her head wrapped in that bloody rag. Where's Georgie? She hasn't been to see me. Where's my baby? Promise me, Andrew. Bury me next to Daisy."

"I promise, Daddy." Andrew's voice cracked.

The next two days the old man slept. The morning of the third day Edward visited Andrew in his office. "You might want to come up and sit with your daddy. His breathing is hard. It's the death rattle. Ain't gonna be much longer."

For two hours, Andrew and Edward sat quietly in the room. The old man's labored breathing slowed and eventually came to a stop, peaceful.

Andrew walked to his daddy's bedside and kissed his forehead. "Goodbye, Daddy." Andrew wiped his eyes. "I better go in town and ask Mr. Martin to bring out a coffin."

Later that day, Mr. Martin arrived with the box. Edward and Andrew assisted him in dressing the old man and putting him in his final resting place. They sat the coffin up in the front parlor and waited for friends and family to call. Edward spent the remainder of the day orchestrating the kitchen and sampling what Mary and Sadie had prepared to serve the guests, making sure it was fit to be served.

The old man had a rich history of cultivating loyal business acquaintances and friends. Word got out that John Gordon had gone to meet his maker, and for the next two days, the house overflowed with folks coming to offer their condolences. Andrew greeted each guest and took special care to say the burial would be private.

The morning of the third day, Reverend Grandison arrived early. "Good morning, Andrew. I'm so sorry to hear about your father."

"Thank you, Reverend. I'm glad you are able to join us."

Grandison walked over to view the remains. Mr. Martin fussed with flowers and the black bunting around the bier.

"Mr. Martin we'll need your hearse to carry the coffin out to the burial site," said Andrew.

"Of course. But if I recall from your mother's service, it's not too far of a walk. We could use some of your workers as pallbearers."

"We're not using the same site."

"I see. I'll go out and pull the hearse closer."

"Thank you." Andrew turned back to Grandison. "Reverend, we're taking two other wagons out to the burial site. You can ride with me. Edward, you and Luther follow in the second wagon."

They loaded up and processed out, with Andrew's wagon leading the way followed by the hearse then by Edward and Luther.

Andrew led them up to the northern end of the plantation where a rugged stand of trees on a hill unfolded before them, thick with full-grown pines, maples, and magnolias.

Luther and Edward bounced along the bumpy road. Edward slowed the wagon when they got to the foot of the hill. "That's a mighty big hole," said Luther.

The thick green trees were just beginning to show a hint of their fall colors. Edward stretched out his bad leg, comforted by the morning sun. Up on a hill, with a view overlooking Wilmington Manor, a grave had been dug. Ryland and a few other slaves stood with shovels and picks.

The group of mourners walked up the slight incline, careful not to lose their footing under the grass still wet with dew. At the top, Edward was surprised to find two coffins already in the hole. But the surprise lasted only a few seconds. Andrew loved is daddy and wanted him to have his peace. Ryland assisted by a few other slaves, unloaded the old man, struggled to get the coffin up the hill, and set it beside the hole. Mr. Martin and Reverend Grandison exchanged strange glances.

"We're ready," said Andrew.

"Is your sister not joining us?" Reverend Grandison asked.

"She is not. Unfortunately, she is quite grief-stricken. You may proceed."

The reverend started with a song. He bellowed out some tune

about glory in the great by-and-by.  After which he recited the Twenty-Third Psalm.  He talked about the old man's life and ended with the Lord's Prayer.  After a moment of silence, they lowered the remains of old man Gordon into the hole and began to cover the three coffins with loose earth.

Late that evening, Edward rested in his cabin.  He looked forward to the time of day when he could put up his leg and massage his hip.  The slight tap on the door he recognized as Andrew's.  "Come on in."

Andrew entered, bolted the door, and exhaled.  "Everybody's gone, and the house is quiet again."

"I'm surprised Anna didn't object to you burying your daddy out on that hill.  Did she know you were going to dig up Aunt Daisy and Little Sally and put them with him?"

"She wanted him in the family plot next to mother.  I made Daddy a promise on his dying bed, and I intended to keep it.  Anna's so fond of calling me the lord and master of Wilmington Manor.  I reminded her that I am indeed the lord and master, and that it was my decision, not hers.  She refused to attend.  I let her know it would take place with or without her."

Edward walked over to Andrew and put his arms around him.  "You know this means there is no longer a reason for me to be in the big house.  Everyone will be watching you and me."

"I know.  There's a bed here.  We'll just have to make good use of it."  Andrew pulled his shirt out, unbuttoned it, and led Edward over to the bed.

## Chapter 30
### June 1862

**Andrew** took a long draw on his pipe and exhaled heavy smoke through his nostrils. A breeze came through the cabin's window, and the smoke floated off and disappeared.

"You mighty quiet tonight," said Edward.

"Got a lot on my mind. The war has been going on for over a year now. Don't seem like there's an end in sight. Davis says he's determined to preserve the South, and Lincoln is equally determined to keep the Union intact. The stakes are mighty high."

"Folks didn't think it was gonna last this long, right?" Edward paused to rub his hip. "I'm glad we spend time here instead of up at the house. Anna is always watching me."

Andrew chuckled, but his laughter turned to lament. "I don't know what I'm gonna do. It's hard to get the tools and other supplies needed to keep this place running. Mostly everything is going toward the war effort. I don't have the labor. Most of our slaves done run off to join the Union or just plain run off." It was more than the managing of the plantation that weighed on him. "Edward," Andrew ventured.

"Yeah."

"War changes everything. There are no more cotillion balls or barbeques. Not that I liked those things, but I guess I liked knowing those sorts of things, our traditions, carried on. I guess you don't miss something until you no longer have it."

"I wouldn't know about all that," said Edward.

"I'm sorry. That was insensitive of me."

"What else? There's something else."

"I should do more to help. My military training could surely benefit the Confederate Army. But that would mean leaving, and, although I trust the new overseer much more than I did Nimrod, the idea of leaving Jasper and Anna in charge of the plantation worries me. This whole place will go down without proper leadership. Then, there's you. Us."

"What do you want me to say? You want to leave me to risk getting killed in a war to keep me and my people enslaved. What do

you want me to say, Andrew?  You going on about missing cotillions.
I'm a slave — a cripple slave.  How much pity do you expect me to give
you?"

"Get out your book," Andrew said, hoping that would get his
mind off his worries and cut the tension.  He had warmed to the idea of
Edward gaining some literacy skills, and in their private moments, had
been helping Edward with reading and writing.  "I've got something
special I want you to read."

"What is it?"

"Let's practice reading, then I'll show you."

After they had spent time sounding out new words, making
sentences, and turning sentences into full paragraphs, Andrew put away
the book.  "Now look at this."  He pulled a folded paper from his pocket
and handed it to Edward.

Edward looked at the words and began to read.  "You defy low-
gic."

"Logic," Andrew corrected.

Edward started again.  *"You defy logic.  On the coldest day, you
warm me like the hottest ember.  In the noonday heat, you cool and
refresh.  In the middle of a tempest, you calm and protect me.  I cannot
be without you."*  He looked up to Andrew.  "What is this?"

"I wrote it for you.  We've been reading other people's poetry.  I
thought I would try writing my own."  He touched the paper.  "This
describes how I feel about you.  I hope you won't leave me like Georgie
did."

Edward stood.  "This is very nice.  I don't know what to say."

Andrew paced nervously.  "What I was trying to say earlier is
that so much has changed so quickly, starting with Georgie leaving.  And
then Daddy died.  We buried Uncle Buck last week.  In the middle of it
all, Zula had her little boy.  I can tell she's thinking about leaving.  It's
not the parties I'm missing, it's the folks who cared about me."

"I'm sorry I got angry, but sometimes I don't think you
understand how I feel."

"I do understand.  More than you know."  Andrew pulled a
packet from his pocket.  "These are for you."  He handed Edward the

envelope.

"What's this?"

"Your papers. You're a free man now. If I decide to go fight, I want to make sure you have your freedom."

Edward limped toward him with his arms stretched wide. They embraced.

"Please forgive me for not doing it sooner. I was afraid you would leave me like Georgie did."

"Thank you."

"I ho ... ho ... ho ... hope." He tried again. "I hope you'll s ... s ... s ...." Edward rubbed Andrew's neck. "I hope you'll stay," Andrew forced it out.

"I'll stay," said Edward."

**\*\*\*\*\*\*\*\*\***

The noon sun was high in the cloudless sky. It was a warm day, not blistering hot like the days that were sure to come. With the workforce diminished, Andrew hoed, chopped, and hauled alongside the remaining slaves. He'd worked up a good sweat. He would need a bath later, or he'd smell as bad as Nimrod. He came in from the fields for his mid-day meal. Luther had set up a small table in the foyer and was polishing silver.

"Shine 'em up good," said Andrew. "If this war doesn't end soon, we may need to sell the whole lot." He picked up a candelabra and examined it. "Whose horse is that out front?"

"There's a gentlemen here to see you — a Confederate soldier. He's waiting in the front parlor."

"What?"

"Ya sah. He say his name is Captain Emmett DePriest. Said something about you and sharpshooting."

"He's an old classmate of mine. I best go see what this is all about." Andrew let out a heavy sigh. "It's hot as hell, and I'm tired," he mumbled. "I want some food and rest right about now."

Andrew walked into the parlor to find Emmett seated with proper military posture, his back straight against the back of the chair, knees together, and hat resting in his lap. Andrew wondered just how long he had been in that position. But that was Emmett, military to the core. In spite of his crisp pose, Emmett looked haggard and tired. He had always been a scrawny bean pole of a man. But now sunken cheeks and deep-set eyes revealed exhaustion and possibly hunger.

"Emmett," Andrew said, walking briskly toward him extending his hand. "This is a surprise. What are you doing in Charles City?"

"I'm here on official business," Emmett replied, shaking Andrew's hand. "I am a Captain with Company H of the Twenty-third Regiment Virginia Infantry, also known as the Richmond Sharpshooters. We need your help. I'm sure you know this war is going on much longer than expected. The North has proven to be a worthy opponent. The losses have been great on both sides, and there is no end in sight. I suspect it will get much worse before it is finally over."

Andrew sat listening intently to Emmett's wartime tales, while the sour feeling of envy took up residence in his stomach. Emmett had not changed since their college days. He got right to the point of his visit. He asked no questions about wellbeing, family life, or any of the minor pleasantries of polite conversation.

"We are forming an elite fighting unit made up of enlisted men. Because of your skills and training at military school, I have been granted special permission to recruit you and others like you. Are you still as skilled with a firearm as you used to be?"

"I am," Andrew responded.

"Will you join up with us? I can't promise that you'll be exclusively with the Sharpshooters, but we need you on our side nonetheless. You might spend some time training pickets and new recruits."

"I'll need to discuss it with my sister and the overseer. We'll have to develop a plan to keep the plantation running."

"I understand. But please keep in mind that if we lose this war, you will have no plantation left to run. I'll need an answer within three days. We head out to join up with another company near Ashland on Thursday morning. Our intelligence tells us that the Yankee Army is planning to take Richmond soon, and we plan to stop them. We leave from Tredegar Ironworks at 9:00 a.m. sharp. If you decide to join us, you'll need this."

He handed Andrew a parcel wrapped in brown paper tied with twine. Andrew snapped the twine, and the paper unfolded to reveal a gray uniform. He ran his hand across the material.

"I guessed at your size from what I remembered of you from military school. I hope it fits. You'll get other supplies later. They're issuing us brand new P1858 Enfield rifle muskets," Emmett rose. "I've got to be going."

"Won't you stay and have something to eat? You know you're more than welcome."

"No, thank you. I've got plenty to do today."

They walked to the front porch in awkward silence. Emmett descended the steps and mounted his horse.

"Thank you for thinking of me."

"Hope to see you Thursday," Emmett said and rode off.

Andrew had not been given much time to think about the proposal, but he had made his decision the moment he ran his hand across the uniform. Seeing it and knowing it was for him brought back all the memories he had suppressed about his glory days at military school. After graduation, Emmett made a career in the military while Andrew returned home to run the plantation. It was shortly after graduation when Daddy's health began to fail. Mother had shamed him into rejecting the teaching position the school had offered. He rarely thought about those days. They only served to remind him that he had become nothing more than a glorified overseer.

Persuading Anna to leave her place at the window, to give up her lookout for Georgie and take on more responsibilities, was not as difficult as Andrew thought it would be. He showed her the books and instructed her on the accounting procedures, like how to record major property changes, and she seemed eager to learn. He gave Jasper special instructions on how to run the plantation and care for the few remaining slaves. He wrote a new will freeing all the slaves upon his death, mandating the sale of the plantation, and establishing a trust for Anna that would be managed by Jessup.

All affairs were in order except for one final detail. In the early evening, Andrew lit a kerosene lamp, poured a brandy, and carried them to the library. He pulled the ledger off the shelf, its weight landing on the desk with a heavy thud. The war had fueled rumors of freedom among the slaves, and many had run off to join the army or had headed north, depleting his labor force to almost nothing. He recorded losses almost daily. He flipped to the page with Georgie's name and stared at it as he had many times before, unable to write the words he knew belonged beside her name. He stood with both hands on the desk, still staring. Finally, he moaned and wrote "dead." A tear fell and splattered on the page blurring the freshly scrawled ink.

The night before Andrew left, he and Edward lay in Andrew's bed. They both remained awake, locked in each other's arms. It might be the last time they would be together. Andrew suspected Edward was thinking the same thing. Andrew rubbed his face against the black curly hair on Edward's chest. He kissed his chest and torso. He slid down Edward's body and took him deep into his mouth. The thick foreskin stroked the roof of his mouth. After a while, Edward pulled back and repositioned himself to reciprocate. The activity was intended to be foreplay, but the intensity of it resulted in a climax for both.

Night drifted into morning. Andrew rose, washed and put on the gray trousers, frock coat, and hat. He was about to button the jacket, when Edward limped over. "Let me finish that for you."

Edward pushed the brass buttons through the holes, tears streaming down his face. Large teardrops splattered on his hands, wetting the shiny buttons and dampening the heavy fabric. Andrew tried to fight back tears but could not. They wiped their faces and embraced once more.

Andrew went down the front stairs, and Edward went down the back. Zula, with her little boy, Simon on her hip, along with Sadie, Mary, Ryland, and Jasper, had all gathered to see him off. Anna stood on the front porch, too. Ryland had saddled and brought one of the horses from the stable for him. Edward walked around from the back of the house to join the group. Andrew exchanged a few words with Anna and stepped down into the group.

"Thank y'all for coming out to see me off. Take care of each other, and I'll be back as soon as I can." Andrew mounted, saluted the group, stole a final look at Edward, and rode off.

He rode to Richmond under a clear morning sky, crisp blue spattered with white clouds. A warm breeze refreshed. A horse coming from behind startled him, like the night he and Edward were jumped by Onie and Clayton. He reached for his pistol only to realize that it was Jessup trying to catch him.

"Jessup! What you doing riding like a wild man? You fixing to get yourself shot coming up behind me like that."

"I'm sorry Andrew, but I had to catch you before ya got off. I stopped by the plantation this morning, and Anna told me I'd missed you. I'll handle the trust for Anna and all the arrangements you made in your will. Don't you worry about nothing. Just get your ass back here safe."

"I'm gonna do the best I can."

"The main reason I wanted to catch you was to give ya this." He reached in his satchel, pulled out a book, and handed it to Andrew. "I want you to read this when ya can. This here poet, Walt Whitman, is trying to change things. You know, change the way people think about us. He wants to let the world know that it's all right for a man to, well, you know — care for another man."

Andrew looked at the book. *"Leaves of Grass.* I'm not familiar with it." He put the book in his satchel. "Thank you, Jessup. You have no idea what this means to me. When I get back, we've got to have a good meal, some good whiskey, and a long talk. There's a lot I want to tell you."

Jessup smiled, and the two rode into Richmond together.

* * * * * * * * * *

Andrew and Jessup parted ways when they entered Richmond.

"I've got to head on over to Tredegar," said Andrew.

"Remember what I told you." Jessup leaned over and cupped his hand around the back of Andrew's neck. "Keep your ass safe."

"I'm gonna try."

They tipped their hats and separated.

Andrew arrived at Tredegar and was greeted by Emmett and two other soldiers seated at a makeshift table – a door supported by two barrels – registering new recruits. Wagons, soldiers, civilians, horses, and farm animals scurried all around them kicking up dust. The random movement, coupled with the heat and stench, suggested complete chaos.

Emmett walked over to where Andrew was tying his horse. "Glad you decided to join us. Come on over to the table. You'll need to sign these papers."

Andrew examined the papers and signed in the places Emmett pointed out.

"Your rank will be corporal. I hope you understand. You have not been involved with the military since we left school, and there have been men fighting since this war began. We have to promote them first, when we can."

Andrew was hoping for a higher rank. One step above a private didn't match his training or expertise. "I understand." He tried to hide his disappointment.

"For the time being, you'll be with me. Like I said when we met, I got special permission to recruit you and a few others. We'll be training sharpshooters and pickets, and will coordinate top secret operations and special reconnaissance. There may be opportunities for promotion in the future. Things have changed since I spoke with you. We will not be heading to Ashland right away."

"I'll do whatever I can." Andrew wanted to loosen his collar. The uniform had already become uncomfortably warm.

"Walk with me for spell." Emmett motioned toward a private area. "We need you and thousands more like you. McCellan has taken Norfolk and Yorktown, and he's positioning himself to do the same in Richmond. We must defend our capital. Richmond must not fall to the Yankees like New Orleans."

"I read about the fight for Norfolk." Andrew ran his finger around the top of his coat collar to offer some momentary relief.

"It is hot, and these uniforms were not designed for comfort," said Emmett. "But surely you remember that from our days in military school."

"I do."

Emmett had always been distant and strictly military in his dealings, but there was a bite in his tone. Maybe it was the stress of the war.

Emmett continued, "Our Merrimack could hold her own against the Yankee's Monitor. The two have battled several times, always a stalemate. When we lost Norfolk, the Yankees destroyed the Merrimack. The James River is now open to Federal Navy ships. We must hold Richmond." Emmett's eyes widened, and the pitch of his voice rose. "The General Assembly and Mayor Mayo have vowed to defend this city at all costs." He clenched his fists.

\*\*\*\*\*\*\*\*\*\*

The next day, Andrew awakened early to the morning bugle, coupled with Emmett's shouts.

"Everyone up! We're moving out," the officer repeated the same orders several times.

By the scant pink light on the horizon, he thought it to be around 6:00 in the morning. And if he had his days right, today was June 26. The message being spread throughout camp was to gather right away. Emmett's urgency created a sense of chaos. Andrew forwent his usual morning cleaning ritual. Instead, he rinsed his mouth with water from his canteen and splashed some on his face. He ate a few pieces of hardtack and washed it down with some of cook's tepid coffee. He and the other men stumbled into formation, some still organizing their clothes and equipment.

"We're heading to Mechanicsville Turnpike to serve as skirmishers and sharp shooters." Emmett rubbed his hands as he walked to and fro in front of *his men*. He seemed to like referring to them that way. "Their pickets are an inexperienced bunch, and Lee wants men like us to shore up the line and turn back the Yankees."

"Pickets?" A voice yelled from the back. "I thought we were an elite group here for special assignments. Any green recruit can be a picket."

"We're here to follow orders, soldier," Emmett retorted.

Andrew was disappointed in his first assignment. It was nothing like Emmett described when he recruited him.

The bitter after taste of coffee still hung in his mouth when they finally headed out at 8:00. The morning sun warmed him as he mounted up and began trotting in formation with the regiment. The pleasant weather brought out the civilians. Curious on-lookers and newspaper reporters gathered on the hillsides of Richmond to see and hear what they could of the battle.

After a long march in the heat, the troops arrived at an open green space where it was suspected the Yankees would launch their attack. The area was peaceful, surrounded by stands of full-grown trees with thick undergrowth. It seemed a better place for artists and poets to gather than armies equipped with cannons and rifles.

"Lookie up yonder. Ain't that General Lee *and* President Davis under that thar tree?" It was not the first time the undisciplined hillbilly had broken formation and order. His high-pitched Appalachian accent grated on Andrew's nerves. He was baffled as to how the man had gotten into this elite group.

"He must be one hell of a good shooter," Andrew reasoned.

"Get back in line, Private," Emmett yelled at the young recruit.

General Lee was positioned on a higher ground to see the battle. Andrew was surprised to see President Davis, with a small group of civilians, most likely staffers, in such close proximity to the fighting.

"Take position in those thickets and trees," Emmett barked out. "And wait for my orders to fire."

Andrew and the other sharpshooters headed for cover. Hours passed before blue uniforms were seen advancing toward them. The time had come; a sour taste crept from Andrew's stomach to the back of his throat – bile. It made him want to retch. Several times he tried swallowing, but his mouth was dry. His body trembled, and his teeth chattered. His undergarments were drenched with sweat and clung to his clammy skin. Death waited ahead. Was this his last hour, or would he survive another day? He couldn't let fear control him. He could not let Emmett see the fear. He swallowed again and aimed, ready for battle.

"Fire!" Emmett's command came.

They let lose a barrage against the Yankees, who took cover and fired back. Bullets whizzed through the air like rain, snapping tree limbs and penetrating flesh. The smell of gunpowder filled the air. The fighting commenced in fits and starts. After a while, the Yankees fell back, and for a few hours, Andrew's little corner of the battle was quiet. But from the sound of it, fierce fighting pounded all around them, up and down the Chickahominy River.

Early dusk snuck up with an unwelcome dimness, just as Emmett came crawling on his belly through the thickets to reach Andrew. "We've been ordered back to Richmond."

"Back to Richmond?"

"Yes. It's too quiet here. There is concern that McClellan may have circled around to take the city. The defenses around the city are thin, because we're spread out between here and Ashland."

They crawled through the undergrowth together, headed back to the field headquarters. The rifle, saber, and heavy uniform weighed on Andrew, but he did not want to appear weak.

Emmett stood. "We're in the clear. Let's hurry."

"I don't think so. We're still mighty close to ..." The sniper bullet cut through Emmett's chest. He fell onto Andrew. "Emmett! Oh God. Hold on. I'll get you to safety." Andrew crouched over and stayed low, pulling Emmett behind a tree. Blood poured from his chest-wound.

"It's no use Andrew. Go on. Send the stretcher bearers for me. I'm done for anyway. It's bad. I can tell. It seems you've beaten me yet again." Emmett grimaced and propped himself up beside the tree.

"Beaten you?"

Another bullet whizzed by. A Yankee sniper had them in his crosshairs. Andrew stayed low behind the tree.

"You were always better, better at debate, recitation, sharpshooting, hand-to-hand combat. Everything." Emmett coughed and spat up blood. "The school wanted you to teach instead of me. Everything I wanted you got and turned your back on."

"Not now Emmett. We have to get you to the field hospital."

He licked his lips and pointed his finger. "I wanted to be like you. Wanted you to like me." Emmett smiled, showing blood-soaked teeth, his voice fading. "You and your friends couldn't be bothered with a poor hick like me, but I wanted you."

"I didn't know. We can talk about these things later." Andrew wiped the blood from Emmett's mouth.

Another bullet whizzed through the trees. The day's final rays of sunlight reflected off metal on a rifle exposing a Yankee sniper positioned in the thick branches in a grove of trees. Andrew aimed and pulled the trigger. The sniper fell from the tree and hit the hard ground with a thud.

"You've beat me at everything, even soldiering. You stayed down." His voice was no more than a whisper.

"Hold on, Emmett. I'll get you to safety."

Emmett touched Andrew on the side of his face. "Stay safe." His arm fell limp, and he slumped over.

Andrew closed Emmett's eyes and crawled to safety.

Andrew began the solemn trip back to Richmond with the regiment. The full moon offered some illumination in the pitch-black night. The repetition of horses' hooves clopping and soldiers marching numbed Andrew's senses.

Captain Austin Franklin trotted up beside him. "You're Corporal Gordon, right?"

"That's right, sir."

"I know Emmett DePriest recruited you personally. I'm sorry to hear about his death."

"Yes. It's a tremendous loss." Andrew did not feel much like conversation.

"Out of the two hundred and ten men who left with us this morning, little more than half of us are returning. The known dead total fifty-one, twenty-seven are wounded, and eight unaccounted for. So many dead and wounded. The Richmond women's clubs and organizations have come forth to offer care and comfort as best they can, and the Virginia Central Depot has been transformed into an initial care station to assess the needs of the wounded and sick. The city is overwhelmed. I wonder if our leaders know what the hell they're doing."

Someone called for Captain Franklin. "You take care of yourself, Gordon. We're glad to have you." He galloped ahead.

Andrew made the remainder of the trip in silence, grateful for the solitude. Hours later, it hit him that he had killed a man. Maybe more than one, but he couldn't know for certain, when everyone around him was shooting, too. The Yankee sniper's death was deliberate. He aimed, fired, and watched him fall. He was somebody's son, husband, or father.

As the troops entered the city limits and made their way farther in, Andrew witnessed the heart of Richmond in utter panic. Families were leaving in droves, their wagons filled with belongings. One horse had dropped dead on Broad Street leaving what appeared to be a father, mother, and three children stranded with their wagon load of possessions. The Yankees were within striking distance, and word had circulated. Groups of emboldened slaves were leaving on their own and seemed to be daring anyone to stop them. Worst was the number of sick, wounded, and dead soldiers piling up in the streets. Churches and lodges had been converted into hospitals and morgues, and they were piled high with bodies.

Captain Franklin led the troops up Broad Street, then over to Grace Street to Saint John's Church. They remained in formation along with other soldiers gathered in the churchyard, spilling into the streets. Three higher-ranking officers addressed the troops with fiery speeches of encouragement and briefings on the status of the battle. Choosing Saint Johns, the site of Patrick Henry's famous "Give Me Liberty or Give Me Death" speech, for this gathering was no mistake. It was the perfect location for rallying southern causes.

Andrew and his small regiment were to stand ready to defend Richmond's northern border, along with others spread out around the city protecting other key entry points. Being away from the line of battle, he could at least sleep tonight without the worry of sniper fire. Emmett's dying words haunted him. "What did he mean, he *wanted* me?" Sure, he had made friends with Ross McCabe and Joe Carter, but they had so much in common. Theirs was a natural friendship. He had not intended to slight Emmett. "He wanted me and wanted to be like me." Andrew drifted off to sleep replaying Emmett's final words.

The next day, Andrew and his regiment were granted some rest. He spent the day cleaning his weapons and started a letter home. "Dear Anna," was as far as he could get. That night, the soldiers were divided up in pairs to patrol the streets. If there was a God, Andrew believed he was laughing at him right now – the Appalachian was assigned as Andrew's patrolling partner.

"Make sure you boys stick together and watch out for each other, Captain Franklin instructed them.

"Not to worry, sir." The hillbilly turned to Andrew. "I'll stick to you like a tick on a hound dog. Yes siree, like stank to a shithouse."

"That's reassuring," said Andrew.

The Appalachian extended his hand to Andrew. "I'm Cody, sir. Cody Clatterbaugh."

"Nice to meet you, Clatterbaugh."

They headed out for their two-hour patrol. The first hour passed, uneventful. Cody was not as annoying as Andrew had anticipated. Two drunks staggered out of a local tavern and ran into them, knocking into Andrew's right shoulder. One of them confronted Andrew. "You boys done heard the news?" His balance was wobbly, but he held tight to a bottle.

"What news?" Andrew was in a sour disposition and had no patience for this man's folly."

"Our boys done pushed the Yankees back across the Chickahominy," the second drunk slurred out.

"Well, that is good news." Andrew brightened. Maybe this wasn't a lost cause after all. As the good news spread, cheers and jubilation erupted.

The following day, Captain Franklin gathered the regiment and gave a report from the front lines: "The fighting is still going on. McClellan is retreating, but Lee is chasing him, determined to split and humiliate the Army of the Potomac. Unfortunately, it's not going as planned. The Yankees may be in retreat, but they're putting up a good

fight as they leave. There was a fierce battle yesterday at Glendale. Our boys couldn't overtake them. More wounded will arrive today."

Andrew spent the day patrolling the streets of Richmond with Cody. The regiment gathered that evening at Tredegar. Many shared their frustration that they had not seen more of the battle. "The news is not good," Captain Franklin relayed to them.

"Is the Yanks headed back to Richmond, sir?" Cody yelled from the back. "We is ready to whoop 'em if they comes thisa way."

"No," Captain Franklin continued, "they're still in retreat, but they put up a tremendous fight at Malvern Hill today. They outgunned us at every turn. Today's battle cost us over five thousand men, dead or wounded. We may be called to the front tomorrow."

The call to the front did not come. Andrew and his fellow soldiers waited in formation in the driving rain while Captain Franklin barked out orders. "McClellan has marched his army along the banks of the James River. They headed east and have taken refuge at Harrison's Landing," We're to stay here until further notice."

With the Yankees' retreat and no activity over the next days, it became apparent that the campaign to take Richmond had ended in victory for the Confederates. But there was no celebration in the streets of Richmond, no brass bands playing songs of jubilation. The only parade was the constant flow of ambulances and dead wagons delivering more bodies.

*July 4, 1862*

*Dear Anna,*

*I've been in my first fight. It seems General George McClellan had been gathering the Army of the Potomac south of the Chickahominy River. His plan was to take Richmond. We beat them back. Lasting from June 25, to McClellan's retreat on July 1, they have already named this The Seven Days Battle. The fighting was heavy around Richmond, from Ashland to Charles City. I hope you are well and all at Wilmington Manor are untouched by this terrible war. The human carnage is like nothing I have seen before. Thousands from the North and our beloved South are wounded or dead. Let everyone there know that I am safe.*

*Andrew*

He was proud that he had been a part of the defense of Richmond.  He hoped somehow Daddy was proud of him, too.

## Chapter 31
### September 1862

**Maggie** and Jessup sat on the settee watching the last customers leave. She was tired and glad to have the place quiet. Now, she could kick off her shoes, relax and enjoy some time with her closest friend.

Jessup repositioned himself, leaned back, and stretched out his legs. "This war has changed everything, but your business don't seem to be hurting."

"We keep busy, but it's more soldiers than businessmen nowadays. Did you enjoy your time with that officer the other night?"

"I'm still smiling, ain't I?"

"You little devil."

"Yes. Yes indeed I am." Jessup drew on his cigar and blew a smoke ring. "I commend you on your ability to bring together the Union and Confederate sympathizers under one roof. And right here in the capital of the Confederacy. You've created a neutral territory, Miss Maggie."

"Peace is a requirement to get in," she said. "If a solider, or anyone for that matter, wants to spend time with one of my girls, he's got to leave the war at the door. Actually, I think they need and welcome a place where war and killing are not part of the agenda and folks with differing opinions can once again be friends."

"Many a night I have watched two men leave here engaged in friendly conversation, head off in different directions on foot or on horseback, probably both knowing that someday they might face each other on opposite sides of a battle line. This war is something, I tell ya." He stubbed out the cigar.

"Well, darling," she said, taking the combs from her golden hair and letting it fall below her shoulders, "I think I'm gonna call it a night and go on up to bed."

"All right, Maggie. I'll see ya later. I may sleep here tonight."

"You know your room is always ready." She leaned over and kissed him on his cheek. "Other than my girls, you are the only family I have. This place may be a whore house, but it's my home. I want you to feel at home here, too."

"Thank you, Maggie. I think of you as family, too. You and Andrew are the only two people who really know and accept me."

"You have been talking about this Andrew Gordon for years, and I have never met him," she said, changing her tone to a more light-hearted timbre.

"He's off fighting in the war right now, but when he returns, I'll make sure the two of you meet."

"You must." She winked, turned, and headed up the staircase.

She sat at her dressing table looking at herself in the mirror, unbuttoning her dress. The reflection of the Confederate officer in her bed watching surprised her. "I didn't know you were here. I would have come up sooner."

"It's all right. I came up the back stairs like always," he said. "I knew you'd get here eventually."

She was tired and wanted to sleep. She pulled back the covers to crawl up next to him and found him already naked.

He stroked his hard cock, raised his eyebrows, and smirked, "See what being in the same room with you does to me."

"Good Lord," she thought. "Being a good prostitute means being a good actress."

After it was over she nuzzled her head into the well of his arm and rubbed his chest. "Are you keeping yourself safe – away from the battle lines?"

"My men and I have been in a few battles, but so far I'm still alive." He chuckled.

"I'm glad." She kissed his nipple and played with his chest hairs. "You lost many men?"

"A few."

She stroked his cock. "When will you be back here again?"

"I'll be around awhile. My men and I are to guard a supply train coming through Richmond tomorrow night. Lee is mighty low on supplies."

"Will you be fighting alongside Lee?"

"No. We're just guarding the train while it's here." He pulled her closer. "So, once it pulls off, maybe I'll make my way back around here."

"What time will you come? I'll have some food ready and make sure no one is around."

"The train is scheduled to pull out at eleven o'clock. I'll come around after that."

She gave his cock a gentle squeeze. "I look forward to it."

They slept for a few hours, and then she roused him, "You need to get back before they accuse you of desertion."

"My best friend knows where I am. He won't squeal. The others think I'm out looking for deserters. But you're right, I should head back."

He dressed, and she walked with him to the back stairs. She kissed him and whispered, "See you tomorrow after eleven o'clock." She watched him ride off and hurried back to her room and rummaged for a disguise. She needed to dress like a grieving widow.

She had seen her Union contacts a few days earlier, wearing her black, feathered hat, a sign that she had nothing to report; therefore, they had not rendezvoused. Now she had important news. She donned a simple black dress, black hooded cape, strapped a holster around her waist, and headed out. She mounted, directing the horse toward the damp streets of Richmond, blanked in a light fog. A few drunks staggered out of bars and taverns. At the funeral parlor, Maggie dismounted and walked the horse to the alley. With the war dead coming in droves, the Martin brothers had opened a second parlor in the heart of Richmond. She lowered her head, walked to the front door, and knocked lightly.

Hurley opened the door. "Yes ma'am. Can I help you?"

She raised her head. He ushered her inside.

"You coming here is risky," he warned.

"Too important. Are we alone?"

"Yes. Other than them." He motioned toward the three dead Confederate soldiers in open coffins. "And they ain't talking."

"Lee's supply train is leaving Richmond at 11:00 tomorrow night. He's desperate for supplies. We've got to either intercept the train or blow the tracks.  Whatever it takes."

"We'll see what we can do.  You be careful getting back.  You got a gun?"

"Always."  She opened her cloak to expose her holster and gun. "I'll be in touch."  Maggie turned and darted back into the darkness.

## Chapter 32
### June 1863

**Edward** removed the loose board from his cabin floor and pulled out the hidden sack. His reading and writing books, the tablet and pencil, all gifts from Andrew were safe inside. He opened the book and practiced reading a few sentences, just as he and Andrew had done so many nights. This would distract him. This would be his night's work. Someday, he hoped to show Andrew in person how much he had learned, how hard he had worked, during their separation.

He opened the tablet to begin a new word. He carefully wrote out an "H" just as a small knock on the door made him jump.

"Who's there? Just a minute." Edward stuffed everything back into the sack, dropped the bundle into the opening in the floor, and replaced the missing plank. He shuffled to the door. "I said, 'Who's there?'"

"It's me, Ryland." The small voice barely penetrated the pine door.

Edward opened it to find Ryland standing with a big grin on his face. "What's wrong?"

"Ain't nothing wrong. I come to tell you that I'm leaving at sun up. You coming with me?"

Edward was not ready to make that decision. "Let me think on it. I'll let you know in the morning."

That morning, Edward brushed the briars of Sweet's tail. The horse switched and twitched and seemed out of sorts. Maybe he missed Andrew, too. Edward stepped out of the stable to catch a breath of fresh air and rest for a spell. Thoughts of leaving pressed on him, but he fought off those ideas. With each passing day, though, it was harder to push them aside. Now, Ryland's offer was forcing him to make a decision. For all he knew, Andrew could be one of the missing or unknown dead. Edward returned to his work in the stable and continued the battle in his mind. Daytime work had a way of keeping him distracted. The nights taunted him the worst.

Ryland walked in with a few things tied in a tattered blanket. "You coming with me? It was official on January 1, 1863." He emphasized the year. "That was months ago. We free. I waited for winter to end. Now the weather done broke, and I'm done here. I want to see what freedom is really like. If I'm lucky, I'll find Georgie. Come with me. Ain't nothing here for us."

"I thought about it. I'll give it a few more months, and then I may leave, too. Good luck to you, Ryland. I hope you find her."

"Good luck to you, too. I hope he comes back." Ryland extended his hand to Edward.

Ryland's reference to Andrew shook Edward. He wondered what Ryland knew and who else might know.

"It seems like I'm leaving just in time," said Ryland.

"Why you say that?"

"Look over yonder."

A small band of mounted Confederate soldiers rode toward the main house. One man dismounted and nearly knocked the door down with his pounding.

"That can't be good," said Ryland.

"You reckon they bringing news about Andrew?"

## Chapter 33
### June to October 1863

**Anna** jumped, startled by the loud knock. She looked up from the ledger, her heart beating faster with each bang. She turned to Jasper, who had pushed the ledger forward and moved to a window. "What in heaven's name could all that be?" Anna asked.

He shrugged. "I can't see from here."

They left the office together and walked out into the foyer, standing behind the door while Luther opened it.

"I'm looking for the owner of this here plantation," a man said in a deep southern drawl.

"That would be Miss Anna. I'll get her. Who shall I say is calling?"

"Don't you worry none about who I am, boy. You just fetch her."

Anna stepped into the doorway to face a Confederate officer. "My name is Anna Gordon. I'm in charge of this plantation while my brother is off fighting. And, I thank you not to order my slaves around. What can I do for you?"

"In case you don't know, they ain't slaves now." He stepped inside.

"I don't' recall inviting you in," she said.

He took another step in.

"Now just a minute," said Jasper, walking up.

"It's all right, Jasper," said Anna stepping between the two men. "State your business here."

"My name is Sergeant Brent Toddy, and I'm here on official business on behalf of the Confederate Army. This property is being temporarily confiscated by the Army for use as a command post."

Anna stared at the man's badges, trying to understand his statement. She had heard of the Army taking over public buildings for such purposes, but never private homes. "This is an outrage," she responded, trying to remain composed. "You are not taking over my home, and I am certainly not leaving it!"

"Yes, Miss Gordon, we are taking it, and yes, you are leaving this main house.  You and anyone else living here can take up lodging in one of your slave houses.  You may continue to go about your business as long as you *and* your niggers stay out of our way."  His cadence methodical and slow, the man reeked of arrogance and contempt.

Anna turned to Jasper.  "Go up to Richmond, and tell Jessup what's going on.  See if he can stop this," she said.

"A brigade will be here by noon tomorrow," the Sergeant informed her.  "Others may follow.  There's nothing your Jessup or anyone else can do about it."

"We'll see if indeed you move in at noon tomorrow, but until then, I'm still the mistress of this house.  And I'll thank you kindly to get off my property."

Sergeant Toddy reached for the door, turned and said, "We'll be taking over the entire house."

"The lady told you to get out," said Jasper.

With that, Toddy left the porch, remounted and rode off with his small band of soldiers.  He glanced back as he turned his horse onto the main drive.

That evening, Jasper returned from Richmond.  "I'm sorry, Anna, but you will have to temporarily relinquish the main house to the Army.  This place is secluded.  Its proximity to the James River makes it ideal for Confederate spies to travel here.  That's why they want to use it."

"How long will this go on," she asked.

"I don't know.  Jessup agreed to write a letter to the Secretary of War, James Seddon, to see if this can be avoided or at least kept to a minimum."

The next morning, Anna gathered a few of her necessary belongings and carried them to the cabin that had been occupied by Georgie.  It was the best available.  Zula, Sadie, and Mary helped her move.  Edward moved into the cabin that had been occupied by Uncle Buck and Aunt Daisy.

"They coming, Miss Anna," Luther announced.

Anna parted the curtain to see the approaching brigade.  It was a little after the noon hour when Sergeant Toddy rode up with three other officers, just as he had promised.  Soldiers, too numerous to count, followed on foot and horseback. Anna moved to the front porch, where an officer dismounted and greeted her.

"Miss Gordon, my name is Colonel Garrison DuBerry. I want to thank you for allowing us to use your home," he said cordially.

"*Allow*? It doesn't appear to me that I have much choice, now do I, Colonel DuBerry," she said, glaring at Sergeant Toddy.

"Your sacrifice will benefit our effort to preserve the South. It will not go unnoticed."

"This is our family home. My brother is a soldier in the war, and we intend to return to it someday. I do hope that you and your men will respect it as such."

"We will Miss Gordon. I assure you we will."

She stepped aside, and Colonel DuBerry and his officers entered Wilmington Manor. At that moment, Anna became an outsider in her own home.

The soldiers set up camp on the far southern grounds of the plantation. More infantry and wagons arrived. Tents, horses, and men now covered the undeveloped acreage. Colonel DuBerry and other high-ranking officers resided in the main house. An endless stream of men came and went, both day and night.

Anna adjusted to her new lifestyle faster than she expected. Even with an endless stream of men coming and going, she settled into a routine after a few weeks. She had even started to look forward to dealing with Sergeant Toddy. Their interactions, though minimal, had moved from outright dislike for each other to cordial greetings. She accepted that he was a soldier following orders and fighting a war, a war worth fighting.

Being in the presence of so many men reminded her of what was missing in her life. Her thoughts on the matter grew from mere recognition that she was a spinster to a longing and aching for the affections of a man. She watched them line up for drills, take their meals, clean their rifles, and dig latrines. From a distance, she watched them at the end of the day when they took off their shirts and loosened their trousers and was stirred by their male physiques. At night she touched herself in ways she had not done before. Her voyeurism provided only a temporary satisfaction.

One evening, at sunset, Anna walked behind the kitchen on her way back to her cabin. Sergeant Toddy stood beside a tree facing her but with his head down, relieving himself. Startled, Anna stood very still, transfixed on his anatomy. She had never seen that part of a man before. Even now, she could hear her mother telling her that proper ladies did not discuss such things. The woman would roll over in her grave if she could see her daughter entranced with the yellow stream pouring forth and the instrument from which it flowed. Toddy looked up, and Anna lowered her head in embarrassment.

"Please forgive me. I didn't know anyone was back here. I'm so sorry," she said and hurried away, her cheeks hot.

The next night, she sat up counting what little money they had and trying to decide what supplies to buy and what to forgo, when a soft knock came to the door. She hid the Confederate notes in a tin box and placed it under some papers on a shelf. Andrew would be furious when he found out she had mortgaged the plantation. She couldn't imagine who would call on her at night but hoped an unexpected visitor would help take her mind off financial woes. She opened the door to Sergeant Toddy.

"Why, Officer Toddy. What may I do for you? Am I to be evicted from this place, too?"

"I beg your pardon, Miss Gordon. I don't mean to disturb you, but I would like a moment of your time."

She hesitated.

"May I come in?"

"Why, yes. Please do."

They sat at the small table in silence for a moment. He fiddled with his hands.

"I meant you no disrespect," he finally muttered. "War can change a man. I've been hardened. I've forgotten my manners. I hope that my own sister would have behaved as you did, if she were in the same situation. My mother would be ashamed of me. Please forgive me. I do hope you are comfortable here."

"Well, I'm as comfortable as I can be, considering the

circumstances."

"It's a well-built cabin. Not like the others."

"Yes. My daddy had it built special for …" The thought of Georgie caused her throat to close up for a moment. She refocused on the man seated before her.

"This war has disrupted so much."

"Yes it has. This used to be a very successful tobacco plantation. Now we plant and harvest more potatoes than anything else. They're a cheap food source. I find myself in the kitchen cooking or hoeing in the field." The comment reminded her of her cracked and calloused hands. She concealed them in the folds of her dress.

"I best be getting back. May I call on you again?"

Warmth rose from deep within her core and lit her cheeks. It had been so long since a man had uttered such words to her. She recalled earlier flirtations with young men at special gatherings. The Honeysuckle Cotillion, the Winter Ball, the Dogwood Ball, and the Magnolia Dance — all seemed like ancient history now.

"Yes. You may call again. I would like that very much."

He rose to leave and bowed. She held the wide pleats in the skirt of her dirty dress and curtseyed to him. Such formal behavior seemed ridiculous considering their desperate conditions, but the mannerisms reminded her of a time she hoped would return.

His visit increased the longing she had already been experiencing. That night she replayed his company in her mind. She delighted in his masculinity and the velvet tone of his voice, the way the knot in his throat moved when he spoke. She pictured the cleft in his chin, his nose, and his thick eyebrows. She pleasured herself to these images, then drifted off into a blissful sleep on damp sheets.

For the next few days, she and Officer Toddy exchanged pleasant glances, while lustful thoughts simmered within her. Three nights later a soft knock returned to Anna's door. Her heart jumped; she hoped it was him. Since his first visit, she had taken to brushing and neatly pinning her hair each night in hopes that he might come again.

She opened the door, and Toddy stepped inside, closing the door behind him. They dismissed any formal greeting. "I won't force myself. I promise. I won't. I'll leave right now if you want me to. But, if you want, I'll stay awhile," he said.

His breath smelled of whiskey and tobacco, making her head swim. Blood pulsed through her every fiber, and the hunger between her legs seemed unbearable. She released her inhibitions and took a step toward him. "I want you to stay."

He pressed his lips against hers, gently at first then harder with more passion. She received his tongue. She wrapped her arms around him and held him tight, exploring the strength of his back, his broad shoulders, and strong arms. He kissed her neck, his whiskers rough on her skin. She liked it, felt starved for all the pleasures he brought. With clumsy fingers, he unbuttoned the row of tiny buttons that ran down her back. She stepped back from his embrace and removed the dress. He kicked off his boots and removed his shirt and trousers. She looked up, and there it was protruding forth. She stared at it wondering what it would be like to touch it. He moved toward her, and she embraced his naked body, it pressing against her thigh. Dizzy with nerves and passion, she was grateful when he led her to the bed. He climbed on top of her and entered her slowly. It hurt at first, but the searing pain eventually turned to pleasure. The deeper he pushed inside, the better it felt. His pleasure – his moans and the soft look on his face – excited her. She ran her hands through his thick hair pulling him closer, while sweat trickled down his unshaven face and onto hers. The sinews of his arms and legs tightened and stretched with every movement. Anna reveled in his body and power and then in his exhaustion from their climax. He stayed on top of her until their heavy breathing returned to normal. He rolled off and lay next to her, but she wanted more.

Anna looked forward to their late night and very early morning trysts. At least twice a week Toddy came to her cabin, and she eagerly received him. They kept careful watch to ensure no one saw him enter her cabin, both for her reputation and his. The risk was worth it. He had awakened a part of her that had lain dormant. She vowed it would never be suppressed again.

The summer passed, and early fall brought on a landscape painted with leaves of yellow, red, and orange. She snuggled close to

Toddy in the mid-October chill. "We got orders to move out," he said. "They came yesterday. We pull out day after tomorrow. A turn of events in the war requires our attention elsewhere."

"I knew this would not last forever. Isn't it funny? I fought as hard as I could to keep you from coming. Now, I'm sad to see you go. Will you come back?" She hoped she didn't sound desperate.

"I will. If you'll have me." He got up and pulled on his clothes.

"Of course I'll have you. I'll wait for you and pray for your safety." She put on her robe and knotted the belt then paused searching for the right words. "I want you to know that I have never done anything like this before. You were the first. I won't bring any shame to you and your family."

"I know. I shall return and speak to your brother."

She parted the curtain and looked out.

"No one is around," she whispered and opened the door.

"I'll try to come by one more time before we leave."

He kissed her quickly and exited.

Anna peered through the window to watch him walk away. She gasped to see MawNancy standing in the darkness watching him leave, too.

## Chapter 34
## October 1863 to January 1864

**Anna** looked at her reflection in the full-length mirror while Zula buttoned the back of her dress.

"My goodness, Miss Anna, you getting big," said Zula.

The words hung like an iron weight ready to crush Anna at any moment. It had been only a few weeks since the army pulled out. She was glad to be back in her home but missed the secret moments she shared with Sergeant Toddy. Anna fought back tears. Zula hadn't meant to point out the obvious, but she had. The slight discomfort in her breasts, her loss of appetite and general malaise, she had attributed to her recent and new sexual activity. And to missing Sergeant Toddy. She had convinced herself she was out of sorts, love sick. But after a few days, she went to see Doc Prichard. It pained her to tell him about her time with Sergeant Toddy.

"The baby should be here in the summer," Doc Prichard told her. "Probably late June or early July. You should write this young man and tell him he's got to come back and do right by you."

"I'll write him," she said, tears streaming down her cheeks.

"Anna, these things happen more than you know. You'll be all right."

"But, my reputation." She wept.

"Well, if he comes back, and y'all get married, no one will have to know."

She wrote Sergeant Toddy and informed him of his pending fatherhood and insisted that he return immediately. After a few weeks, she grew anxious that he had not returned her letter, or shown up prepared to take his wedding vows. After a few more weeks, her letter was returned with a note informing her that Sergeant Toddy had been killed in the Battle of Rappahannock Station on November 7, 1863.

She decided to conceal the pregnancy as long as possible, and when her belly was completely swollen, she would keep away from the public. After the child was born, she would pass it off as Zula's. That way she would have the child near her but would not have her pristine reputation stained among friends and family. The war would end eventually, and *everything* would go back to the way it used to be. And when it did, she would be ready to resume her place in proper society.

Winter came early and stayed long. Christmas went by, mostly unacknowledged. The January cold stung Anna's face as she walked across the yard to the kitchen. She stood in the doorway for a minute staring at Zula, Mary, and Sadie. She was not accustomed to asking for help. The people to whom she was so used to giving orders could now easily refuse her request. She searched for the right words. "I know y'all are free to leave here whenever you choose. I don't know what your plans are, and you don't have to tell me anything if you don't want to." She paused for a reaction, but the three women said nothing. "You see." She hesitated, took a deep breath, and let it out. "I'm fixing to have a baby." She made the statement if she were revealing new information to them. Deep in her heart, she knew they had known for as long as she had. "So, I'd be mighty grateful if y'all would stay on here at least until after the baby is born."

"We was thinking we would leave after the winter, but I reckon we can stay on till after the baby comes," said Mary. "What y'all think?" She gestured to the two other women.

"I'll stay," said Zula.

"I will, too," said Sadie.

"Thank you." Anna sat down for a moment, exhausted in relief. She decided that if Zula left, she would claim the child was a light-skinned Negro she was raising out of the goodness of her heart because the parents had run off and left it.

Winter eased, and spring came. Anna ventured out only as far as the front porch to enjoy the warm days after such long, cold ones. When she spotted visitors coming, she would retreat into the house before they could get a good look at her. Anna spent most of her time rocking on the porch. Her only real visitor was Dr. Prichard, who made weekly visits. Jasper, Edward, and the few male Negroes who were still around spent their time out in the fields.

Mary brought her a cup of tea. "Where's my china cup? Why'd you put the tea in this tin cup?

"That china cup's cracked at the bottom. You said it made the tea taste funny," Mary reminded.

"That's the only real piece of china I've got left. I had to sell it all and the silver just to keep this place running. I don't mind the taste. That cup was from my mother's favorite pattern. I want to use it."

**********

Zula scrubbed sheets in the wash house. Busy with her chore but a thousand miles away in her mind, she froze when MawNancy walked in. The sight of the old crone – her curved back and toothless smile – unsettled most, but rendered Zula immobile.

"I needs yo hep," MawNancy said, leaning on her walking stick for support.

"You need something? You need something washed, MawNancy?" Zula stammered.

"Dat ain't de kind of hep I'm a talking 'bout." She grinned, exposing her gums and the imprint of where teeth used to be. "I needs some of her hair."

Zula saw no reason to get on MawNancy's bad side. "All right, I'll get you what you need."

As she was leaving, MawNancy turned and smiled. "Chile, MawNancy ain't gonna never hurt you."

A few days later, Zula found MawNancy seated outside her cabin rocking and looking far off. Zula was happy not to have to knock on the door, or worse, go inside the cabin rumored to be filled with spells and human bones. Hesitant to disturb the old woman from her sleep, Zula stared at her, about to call out her name. On her own, as if she sensed Zula's presence, MawNancy opened her eyes. Zula delivered the clump of hair folded in handkerchief. MawNancy accepted it with a nod. The exchange was done in silence. Zula turned to walk away when MawNancy asked, "When dat baby gonna come?"

Word of the pregnancy had leaked out, despite Anna's best efforts to hide it. Zula thought it best not to lie. "Doc Prichard say June or July."

MawNancy reached into her apron pocket and pulled out a bottle of brown liquid. Black, leathery skin wrapped each finger of the hardened hand. It was a silent plea for an accomplice. Zula took the bottle. In the exchange, her hand touched MawNancy's and sent chills down her spine. Those hands had mixed death potions for a long time, their lifeless skin now calloused to the poisons and unfit for human touch.

"Put a little drop of dat in her food. Not too much," MawNancy warned. "Just a drop. Can't let her know its thar. Don't need to be every day. Just every now and den."

"But ..."

MawNancy held up a finger, silencing Zula. "She de cause of Daisy's suffering and death. My old friend, Daisy. Now, she got to pay."

Zula agreed to the old woman's request, not knowing exactly why she had. It may have been out of fear of MawNancy, vengeance for Aunt Daisy, dislike of Anna, or a combination of all three.

## Chapter 35
## February to April 1864

**Andrew** spent the morning digging the foundation for his hut –
his new home – with the Army of Northern Virginia. Like the others
around him as far as the eye could see, the shanty would be a log hut
with a shelter tent roof. He stopped for a moment to catch his breath
and take a swig from his canteen. Despite the February cold that blew
across the Rappahannock River, he was sweating.

"How do?" said a soldier as he walked up and dropped his gear.
"They told me I'm to share this space with you. I'm Beauregard Fairfax
Montehugh." He extended a large, bear paw of a hand. "That's a hell-
of-a mouthful, so my friends just call me Beau or Monte." His deep
southern twang harkened of Kentucky, where Andrew once visited
relatives.

"Which do you prefer? Andrew asked, struck by the man's solid
frame and piercing blue eyes, which stood in contrast to his full head of
reddish brown hair and matching thick beard.

"Given the choice between the two, I kinda cotton to 'Beau.'"

"All right, Beau, I'm Andrew Gordon. Glad to know you."

Beau grabbed a shovel and commenced digging. "Damn, this
ground is hard."

"Yeah. I'm glad to have the help. I thought I'd dig a trench the
specifications of the hut and then build the four walls. I marked it off to
fit two beds. They told me somebody was coming to join me. I figure if
we start the walls a few feet below ground, it will give us a little more
stability."

"Sounds fine. We sure don't want the damn thing falling down
around us. I'll get a pick. Maybe that'll help loosen the ground first."

Beau swung the pick into the earth. "Have you seen much
action?"

"A little." I've been everywhere it seems. I started out with
Company H of the Twenty-third Regiment, Virginia Infantry. I helped
defend Richmond in the Seven Days Battle. I get called on for special
assignments, mostly sharpshooting. I fought with Fritz Lee at Kelly's
Ford. It was quite a battle. I don't know why the Yankees turned back

just when they had us, but I'm glad they did. I'd be dead or in a Yankee prison right now, if they'd kept after us. I've done a few raids with Jeb Stuart and his Calvary. Now, I'm here training sharpshooters and pickets."

Beau was about to take another swing but stopped short. "Look yonder." He pointed to the sky. "The Yanks got their balloons up scouting our positions."

"Yep. It's something ain't it? The Yankee Army of the Potomac on one side of the Rappahannock, and here we are the on the other side. Just down yonder is the river's narrowest point, ain't no more than about 150 yards of water separating us. After you've been here a while, you'll hear us cussing at each other. Sometimes there's singing competitions."

Two balloons floated high overhead. Beau threw down the pick and waved at the occupants as if he were signaling a train. "Howdy," he yelled. "How's your sister? Tell her I'll see her tonight. Your mama, too." The soldiers around laughed and waved.

Andrew grinned. "Keep digging, will you?"

"I don't know why we haven't shot down those damn things," said Beau, grabbing the pick.

"We tried. They're positioned too far back and too high up." Andrew worked and talked at the same time. "Some of the others will help us with the walls once we get the trench dug. It might not be finished, but we should be able to sleep in it tonight. I've been bunking with two other soldiers over yonder. I don't want to have to do that another night if I can help it."

"Why?"

"One of them calls hogs all night long. I can't get no sleep."

"Oh." Beau wiped sweat from his brow. "I don't think I snore. But, if I do, just wake me up or turn me over."

"Where you from, Beau?"

"Wise County, southwest Virginia. My family owns coal mines. We got distilleries, too. You ever heard of Montehugh Whiskey?"

"I've heard of it and enjoyed it on several occasions."

"Well, that's us. Glad you like it."

Beau was truly from one of Virginia's, if not the South's, richest families. "Mother must be spinning in her grave about now," thought Andrew.

By the end of the day, the log hut was almost finished, with three of the four walls up.

"It's suppertime. Let's go get something to eat," Beau suggested.

They lined up, got a plate of food, and found a space on the ground to sit.

Beau stirred the food and sniffed it. "Looks like some kind of stew."

"I don't know," cautioned Andrew.

Beau put a big helping in his mouth then spit it out. "What is this shit?" He coughed and reached for his canteen.

"Just as I suspected, it's cush," said Andrew. "It takes some getting used to. When it's all you got, you get used to it fast."

"What the fuck is cush?" Beau frowned and wiped his mouth.

"Bacon grease, hardtack and whatever else they can find stewed down. So you see, it is kind of a stew," Andrew smirked and took a bite. "Eat it in small bites. It's the only way I can get it down."

"I ain't eating this shit. Let's rig up some poles and go down to the riverbank and catch us some shad."

"Sounds good to me. But you better eat a little of it in case we don't catch anything. Don't think about it. Just eat it."

"Hell naw. Fuck this nasty shit. I'll take my chances with the fish." Beau, tossed the plate aside. "It's a damn shame. We're out here risking our lives, and they can't even feed us proper. How they expect us to fight half starved? Look at the horses and mules. They ain't had good forage in months. The sons of bitches so scrawny, they can't half way pull the supply wagons. Shit. Pretty soon they'll have us pulling the goddamn wagons." Andrew took an instant liking to Beau's contrasts. Despite his rich pedigree, he could make a sailor blush with his gutter talk.

Andrew and Beau got lucky at the river's edge, pulling in shad and catfish. They built a small fire and cooked a fine meal. Andrew hadn't realized until tonight that soldiers on both sides had taken to feeding themselves from the river that ran between them instead of relying on their armies.

"Can I trust you, Andrew?" Beau asked. "You'll keep quiet about something if I tell you?"

"I will." Andrew was curious. He needed a diversion to break the drudgery of war.

"When we get back to the hut, we can have a drink of whiskey."

"What?" Andrew whispered. "You know Lee doesn't allow that. How'd you get whiskey past inspection?"

Beau smiled. "My sister," he leaned in, talking low. "She sends me jars of preserved peaches. She pours whiskey in with the peaches. I eat the peaches and drink the whiskey, or as I like to call it, *peach nectar*."

"Well, what are we waiting for?" Andrew jumped to his feet. "I know our little shanty ain't finished, but I'm willing to stay in it tonight. We'll just cover up good with the blankets and shelter tent."

"All right by me." Beau stood and brushed the seat of his pants. "One side will have to be all shelter tent for a while anyway, so we can add a chimney later."

They walked back to the hut. It had not occurred to Andrew until now that he had no one who cared enough to send him anything. Edward would if he could, but he had no way of gathering items to send him.

*********

Winter slowly turned to spring, and rumors of an upcoming battle spread daily. Andrew sat huddled on his bed, its plank supported by empty hardtack boxes. He pulled out the book Jessup had given him and re-read his favorite passages, thinking of the day when he and Edward could share Mr. Whitman's works. When he missed Edward the most, he tried his hand at writing poetry, recalling the first time he saw Edward struggling to walk with shackles digging into his flesh. He tried to put into words Edward's strength and bravery when he fought to protect him and Edward's gentleness when he helped to nurse Andrew back to health.  He had written five lines and read them often.

> *To see you is to visualize strength and gentility*
> *To hear you is symphonic*
> *To touch you is ecstasy*
> *To kiss you is intoxicating*
> *To know you is to love you*

He felt rather proud of his creation, not for its literary quality but because of Edward.  He was grateful to Edward for inspiring his sensitive side that had lay dormant for so long.  He finished a letter to Edward, just a few lines he knew Edward could make out.

*April 29, 1864*

*Edward,*

*I hope you are well.  I am fine.  I will tell you all about the war when I get home.  Wait for me.*

*Andrew*

The shelter tent flap pulled back, and Captain Bill Norton, the Provost Marshall, stuck in his head.  "Gordon?"  He asked.

"Yes sir," said Andrew crawling out of the hut to meet him properly and avoid the man from seeing what he was reading and writing.

"We're executing a deserter at noon tomorrow," said Captain Norton.  "We drew lots to determine a representative from each regiment to serve on the firing squad.  Your name was pulled.  Do you know the procedure?"

"Yes, sir.  I do."

"Good.  Just to be clear, all rifles will be preloaded, and only one will have a blank.  No shooter will know if his gun contains the blank."  Andrew remained silent.  Captain Norton shifted his stance and exhaled.  "I know this is a hard thing to do, but it's got to be done."  His tone was more sympathetic.  "We done got all these new soldiers because of the Conscription Act.  They don't want to be here; the damn conscripts have been deserting in droves.  General Lee wants to send a message that desertion will not be tolerated.  This one had his mama send him civilian clothes.  He changed into them and snuck off.  The fool's so damn stupid, he walked in a circle and came right back to us. To make matters worse, this is a man with military training. He should have been glad to serve our cause."

Andrew met the next day with dread. He ate nothing at breakfast; his nerves gnawed at his stomach, chasing away any hunger. Time seemed to crawl to the appointed time. At eleven forty-five, Andrew walked with the other members of the firing squad to the appointed place in the field, picked up his assigned rifle, and took his place in line while a small band played a dirge. The Yankees on the other side of the river gathered at the edge of the riverbank to watch. Some removed their caps and stood at attention. The deserter, his hands manacled in front of him and his head bowed, walked behind his coffin, which was carried by four soldiers. They put the coffin on the ground and positioned him beside it. With his head still bowed, he sobbed. The Chaplain stepped in front of the deserter, said a few words to him, and moved away. The deserter raised his head. Despite the shadow of a beard and hollowed cheeks, Andrew recognized the shaking man as Sidney Fairchild, IV. Andrew blinked back tears and shock. The Provost Marshall bandaged Sidney's eyes with a white handkerchief, while Sidney cried harder. He pissed his pants and dropped to his knees. Two soldiers stepped in and stood him up, while he began blubbering the Twenty-third Psalm. The Provost Marshall raised a red scarf he had tied around his neck. Andrew didn't want to pull his trigger. They would know if he didn't fire, and he would be disciplined. He prayed he had the blank cartridge in his rifle, or that his rifle would misfire, or that some miracle would stop this. The firing squad took aim. The Provost Marshall waved the red scarf as the signal to fire. Andrew closed his eyes and pulled the trigger. All guns fired. He opened his eyes. Sidney lay dead beside his coffin.

*********

Andrew sat with his back against the corner of the hut facing the sun with his knees pulled up to his chest.

"You all right, Andrew?" Beau asked walking up.

"I knew the man we executed. We were in military school

253

together."

"Hell, Andrew. I'm sorry."

"We weren't close, but I knew him. Why did they have to execute him? Why not just cashier the deserters?"

"Cashiering them would be giving them what they want. Come on with me. We could both use some cheering up. I got a box from home with soap and a brand new razor. Let's go down to the river and get us a bath and then boil some water for a hot shave. We'll get rid of these whiskers and see what we really look like."

"That water's cold," protested Andrew.

"My sister also sent some *peaches*," Beau winked. That'll warm us up. Anyway, it's April 30, and I need to celebrate."

"What are we celebrating?" Andrew stood, and they walked toward the riverbank.

"Today's my birthday. So you see, a bath, shave and some peaches are in order."

"Well, happy birthday."

"While we're at it, we might as well boil these under shirts and under drawers," said Beau, pulling at his clothes. "Kill some fucking lice."

The water was not as cold as Andrew expected. He shaved but kept his mustache. Beau shaved his whole face to reveal strong features and a distinguishing dimple in his chin, rugged and handsome.

"Stonewall Jackson had his wife and new baby brought in for a visit. Mrs. Jackson is putting together some kind of service for the troops," said Andrew taking a swig of whiskey from the peach jar.

Beau's blue eyes got wide. "I ain't interested in going to no damn church service."

"All right," chuckled Andrew. "He was one of my professors at military school. He didn't have the nickname 'Stonewall' then. I thought I would try to be supportive."

"I'm just fine right here in this shanty with your company and this peach nectar. Here take this." Beau reached in the care package and tossed Andrew a cigar. "The inspectors must not have seen these or the greedy bastards would have kept them."

They lit up and continued passing peach nectar between them.

"So, what military school did you attend?" Beau asked.

"Virginia Military Institute, class of 1856."

"I went to West Point."

"Really. What year did you graduate?"

"I didn't. I didn't do so well with their *demerit system*." Beau laughed. "I had so many damn demerits by the end of my second year, I spent all of my free time working them off. I started sneaking out to the local tavern when I should have been working. One of my superiors caught me and told me I'd be getting more demerits if I didn't high tail it back to the barracks. He embarrassed me in front of everybody in the tavern. Anyway, I suggested that he gather up all my demerits and shove 'em up his lily-white ass.

"Beau! They could have disciplined you severely for that, maybe even court-martialed you."

"They tried, but having the last name Montehugh has its benefits. My daddy and granddaddy graduated from West Point. Daddy graduated with the governor. So, they used their influence. They didn't discipline me, just threw out my ass. Needless to say, my daddy was none too happy with me." He passed the jar to Andrew. "There's a swallow left. Finish it off."

"You're something else."

"I've always been a hellion, and I always will be. Bunking with me might be hazardous to your reputation." He smiled and raised his eyebrows.

*********

The next morning, Andrew awoke to Beau's nudge.

"Wake up, Andrew. We got orders to move out. I got a couple horses for us. I got the best I could find, and that ain't saying much."

Andrew sat up and rubbed his face. "What's going on?"

"That new Yankee General, Joe Hooker, done out-smarted Lee. While we were over here executing deserters and having fucking prayer meetings, Hooker moved his army across the Rappahannock below us and the Rapidan above us. They're surrounding us."

"But we can see them across the river," said Andrew.

"That was part of his plan," Beau continued. "He left just enough of them over there to make us *think* the entire army was still in place. It seems like Abraham Lincoln done finally appointed himself a General who can take Lee to task. He's forcing us out of our defensive position."

Andrew yawned and stretched. "They finally figured it out. Lee out-maneuvered John Pope, George McClellan, and Ambrose Burnside." He gathered his belongings. "I hate to say it, Beau, but if Hooker has split up his whole army, gotten them across two rivers, and we didn't know anything about until now, we might be in for a tough time with the Yanks."

"I guess they don't call him 'Fighting Joe' for nothing. We're gonna be fine. We can lick 'em. Get your haversack. They're handing out rations. It better not be any of that cush shit."

Cherry blossoms and forsythia peeked through the thick morning fog, and birds welcomed the day. They started out four abreast on foot and two abreast on horseback.

Captain Norton sprinted through the troops barking out orders, separating the pickets from the Napoleons and putting as much organization to the chaos as he could. He galloped up beside Andrew. "You ready for this, Gordon?"

"Yes sir."

"I hear that you knew that fellow we executed."

"He was a classmate."

"I'm sorry. Had I known, I would have relieved you from the firing squad."

"Thank you, sir. Where are we headed?"

"Chancellorsville. I suspect this will be big. Good luck to you." He galloped off, cussing some group back into formation.

They bivouacked that night and started out again the next morning. Andrew had been told Lee's and Jackson's strategy was to surprise the Yankees by getting around to Hooker's right.

"Where the hell are we?" Beau asked.

"We're in the Virginia Wilderness. The thick brush is almost impossible to navigate," said Andrew.

"That's for damn sure."

"I suspect we're near Chancellorsville. If I remember correctly, the Chancellor House is not far from here." Andrew remembered the area from maps and from a visit he had made while in military school.

The commanding officers spotted Yankee regiments bivouacked just off the Orange Turnpike near Chancellorsville and sent back word to the troops that they would stage a surprise attack late that afternoon. Some soldiers read their Bibles or prayed. Others wrote what they knew could be final letters home. Andrew and Beau cleaned their guns and checked their ammunition. Afterward, they sat in silence, waiting for the orders to come. After a lunch of hardtack and bitter coffee, the soldiers began their approach. They found the Yankees, relaxed, playing cards, and cooking their evening meals. The Confederates snuck through the woods, positioned themselves, and waited for the command to attack. Andrew and Beau crawled on their bellies until they reached tall brush that hid them. Andrew's breath came fast and hard, and sweat clung to his forehead. He was ready to do battle and scared at the same time. His heart pounded, and a sour taste rose in his throat.

"Here we go," whispered Beau. "You ready?"

"I am. Do you think they're as afraid of dying as we are?" Andrew asked.

"If they're human, yes."

The Major motioned for the bugler to sound. The blast pierced the air as did the pickets' first shots. Andrew and Beau followed onto the battle line. They swooped down on the unsuspecting Yankee regiments, startling them with gunfire and the rebel yell. Some Yankees gave fight but most retreated without time to gather their guns. Bullets whizzed, splintering trees and soldiers. Andrew took aim at Yankees standing their ground. He recognized the Union soldier in his cross hairs as Ross McCabe, his classmate from Connecticut. Andrew froze. A bullet pierced his upper left arm, the pain knocking him to his knees. He regained his balance and another tore into his left leg. He crawled back to the line of battle and looked for Beau. He was losing blood fast. The shot in the arm must have severed an artery. The battle swirled around him. He couldn't make sense of direction, and his vision blurred. He lay in a haze hoping someone would find him.

Confederate victory whoops and hollers permeated the quiet, letting Andrew know the skirmish had ended. He made out ghostlike figures with stretchers searching through the human carnage and dead horses for survivors. They may have passed him twice. He couldn't tell if he was dreaming or if the foggy scenes in his head were real. Twigs snapped next to his ear, and a boot stepped down beside his head. Andrew tried to ask for help but was too weak. With his boot, the stretcher carrier turned over Andrew. With all of his strength, Andrew managed to grab the man's leg.

"We got a live one over here," the stretcher carrier yelled.

They tied tourniquets on his wounded arm and leg and carried him to the field hospital. He lay on the stretcher waiting for the doctor, his wounds throbbing and his body aching. He waited for what seemed like hours, the torment of the wounded all around him. Death walked among them, silencing some of the moans. He closed his eyes and longed for Edward to ease his pain.

Andrew woke when they lifted him and carried him into the surgeon's tent. Everything around him lay under a veil, out of reach and focus. The sun had set, and kerosene lamps lit the tent. He lay on his back staring at the ceiling.

"The bullet shattered the bone. I'm going to have to take it off just above the elbow," said Dr. McGuire to his assistants.

"What about the leg?" Another voice asked.

"I can save the leg, but the arm is too damaged."

Andrew sat up. "No!" The attendant pushed him down. He flailed his legs and good arm. "No! Goddamn it, don't you take my arm! Remove the bullet!"

"I'm sorry, son," said Dr. McGuire. "It's too far gone."

Andrew fought them off with his good arm.

"Get the morphine," said Dr. McGuire.

Somebody stuck a leather strap into Andrew's mouth.

"Bite down on it," a voice commanded.

The saw tore into his flesh; awareness hung somewhere between the hard table and heaven which seemed to have its doors open wide. The saw penetrated deeper with each motion. Three men held him down, but he couldn't have moved regardless. He had tried and failed. The blade reached the bone and got hung up. And that was the last moment of his amputation he remembered.

*********

A commotion woke Andrew. The stretcher carriers and surgeon rushed in with a wounded soldier. They hovered around the victim for what seemed like a long time. Beau ran up to Andrew's cot. "Oh my God. Andrew, I've been looking all over for you. After we got separated in all the fighting, I didn't know where you were. Are you hurt bad?"

Andrew didn't respond. Beau kept talking. "I just helped bring in Stonewall Jackson. They decided to keep after the Yankees. Everything got all fucked up in the darkness, and we ended up shooting at each other. Jackson got caught in the middle trying to stop us. He took three bullets — one to the right hand, one to the left arm, and another to the left shoulder. Dr. McGuire says they gonna have to amputate his arm. Andrew? Andrew, can you hear me?" Andrew could tell by the voice it was Beau, but couldn't make out his face.

Drenched with sweat, Andrew's blanket stuck to his naked body. He pulled it down to expose his severed arm.

"Ah hell and damnation," said Beau. He touched Andrew's cheek. "Nurse! Nurse, come quick! A fever done set in."

*********

"Wake up, Andrew." Beau's voice seemed to come from far away or from behind a closed door. "Come on, wake up. They tell me you been sleeping since I left you days ago. You got to get up and move around to get your strength back. You've been too sick to transport to the Richmond hospital. Your fever done broke, and I'm not just gonna let you lay here and die."

Andrew opened his eyes to find Beau not far away but standing next to his cot. Andrew moved but froze fearing his head would split from the pain. He closed his eyes hoping for some relief.

"Naw. Come on now," insisted Beau. "You've got to get up."

"I hurt all over. My head is killing me."

"I'll help you." Beau moved forward to assist.

"Be careful of my arm. It's still throbbing."

"I will." Beau lifted Andrew's upper body and moved his legs, placing his feet on the ground.

"Let me just sit here a spell. Everything is spinning."

"Take your time."

Andrew sat on the side of the cot and rubbed his forehead. "I'm maimed, Beau. What good am I to anyone now?"

Beau pulled up an empty hardtack box and sat on it. "I did most of my fighting the last two days. By the end, the battlefield probably stretched for twelves miles with fighting from Fredericksburg to Wilderness Church. I can't say who won; the dead I could see numbered in the hundreds from both sides. The Yankees retreated, so, I guess we can claim victory. I stepped over dead men laid out in all sorts of positions —mouths agape, eyes bulging, and bodies bloated. Some had all or parts of their heads blown off. Others were so badly wounded all they could do was lay there and wish for death. I can still hear the pop of gunshots, the whiz of bullets flying by me, the wail of horses dying from broken bones and gunshot wounds, and the thundering cries of butchered men. All around me our comrades dropped like flies, Andrew, and those of us still standing fought on. Blasts from the heavy artillery set the thick woods ablaze; smoke from the firing Napoleons hung thick in the air, making it almost impossible to see or catch a full breath. At one point, the battle lines merged, resulting in hand-to-hand combat. I killed two men with my saber and one with the butt of my rifle. It's a terrible thing to watch a man die knowing you caused it. But it was kill or be killed, and I like living. All of this maiming and killing just so the south can keep its slaves." He repositioned his seat directly in front of Andrew. "Look at me, Andrew. Be mighty thankful all you lost is an arm. In the last few days, thousands lost their lives, and this war is far from over."

"I guess I am feeling sorry for myself. I'll get my boots and try to walk a bit."

"What about your leg?"

"Just a flesh wound. Not as bad as it looked. Sorry I can't say the same for the arm."

"Want me to help me with your boots?"

"No!" Andrew was defiant. "I'm gonna be this way for the rest of my life. I got to learn how to get along on my own. Might as well start now."

He slipped on his boots and, after much effort, tied the laces in a knot. "I'll figure out a better way later. I can see now they're going to be hell to untie."

"It's not a shame to ask for help."

Andrew did not respond. He tried to stand but fell back.

Beau grabbed his good arm. "You gonna let me help you now?"

"Yes."

"Let's take it slow until you get your bearings straight."

Leaning on Beau, Andrew started with baby steps. After a few minutes, he was able to make slow regular strides.

They walked away from the moans of the suffering and the hustle of stretcher carriers and ambulance wagons. As they approached a ravine, a foul smell filled the air. "Must be a dead animal," said Andrew. The scent grew stronger with each step. In a gully was a pile of mangled arms and legs—the aftermath of amputation. Some still wore their boots or shirtsleeves. The entire mound seemed to move. Andrew closed his eyes, thinking it was his imagination. He looked closer to see it was covered with flies and maggots. "I guess my arm is in there somewhere."

"Ah fuck," said Beau. "Let's get the hell away from here."

They walked in silence for a while. "So, what are you going to do, now? Go home?" Beau asked.

"I think I'd like to stay on a while and keep training the sharp shooters and pickets, if they'll let me."

"Oh, I'm sure they'll let you. After this slaughter, they need all the men they can get. I can't wait for my time in the army to end. As soon as I can, I'm getting the hell out of here."

"Let's get some shade under that magnolia tree," suggested Andrew. "I need to rest a spell." He leaned against the tree and wiped his brow. "I am fortunate not to have many of the infections that come after amputation."

"We're both damn lucky not to have contracted the cholera, scarlet fever, pneumonia, or small pox that have killed just as many of us as the Yankee bullets have," Beau added.

"So," Beau ventured clawing at his whiskers. "Who's ... Edward?"

"Why do you ask?" Andrew tried to appear calm and not surprised by the question.

"During your delirium, you kept calling for him."

"He's someone very close to me."

"Is he a family member?"

"Not in the way you might think."

"I see." Beau looked out over the field and seemed to be in deep thought.

"By the way, I put your satchel under your bed at the field hospital. When it looked like you might not make it through that first night, I looked through it to see whom I might have to write. I saw Whitman's book and your poetry. Edward's a lucky man. I, too, like Mr. Whitman's book. Pity we didn't know sooner. We could have used more than my sister's peach nectar to keep warm this winter."

Andrew blushed.

"There's no one around," said Beau, scanning the area. He leaned over and kissed Andrew.

## Chapter 36
### July 1864

**MawNancy** visited the kitchen a few times each day to find out if the labor had begun. That morning she showed up to find Mary frantic. Pots of water boiled, broth simmered, and Zula folded gauze.

She stepped into the kitchen. "Is it time?"

"Sho is. She started paining pert near an hour ago. Jasper gone to fetch Doc Prichard," said Mary.

MawNancy hurried back to her cabin. She had moved so quickly, she could hardly catch her breath when she entered the room and laid out her tools. She placed an effigy of Anna on the table. After lighting a candle on each side of the doll, she stuck a long needle into its belly. Using a long bone, she slowly beat the drum she had made by stretching animal skin over a small barrel. She chanted and drummed.

Hours later, Anna's cry echoed around the plantation. MawNancy knew it was over. She walked to the kitchen to get the news and sat at the table, something she had never done before. Exhausted, she had to sit. She had been drumming and chanting nonstop for over twelve hours.

"Was it hard on her?" MawNancy clasped her hands and rubbed her palms.

Mary put the coffee pot on the stove with a loud clang. "It's late MawNancy. It's after ten o'clock. Poor thang was in labor for over twelve hours. After dat coffee takes the heat, I'll take some up to Doc Prichard, and we all need some sleep."

"What happened?" MawNancy was defiant.

The room fell silent. Finally, Zula said, "Doc Prichard say he done delivered many babies, but he ain't never seen birthing so hard on the mama like this. It took a long time getting here, and she was paining the whole time."

"You might as well burn them bed linens," said Sadie. "They all soaked with sweat and blood. They ain't never coming clean."

"It slipped out of her just a little while ago," Zula continued. "Doc Prichard, he just stood there holding it and looking. Then he say, 'Oh my God.' That's when I looked at it. I hid my face in my apron."

"What it look like?" MawNancy wanted every detail.

"Zula got a good look at it," said Sadie. "Mary and I turned away."

"Well," Zula rocked as she prepared to tell what she saw. "It didn't have no skin. You could see the flesh. One eye was smaller than the other. The forehead was really big. No wonder Miss Anna was in so much pain. Its nose looked like it had been smashed in, and the mouth was twisted, the cord still dangling. It started to move and make noises. Doc Prichard put his hand over its nose and mouth to shut off the breathing. After a while, it stopped moving. He wrapped it in a blanket and told me to take it outside and have somebody bury it. I didn't want to touch it. So, he took it out to the barn. Somebody gonna have to bury the poor little thing tomorrow. When Miss Anna heard him say it had to be buried, she sat up screaming, 'No! No! No! No! It can't be!'

"She fell back on the bed and just wept," said Sadie. "I kinda felt sorry for her."

"It's a shame dat baby being born like dat. Dat child ain't never hurt nobody. If you had something to do with all dis, you going straight to hell, old woman," said Mary.

MawNancy looked up and grinned. "We already in hell."

MawNancy made her way back to her cabin, but her curiosity got the best of her. She walked back to the barn, crept over to the bundle in the corner, and pulled the blanket away. The sight of the thing knocked her back a step. She composed herself and stared at it. She smiled. The smile turned to giggle, and the giggle to laughter. She'd done it. She had settled her score with Victoria, and now with Anna. She was pleased.

## Chapter 37
### July 1864

**Anna** hugged the tear-soaked pillow. Doc Prichard's hand rested on her shoulder, one more weight pressing down. "Child," he said, so low she had to focus to hear him. He brushed a lock of hair from her face. "You have an infection or something that was passed on to your baby. And that infection affected the development of your child. It could not live. This wasn't your fault, Anna."

"Infection? What kind of infection?" Anna asked as the tears rolled down her face.

He swallowed hard. "I don't know, my dear. These things are rare, but they do happen. It may have been something you were exposed to, or it could have come from the father. But, we'll look after you. You've got to know that you did nothing wrong. This is God's will. I'll stay the night, and we'll talk more in the morning. Right now you just rest and get your strength back. You're not alone. I'll be right down the hall in Andrew's room, and tomorrow I'll write Andrew and tell him he needs to come home. This is a family emergency. Surly he can get some leave to come home for a spell."

Anna turned her face away from him and sobbed into her pillow. Between wails, she said, "I'm being punished. I'm being punished. Oh, my baby. I'm being punished." She cried until she finally drifted off to sleep.

Anna woke in the wee hours of the morning. For a brief second, it all seemed like a bad dream until the pain between her legs reminded her that she had indeed given birth. She didn't know if her child was a boy or girl. Even though it was dead, she wanted to give it a proper name. She had already picked the names. A boy would be named Brent after his father, and a girl would be named Victoria after her mother. She put on her robe and slipped her pistol into the pocket. Since the war began, she'd taken to carrying it for protection from thieves, deserters, or Yankees. She worked to get down the stairs, taking one step at a time and supporting herself with both hands on the banister. Each step agitated the fresh pains of childbirth. The cold wood floor shocked her bare feet, but the earth was surprisingly comfortable when she finally reached the outside.  The barn door moaned as she opened it, and after a minute, her eyes adjusted to the blackness.  A basket holding the baby sat in the corner waiting for its morning burial.  She carried it back to her room and set it on the bed beside her.  She was eager to hold it but afraid of it, too.  Still covered with the blanket, she picked it up and cradled it in her arms.  She closed her eyes and rocked as if it were alive and needed comfort.  She swayed and hummed and mothered her baby. The blanket slipped from its face, and when Anna opened her eyes, there, in her arms in full view, rested the monstrosity that had grown inside her.  A chill spread through her bones, and her skin moved.  The evil she had poured on others and the poison she had spewed over the years had festered inside her for nine months and had created the monster she was cradling — her own flesh and blood.  She covered its face.  She reached into her robe's pocket and pulled out the pistol.  She placed the barrel in her mouth and pulled the trigger.

## Chapter 38
## August 1864

**Edward** ventured out in the storm. It had been raining steady for almost two weeks. He wasn't particularly fond of the rain, but he had some decisions to make. He needed the solitude of the walk and the rain to clear his mind. He was surprised to see MawNancy walking ahead. He followed her, still alone in his thoughts which now included her. What was MawNancy's business on a morning like this?

The storm intensified, and the strong winds came in waves. It drenched them, and the gusts whipped their clothes in every direction. MawNancy walked slowly and calmly through the storm until she came upon the big tree, the unknowing participant in Edward's attempted death sentence.

Edward watched as MawNancy encircled the tree's base with large bones she removed from her satchel. Her mouth moved, but he wasn't close enough to hear the words. She threw her head back so hard it might have broken a different person's neck. The powerful rain beat on MawNancy's tough, black face. She raised her arms and reached for the storm clouds. She waved her arms, and the wind blew harder. She appeared to be in command. The tree swayed. With each powerful howl of wind, it leaned and then righted itself. MawNancy and the tree seemed to be at war. With the next gust, the tree leaned hard, and its massive roots screamed as the force pulled them from their earth-bound home. Slowly and gracefully the tree fell to its side, its massive limbs impaling the ground. The roots that were for so long anchored deep into the earth now reached heavenward like the ghastly claws of a phantom resurrecting from the grave.

MawNancy collapsed. The wind and rain continued to whip her as she and the tree both lay on the ground.

Edward ran to her as quickly as he could. He turned her over to see nothing but skin over bones. Her body deteriorated as soon as life went from her. Lighting struck the big tree, and flames and smoke erupted from it. He tried to lift her, but the force of the wind was too much. He struggled back to the house to get Jasper. The storm grew too intense for them to go back out, and they made the decision to stay

James Laws

under cover.  The next morning they went to retrieve her body.

"When did you say this happened?"  Jasper asked.

"Yesterday morning.  During the storm."

"My God.  It looks like she has been dead for weeks."

MawNancy was only recognizable from the clothes and bone necklace she wore. They dug a hole next to her, and since Jasper wouldn't touch her, they shoveled what was left of her into it.

Edward wasn't sure if he believed in God or Jesus or any of the saints, but he was sure he had witnessed a supernatural force the day before.  A simple prayer rose in his throat and before he could reconsider, the words tumbled out: "Lord, MawNancy's worn out."

Jasper removed his hat, bowed his head and closed his eyes.  A light breeze ruffled the small outer branches of the felled tree.  "Give her the rest and peace she deserves."

The two men stood in silence while a dead calm settled the tree.  With a nod, Edward and Jasper began shoveling earth over MawNancy's lifeless form, like he was planting one of her exotic dried seeds.

## Chapter 39
## August 1864

**Andrew** was asleep on his cot when a shot woke him. This wasn't late night sniper fire but a single shot that pierced the night in a personal way. He hoped some lucky soldier had harvested a deer, but, more likely, his life had ended. The war's emptiness overwhelmed him. He longed for home. Beau had been transferred to Tennessee. Andrew was glad that Beau would be closer to his home in southwest Virginia, but he was sad to lose their friendship. Andrew was of little use now. Maybe he would act on his medical discharge eligibility and head for Wilmington Manor.

He filed the paperwork the next morning with his senior commander. In only a few days, Captain Norton delivered his official discharge papers, ending Andrew's tenure with the Confederate Army. He'd seen enough of war and death. What the Union's bullets and cannons didn't kill, diarrhea, infections, and other diseases did. He longed for Edward's arms. He said his goodbyes and headed south.

He stowed his meager belongings in a saddlebag and tied it to the horse. He planted his foot in the stirrup and instinctively reached for the horn with his left hand. He had no left hand. He awkwardly fumbled with his stump. With one foot in the stirrup, he hopped along beside the horse hoping to keep it from moving into a trot and dragging him. He hoped no one was watching. He'd ridden horses since childhood without even thinking. Now riding was one of his daily challenges. He mounted and reached for the reins with his good arm. He spurred the horse, and headed south. After a spell, his muscles took over, balancing with only his legs and controlling with his right arm. He had beaten his stutter, but he couldn't will another arm to grow. He didn't want to stop, but the effort exhausted him. He had to rest often or walk beside the horse. The sun was still high when he reached the northern line of Caroline County. A rickety wagon came up behind him on the packed dirt road. He walked his horse over to the side of the road to let it pass, but the wagon stopped. A shriveled old driver yelled to him, "Whar ye headed, soldier?"

"Richmond."

"Well, I'm a-going as fer as Hanover.  Hitch yer hoss to my wagon, and climb in the back and rest a spell.  Ye can take a load off fer a few miles.  Least I can do fer one of our boys.  I see ye done lost yer arm.  Goddamned Yankees."

The old man was hauling a load of hay.  Andrew got in the back and took advantage of the soft bed.  He put his hat over his head to shield his face from the sun and fell asleep.

**\*\*\*\*\*\*\*\*\***

Edward had received no word about Andrew in months and feared he was dead. Wilmington Manor no longer held him in any way. All that he cared about there were gone: Aunt Daisy, Uncle Buck, Georgie, and Andrew.  He was free and ready to head north to a new life.  He wrote a note and put it in the pipe box he made for Andrew several Christmases ago, in case he did come home. *Going north.  I will write.  Edward.*  He folded the paper around a pouch of tobacco and placed it in the box.  He went to Andrew's office and reached for the ledger.  For Georgie, himself, and every slave listed among the property, he would burn it.  Footsteps headed his way, and he had nowhere to hide the ledger.  He put it back on the shelf just as Jasper entered.

"Well, Mr. Jasper, I think it's time for me to go," said Edward.

"Yea.  I don't know how much longer I can hold on.  I feel obligated to wait for Andrew to come back."  Jasper brushed at the few remaining wisps of hair on is bald crown.  "We ain't heard from him in so long, I'm beginning to wonder if he's still alive.  I wrote him about Anna, but with things the way they are, it ain't no telling if the letter will reach him."

"I'd like to take one of them horses.  I can't pay you right now, but I'll send the money as soon as I'm settled."  Edward didn't want to ask but had no choice.

"Take any one you like.  Don't worry about the money.  I know you like that Arabian of Andrew's.  Take that one if you want."

"Sweet?"

I don't' know his name, but you been taking such good care of him, waiting for Andrew to return.  Take him if you want.  Andrew might not ever be back. If he comes back, I'll tell him I gave Sweet to you."

"Would you let him know that I'm heading north, and once I get settled, I'll contact him?"

Edward had not thought about taking Andrew's favorite horse, but he liked the idea. He might get caught between battles as he traveled, but he couldn't wait for the war to end. His spirit was ready to go. Sweet would give him the best chance of making it to the other side of the war alive. He gathered his few belongings: the reading books Andrew had given him, the pipe and tobacco, and the two pistols he took from Onie and Clayton the night of the ambush. Andrew had never asked about the guns. Edward had kept them hidden all that time, at first in the barn and later under the floorboards of the cabin along with things he had gathered for his escape: long drawers, wool socks, winter coat, razor, extra pants, and a shirt. His escape plot had never materialized. He now headed out a free man and could carry more in order to be prepared for the coming winter months.

Edward alternated walking and riding, his hip bothering him if he rode too long. He kept a vigilant watch as he traveled, on the lookout at all times for angry Confederate soldiers. Between walking, riding slowly, and resting in between, he only got as far north as the southern border of Caroline County that first day.

A wagon in need of repair drawn by a bedraggled horse headed toward him. Edward walked his horse to the side of the road to let it pass. The old driver spat at Edward as he passed. The wad landed at his feet, a mixture of tobacco juice and phlegm. Edward stared at the old geezer straight in his eyes. The wagon passed, and Edward saw a Confederate soldier sleeping in the back. Edward couldn't see his face – it was covered by a hat – but he could see his shirt sleeve neatly folded and pinned where an arm should have been. Edward mounted Sweet and galloped away in case the driver and the one-armed soldier decided to come after him.

*********

Andrew and the farmer traveled to Hanover. After a long and bumpy ride, the old man pulled the wagon to a stop. "Hey mister, wake up. This here is as fer as I go."

"I'm awake. I closed my eyes to shield them from the sun, that's all. Thank you for the lift."

"You take care, son. And be careful. Thars Yankees and niggers everywhar, like the one we passed back yonder."

"What do you mean?" Andrew asked. He jumped down and untied his horse.

"I reckon you didn't see him. Thar was a cripple nigger walking a real fine hoss. I don't know how he come across such a nice animal. When he seen us, he got on that hoss and skedaddled. Yes siree, he skedaddled something powerful."

He thanked the old man and mounted up for his journey home. His arm throbbed, as it tended to do from time to time. He thought it best not to try to ride the distance to Wilmington Manor.

"Is there a place where I can get a room for the night?" he asked the driver.

"Go down yonder a little ways to Lizzy Reynolds' place. She got rooms fer rent. Tell her I sent ya. Name's Joe Ellis."

"Thank you, Mr. Ellis."

"Yer mighty welcome, son."

War and poverty had ravaged Lizzy Reynold's place. The large house needed a coat of paint and new shutters. Still, Andrew admired its elegant structure and details. He tapped on the door, which opened against the weight of his soft knock. He hesitated to walk inside. In times of war, people sometimes shoot first and ask questions later. He knocked again. "Hello. Is anybody home?"

A woman came around the side of the house with a pistol in her hand. It wasn't aimed at him, but it was clear she wanted him to know she had it. "What can I do for you?" she asked.

"Joe Ellis sent me. He said you got rooms for rent. I just need one for the night."

She looked at his half arm. "One dollar," she said, brushing her disheveled hair back from her forehead. "You can stay the night. I ain't got no food. All's you get is the room. Thar's water in the well, if you want it."

Andrew dug into his pocket and handed her a coin. War, desperation and hunger showed in the lines of the young woman's face and in the hollow of her cheeks. She looked exhausted, beaten down by hard times. Whatever spirit she may have possessed looked to be broken. She took the money and handed him a key.

To his surprise, the room was clean and the sheets washed. He kicked off his boots and sat on the side of the bed, eating the hardtack and molasses he had brought with him. Later he went down to get water from the well. The woman was sitting at the kitchen table.

"I thought I'd get some water."

"Help yourself."

She was still sitting at the table when he came back inside. He offered her a piece of hardtack, and she grabbed it, shoving it in her mouth. He thought she might choke. She finished and brushed the crumbs from the table into her hand and licked them from her palm. He wanted to offer her more, but he had nothing more to offer. She buried her face in her apron and cried. He held her hand, and they sat in silence.

The next morning Andrew rose early with spryness in his step. Despite sharp hunger pains, he prepared for the last leg of his journey with energy and new hope. Home awaited. So did Edward.

## Chapter 40
## August 1864

**Andrew** arrived home to a desolate place. The grounds were overgrown, there was very little activity, and a gloom hung over Wilmington Manor. No one rushed to greet him. There were no little pickaninnies hailing his arrival. He approached the house slowly, dismounted, and entered the front door. The house almost looked as bad as the boarding house he stayed in the night before. He walked into his office.

"Anna!" he called out.

He stood dumbfounded. "Where is everyone? What happened here?"

Eventually, Luther came in the back door from the kitchen.

"Finally, a familiar face," said Andrew, startling Luther.

"Mr. Andrew! Lord have mercy. Welcome home, sir."

"Where is everyone?"

"Dey done gone, sir. Just 'bout everybody. Scattered like dust in de wind. In every which direction."

Jasper entered the front door. "I saw the horse outside and hoped it was you. Welcome home. You're back just in time. You must have gotten my letter"

"Just in time for what? What letter? Where's Anna?"

"Come on in the other room, and let me tell you what's happened," said Jasper. "Luther, see if Mary and Sadie can rustle up some food."

Andrew listened as Jasper told him everything that had happened since he left. He took it all in; the temporary occupation, Anna's pregnancy, the birth, her suicide, and the debt. "Where's Edward?" he asked.

"Gone too. Left day before yesterday, heading north. He took that Arabian he was so fond of. He offered to send money back to pay for it. I let him take it and told him not to worry about the money. Thought you wouldn't mind. I know it was yours, but we didn't know if you was ... well, coming back. I'm surprised you didn't pass him on the road somewhere."

Andrew felt sick. His head began to spin. "Oh dear God," he said. He remembered the old man's words. *"Well, I reckon you didn't see him. Thar was a cripple nigger walking a real fine hoss. I don't know how he come across such a nice animal."*

Andrew cursed the old man for offering the ride. He cursed himself for resting in the back. He was only a couple days' ride away. He had to find him. He had to go back. "I'll head back out now to see if I can catch him."

"Andrew," said Jasper. "This place is in debt. You need to go up to Richmond to see what can be done to save this plantation from being taken by the bank. You need to take care of that first thing in the morning. That's why I say you're back just in time."

"But I've got to stop him before he gets too far."

"Andrew," said Jasper sounding very exasperated. "The bank is only a few days away from taking this place over. Anna had to mortgage the plantation just to keep potatoes on the table. You've got to straighten this out before you head back out to find Edward. Jessup has done all he can do to hold this off, but he has to answer to a board of directors. You, as the owner, must step in to sign a new loan, or find some financing."

Andrew didn't like the idea of letting Edward slip away from him, but he also had to save his home, so he gave in. "I guess you're right. I'll see Jessup first thing in the morning."

No one had said anything about his arm. Finally, Jasper asked, "How'd you lose your arm?"

"Battle at Chancellorsville. Bullet shattered the bone."

That night he rested in bed alone. For months, he had envisioned his return and his first night back with Edward. The bed was not as inviting as he had hoped. He fretted all through the night. He wanted to head back to find Edward, worried that he might get hurt by Confederate soldiers. But he knew that he had to stay at least one more day to try to save the plantation. In the early morning hours, he finally drifted off to sleep.

He rose early and headed for Richmond to find Jessup. There was little activity in the bank, and the once large staff of clerks, tellers, and assistants had dwindled down to Jessup and two clerks.

"I know someone who might make you a loan to get you out of debt," said Jessup.

"I'm glad to know there's someone who might be able to help. Who's got money to lend these days? Times are hard for us and all of our friends."

"Now don't go getting all high-and-mighty on me. I can get you a loan from Maggie Dumont."

"Maggie Dumont? You mean the …"

"That's right," Jessup interrupted him. "Times may be hard, but a good tumble is still a valued commodity." He took a draw on his cigar and blew smoke. "Maggie accommodates soldiers, northerners, and southerners. Her business is thriving. I consider her a friend, and I trust her. Do you want me to approach her about the loan or not?"

"I do. I can't lose Wilmington until I'm ready to get rid of it. I apologize if I sounded ungrateful. I was just surprised, that's all."

"I talk so much about you, she's looking forward to meeting ya."

"I look forward to meeting her. Seems like now we'll get the chance."

They sat in silence for a minute. Finally, Andrew said, "Now that we have taken care of business, let's talk about a few personal matters."

"All right. What's on ya mind?"

"I want to tell you everything. I want to tell you about Edward."

Jessup smiled and leaned back in a more comfortable position. "Edward? Who's Edward?"

Jessup sat speechless. His lack of response made Andrew worry that he would be non-supportive. "Well, say something won't you."

"I'm sorry Andrew. You just shocked me is all. You sho kept that from me all this time."

"I wasn't sure how you'd respond. You know with him being … Well, you know."

"Andrew, you are the only friend I have, other than Maggie. I understand this need we have more than anybody else. Course I support ya. I got a question." Jessup leaned in close to Andrew's ear and whispered, "What's it like with one of them?"

Andrew smiled. Jessup's eyes twinkled with anticipation. "Come on. Tell me," he prodded Andrew. "Stop blushing and tell me. I tell ya all my secrets."

Andrew overcame his embarrassment, leaned in to Jessup ear, and said, "We make love. It's special."

Andrew blushed, smiled and they snickered like mischievous schoolboys. It had been a very long time since he laughed.

Andrew's demeanor turned serious. "I love him, Jessup. I realize that more than ever now."

Jessup looked distracted.

"I don't mean to go on and on about me. How are things with you?" Andrew asked.

"I guess everything's all right."

"How are things with that fellow from Philadelphia?"

"I'm a little disappointed with Thelton. I reckon I expected a little more than he's capable of giving."

"What do you mean?"

"I might not have told ya, but he likes both, and when he's here, I find myself competing with the women for his attention. He doesn't respond to my lettahs, and sometimes he comes to town and I don't even know it until after he has been here for a few days."

"I'm sorry, Jessup."

"When we do get together, it's mighty nice. He's intelligent, damn handsome, and fun in bed." Jessup offered up a heavy sighed. "But now I know he's just in it for the physical relations. I just have to keep reminding myself of that."

"You'll find someone. I know you will."

"I hope so. I getting tired of being the life of every party and going home alone."

As they prepared to part ways, Jessup said, "Oh and one other thing. Just in case I didn't make it clear, as far as Edward is concerned, I'll do anything ya want me to do to help you find him."

Andrew rode home, content that he had solidified his friendship with Jessup and had begun the process of removing some of the debt attached to the plantation. Now, he had to find Edward. Unfortunately, he needed to be in town a few more days until the deal was finalized with Maggie, assuming that she would even agree to make the loan.

## Chapter 41
## August 1864

**Edward** got as far as the northern end of Spotsylvania County. He found a place to settle in and made a meal out of apples, plums, pears, and the biscuits that Mary and Sadie gave him. He finished eating, and, with a pistol on each side concealed under leaves, drifted off to sleep.

He was awakened by someone kicking his feet. "Well, lookie here what we done found," said a male voice.

"Wake up, boy," said another one with a kick to Edward's foot.

Edward sat up and found himself face-to-face with Nimrod and Onie wearing Confederate uniforms.

"I'll be damned," said Nimrod.

"I thought we took care of you with that noose a few years ago," said Onie. "Anna Gordon paid us good money to help her with you and that Georgie. But the bitch left before we could finish her off. I was gonna fuck her one more time then snap her neck."

"We'll just have to finish what we started," said Nimrod. He pulled a knife. "Besides, I owe you something for breaking my nose."

"We ain't got time for this," said Onie. "We got to keep moving. If they catch us, they'll execute us for desertion. I don't know what the hell you was thinking, shooting one of our own men over a damn piece of bread. I tell you, we got to move on."

"This won't take long," said Nimrod. An evil grin spread across his face. He walked toward Edward displaying the blade. The grin dissolved when Edward pulled the pistol from under the leaves and pointed it at him. One shot in the upper chest and Nimrod dropped to his knees. He fell face-first. The knife punctured his jugular. His body shook and convulsed, and blood gurgled out and onto the dry leaves.

Onie reached for his gun. Edward's was already cocked. Onie threw up his hands. "All right now, boy. You mind yourself. Just let me be, and I'll go on."

"This is for Georgie." Edward aimed.

"Huh?"

Edward pulled the trigger. After watching them die, he

searched them for money, took their weapons, packed his belongings, and kept traveling north. The shots may have attracted someone's attention, and he did not want to have to explain two dead Confederate soldiers. He gathered his belongings, mounted Sweet, and headed north.

After two days, he arrived in Alexandria and finally reached the Potomac. The still waters glistened in morning sun. Hiding behind the thickets and trees, he looked up and down the riverbank for a bridge or a shallow crossing but found neither. He couldn't swim, and his only hope was to stay mounted on Sweet and hope the horse could get them both across. He mounted and walked Sweet toward the water. There were only a few feet in when five Union soldiers galloped from their hiding places.

"You can't cross here. Unless you want to drown," one of the soldiers yelled to him. "The undertow will pull you down."

"I'm trying to make it to Washington." He felt foolish for trying to make the crossing.

"We're heading in. Ride in with us. It's safer that way."

Edward walked Sweet up to the soldier. "Thank you."

"That's a fine looking animal you riding."

Edward rubbed Sweet's head. The soldiers headed down the riverbank. The pace was slow, but he struggled to keep up. His hip throbbed. After a mile, they came to a bridge and safely crossed the Potomac. Edward breathed a sigh of relief.

"I'm not sure where you're headed, but if you keep in that direction you'll enter the city." The soldier pointed and again looked admiringly at Sweet.

"Thank you, Sir. I appreciate your help."

The city bustled with early morning activity. White and colored people went about their business. The constant walking and riding irritated his bones, and his hip pained him. He needed some medical attention.

"Excuse me, folks," he finally got the nerve to ask one of the many sophisticated looking colored people. "I'm in need of some medical help. Can you tell me where I could find a doctor?"

"Of course," the man responded with a smile. "We'd be happy to."

"You want Freedman's Hospital," the woman interjected.

"Just continue straight on up this road for about half mile and make a right. You can't miss it," the man instructed.

"It's a nice colored hospital. They can help you there. Good luck to you," said the woman as they walked away.

After stopping and asking for directions twice more, he found the hospital. The staff diagnosed that his discomfort was due to the sudden increase in the use of his legs. The constant riding and walking was not good for his joints. They prescribed a few days rest and a decrease in the amount of time he spent mounted on a horse. He worried about making it on up north if he couldn't ride, but the pain in his hip and leg convinced him to heed their advice and rest.

He woke from a nap and sat on the side of the cot just in time for the evening meal. The woman carrying the food trays broke into a broad smile when she saw him. She ran to him and knelt beside the cot. "Edward? Edward, is it really you? It's me. It's Georgie." She grabbed his shoulders, cupped his face, and threw her arms around his neck.

"Georgie?" He was groggy from his nap. "This must be a dream." He embraced her. "It's really you. Oh, thank God you're all right. We didn't know what had 'come of you."

"I made it this far, and some folks took me in. The colored folks here have been so kind. What are you doing here? What's wrong?"

"Oh, I'm all right. It ain't nothing much. This old hip of mine is giving me problems."

"Hip? What's wrong with your hip?"

"After you left, I had a little trouble, with Nimrod. I'll tell you all about it later. The doctor says a few days rest and I'll be fine."

She looked very different from when he last saw her. The disheveled shadow of a woman, who was ailing in the mind when she escaped Wilmington Manor, no longer existed. She was beautiful and full of life.

She sat beside him. "I'll be back as soon as my work is done, and we'll catch up. You eat this, and I'll see what I can find special for you."

It reminded him of old times when she and Aunt Daisy saved special things from the kitchen for him. Later that evening, they relaxed and drank ice water flavored with lemon and orange slices. They ate cake and shared their stories.

"How'd you end up working at this hospital, Georgie?"

"My friend, Elizabeth introduced me to lots of people. I attend the Baptist church on Sundays. Mrs. Regina, one of the ladies at the church helped me get this job."

Edward put the last morsel of cake in his mouth and washed it down. "From what I could see, there are lots of fancy colored folks up here."

"Oh yes and she's one of them. She almost runs the church. She's a member of every club and auxiliary that the church has. Her husband, James, is a deacon. They took a liking to me and helped me get a job here working in the kitchen."

After a few moments of silence, she lowered her head. "Tell me about the rest of the folks at Wilmington Manor."

She listened to the chronology of events that took place after she left. When he finished, she sat speechless.

"Georgie, I hope I haven't upset you, but I thought you ought to know."

"So, she shot herself?"

"Yea, she did. Put the pistol in her mouth and did it. And, we ain't heard from Andrew in a long time. I'm afraid to think about what may have happened to him."

"I'll pray for him." Sadness washed over her.

"I've got to go on north." He hoped the change in conversation would lighten her spirit. "I want to get away from this country. I want to keep on until I reach a place where people think and act different than the way they treat us here."

"Canada? I've heard them talk at church about some of the members who continued on north into Canada."

"I don't know. Somewhere. I've got to get out of this country. I can't breathe here."

"Well, from what they tell me, you can't walk to Canada. And, with your hip the way it is, you can't go by horseback either. I guess we'll have to see about putting you on the train. I'll talk to my friends, Elizabeth and Mrs. Regina at the church and we'll see what we can do."

At the end of his second full day at the hospital, Georgie rushed to his bedside full of news. "We've found a buyer for the horse. He's offered a fine price, but then it is a nice animal. That was Andrew's special horse. How'd you come to bring it with you?"

"The new overseer told me to take it. I'm still gonna send money back to pay for it."

"Also, the men at the church put in a little of their own money to get you a ticket to Canada. They've already sent a letter to some church members who live in a place called Ottawa."

"Oh, thank you, Georgie. Please let them know that I will pay them back."

After a few days his hip felt better. He left the hospital walking with a cane. It eased some of his discomfort and helped with his balance.

"Georgie," he said, as he was about to board the train. "I got one more favor to ask you. I don't know if Andrew is dead or alive. We ain't heard nothing from him in months. Just in case he is still alive, I'm going to write him and tell him where I've gone. But, would you write him and tell him, too? Just in case one letter doesn't get through to him, the other one might. Anyway, you need to let him know that you are alive and safe. He loves you."

"I know. He loves you, too."

Her revelation shocked him. First Ryland and now Georgie.

"Yes, he does. I feel the same way about him."

"I'll write." She embraced him and kissed him on the side of his face.

"Georgie," he whispered in her ear. "Ryland is looking for you. If he finds you, give him a chance. He's a good man, and he cares for you."

She separated from his embrace and smiled. "I know. You take care, and let me know that you got there safe."

He did not want to leave her. Their reconnection provided the foundation he needed to move toward his new life. He hoped she felt the same way. Wilmington Manor may have been a plantation, but in a strange way it was home. It was where they loved and supported each other. It was where they formed a family.

He settled into his seat on the train.

## Chapter 42
### August 1864 – April 1865

**Edward** snuggled into his window seat to get a good view of the countryside.  He stretched his legs as best he could, worried that sitting too long might irritate his hip.

"'Cuse me, sir.  Is this seat taken?"

He took his attention from the window to see a beautiful young Negro woman motioning toward the vacant seat beside him.

"No, Ma'am.  Please, sit here."  He'd not thought about having to interact with a traveling companion, a stranger.  His mind raced sending jolts of nervous energy to his chest.

She settled into the seat, placing her cloth satchel on her lap and delicately folding her gloved hands on top of it.  The satchel looked as if it might burst at any moment.  She wore a starched dark-green print dress with a matching bonnet.  The hat, with its large bow tied under her chin, framed her brown-skinned face, accenting her large black eyes and perfect smile.  "My name is Topsey.  Topsey McDaniel."  She extended a gloved hand.

"Pleased to meet you, Miss McDaniel.  My name is Edward."  He shook her hand.  Topsey appeared delicate and refined, but he could tell energy and excitement percolated just below her surface.

"Thank you.  I'm *Mrs.*  I'm on my way to Canada to meet my husband, Augustus.  We call him Gus."  She interlocked her fingers to push her gloves more securely over each finger.  "Gus went up and got settled while I stayed behind with family.  Now he done sent for me.  I'm pleased to meet you, too, Mr."  She paused.  "What is your last name?"

"I don't have a last name."

"Now, that just don't seem right.  How you not have a last name?"  She smiled revealing perfect white teeth.

"I don't want to take no slave owner's last name."

"I understand."  For a few seconds, some of the energy seemed to leave her, overcome with sadness.  "It's quite a few day's travel betwixt here and Canada.  Mayhaps we can come up with a last name for you by the time we get there."  Excitement and energy bubbled to the surface.

"We'll see."

The distant call of the conductor's: "All aboard!  All aboard," echoed through the car.

The train lurched forward and began to roll, slowly picking up speed.

Edward parted the curtain to look at the folks on the platform waving.  He glimpsed Georgie wearing a broad smile and waving a white handkerchief.  He kissed his fingertips and pressed his hand to the window.  "Stay safe," he whispered.

The train gathered more speed.  The things up close whizzed by, but the trees in the distance seemed to move slowly, almost following the train.  "I hope this contraption is safe."  Edward hoped he didn't sound stupid, but it was his first time on a train.  "I don't know how something this big and powerful can stay on them little rails without falling off."

"Don't you worry.  We'll be just fine.  White folks ride these things all the time.  I ain't heard tell of them coming off the rails yet." She adjusted her gloves, pulling them snugly over her wrists.

They changed trains in New York City to head to Albany. Edward hobbled through the train station with Topsey gazing and pointing at every sound and sight.  He wished she would stop.  They may have been ignorant and scared, but they certainly didn't need to act it.  By the grace of God and the help of a few bystanders, they made the right connection.

Hours passed and Edward had shifted in his seat more times than he cared to remember.  Once they reached Albany, they would change trains again to head to Ottawa.  Edward was eager for the stop to stretch his aching hip.  The pain became unbearable, and his hip would not let him wait any longer.  "Mrs. McDaniel, would you excuse me please?  I need to stand for a while.  My hip is bothering me."  She grabbed her satchel, holding it tight to her breast, and stepped into the aisle.  Edward limped from one end of the car to the other, stiff from having sat so long.  When he returned, Topsey stood to make way for him to get to his window seat.

"What happened to your hip?"

He was surprised she felt familiar enough to ask. "They tried to lynch me. When my ... When the rope was cut, I fell and injured up my hip."

"Oh dear Lord." She lowered her head and energy seemed to drain from her. "I think I'll walk a spell too."

She took her satchel with her, holding it tight as if her life depended on its contents. She returned to her seat just as the train lurched, causing her to stumble. The satchel flew from her arms. She shrieked and lunged for it. It landed in the seat, the contents spilling out everywhere. Gloves – every kind and color, red, blue, green, polka-dot, gingham, long and short. She seemed panicked as she reached for them, grabbing as if they were baby chicks escaping from a pen and stuffing them back into the bag. Edward tried to help, but she rebuffed him and snatched them away. "They're mine! I'll get them," she snapped. For close to an hour, she sat cradling the satchel of gloves and rocking. Edward was reminded of Georgie when her mind was ailing. He wanted to help but did not know what to say or do. He pulled out a book to pass the time.

She stopped rocking. "You know how to read?"

"I do."

Her energy and excitement seemed to resurface. "I can't read, but I'm gonna learn as soon as I get to Canada."

"Are you hungry?" Georgie had supplied Edward with enough ham, chicken, corn pudding, greens, biscuits, and cake to feed an army. Topsey clearly had nothing but a satchel full of gloves.

"Yes. I realize that I didn't think of packing much other than my clothes and my ..."

"It's all right. I've got plenty."

"Oh, thank you, Mister," She giggled and seemed to return to her old self. "We still got to get you a last name. What was your mama's name?"

"They tell me it was Betty."

"Edward Betty. That don't sound right. What about yo daddy?"

"William."

"All right. What about Edward *Williams*?"

"He smiled. That does sound kinda nice. I'll think on it." He unwrapped the food to share. You going to have to set your bag on the floor so you can eat."

She lowered her eyes. He feared she might retreat into herself again.

"It's all right," he said.

She seemed reluctant but placed the satchel on the floor, and he placed a napkin in her lap.

They ate. He talked about Georgie, and Topsey beamed on and on about Gus.

"My goodness, that Miss Georgie sure can cook," Topsey said picking the cake crumbs from the napkin and eating them off her gloved finger. A change had come over her. She looked more serious. She shook the crumbs from the napkin, folded it, and handed it back to Edward. Looking him in the face she said, "I ain't crazy. I just..."

"It's all right Mrs. McDaniel. We *all* have scars, on the outside and on the inside. Ain't no shame in it. We didn't do this to ourselves. Others did it to us."

"I got scars both places." She peeled off her gloves to reveal a hideous brand on the top of each hand.

"Me, too. My back is covered."

Topsey shifted to face him. "A few years before the war, my missus said I stole her pearl necklace. I told 'em I didn't do it, but 'course, you know they didn't believe me. They put me out of the big house and made me work in the fields. But 'fore they did, massa, he took and held me down while Missus stuck the hot poker on each of my hands. Said they wanted folks to know I was branded as a thief. Now what the hell did they think I gonna do with a pearl necklace, wear it around the big house or in the field and think nobody was gonna notice."

She rubbed her hands. "My man, Gus, kept telling me he was gonna fix it, make it right. But he can't make my hands pretty again, and I just can't bear to look at 'em." Tears streamed down her face. "Every time I get some extra piece-goods, I make me pair of gloves."

"From the looks of 'em, you mighty good at sewing."

"Thank you. I make all my dresses and hats, too. After a while missus let me back in the big house to help her out with things. She said I had learned my lesson. One night she caught massa going through her jewelry and putting it in his pockets. They got to fussing and it come out that he took the necklace and other pieces to pay debts. I stood in the doorway and heard it all. They just looked at me and told me to get out. Missus never said she was sorry for what she did to my hands. I told Gus about it, and he told me not to worry. Said he was gonna fix it, make it right. Them was always his exact words 'fix it, make it right.' The war came, and all the slaves was gone except for a few of us. I told Gus that we needed to move on, but he say we can't go yet, because he still got to fix it, make it right. Massa went off to fight and came back in a pine box." Topsey began to rock and tap her foot as she continued to tell the story. "I was sitting in the small parlor with missus and massa's body when Gus come in with rope and a big can. Missus yelled at him to get out. She said he had no place in the big house. Gus knocked missus to the floor with the back of his hand. He picked her up and tied her in the chair, even tied her legs. He took that can and poured kerosene everywhere. He doused Massa all inside the coffin, the heavy blue velvet drapes, furniture, everything. I begged him to stop, but he was like a wild man, like some demon got in him and took over. He pushed me away. He kept on saying 'I gotta fix it, make it right. Fix it, make it right,'" her voice in rhythm with her rocking and foot-tapping. "Then he took the rest of that kerosene and threw it in missus' face. He waited for her to come to and then said to her 'Wake up. Damn it all. You gonna see this.' Gus pulled me to her and shoved my hands in her face, and he say, 'Now y'all gonna pay for what you did to my Topsey.' Missus looked at us, her hair and dress dripping with kerosene and said, 'Go to hell.' Gus said to her, 'Might be, but I'm gonna send y'all there first.' He used the flame from the lamp and lit Massa's body. Then he threw the lamp against the wall, and the floor and drapes went up in flames. He pulled me out. Gus had placed a hammer and nails outside the door. He closed the door and nailed it shut. He told me to hurry up stairs and get Missus' jewelry box. I wouldn't do it, 'cause I ain't no thief. Gus ran up and got the box.

"He had the buckboard loaded and waiting. We pulled off heading north, and that's when Gus turned to me and said, 'I told you I was gonna fix it, make it right.' The big house was made of timber. I looked back, and the whole place was a ball of fire. To this day, I can still hear missus wailing. And the smell of massa's body when it took fire. Sometimes it comes back in my dreams. I wake up a-hollering. Then I remember my Gus." Topsey picked up her gloves and put them on, making sure the tops were pushed up over her wrists. She dug deep into her satchel and pulled out a pearl bracelet and clasped it around one wrist. Then she pulled out a gold bracelet and clasped it around the other. She continued her rhythm of rocking and foot-tapping, held up her gloved, and now adorned hands, examined them, and said "My hands is pretty again. Yes siree, my Gus fixed it, made it right.

They sat quietly, comfortably. Finally Topsey asked, "You got people in Canada, Mr. Williams?"

Edward laughed. "You bound and determined to give me a last name, aren't you? I don't have anybody there that I know. My friends have made arrangements for me to stay with a family from their church. We'll meet for the first time when I step off this train. I don't know what's in store for me, but it's got to be better than the life I've had so far."

"It's gonna be fine. My Gus say things is a lot better for colored folks in Canada."

"I hope I can find work. With this bad hip, my opportunities are limited, but I got to try."

"Don't you worry. Them people you gonna be staying with ain't the only folks you got in Canada." She flashed her perfect smile. "You got me and Gus now."

They arrived in Albany, New York, to have a three-hour wait for their connecting train to Ottawa. They slept sitting in the waiting area and made the connection with little difficulty.

The conductor walked the aisle. "Excuse me, sir," Edward stopped him. Could you tell me when we cross the line into Canada?"

"We just did. About ten minutes ago." The portly conductor

pulled out his watch.

"Thank you, sir." Edward turned his head toward the window to look at the countryside. A tear rolled down his cheek. "I'm free." He rested his head on the back of the seat allowing the feel of freedom to sink in. "Mrs. McDaniel, I've decided."

"Decided what?"

"My last name will be Freeman. I'm Edward Freeman."

Topsey smiled and rubbed his hand. "I like that. It's mighty fine."

Edward drifted off to sleep.

Topsey stirred him from his slumber. "We're just about there, Mr. Freeman."

"Next stop, Ottawa. Coming into Ottawa." The conductor rattled the quiet train car as he walked the aisles. The train rolled to a stop.

Topsey craned her neck to look out the window. "There's my Gus." She pointed to a strapping dark-skinned man in work clothes and heavy boots. Edward wondered what kind of work Gus did. By the looks of him, seemed strenuous. Too strenuous for Edward. He rubbed his hip while he and Topsey gathered their belongings and left the train.

Topsey ran to Gus and threw her arms around him. He picked her up and spun her around. Her smile was broader than he had seen it. "I can't believe I'm finally here. Gus this is Mr..."

Edward limped closer and extended his hand. "I'm Edward. Edward Freeman."

Gus extended his big hand. "I'm pleased to meet you."

Topsey seemed giddy. "You look us up if you need us," she said, pointing out her trunk to Gus. "Careful with that, Gus. All my dresses and hats are in there."

Edward looked around for the people Georgie had arranged to meet him. Her friends at the Baptist Church had written and telegraphed ahead and made arrangements for a family of escaped slaves to take him in. Topsey and Gus gathered her few belongings and went on their way. Folks greeting and saying farewell to travelers filled the platform with hugs, kisses, handshakes, and backslaps. Everyone seemed to find their people, except him. Alone and anxious, he realized he hadn't considered the possibility that his connections might not show up.

"Pardon me. Are you Edward?"

He turned to find a tall, thin, brown-skinned man wearing wire-framed spectacles and a black suit. "Yes sir. I am."

"Well, how do? I'm Elmer. Elmer Bennett," he said extending his hand and breaking in to a broad grin.

"It's nice to meet you, Mr. Bennett."

"Nice to meet you too, son. I'm always glad when one of us makes it this far north. My family and I done helped many get settled up here. You gonna be fine. Don't' you worry about a thing. My carriage is just over yonder."

A bundle of energy, Mr. Bennett seemed to slow his pace after seeing Edward's limp and cane. Sensitive about his limp, Edward tried to walk faster. He didn't want others to think of him as a cripple.

"I've got this bad hip, and it slows me down." Edward felt the need to say something about it.

"Like I said, son. You gonna be just fine. Get on in."

They were about to pull off when a white lady waving a handkerchief called out in their direction, "Mr. Bennett. Oh, Mr. Bennett, wait a minute please."

"Well, how are you, Mrs. Wiley," he said tipping his hat with one hand and holding tight to the reins with the other.

"Oh, I'm just fine. I want to thank your wife for the fine job she did with my linens. That was my mother's tablecloth. It's so special to me. I thought that coffee stain had ruined it, but your wife worked a miracle. It looks brand new. Do tell Mrs. Bennett I said thank you."

"I will, Mrs. Wiley. And thank you for your business. You have a good day," he said as they pulled off.

"Well, I'll be," said Edward. "I ain't never heard a white person call a Negro mister and missus."

"It's different here. Trust me when I say your life will be much better."

Edward exhaled; he had made the right decision in coming to

Canada. They drove on.

"Looks like they're all gathered to greet you," Mr. Bennett said as they pulled up in front of the house. "That's my wife and her two sisters on the porch."

The white three story frame house with dark red shutters and the fence with gleaming white pickets looked like something out of Andrew's story books.

"I'll get your bag," said Mr. Bennett.

"That's all right. I can manage," said Edward, determined not to appear helpless.

The women came down to the carriage to meet them.

"Y'all gather around," said Mr. Bennett. "I want to introduce you to Edward. This here is my wife, Virgie. These are her two sisters: Bernice, and this here is Willy."

"It sure is nice to meet y'all," said Edward. "Thank you for opening up your home to me."

"My goodness, child. You are welcome here," said Virgie. "Since we escaped from that evil plantation in South Carolina, we done helped many Negroes — free and escaped slaves —settle up here. Does my heart good to see colored folks settle into a new life. I can't even begin to count all we've helped. Let me think now ..."

"Oh good heavens, Virgie," interrupted Willy. "You fixing to talk the man to death, and he ain't even got in the house yet."

"Come on in, Edward," said Bernice. "We done cooked up a nice welcome home meal for you," she said as they turned to walk up to the house. She stopped without warning, turned to look him in his face, and said, "We want you to know that you are at home here. Understand?"

"Yes indeed," the others chimed in. "You're home now."

"Yes. I understand, and I thank you."

"Good. Elmer, get the man's bag," said Bernice.

Compared to Wilmington Manor, the house was modest. But for colored people, it was truly grand, complete with an entry foyer, front parlor, dining room, and office. Spotless, gracious rooms greeted him at every turn.

"Your room is on the third floor. When Mrs. Regina wrote us about you, she didn't make no mention about your leg. If we need to move you down to the second floor, we can do that," said Willy.

"No. I don't want to be no trouble." He was startled by her candor. "I'll be just fine. I had to climb a lot of stairs back at the plantation. So, I reckon I done got used to it." He liked the idea of being on the upper floor. It might give him some privacy when he felt the need to be alone.

"All right now. But it ain't no trouble. You just let us know," she said.

"You go on up and unpack, and then come on down for something to eat," said Virgie. "You're the first door on the right.

Edward cleaned up and joined them in the dining room, where he was met with a table laden with fried fish, potato casserole, green beans, and apple pie.

"What made you settle on Canada, Edward?" Virgie asked as she passed him the platter of golden fried fish.

"I didn't think there was any place in the States where I could truly feel free. I heard about Canada and decided to come here."

"Tell us about yourself," she said.

They ate, and he told his story.

"That was a mighty fine meal," said Elmer leaning back in his chair and patting is belly. "Edward, come on into the parlor with me. You smoke a pipe?"

Edward smiled broadly. "Yes, sir, I do. I'll go up and get it."

"No. Don't trouble yourself. Take one of mine already down here."

"Take the corncob. It has a nice draw." Elmer sat back in the chair and stretched out his legs. "You know, we were thinking before you arrived that you might help us out with the business until you get settled."

"I'd be most grateful for the work. What type of business do you have?"

"The women are very skilled at laundry, ironing, and mending. Skills they learned on the plantation. We take in everything from clothes to linens. Them Chinese folks ain't got nothing on us," he chuckled. "I need help with the pickups and deliveries."

"All right. I can start tomorrow."

"You think it will be too much on your leg."

"I do my best not to let this injury stop me. I gotta do my fair share."

"Then we have a deal. We start first thing in the morning," he said extending his hand to Edward."

The ladies entered and took their seats.

"Edward, thank you for answering all our many questions over dinner. I hope you don't think we were prying too much," said Virgie.

"You? Prying? Who would ever think that about you, Virgie?" Willy said.

Virgie ignored the sarcasm and continued, "I enjoyed hearing about your life and friends on the plantation in Virginia and how you hurt your leg. Every story is different but ends in freedom."

"We all started out on a cotton plantation in Charleston, South Carolina," Elmer began. "Virgie and me jumped the broom on December 27, 1845." Pride punctuated each word. "Life on that plantation was just about like it was on any other. But when the old massa died, his son took over and brought on a new overseer. Things got mighty bad. That man was as evil a man as I have ever seen. The young massa was too busy chasing women, drinking, and gambling. He'd gotten his daddy's money, and he didn't care nothing about the plantation or the slaves. In early March of 1848, we took off on the Underground Railroad."

Willy took over, "We was almost caught three times. The Lord was with us, and we made it out. Our closest run-in with them catchers was in Washington. That's what caused us to keep moving north to Canada. Oh, have mercy, Jesus. I remember it like it was yesterday," she wiped her eyes and folded her arms across her breast and rocked.

"You see," said Virgie. "When we made it to Washington, plans were made for about seventy-five slaves to escape on a schooner named *The Pearl*. Word spread through the Negro community quickly. The boat was anchored at a hidden place and would be leaving the next night. It sure sounded better than all the walking and hiding we'd been doing."

"The morning of the departure," Bernice took over telling the story. "Willy came down with a severe case of whooping cough and couldn't make the trip. We certainly weren't going to leave without her, so we decided to continue to hide out and leave later. Meanwhile, white folks had gotten word of the plan. The catchers waited and trapped everybody."

"Those slaves were removed from the boat and held in cells and pens until they could be reclaimed," said Elmer. "We had been thinking about settling in Pennsylvania or Boston, but after *The Pearl* incident and hearing how those good colored people were treated, we didn't want to take the chance of being recaptured and having our family split up. So, we set our minds on Canada."

Edward sat riveted both by the story and how they handed off parts of it to each other as if rehearsed.

That night, Edward sat on the side of the bed looking out at the half moon and reflecting on the successes of the Negro folks he had encountered. Georgie had gotten a job, learned to read and write, and settled into a new place in the world. Elizabeth managed a successful business making dresses for the President's wife. The good colored people at the Baptist Church were like these folks who had taken him in — kind and decent and taking care of themselves and others. He would find his place. If only he could begin his new journey with Andrew beside him.

Weeks passed. Edward wrote to Andrew, but no response had come. He settled into the routine of helping Elmer with the laundry deliveries, and weeks turned into months.

"I reckon that about does it for today," Elmer said as he and Edward loaded the last laundry bags on the back of the wagon one blustery November day.

"Yes, sir. We can head home now." Edward was happy with the way things were working out for him. He appreciated the job and the roof over his head. He'd even run into Gus and Topsey a few times and could comfortably call them friends. Even still, he wanted more independence.

"You all right, Edward? It seems like your mind is somewhere else today."

"I'm fine. I just been thinking."

Elmer didn't say anything.

"I been thinking about how I can best make my way in the world," Edward continued. "I been here for a few months, and I think I need to do something more."

"You seem to have caught on to our business. And you know you're welcome to be with us a long as you like."

"I'm mighty grateful, but I think I should be doing more to help out with the expenses and to make my own legacy."

"What do you want to do? I hope you ain't thinking about leaving Canada and going back to America."

"Oh, no sir. I'm staying here. Although I got to admit, it gets mighty cold up here and early in the season. I'm grateful for what you pay me. I've been able to save a little money. I'm grateful I found that good doctor who helped my leg. The new shoes have made all the difference. I hardly even use the cane anymore."

"So, what do you want to do?"

"See that tavern over yonder. There was a sign in the window yesterday asking for help. I talked to the owner, and he told me I could start waiting tables some evenings and Fridays and Saturdays. I think I'd like to try it. It won't interfere with my work for you."

"That's fine. Fine indeed," Elmer slapped the horse with the reins and pulled off. "I'm a firm believer in hard work, and I respect a man who is willing to do it. Let's get home and tell the ladies the good news."

"Working in a bar where they serve strong drink? Are you sure you want to do that, Edward? Virgie asked.

"I think it will be just fine. And I could use the extra money."

"But in a tavern?"

"Oh, for heaven's sake, Virgie. Don't you go getting all high-and-mighty. You know we make a nice income off of our homemade wine and Elmer's corn liquor."

"Our spirits are used for medicinal purposes."

"You don't believe that any more than I do," said Bernice. "Congratulations, Edward.  You take that job for as long as you like. Medicinal purposes my foot," she chuckled.

## Chapter 43
## April 1865

**Edward** swept the floor as the last customers left the tavern. Felix, the owner and bartender said goodnight to everyone by name, making his place feel like home.

A man with a bloated belly sat at the back table. Edward couldn't place the face and would have remembered the huge stomach on the man if he had met him before. The man sat staring at his untouched plate of food, his full head of black and silver hair bobbing with each breath. He appeared to be working at not tipping into his food.

Edward put down the broom and walked over. A stench – piss – overwhelmed him as he got near the man. "Excuse me, sir, is there something else I can get for you?" Edward asked, keeping some distance.

The man did not respond. The bottle of rye he had been nursing for most of the evening was half full. Again Edward said, "Excuse me, sir," and touched him on the shoulder. The man fell face-first into the plate and knocked the bottle to the floor, splattering broken glass and whiskey all around the table.

"Ah, hell," said Felix, walking from behind the bar, untying his apron, and throwing it on the closest table. "Here we go again. Every few months he comes in here and drinks himself into a stupor. We don't see him for another two or three months. Then, he shows up and pulls the same shit."

"Who is he?" Edward asked, lifting the man's face from the mashed potatoes and stewed chicken.

"He's got a business he runs outside of town, if you can call it that. He don't take care of the place. But travelers still seem to go there to bathe and clean up, mostly in the summer. Help me get him in his wagon. He can sleep in the back and take himself on home when he wakes up."

They lifted the man into the back of his wagon.

"It's a cold night, and I don't feel right just leaving him in the back of the wagon to sleep it off. Where does he live?"

"About a mile down yonder," said Felix, pointing east. "You can't miss the place. It's all filled with barrels and wash tubs."

"I'll take him home."

"You be careful. He can be a real scoundrel," warned Felix.

Edward tied his horse to the back of the man's wagon and started out down the road. When they arrived at the house, the man came out of his stupor enough to walk a little with Edward's help. Once inside, he fell across a bed in the front room. Edward lit a lamp and put wood in the stove and stoked the fire. In the midst of clutter and filth, in a dark corner, sat a large chair with an ottoman. Edward sat down, propped up his feet, and drifted off to sleep.

A few hours later, Edward woke to the man sitting on the bed staring at him and nursing another glass of whiskey.

"How you feeling," asked Edward.

"Who the hell are you?" the old man responded, taking a swig from the glass.

Edward sat up and took his feet off the ottoman. He rubbed his face and remembered Felix's warning.

"I'm the one who brought you home and sat with you to make sure you didn't drown in your own vomit. Who the hell are you?"

The man bristled at the response. Edward got up and headed for the door.

"My name is Ezra, Ezra Burr." The man softened his voice.

"Please to make your acquaintance, Mr. Burr. I'm Edward."

"You got a last name?"

Edward remembered Topsey and smiled. "Freeman. Edward Freeman."

He stepped out the door into the yard and brisk cold, and Ezra followed. Edward untied his horse from the back of the wagon and looked around at the washtubs and barrels for catching water. A barber's chair stood ready under a shed.

"They usually just let me sleep it off in the back of my wagon," said Ezra. "I done woke up rained on and snowed on and in all sorts of shape. I guess what I mean to say is thank you. It's been a long time since anybody has shown me a kindness." He hesitated a moment. "I ain't always been like this. I do have some manners in spite of what folks might have told you," he said taking another swig.

Edward looked at the glass.

"This is my breakfast," Ezra explained. "It cuts the pain and helps me to start the day. Yes, siree. We been lovers a long time, and she's been mighty good to me." He kissed the glass.

"If you want to thank me, how about you let me take a bath in one of them tubs sometime after it gets warm."

"You don't look like you need no bath."

"Well, I don't. It's just that I like the idea of privacy. I share a house with three women and to be able to soak in a tub without worrying about being walked in on ..."

"I see. You don't have to wait for the warm weather. I got three tubs set up in the back room. Help yourself. Start a fire in one of them stoves back there, and heat some water. I don't give a damn. Ain't nobody else coming 'round here these days," Ezra mumbled and walked back into the house.

Edward searched for kindling and started a fire in one of the stoves. Surprisingly, the water pump wasn't frozen. He carried the cold water to the house and waited for it to heat. He walked around out back and looked over the place. It seemed to have a nice amount of acreage for planting crops, and the equipment for the public baths was in good shape. The place just needed minor repairs and cleaning up.

He stripped and stepped into the warm soothing water. He leaned back and let the water reach his neck. He thought of Andrew. He remembered their first night together. He imagined Andrew's strong hand massaging his neck and stroking his back with the soft cloth. His mind drifted back to their times together. The long soak relaxed and energized him at the same time. Lots of folks would appreciate a hot bath being prepared for them. Why had Ezra let the business go down? His mind raced. Maybe he could run it for Ezra. Or maybe he could buy the place. He had a little money, but probably not enough. But maybe he could work out a deal.

Edward shared his thoughts with Elmer and the ladies that night over dinner.

"I think it's a grand idea," said Elmer. "I remember when the place was thriving, before the man took to drinking, let it get run down, and started to run his own customers away with his disagreeable disposition."

The ladies agreed.

"I don't know if he'll sell it to me for what I've got."

"You won't know until you ask him," said Bernice.

"I'll ride out there on Sunday," said Edward.

Edward arrived at Ezra's mid-day on that following Sunday afternoon in a bitter cold front, one that felt like it would settle in and stay until spring. Edward enjoyed the crisp air, found it invigorating.

"You back for another bath?" Ezra yelled before Edward could get off the horse.

"No sir, Mr. Burr. I come to talk to you."

"Well, do tell. I ain't had a visitor in quite a spell. What you want with me?"

Edward dismounted and walked up on the porch. "I want to talk to you about this here place you got."

"What about it?" Ezra asked. A glass of whiskey sloshed in his hand.

"I want to buy it from you, if you're willing to sell. I don't' know if I can afford it, but I got to ask you. I come to like it. I come to like it a lot. How much you want for it?"

"Come on in. It's too cold for talking business out here. Ezra stepped inside and Edward followed. "How much you got?"

"I ain't got much, but I done saved about two hundred dollars. Mr. Bennett is willing to loan me a little more if I need it. I thought maybe we could work out a deal where I could pay you off over time."

Ezra sat back in his chair rolling the glass between his palms. After a minute of silence, he said, "I tell you what I'm willing to do. I'll take your two hundred dollars and give you this place, but there are some conditions with the deal. You got to agree to let me stay here and drink as much as I want for the rest of my life. I guess you done figured that ain't gonna be much longer. And, when I die, you got to promise me a decent burial out yonder in that field. I done picked my spot and marked it off."

Edward could hardly believe his ears. "I'll go in town first thing in the morning and get the papers drawn up," he said smiling.

They sat in silence for a moment; Edward looking around his new property and Ezra at his glass. "What's wrong with you?" Edward asked looking at the large protrusion in the man's stomach.

"Don't know. The doctors say this thing in my belly is gonna eat at me until it kills me. The pain gets worse each day. That's why I drink. It numbs the pain. The folk in town don't understand that."

"Seeing as how we gonna be living together," said Edward, "I'll help you any way that I can."

"Have a drink with me to seal the deal." Ezra got up to get another glass.

"You mind if I look around the inside."

"Look it all over. You gonna own it soon enough."

Edward remembered the front room from his first visit. The house was bigger than he thought. The first floor was also home to a very large kitchen, and a backroom for storage that could also be a bedroom if necessary. Each room seemed more cluttered than the next.

The upstairs housed three large bedrooms. The thick coat of dust suggested these rooms had not been used in a very long time. Ezra probably spent most of his time on the first floor. Each bedroom had a full-size bed with minimal furnishings. It would all have to do for now. In addition to needing a good cleaning, the house also needed a coat of paint, inside and out.

*********

The next week, Edward left Elmer and the ladies and moved in with Ezra. He used Mr. Bennett's buckboard to bring his few belongings to the house. He sat for a few minutes, taking in the view and surveying *his* new property. In spite of its outer appearance, it was a well-built house, solid and sturdy. He was proud. He'd found work, and now he had a home.

"You sure got things cleaned up around here. This place ain't never looked this good," said Ezra looking around the front room.

"I'm glad you're pleased. I been doing as much as I can in my spare time. Until this place starts to make some money, I got to keep my job at the tavern and with Mr. Bennett's laundry service."

"I noticed the way you done changed things outside."

"I thought if I could build those walls to offer more privacy, the place might attract more women customers when the weather breaks."

"That's a good idea. It's a shame you didn't show up sooner. I could have used a partner like you. You be careful out there working in the cold. Frostbite is a terrible thing. Make sure you're covered up good."

"We got nine or ten tubs for bathing, a space for cutting hair and shaving, and three outhouses. We just ain't got no customers."

Ezra smiled and raised his bushy eyebrows. "It's gonna be all right, Edward. Now that you done had them handbills made and placed all over town, business is picking up."

"What do you mean?"

"I got a something for you. Some farm hands and men from out in the country came in today. I took care of 'em. Collected the money. It's all right there. You can count it. I wouldn't cheat you."

"Oh, I ain't worried about that. I know I can trust you." Edward picked up the coins. He jangled them and imagined a week's worth, a year's. A smile spread across his face.

"You were right, most folks don't mind paying extra for hot water. Congratulations, Edward. You are officially in business. Let's have some tea to celebrate."

"Tea?"

"Yes, tea. I think I done drank enough whiskey for a while. I'm kinda excited about having you around and seeing this take off. I ain't trying to stop drinking all together, mind you. But, I'll try to wait until after the customers are all gone before I take my nips."

Business picked up, but still not like Edward had hoped. He and Ezra sat by the fire one Sunday afternoon when five farmers rode up. Edward parted the curtain. The elder looking of the five dismounted and knocked on the door. Edward opened the door, and a blast of cold air chilled the living room.

"Afternoon," he said.

"Afternoon," Edward and Ezra replied.

"What can we do for you?" Edward asked.

The elder man took off his hat. "My daughter is getting married in a few hours, and my wife said we better not show up unless we done got cleaned up. We been digging a well the last few days to make sure we got water. I ain't had no time to be worried about no wedding. Can you help us? We need to get cleaned up, and we ain't got a lot of time. If you got some clean shirts and pants, I got money to buy them too."

"I'll do the best I can, but all the tubs are empty. Don't get much business in the winter and especially on Sundays." Edward did not want to panic. He knew if he helped these men they would spread the word about his business. He was glad he had learned a little about mending, washing, and ironing from the Bennett household. He always kept a few extra shirts and pants to sell.

"I'll start to shaving while you get the tubs filled," Ezra piped in. "I got some hot water on the stove in the kitchen. I can use that to whip up a shaving lather. You boys get on off them horses. We'll get you fixed up. We might need some of you strong young ones to help carry water."

In no time, hot water filled the three inside tubs. After their haircuts, shaves, baths, and fresh clothes, the five mounted up.

"Thank you. You can expect us most Saturday evenings," said the father. "I got a few men who work for me. I'll bring them around, too." They trotted off.

"They look a hell of a lot better than they did when they come up," said Ezra.

*They sure do* thought Edward. It had been years since he had touched another man. When his urges got strong, he satisfied himself, but that was no substitute for Andrew.

"We make a pretty good team. Seems like steady customers going to be coming again," said Ezra.

"We do make a fine team." Edward sank into the rocker.

"I think we done earned us a real drink. You sit still. I'll get it."

**\*\*\*\*\*\*\*\*\***

Edward stood on the hillside, looking at all the people who came out to help bury Ezra.

Felix from the tavern meandered up. "What are you thinking so hard about?"

"I can't believe it is spring already.  We done got through a long hard winter."

"Yep, early April already. And can you believe its 1865?  If we take care of ourselves, you and me might live long enough to see the new century come in."

They stared at the fresh earth.  "You did everything that you could, you know," Felix broke the silence.

"I know."  Edward rubbed his foot over the dirt.

"You never did tell us how he died."

"He had cut back on the drinking when we were busy.  He stayed sober long enough during the day to cut the men's hair and give them a shave.  Once January and February set in and the business slowed, he took to drinking more.  The winter weather kept him inside, with no distractions from his pain.  One night in late February, I came in from the tavern, and he was sitting in front of the fire with his arm hanging over the side of the chair, a bottle of rye tight in his hand. I tried to wake him, but he was dead.  I put him in the back of the buckboard and took him to the funeral parlor.  The undertaker dressed him and put him in the box for me.  It was so cold at the time, I covered the box and kept him under the shed, waiting for the ground to thaw.  By the way, I want to thank you and the other men for coming out to help me dig the grave."

"It's a mighty fine thing you have done putting him away real nice.  We were glad to help.  He would be pleased to know just how many folks cared enough to show up."

"He picked his spot and told me where to put him."

"Come on, Edward.  Let's go on back to the tavern for something to eat.  The other men can finish up with the burial."

"I'll come eat shortly.  I need to stay until they fill it.  You go on ahead.  I'll be there directly."

**Chapter 44**
**April 1865**
**Andrew** looked up as Luther entered the study. "You ought to put some oil on that door hinge. It startles me every time."

"Beg your pardon, Mr. Andrew, but Mr. Jessup is here to see you," said Luther. I'll oil that hinge, directly."

"Bring him on in here," said Andrew, his somber mood brightening.

Jessup walked in and over to Andrew's desk. "Howdy, Andrew. I hope you don't mind my coming by like this."

"Course not," he said, realizing that Jessup was not his usual cheerful self. "You know you're always welcome here anytime."

"What ya doing?"

"Nothing. Just sitting here pondering one thing or another."

"Sounds like we both in a bad way. I needed to see a friendly face is all. I rode out hoping you might be in."

"Where else would I be, Jessup, but sitting right here. The fall and winter done come and gone, and I'm still here at this plantation." He rubbed his stump.

They sat in silence, staring at the small fire. The flames danced, the wood popped and sizzled, and smoke escaped up the flue.

"I've been so preoccupied with preserving Wilmington Manor, I haven't had time to really try to find Edward," Andrew said breaking the silence. "Lord only knows where he is now. Sometimes I miss him so much, it hurts."

"So, I guess that means you ain't heard nothing from him."

"He told Jasper that he would write, but nothing has come so far. I worry that something may have happened to him. Maybe he got caught by Confederate soldiers or between battle lines. Maybe he's dead. I don't know."

"I know you miss him, and I know you've had a lot on your shoulders this last year. I hope the loan from Maggie helped."

"It did, and I'm grateful to both of you for all your help. Anna had run up so many debts. I don't blame her for the shape the place is in. I know she did the best she could with the resources she had."

Andrew massaged his forehead.

"Are things a little better now?"

"Yes. And this year, we're going to raise tomatoes, beans, corn, potatoes, and other produce. I've started raising chickens. Folks are clamoring for fresh vegetables and meat. I've been able to repay Maggie most of what I owe her. Jasper stayed on, and so did a few of the field hands. I have to pay them as best I can. You know they ain't slaves now."

"Yep. A lot sure has changed, and I suspect more change is coming."

"We'll just have to deal with it, Jessup. Just think about it. Wilmington Manor was once one of the finest tobacco plantations in the south. Now it's a chicken farm with free Negroes and poor whites doing the work. I'm sure Daddy's rolling in his grave right about now," he chuckled.

"I'll bet he is."

"But you didn't ride out here to listen to me unload my woes. What's on your mind? Seems like something is eating at you."

"I wasn't gonna bring it up. I'm all right."

"What is it?" Andrew prodded. "You're not all right. I can tell."

Jessup sighed and rubbed his face. "I told ya all about my friend, Thelton Taylor. Remember?"

"I remember. He's the one you met at Maggie's."

"Yea. He up and got married last month. I got a lettah from him today saying ..." Jessup's voice cracked and water welled in his eyes. "Saying he didn't want to see me again." His elbows planted firmly on the chair arms, he rested his chin on his interlocked fingers, and tears fell freely.

Andrew knelt beside the chair and put his arm around his distraught friend. Jessup rested his head on Andrew's shoulder and sobbed. "Oh Andrew, I'm not ashamed of what I am, but what's to become of me? There is no place for me, you, and others like us in this country." He spoke through sobs and gasps for air.

"Come on now. You're the one who's always pushing me to live life to the fullest."

"I know, but it gets hard sometimes. So damn difficult." Jessup wiped his eyes.

Andrew stood and poured some whiskey. "Sip this."

"I'm sorry for carrying on like this. I'm a damn fool. Where the hell's my pride?"

"Ain't nothing foolish about being human, Jessup. I got two words for Mr. Thelton Taylor."

"What's that?" Jessup asked, looking up from the glass.

"Fuck him."

"I did." Jessup snickered, changing the mood, if only for a moment.

Jessup finished his drink. "I best be getting on back down the road. It's getting late."

"Jessup," said Andrew as they reached the front door. "You're my best friend. You're always welcome here. Where *I* call home, *you* may call home."

"I feel the same way about you, Andrew. We're family. You and Maggie are all I've got. By the way, ya mustache looks nice.

"I thought I'd try a different look. I let it grow out once when I was in the war."

After saying goodnight to Jessup, Andrew retired to his bedroom. He reached for his pipe but couldn't find tobacco. He looked everywhere. Finally, he opened the chest Edward made for him, thinking some forgotten stash might be hidden there. Inside rested the note from Edward and under it, a pouch of tobacco. His heart stirred. He lit his pipe and read Edward's words over and over.

*********

Andrew opened drawers and emptied papers on the floor, tearing his office apart.

"Is there something I can help you find, Mr. Andrew?" Luther asked.

"I'm heading up to Richmond to meet with the family lawyer, and I want to take the will I wrote before I went to war. Where would Anna have put such an important document?" He stood with his good arm folded over his stump. "Come up with me to her room."

The room had been closed since her death. The bloodstained carpet was removed along with other signs of her agony. Staleness greeted them when they entered.

"Start looking over there and set aside any envelopes you find," instructed Andrew. Luther wouldn't know a will from a shopping list. "I'll start over here in her dresser."

After a few minutes of rummaging, Andrew stopped looking.

"Did you find it, Mr. Andrew?"

"No. But I did find something else," he said holding the letter he had sent to Edward. It had been opened and read, but not delivered to Edward. "I'll be damned. She never gave it to him. He must think I'm dead. Maybe if he had gotten the letter he would have waited for me."

"I beg your pardon, sir."

"Oh it's nothing Luther. I'm just mumbling to myself. I'm gonna head up to Richmond today. I need to take care of some business and get some seeds. It's early April, and we've only planted half the crops. Close up this room for me, and I'll see you later tonight."

The ride to Richmond was pleasant. Signs of spring and new life greeted him around every bend in the road. White, yellow, and pink buds sprouted on the trees and plants. Birds chirped, and wildlife scurried. But as he entered the city, the ravages of war marred the landscape. The smell of smoke and gunpowder and the ghosts of buildings surrounded him. The Shockoe District was not bustling, as it did before the war. The sounds of immigrants and hired out slaves hard at work in the factories and warehouses had been silenced. Many buildings had been burned, leaving only shells as evidence of their existence. The city was now a collection of collapsed roofs, walls, abandonment, and decay.

"Good to see you, Andrew," said Mr. Horsley as he hoisted the seed on the back of the wagon. It's nice to know a few of us are holding on. You seem to get on just fine with just one arm."

Mr. Horsley's candor surprised Andrew. Most folks tried to avoid looking at or mentioning his arm. "I've found that you can get used to anything."

"I reckon you're right."  Mr. Horsley shook his head in disappointment.  "Seems like we all gonna have some adjusting to do."

"What do you mean?"

"From what I hear, the war is turning in favor of the North. Richmond has been overtaken by the Union, and, as much as I hate to say it, the South is losing, Andrew."

"It don't look good, but we can keep hoping."

"I hear tell that Abraham Lincoln is at our White House right now.  If that ain't a bad sign, I don't know what is."

"You mind if I leave my wagon here for a spell.  I think I'll walk over to Clay Street and see if I can catch a glimpse of Mr. Lincoln."

"Sure.  Help yourself.  I'll watch the wagon.  But, don't walk. Take my horse.  I'm not going anywhere."

Andrew stopped in front of the building.  A crowd of people had gathered – Negroes and whites.  Lincoln and his son walked out on the front porch, and a great applause erupted, mostly from the Negroes. He and his son walked down the steps and into the street; the Negroes began to sing a tune Andrew had heard coming from the fields many times before.

*God done set his people free, God's gonna build up Zion's walls.*
*Great day.  Great day the righteous marching.*

He used to like it, them thinking of their freedom as a spiritual place.  It must have given them comfort.  But today it meant something different to them, and it scared him.

*This is the day of jubilee, God's gonna build up Zion's walls.*
*Great day, God's gonna build up Zion's walls.*

## Chapter 45
### April 1865

**Andrew** sat mounted on his horse watching his field hands plant the crops, the rich brown earth soft from the spring rains and easy to turn. Daddy had always been proud of the quality of Wilmington Manor's earth. Andrew never loved the place like Daddy did. If he didn't leave soon, he feared he would be tethered there forever. Hard-riding hooves interrupted his thoughts. Andrew looked over the field; Jessup was galloping hard toward him.

"Andrew! Andrew!" Jessup yelled and waived his hat.

He was shouting something else, but Andrew could not make out the words.

"Andrew," he said gasping for breath as he rode up to him. "It's over. It's over, I tell ya. Lee surrendered to Grant this morning."

"Y'all hear that," Andrew yelled to Jasper and the others. "The war is over!"

A round of yelling and backslapping broke out among the workers.

"Come on up to the house, Jessup. I don't know if this calls for a celebration or mourning."

"What you mean?"

"We'll celebrate the war ending and mourn the South's loss. Seems I lost an arm and a lot of men lost their lives." He rubbed the back of his neck. "All for nothing."

"I stopped in at the house looking for you. Luther said you was out here. He asked me to give ya this here lettah. Said it come for you this morning. Want me to open it?"

"I can do it." Jessup handed over the letter. Andrew ripped it open with his teeth and read silently.

"I don't mean to pry, but what is it that's got you to smiling so?"

"This is good news."

"Well, what's it say? Who's it from? Say something, will ya, instead of just sitting there grinning at me. "

"It's from Georgie. She's alive and well. And she's seen Edward."

"What's she say?"

"I'll read it."

*Andrew,*

*I am writing you this letter from Washington. I made it this far north, and some fine people took me in. I found work, and I stay with a nice lady named Elizabeth Keckley. Edward came through here. He wanted me to write you to let you know that I am all right. He is all right, too. He says he will write you. I am sorry for the way I left, but I had to go. I hope one day you can understand. I love you.*

*Georgie*
*1017 12th Street*
*Washington*


"Well, I'll be," said Jessup. "This is truly a good day. The war's over, and you finally have a lead on Edward."

"Let's go on back to the house," said Andrew. "Let's walk. I want to ask you a few things."

"What's on your mind?"

They dismounted and started walking, each leading his horse.

"Jessup, do you think you could sell this place for me?"

"I had a feeling this day was coming."

"With the war being over and all, and hearing from Georgie, I think I can find Edward. I've got to try."

"Course you do. Let me ask around. I think I know someone who might be interested. Give me a few days, and I'll get back to you."

After walking in silence for a few minutes, Jessup said, "I know you need to go, but are you sure ya want to sell this place?"

"I'm sure. The little bit of happiness I experienced here was a part of my childhood. Most of my adult years have been filled with disappointment and Daddy's disapproval. Those who truly love me are living up north or are buried."

\*\*\*\*\*\*\*\*\*

The cuff link slipped from between his lips. He had gotten

pretty skilled at using his mouth and chin to perform tasks, but there was no true substitute for two hands to put on a cufflink. He usually put the link in before putting the shirt on, but in his rush, he forgot. He didn't like asking for help but didn't want to waste time taking the shirt off and starting over again.

"Luther!"

After a minute or two he yelled again, "Luther!"

"Yes, sir," Luther said, appearing in the bedroom doorway, out of breath.

"I need help with this blasted cufflink," he said, setting aside his pride for a moment and feeling bad that the old man had to rush up the stairs for such a trivial matter. "I'm sorry. I didn't mean to alarm you by yelling. I guess I'm just a little excited today, and I don't want to be late for the train."

"That's all right, sah. We sho gonna miss you 'round here."

"Thank you, Luther. But you gonna be just fine. Maggie Dumont is a good woman. She bought the place and agreed to keep you on. She can pay you a lot more than I can."

Luther secured the cuff link in place. "They say she got a place in Richmond. What she want to buy this place for?"

"The place in Richmond is her business establishment. She will keep that, but she wants to make this place her home. She wants to keep her business and home distinctly and clearly separate."

"I 'speck I'll be all right."

"I know you will. Now, I catch the train in Richmond this morning and arrive in Washington late this evening. I hope to find Georgie when I get there. Jessup is handling the sale, and I think everything is in order. But, if anyone needs me or comes looking for me, I'll be staying at the National Hotel."

Jasper was waiting to take him to the station. They drove down the road from the mansion, flanked by the myrtle trees Daddy was so proud to tell him about when he returned from school. Stirred by the breeze, they seemed to be waving goodbye. They rode past the slave shanties where he grew to love Georgie and Aunt Daisy. They rode through the lush field down near the riverbank where Andrew had shared dalliances with Jim Shelton until they both agreed it was too risky with Jim being married to Anna's best friend. Not to mention the fact that MawNancy had discovered their secret. All his memories seemed to bid him farewell. And the stately brick mansion, his mother's showpiece, grew smaller and smaller. After getting some distance away, Andrew looked back at what he hoped would be his last view of Wilmington Manor.

The train ride tired Andrew but probably not more than going by horseback. As the train pulled into Washington, he watched dusk settle over the city. He was glad to have his heavy cape. Even though it was early April, a chill fell with the sun.

"Sign and date here, please," said a short desk clerk with a manicured handlebar mustache as he handed him the hotel guest registry.

"What is today's date?" Andrew asked.

"April 12, 1865."

"Thank you. Would you tell me how to get to this address, please?" He unfolded Georgie's letter and showed the clerk.

"Yes, sir." The clerk explained the streets and turns leading to the address. "Do you need me to carry up your bag?"

"No. Thank you. I can manage."

He woke early the next morning, eager to see Georgie. The morning chill had not lifted. Andrew secured the clasp at the neck of his cape. The streets of Washington were still populated with Union soldiers. Strolling, he sensed optimism in the air coupled with a collective sigh of relief. He turned onto her street, and met two Negro women wearing elegant dresses, walking in his direction. He recognized Georgie from her hair wrapped in the blue fabric he had given her several Christmases ago. He stopped, and the two women walked toward him. Engrossed in their conversation, they did not notice him staring until they were right upon him.

Georgie froze. Her eyes widened.

"Georgie?" he said with a comforting smile.

She remained silent.

"Georgie, this gentleman just spoke to you. Do you know him?"

Asked the other woman.

"Yes. Mrs. Elizabeth Keckley this here is Mr. Andrew Gordon."

"Pleased to make your acquaintance, Mrs. Keckley," said Andrew.

"Likewise, Mr. Gordon. I take it you all know each other from Virginia?"

"Yes," said Georgie. "Andrew is …" she didn't finish.

"I'm her brother," Andrew interjected. "Half brother."

A quick breeze got under his cape, causing it to flare.

"Oh my," Georgie said, seeing his arm stump.

He touched her face with the cup of his hand and said, "It's all right. I'm just fine. Now."

"Mr. Gordon, you are more than welcome to join Georgie and me for supper tomorrow evening."

"I'd be delighted. That is if Georgie doesn't mind."

"I'll fix all of your favorites," Georgie said with tears in her eyes. She flung her arms around his neck.

**********

"Georgie, you've been cooking all day," said Elizabeth as she breezed through the kitchen headed toward her sewing room.

"I want everything to be perfect. I've tried to remember Andrew's favorites and prepare them the way my mama did," Georgie raised her voice to reach Elizabeth in the other room.

"It sure smells good. What you got going in there?"

"Corn pudding, fried chicken, greens beans, scalloped potatoes, and pickled beets."

"Get the good china and crystal out of the cabinet. Use my best tablecloth. It's in the chest. I wish I could help you, but I've got to finish this gown for Mrs. Lincoln. She wants to wear it this evening. Mr. Slade will be here to pick it up any minute now."

"Don't you need to make sure it fits proper?"

"No. We've done all the fittings. I'm just hemming it and adding a little more lace. I'm almost done. She's so particular. I reckon being the first lady of the United States, she's got a right to be,"

Elizabeth laughed.

**********

Georgie stood at the window with Elizabeth. Mr. Slade left with the dress just as Andrew arrived. Georgie untied her apron. "He's here."

They watched Andrew get out of the carriage. "He is a handsome man," said Elizabeth.

"He is. And a good man, too. I almost didn't recognize him yesterday. He grew a mustache."

"What's he waiting for?" Elizabeth asked.

"I don't know. Maybe he's as nervous as I am."

"He's got something wrapped in paper under his arm. I wonder what it is." Elizabeth stood on her toes and craned her neck. "Maybe it's a gift for you."

Elizabeth opened the door. "This is the right place. Come on in," she yelled, beckoning him to come forward.

"Welcome, Mr. Gordon," she said as he approached.

"Thank you for having me, Mrs. Keckley." He looked at Georgie. They embraced. "I've missed you. I'm so glad you wrote."

"I'm glad I did, too. I'm still working on my reading and writing. Elizabeth helped me. After all, I promised Edward I would write you."

"I declare, the smell of your cooking is like heaven," he said. He removed his cape and placed it with the package on a nearby chair.

Accustomed to freedom and socializing with free and educated Negroes, Georgie, at first, didn't know how to interact with Andrew. But after a while, she relaxed and fell into the comfort of being reunited with her brother. They talked about old times and caught up on the news in their lives. Andrew talked about the war, the loss of his arm, and the pending sale of Wilmington Manor. She talked about the illness in her mind at the time she ran away, meeting Elizabeth, and the life she had carved out for herself in Washington. Andrew asked for second helpings of everything and still had room for cake and coffee.

"I was a slave too, Mr. Gordon, said Elizabeth. "I used my skills as a seamstress to purchase freedom for my son and me. I understand

318

the balance that is required when Negroes and whites share the same bloodline."

Andrew asked, "Can you tell me how to find Edward?"

"I was wondering when you were going to get around to that," said Georgie.

He blushed. "I'd like to find him."

"I know," she said, hoping to reassure him that the conversation was all right with her. "I met up with him by pure luck when he came through. He needed assistance at the hospital where I work."

Andrew looked concerned.

"He's fine," she said. "He just needed to rest his bad hip for a few days. We sold the horse and lent him some money to get a train ticket north."

"Where'd he go?"

"He was bound and determined to get out of this country. And, after all he had been through, I don't blame him. He headed for Canada."

"Canada?"

"Yes. Ottawa. He returned the money we lent him, and, in his note, said that he had written you. When no one heard from you, we all thought you might have been killed in the war. I'm glad I wrote anyway. I have Edward's information all written down for you."

"I have a suggestion," said Elizabeth. "I want to see Mrs. Lincoln in the dress I sent over earlier. Why don't we get a carriage and ride around to Tenth Street? Maybe we can get a look at them when they leave the theatre. I know it's a short walk, but let's ride anyway. We can have the driver take us on a tour of the city afterwards."

"That's a fine idea," agreed Georgie.

"The outing will be a perfect end to this lovely evening," added Andrew. But before we go, I have something for you." He retrieved the package. I might not ever go back to Wilmington Manor, and I didn't know what to do with this." He handed it to her.

She removed the wrapping and pulled out the Wilmington Ledger. She ran her hand across it and looked up at him.

"Before you say anything you should know why I brought it with me. I couldn't destroy it. It contains the information about all the folks we love – Aunt Daisy, Uncle Buck, Little Sally, Luther, and Ryan. It's our family history. Look here." He flipped to the first page. "I even added my name." On the first line of the first page, he had added his name, birthdate and across from his name he wrote *second-generation owner and half-brother to Georgie*. "You can do with it what you like. Burn it if you want. It's yours now."

"I've hated this book since I was a little girl. After I learned to spell my name, it became my obsession. I'd look for moments when I could sneak in and flip through the pages, looking for my name," she looked far away, out the window. "But you're right. It contains our history, shameful as it is. I'll keep it to share with my children, if I have anymore. So much has changed. I don't think I hate this book like I used to. I need it to help keep the folks listed in here close to me. Thank you."

"We'd better hurry and get us a carriage," said Elizabeth as she adjusted her cloak.

Georgie placed the Ledger on the living room mantel.

Tenth Street teemed with people. In spite of the late hour and the steady drizzle, the crowd must have gathered for a chance to see the President. After descending from the carriage, Georgie realized that the atmosphere was closer to pandemonium. Women cried, men shouted and cussed.

"Driver, would you please wait?" Andrew asked. "I need to see what's going on here. Something's not right." He stopped a passerby. "Excuse me, sir. Can you tell me what's happening here?"

"It was one of those goddamned Southerners!"

"What has happened?" Andrew asked.

"The President! They done shot him!"

Just then, a caravan of men carried the wounded President from Ford's Theatre across the street to Petersen's Boarding House. Mrs. Lincoln followed, wearing the dress Elizabeth had delivered earlier that day.

## Chapter 46
## April 1865

**Edward** inhaled fresh spring air as he loaded supplies into his wagon and exhaled satisfaction. He filled his days with hard work to distract himself from missing Andrew. He hadn't received a response from the letter he wrote. Some days, he assumed that Andrew had been killed in the war. "Thank you so much. I'll be seeing you," Edward said to the shopkeeper as he loaded the final box of supplies.

"You take care, Edward," the shopkeeper answered, patting him on the back. "It sure is awful what happened to that American President, ain't it?"

"Yes, it is. He was a good man." Edward looked around the street. "It's such a nice day, I think I'll walk around for a bit before I go on back out to the house. You mind if I leave my wagon here?"

"Sure. I'll keep an eye on it. There's something going on up at the performance hall. Go on up there and see what it is. I don't like that fancy stuff, but you might."

The sunset painted the sky pastel as Edward walked past a music hall where a sign said the Civic Society was sponsoring an "Evening of Song and Recitation." He crossed in front of the place as rich sounds of a man singing filled the air. Edward didn't understand the words, but the haunting melody captivated him. The man sang with emotion alongside lush piano chords; Edward imagined the song to be about passion between two people. He stopped and listened, then entered the hall, transported by the melody. Inside, he picked up a printed program and took a seat near the back. According to the program, the singer was Giovanni Belletti, and he had just sung Peter Tschaikowsky's *Wieder — wie fruher.*

Edward read the translation that was printed in the program. It was a challenge but worth the struggle:

*Once again as it was before, alone. Where is my sweet love?*
*Outside shining silver in the light, rustles a willow in the wind.*
*Up above on the heavenly tent the stars shine so mild.*
*Far from the distance of the world your image appears secretly*

*to me.*

*The burden upon me is heavy longingly. I wait for you.*

*Dearly Beloved, I miss you so much. Dearly beloved, Oh think of me.*

Edward didn't know anything about this type of music, but he sat eager for the next song. At the end of the program, he left the performance hall fixated on Andrew, longing for him. Tschaikowsky's melody danced in his mind as he prayed that Andrew's spirit was at peace.

The next day, Edward squatted next a washtub in the barn scrubbing it out. Hooves sounded in the distance, getting closer. Edward remained focused on the tub, readying it for the potential customer.

"They tell me in town this is the place where I can get a shave and a hot bath."

"Yes sir. I'll be right with you," Edward answered, not looking up. The voice sounded familiar.

The man dismounted and stepped into the doorway. Edward put down the scrub brush and stood to greet his new customer.

"This time, you'll have to help me."

Sunlight streamed through the doorway; Edward squinted and realized he was looking into Andrew's face.

For a moment, they stared at each other. Could it really be him? The mustache and stump of an arm confused Edward, but the voice and stance were familiar.

Andrew stepped closer, blocking the sunlight. He put his arm around Edward's shoulder and pulled him close. With his lips pressed on Edward's, he said, "It's me."

Edward's arms held Andrew tight. The memories came flooding back – his scent, the feel of his body, the taste of his kiss. It *was* him.

Edward wanted to talk and listen, but mostly absorb Andrew. They stood embracing, motionless. After a while, Edward rubbed his lips on the side of Andrew's face, exploring his cheeks, neck, chin, and lips. Not letting go of each other they inched over to hay bales, belt buckles loosened and britches dropping below their knees.

"We can go into the house," said Edward, unbuttoning Andrew's shirt.

"I don't want to wait a minute longer." Andrew pulled Edward closer.

The midmorning tryst was gentle, filled with reacquainting caresses and kisses.

That night their lovemaking was more uninhibited and lasted into the early morning hours.

Edward woke to find Andrew staring at the ceiling and snuggled in tight next to him. "Almost three years apart and I've never felt closer to you than I do right now."

"I was just thinking how much you are a part of me. I've been miserable without you. I can't imagine my life without you. I should not have separated us by going off to fight. Can you ever forgive me?"

Edward held Andrew tighter. "Of course. I'm thankful you're back safe."

"I'm not the same as when I left." Andrew tapped his stump.

"Don't matter. We're both alive and have a future together. I'm glad we're here where we can get a fresh start. But I've got to warn you, the winters are damn cold."

"We'll have to keep each other warm." Andrew got out of bed.

"Where are you going?"

"I've got something I've been waiting to share with you."

"I think we took care of that several times last night."

Andrew laughed. "That's not what I'm talking about." He walked to the other side of the room and retrieved a book from his satchel.

Edward marveled at Andrew from across the room. Even with the loss of his arm, Andrew's naked body aroused him.

Andrew returned to the bed with a book tucked under his stump. "A good friend gave me this, and I read this poem several times when I was in the war. It made me think of you and gave me hope for our reunion. It's by this poet, Walt Whitman. It's called *When I Heard at the Close of the Day*." He sat cross-legged in the bed and began to read.

*When I heard at the close of the day how my name had been receiv'd with plaudits in the capitol, still it was not a happy night for me that follow'd,*

*And else when I carous'd or when my plans were accomplish'd, still I was not happy,*

*But the day when I rose at dawn from the bed of perfect health, refresh'd, singing, inhaling the ripe breath of autumn,*

*When I saw the full moon in the west grow pale and disappear in the morning light,*

*When I wander'd alone over the beach, and undressing bathed, laughing with the cool waters, and saw the sun rise,*

*And when I thought how my dear friend my lover was on his way coming, O then I was happy,*

*O then each breath tasted sweeter, and all that day my food nourish'd me more, and the beautiful day pass'd well,*

Edward took over the text, more slowly than Andrew, but determined.

*And the next came with equal joy, and with the next at evening came my friend,*

*And that night while all was still I heard the waters roll slowly continually up the shores,*

*I heard the hissing rustle of the liquid and sands as directed to me whispering to congratulate me,*

*For the one I love most lay sleeping by me under the same cover in the cool night,*

*In the stillness in the autumn moonbeams his face was inclined toward me,*

*And his arm lay lightly around my breast—and that night I was happy.*

Andrew closed the book, placing it on the bureau beside the bed. He nestled up to Edward who pulled the bed covers over them. Edward released a heavy exhale. Andrew sighed. Church bells tolled in the distance, and a breeze ushered in the scent of budding wild flowers.

### Epilogue I

A waiter ushered Jessup through the crowded dining room of the Spotswood Hotel. The war had been over for a year, and folks were eager to return to some form of normalcy. Conversation, laughter, and the smell of good food filled the room.

"In spite of the crowd, we were able to hold your favorite table, Mr. Tillman," the waiter said.

"I do appreciate it," said Jessup taking his seat. "Bring me a bourbon, and I'll be ready to order when ya get back."

"Very good, sir."

Jessup studied the menu. The waiter returned with his drink. "Pardon me, Mr. Tillman, but as you can see, we are unusually crowded tonight. Would you mind if this gentleman shared your table?"

Jessup looked at the strapping man standing behind the waiter.

"Of course not. Have a seat." He gestured to the chair.

"Why, thank you. I came to town to look up an old war buddy of mine, but it seems he ain't around these parts no more." He studied the crowded room. "So, what's a fellow to do here for a good time?"

"There's lots to do. Depends on what ya looking for."

"Just want to have a little fun is all. I'll bet you know how to have a good time."

"That I do."

"What say we enjoy a fine meal and then go out on the town?"

"Sounds like a grand idea. I'm Jessup Tillman." Jessup clenched his cigar between his teeth and extended his hand.

"I'm pleased to meet you, Jessup. My name is Beauregard Fairfax Montehugh, but my friends call me Beau."

"Indeed." Jessup leaned back and blew a smoke ring.

### Epilogue II

Edward and Andrew sat on the bench they had built together a lifetime ago. Over the years it had become a favorite place at the close of each day. Interlocked, their hands were gnarled and calloused from years of hard work. Despite his grief, Edward's soul was soothed by the pure, simple love he and Andrew had shared. Contentment girded his sadness. Edward held Andrew tight stroking his brow and rubbing his beloved's face. He would bury him near the flower garden and plant yellow roses. Edward's bottom lip trembled, and tears fell. He thought of their time together and anticipated the next life when their souls would love again. The crickets provided their early evening chorus with the whippoorwill's descant in the distance. A gentle breeze showered them with petals from the crepe myrtle tree, a lifetime away from the myrtles at Wilmington Manor.

## ABOUT THE AUTHOR

Dr. James E. Laws, Jr. taught the Sociology of Racism and the Sociology of the Black Family at Virginia Commonwealth University.  He has also taught a race relations course at Mary Washington University.  As educator, he has taught education courses at Virginia State University and George Mason University.  Dr. Laws has a Doctorate in Higher Education Administration from The College of William and Mary and a Master's in Public Administration and Bachelors in Sociology, both from Virginia Commonwealth University.  He currently resides in Washington, DC. *Wilmington Manor* is his first novel.

james.laws2@comcast.net

Made in the USA
Middletown, DE
12 August 2018